A MALAYAN AFFAIR

A MALAYAN AFFAIR

ROB HOLLEY

monsoonbooks

First published in 2016
by Monsoon Books Ltd
www.monsoonbooks.co.uk

No.1 Duke of Windsor Suite, Burrough Court,
Burrough on the Hill, LE14 2QS, UK

ISBN (paperback): 978-981-4625-45-6
ISBN (ebook): 978-981-4625-46-3

Cover design by Cover Kitchen.

Cataloguing in Publication Data: a catalogue record for this book
is available from the National Library, Singapore.

Printed in USA

Written in grateful appreciation
of the happy years I spent in Malaya

CONTENTS

PART ONE
THE PLANTER   11

PART TWO
THE PLANTER'S WIFE   65

PART THREE
THE MALAY VILLAGE   105

PART FOUR
THE OUTCAST   167

PART FIVE
THE ORPHANAGE   219

PART SIX
THE ADMINISTRATION   255

PART ONE

THE PLANTER

It was not a marriage made in the most propitious of circumstances. Stuart Mitchell had decided to use his home leave to find a wife and this he did with his usual efficiency but also with his usual lack of grace. Stuart was a difficult man, difficult in almost every way. He had spent nearly all his adult life on rubber estates in Malaya, mostly in remote places where there was precious little social life and few leisure activities of the conventional sort. This had never worried him, as he was self-sufficient and generally indifferent to human society. The isolation also helped him to conceal, even from himself, his inability to form satisfactory relationships with people. He would not have admitted it, but he had never had a close friend in his entire life, and even his parents were relieved when he decided to seek his fortune in one of the far reaches of Empire just after the Great War during which he had served in the trenches and been wounded.

He was well regarded by his employers because he was hard working as well as efficient. The Board of Directors of his company, which met in London every month to check the outputs of its Malayan investments, never failed to be impressed by the figures from his estate and they, at least, appreciated his devotion to rubber and his placing of the production of it above every other consideration in his life. In return, they had ensured he remained in employment during the worst periods of depression in the industry during the inter-war years, times when there had been many redundancies, or retrenchments as they were euphemistically called, among estate managers.

His unfeeling character had never been a handicap in his work

– in fact, quite the reverse, as it prevented him from complicating relations with his workers by the exercise of any undue charity or misplaced loyalties. As a result, the labour force, mostly Tamils from southern India, had long ceased to take liberties either with him or with the company's time and property. However, he did everything he could to maintain their productivity, regarding it as his duty not only to supervise their work, but their pleasures too, whenever he felt it was required.

He made regular visits to the toddy shop on the estate for example, and fined any workers under what he regarded as the undue influence of the palm wine it sold to relieve the monotony of their daily lives. Resentments at these intrusions were dealt with summarily, not infrequently with the use of a fist or a boot. He even extended his concern to their domestic lives when the occasion demanded, and had been known to accompany the native dresser (the estate medical orderly) on his evening rounds of the labour lines to ensure the new contraceptives the company were sending from Britain were being distributed regularly and, more importantly, being used properly. His ability to speak the Tamil language with more than usual fluency enabled him to ensure that the instructions on their use were fully understood. Unwanted pregnancies amongst the female tappers irritated him, they were inefficient and unnecessary when the means of avoiding them were readily available and without cost.

His attitude to women was both uncomplicated and uncompromising. He had had very little to do with them and there had been nothing in his upbringing to make him aware that women might have feelings beyond the most basic, or needs other than those of security and motherhood. After an all-boys boarding school in Scotland and service in the Great War he had gone straight to Malaya where there were relatively few white women and none unmarried. On his long vacations he had never sought them out, preferring to spend his time fishing or playing golf although he rarely devoted much time to either in Malaya when there were much more important ways to fill his daylight hours, such as increasing the productivity of his rubber trees.

His headman, the *kepala*, found him girls from the labour lines whenever he felt the need, sturdy, muscular wenches with fine bodies and shiny black hair. Originally, he had helped himself from the weeding gangs around his bungalow but there had been an unfortunate incident involving a husband, and the company had found it necessary to transfer him. Stuart had resented this as he found it difficult to accept censure of any kind. Now he left the job of procurement to his *kepala* who did it without fuss. The girls would suddenly appear from the back of the bungalow just before he retired for the night. They never expected to be amused or even humoured, and Stuart liked it that way. He often even failed to speak to them as their mouths, stained purple by the betel nut they chewed incessantly, repelled him. By the time he rose for first muster in the morning, about five, they had gone. He never knew if he had been with the same girl twice.

As he stood in the chill light of early dawn in front of the factory watching the *kepala* check and dismiss the gangs, he sometimes wondered which one had just shared his bed. He never caught one staring at him, they seemed as incurious about him as he was of them. They were strangely passive, even inert, creatures. He saw them at various times during the day padding silently amongst the trees or cycling along the gravel paths, cans of latex swinging precariously from the handlebars, but there was never any sign of recognition on their part. Did they talk about him amongst themselves, compare notes, bargain with the *kepala* for more money? He paid as much for a night as they earned in a week, and although he suspected they received only a fraction of what he gave the *kepala*, it ensured there was never any lack of volunteers. No doubt the *kepala* kept the difference, in addition to whatever other favours he exacted, although the girls could never retain the money for themselves anyway, their husbands or fathers would waste that in the toddy shop the same day, of that he was certain.

Perhaps the girls' docility around the estate during the day was the inevitable result of their lives of almost constant drudgery, but he found them just as wooden at night. Only their pale palms, calloused and crazed in deep cracks, showed any animation as they scoured his skin like sack-cloth. The rest of their bodies were totally unresponsive, their eyes dull and expressionless. He never saw a trace of enjoyment or resentment during their exchanges. He presumed the Tamil men liked it that way. Sometimes the whole business filled him with such distaste that he could not bear their touch and took his pleasure with their dusky backs towards him. In this way, he reduced the physical contact between them to a minimum.

In such moments of passion, and even in some more reflective, he was inclined to see their congress as symbolising his exacting rule of the estate, his company's role in exploiting Malaya's resources, even Britain's appropriation and governance of the country, for although no one would describe Stuart as an imaginative man, he was well aware of the reality of empire and the part he was playing in it.

He was in no doubt at all why his countrymen had come to Malaya. It was not to bestow the benefits of their civilisation – to which they liked to point at every opportunity – or the blessings and comforts of their religion, but to make their own fortunes, for whatever they claimed to the contrary it was obvious they were in the country for their own benefit and not that of the natives. Nor was he in any doubt of the part rubber companies like his were playing in helping to channel one of the world's great natural resources from a needy to a wealthier part of the world – and at a price the latter was largely able to dictate. However, although the role being played in this inequitable trade by estate managers like himself was not sufficient to burden Stuart with a conscience, it did at least make him aware of the responsibilities of his position.

He was therefore punctilious in not making the girls pregnant, giving expert advice while, on his instructions, they fumblingly fitted his sheath during their encounters, a task he viewed with some satisfaction, prompted by the thought he was thus providing in-service training for his staff and so following Company policy to the letter, even if – and this little joke was typical of his sense of humour – it was only a French letter. He hoped his message was clear and the experience gained was being taken back to the labour lines for the benefit of their husbands – what was good enough for *Tuan* must surely be good enough for Maniam and Ramisamy. He was convinced the Board of Directors would have been even more pleased with his dedication to their service had they been aware of it.

When he actually formed the idea of taking a wife he found it impossible to say, nor did he really know why, unless it was to relieve the tedium of the evenings in the bungalow which after many years of just his own company were beginning to pall. It certainly was not part of any long-term plan on his part. He just made up his mind he ought to acquire one on his next leave and he began his search almost as soon as he disembarked. His air of self-assurance, together with his mildly exotic aura of the East, made him superficially attractive to women although this attraction did not usually last longer than their discovery of his bleak and cheerless character. This had never been of concern to him in the past as he had never felt the need for women's friendship or even their company for more than the most casual encounter. Now he found he had to exert himself in a way that was quite alien to him and after a couple of unsuccessful golf club dances he began to think wistfully of the *kepala*, and not for the first time he wondered about a local girl, not one off the estate of course, but perhaps a Malay girl from one of the *kampungs*, the villages.

A discreet word here and there should yield something, it always had for the old Malaya hands in the past and he could afford to be generous to her family. It would have to be a family settlement as the Malay girls were not as free and easy with their favours as the Tamils, but there was often a girl available who had made an unsuccessful marriage or had been widowed early. He had to be careful of the social or political implications, however, as although he was scornful of his fellow Europeans, he was not unmindful of the necessity of maintaining white prestige. There were now other considerations too. Life on the estates was not like the old days. Bungalows and amenities generally were now more in conformity with European expectations and companies were beginning to encourage wives from home. Cohabitation with a local woman was not only frowned upon, it was enough to jeopardise promotion. Reluctantly, he came to the conclusion that, everything considered, it might be better if he widened his search in Scotland.

He was indeed lucky to find Valerie. He wandered into a Glasgow pub one wet night and there she was, working part time behind the bar to help her brother who was acting as 'mine host' for a friend. She was ten years his junior, brown-haired and shapely – one of those rare girls, softly feminine but challengingly sensual at the same time, but totally without vanity. What Valerie had seen in Stuart no one knew, she was as sociable as he was reserved, as affectionate as he was cold, as generous-spirited as he was unforgiving. She could have had her choice of any number of men at home but she seemed entranced by Stuart's descriptions of the East and its peoples and her mind was quickly made up.

Stuart hardly had to propose and six weeks later they were on a boat crossing the Bay of Biscay. With the prospect of what she hoped would be an exciting life before her, Valerie refused to admit she had made a terrible mistake, but even on her honeymoon – with Stuart as much in love as he ever would be – he was unresponsive to her gaiety, dismissive of her girlish enthusiasms, and uncaring of her need for tenderness. As for his own needs, their bouts of fierce loving were all he ever seemed to require.

In his turn, he quickly discovered that marrying a girl like Valerie was likely to lead to an unwelcome widening of his social life when he got back to Malaya unless he put his foot down, and he had an opportunity of making his intentions clear on the boat when, in the Red Sea, he declined her request to take part in the fancy dress ball arranged for the second-class passengers.

'I've never been one for making a fool of myself for other people's amusement,' was his gruff response to his wife's plea.

'But Stuart, it's only a bit of fun to help pass the time.'

'Not for me it isn't, I'd rather read my paper or a book any day. You can go if you like but I can't stand these things.'

She hadn't gone. He had known full well that a woman could not do so on her own anyway, so she pleaded a headache to those who asked and did her best to hide her disappointment. In the Indian Ocean he embarrassed her by refusing to make up a foursome for deck tennis in front of their prospective opponents and a crowded deck. She felt uncomfortable for the rest of the voyage and was not sorry when they disembarked in Singapore.

However, all her misgivings were temporarily forgotten in her reaction to the magic of her new country. The expectations of her imagination which had been so breathtakingly kindled in Britain were fully realised. The noise, the bustle, the colour, the variety of the native peoples appealed to her gregarious nature and she was quite entranced by the novelty of it all.

Stuart was gratified by her pleasure and listened with tolerant amusement to all her expressions of wonder. It was almost as if he was accepting personal credit for the fascinations of the British colony and he patiently answered her many questions. He also enjoyed the reaction of his acquaintances to his young wife. He particularly noted, though pretended not to, the response she evoked from the men. It made him look anew at his bride and Valerie did her best to respond. She later remembered the short time they spent in Singapore while Stuart discussed future plans for his estate with the Company's agents before they embarked on the last leg of their journey, as some of the better days she had spent with her husband.

*   *   *

There was no railway in the eastern half of the country as yet, or even a direct road, so they had to resort to the sea again on one of the cramped little steamers run by the Siamese Steam Navigation Company which took them up the coast in typically leisurely fashion. The cabin was without ventilation and during the night its stuffiness drove Valerie onto the little deck where she sat among the throngs of sleeping locals and their various belongings and watched the lightning of a tropical storm fork over the dense blackness of the jungle. She found it difficult to believe that in less than twenty-four hours she would be living somewhere deep within it as to her, at that moment, it had all the mystery and terrors of an unknown planet, a feeling heightened by the unfamiliar scents from the shore, which she could not identify.

The air was heavy and oppressive from the distant thunderstorm but the gentle progress of the steamer generated just enough breeze to enable her to feel comfortable in a light summer dress, although the sleeping figures around her had seen fit to cover themselves from head to toe in their batik cottons, making them look like the shrouded victims of some dreadful disaster which had descended upon them.

She carefully picked her way between the bodies to the prow and looked down into the swirling water to marvel at the sprays of phosphorescence peeling away from the bow like the sparkling trails of a child's firework. Later she watched the sky lighten over the horizon far out across the South China Sea, the sun's red fringe seeming intent on burning off the mauves of the night. Soon, as she well knew, its fierce heat would reign supreme. In the late morning they landed on a modest little wooden jetty in Tumpat, the only port in Kelantan, which was the most northerly state of Malaya on the east coast. It was not quite what she expected after the bustle and modernity of Singapore and made her wonder what might be awaiting her inland.

With all their personal possessions, or *barang* as Valerie heard them called, piled high upon the lorry sent from the estate, they were soon enveloped by the jungle. Occasionally, as they came to a plantation, it relented to reveal row after row of grey rubber trees, but otherwise the scenery was an unrelieved tangle of dark green. It was the lack of open vistas which surprised Valerie the most, the furthest she was able to see at any one time being a hundred yards or so as they went through a native village, or *kampung*, when she had brief glimpses of stilted huts among the palms. The unexpected height of the latter impressed her, their ridged, grey trunks reaching as high as a cathedral roof.

The little villages beneath them lacked the life of Singapore and had a dispiriting uniformity about them: a few huts of planks and woven palm leaves grouped either side of the road over which strayed some chickens and one or two, almost hairless, dogs; an occasional Chinese man, almost invariably in blue shorts and a white vest, wheeling a bicycle banked high with native vegetables; a group of Malay men in sarongs sitting around a marble-topped table in front of a coffee shop of corrugated iron surmounted incongruously by an advertisement for Players cigarettes or Bisto; some brown-skinned children kicking a wicker-work ball on a bare patch of red shale. Only the brilliance of the light and the sharpness it gave to the colours made much of an impression upon her. She wondered what living in such places was like. A couple of women were crouched by the side of the road waiting for a bus, one holding a drooping banana leaf over both their heads against the sun. What were they gossiping about? What could conceivably happen in such places to merit conversation at all?

They came to a river and ran down onto a log slipway. What looked like a shack on the end of a floating platform of similar logs roped to a small launch inched its way across the water towards them. It reversed before settling onto the slipway allowing their vehicle to drive cautiously on board. Half way across Valerie saw her first snakes which, being in the river, she thought were eels which made Stuart and the driver laugh though Valerie thought the latter's smile came only after Stuart's. She detected fear beneath the respect. Once across the river, the road seemed yet narrower and the jungle even more impenetrable.

Towards dusk they slowed by a large board which had once been white but was now encrusted with green algae, standing in the *lalang*, the tall grass, on the verge. It had BUKIT BINTANG ESTATE painted on it under which was Stuart's name and that of the company, United Estates. They turned onto a track of red laterite – the rough soil weathered from ferrous rock which drains well and so was favoured for estate roads – flanked by endless rows of rubber trees. For half a mile or so the lorry ground along in low gear before coming to a bungalow which, after the insubstantial buildings of the native villages, looked reassuringly solid. It was of wood, balanced on concrete piles partially hidden by potted plants. On two sides was a spacious verandah, on the steps of which stood the smiling staff – all two of them – an almost black 'boy' who was obviously Tamil, and a light brown 'cookie' who she thought was Malay but turned out to be Chinese. She was still finding the two races difficult to tell apart.

The verandah led into a sitting room which had doors and open shuttered windows on two walls and a further door on a third leading into the kitchen, beyond which were the servants' quarters, while the fourth led to a wide landing flanked by two bedrooms, the largest of which was obviously Stuart's. It was minimally furnished, the bed overhung by a voluminous mosquito net draped over a metal frame suspended from the ceiling by wire. With so much else to take in Valerie was surprised to find herself wondering why the bed was so large and had an old-fashioned bolster as well as pillows. Later she was to discover that Malayan nights were better endured if the sleepers could spread themselves like the flying squirrels sometimes glimpsed gliding between the rubber trees outside, and a bolster, quaintly called a 'Dutch wife', was placed between the knees to separate one moist leg from the other.

Even in the failing light she was able to see that the bathroom, reached by a back staircase leading down from the landing and stretching back under it, was extremely primitive. It had a cement floor, a slatted wooden bench similar to the one she remembered in her gym changing room at school, and a large earthenware jar in one corner, from which water had obviously to be ladled in lieu of a shower. In the wilds of Malaya's interior – or the *ulu* as the Malays liked to refer to the inaccessible parts of their country – even the most basic domestic plumbing was a luxury it seemed. The jar reminded her of a story she had heard in Singapore of the early days in the colony when a determined young lady, fresh out from Britain, who, having been told the Shanghai jar was the bath, managed to wriggle herself into it on her first morning but, being of ample proportions, was then forced to call for a boy, indeed several boys, to lift her out. She suspected the yarn was one of the perennial chestnuts of the East.

The last rays of the setting sun provided just enough light for her to see that the walls, once whitewashed, had become little more than a battleground for competing armies of green algae and black mould, while the air was dank. It was not quite what she had hoped for after the modernity of the hotel in Singapore but she put a brave face on it so as not to lose face with her husband. She had already discovered to her mortification that the failing he most despised was weakness.

Thirty minutes later, just as she was realising she had not eaten since stepping off the steamer, the magic of the East reasserted itself and the boon of house servants was brought home to her for the first time when a large curry as it can only be made in the the tropics was placed on the table before her by the smiling houseboy. She had not put as much as a toe inside the kitchen either to prepare or to order it, nor would she be expected to do so from now on.

*   *   *

Her husband was missing when she awoke at six the next morning and she did not see him until he returned at ten-thirty for breakfast.

Over the next few weeks she got used to a planter's day: away by five in the morning for muster and, after breakfast, into the factory for weighing the latex until one, a two-hour siesta being followed by a check of the tappers and the field workers before a spell in the office until five or even six. Stuart saw little need to change the working habits of a lifetime. This was the planter's day, Valerie was married to a planter, she had to get used to it. Managing a rubber estate to make it pay did not change simply because the marital status of the manager had changed. That had been made perfectly clear to him when he had applied to the Board of Directors for permission to marry.

What Valerie found more difficult than getting used to a planter's day was getting used to the planter himself.

She had to learn to cope with his undemonstrative ways, his reserve and his need for his own company for part, at least, of every evening despite the fact that she had been alone all day. His self-absorption puzzled her. Had he always been like it or had the isolation of life on remote rubber estates left its mark? Planters had to be self-reliant, she could see that, and as only the very big estates could afford a European assistant, they had to get used to being without another of their kind during the day with whom the problems and frustrations of running an estate could be shared, but surely that should make them even more pleased with some company in the evenings or at the weekends? She heard that other planters regarded the European clubs as a lifeline in this respect no matter how far they had to travel to get there, and that they rarely failed to take local leave in Penang or Singapore whenever they were entitled, but Stuart seemed not to feel the need of either. It made her wonder why he had bothered to marry at all, except for the nights of course.

But it was his unconcern for, perhaps his ignorance of, her feelings which hurt her most. He assumed that as she had chosen to marry him, chosen to come out to Malaya, she was content. It did not seem to occur to him that as she adjusted to new cultures, a new climate, the absence of familiar faces and the unaccustomed loneliness, she would need sympathy, reassurance and, above all, some loving kindness.

He was particularly irritated by her problems with the servants. The Chinese cookie, Ah Gan, and the houseboy, Tambi, a squat muscular Tamil with wavy hair and white teeth, spoke virtually no English. Meeting so few British expatriates they had never felt the need to learn more than the odd word or two and Stuart always spoke to them in Malay or, in Tambi's case, his native dialect. Yet, during the day, they were her only companions and she had to communicate with them to settle the details of the domestic round. It usually meant Stuart having to act as interpreter every time he returned to the bungalow and he obviously found this irksome.

It also did nothing for her authority over the servants who already resented the intrusion of a female presence and the extra work it frequently entailed. Without Stuart, her attempts at communication always ended in frustration mainly because, to many in Malaya, a failure to comprehend meant a serious loss of face, especially when conversing with a woman. Instructions, therefore, were always met by smiles and gestures of assent but rarely followed. Whether this was due to a lack of comprehension or a deliberate attempt to flout her wishes she could never be sure but, as her Malay developed, she suspected it was more often the latter.

Stuart found his wife's initial inability to get on with Tambi particularly frustrating. Tambi had been a mere boy when he had entered Stuart's service and had simply grown into his master's ways. He could anticipate his employer's wishes before Stuart was even aware of them and he found it difficult to remain in the background while Valerie took control of the house and assumed authority over affairs which had been his province for as long as he could remember. He had more sense than to complain to Stuart. He had plenty of experience of his master's short temper and instinct warned him that, for the time being at least, he had to accept a lesser role in the house, but that did not stop him from scoring petty victories when the opportunities arose.

He discovered that Mem did not appreciate his noiseless appearances about the bungalow without warning, and it amused him when his bare-footed approach caught her unawares. Stuart had never minded these intrusions, so Tambi chose to interpret Valerie's need for privacy as disapproval of both himself and the service he provided. She particularly disliked his presence in the bedroom, especially when Stuart was out of the bungalow. For this reason she dispensed with tea and papaya in bed in the mornings and took them at eight on the verandah while she watched the *tukang kebun*, the gardener, although the title somewhat flattered the ancient Tamil who watered the plants.

He spoke not a word of English, or Malay either it seemed, or even of his own dialect as far as Valerie could discover, his only reply to Tambi's constant chatter being a rasping sound in his throat which occasionally changed key. His only garment was a strip of folded cloth around his waist and he was invariably bare-footed. The skin on his chest hung in looping folds under wisps of grey hair while his legs were bent to the point that the space between them prescribed an almost perfect hexagon, making his thighs disappear under his loincloth at an angle that defied human anatomy.

Whenever Valerie spoke to him, he bared gums stained by betel juice and declined his knees still further, so that the hexagon flattened dangerously to a point where it threatened to collapse altogether. But despite these obsequies and his obvious willingness to please, no instructions of hers were ever followed. All her plants were regularly over-watered and only the hot climate saved them. He was also the *tukang ayer*, the drawer of water, and every morning he laboriously carried slopping pails from the stream that ran close by to the bungalow. He cleared the earth closet and filled the Shanghai jar in the bathroom although, despite almost daily remonstrance from Tambi, he rarely remembered either to empty or to clean it, until after Valerie's regular protests about the green slime, Stuart had to intervene.

* * *

After her husband, the next things Valerie had to get used to was
the climate, particularly the heat and humidity, and also how to fill
a long day on an isolated estate. After breakfast she usually went
for a walk. It was the time of day she particularly enjoyed. The
cool freshness was like childhood in all its life and hope, but by ten,
walking had become uncomfortable and, by eleven, all but the most
imprudent had been driven into the shade. By midday even her own
shadow seemed to have taken refuge from the sun as, at that hour, it
was invariably to be found sheltering from its vertical rays beneath
her feet. By the afternoon the estate had been reduced to a still and
sullen silence, save for the singing of the crickets. Then, soon after
six, the sun relented, skipped dusk and departed – to return the
next day as innocently as before.

When the heat became unbearable she walked in the shade
of the rubber trees, which spread out around her in straight lines
from whichever tree she viewed them. They made relatively cool,
shady aisles in the hottest days and, leaning quietly against a trunk
listening to the crickets, she found they were a refuge for wildlife
also – lizards skittering manically across the leaf litter at her
approach, the occasional mouse-deer timidly looking for rubber
nuts, a chattering troupe of monkeys on their way to the next fig
tree, while sometimes a flying squirrel would appear as if from
nowhere to flatten itself against the trunk of a rubber tree before
her. From time to time she saw a tapper, most of them women, who
smiled shyly as she approached but would not speak.

She learned to live with that Western phobia, the leech, which
constantly lurked in the grass, so that on dewy mornings when they
were particularly active, she was able to resist a natural but ill-
advised urge to remove them, and left them feeding between her
toes until she returned to the bungalow. Then Cookie, with an

exaggerated show of mock horror and wonder, and many an "Ah Mem!", sprinkled them – now large and swollen with her blood – with salt, causing them to drop to the floor and contract in their death throes.

After her walk, came a mid-morning breakfast with Stuart who, after the irritations of muster was not at his best, and she learnt not to broach any of her own problems at such a time. There then followed a frustrating period which should have been filled by domestic tasks if only she could have found anything of importance to do. The housework and cooking were more than adequately done by Tambi and Cookie and they interpreted any attempt by her to share their duties as criticisms or, worse, a threat to their livelihood. She roamed from room to room but was able to do very little that Tambi did not follow and immediately undo, and so, unable to make any impression on the bungalow as a consequence, it never felt like a true home.

She made curtains, stitched a series of patchwork bedspreads and ordered furniture and mats from Singapore, but the building stubbornly refused to reflect the character of its mistress. One of the problems was that, like all planters' houses, it was designed for coolness and so built that it could admit the maximum amount of air. It therefore lacked the enclosed, intimate atmosphere of a house in Britain and, in fact, at times seemed nothing more than an open highway for all manner of wildlife, and, much as Valerie enjoyed nature outside the house, she did not appreciate it under her own roof.

It was not unknown for birds during the day, and bats at night, to enter the louvred windows and then fail to negotiate an exit until driven there by the combined efforts of the whole household. Marauding monkeys, looking for a change from their fig trees, were often bold enough to raid the fruit bowl on the dining room table and were only deterred by the regular use of Stuart's shotgun. After dark, green cicadas the size of pigeon eggs blundered their zig-zag way from wall to wall uttering shrill cries of alarm, while small lizards, or *cicat* as the Malays called them, commandeered the walls each evening for their hunting forays. They jousted for the moths and insects around the lights, the vanquished sometimes losing their footing and dropping, as stone-cold as frogs, on anyone below. They laid their eggs in keyholes and behind pictures but, more disturbingly, attracted predators like the house snake.

Although harmless, it was disconcerting to find one of these hunters wound around a wardrobe rail, having been attracted by the heat of the light bulbs kept burning there during the day to resist the damp and mould. On one occasion after she had retired to bed, Valerie was alarmed to find one wrapped along the frame supporting the mosquito net. When the estate generator was switched off at night, and the bungalow was plunged into almost total darkness except for the moonlight filtering through the branches of the rubber trees, it was easy to imagine nature had taken possession of the entire building. It required an effort of will to descend the staircase to the bathroom with just a flickering oil lamp for company.

The creatures with the most invasive persistence were also one of the smallest – the ants, and no obstacle, no poison, nor even a war of ruthless extermination waged by Valerie and Tambi, made the slightest difference to their numbers or their boldness. Day and night, they methodically quartered every inch of the bungalow in a ceaseless search for anything edible which, once found, was carried off in long, seething columns of triumph. A dead cicada could be hauled across the floor, up a wall and over a louvre in a matter of minutes. Crumbs were cleared from the floors, dead moths from around the table lamps, even the dregs of a coffee cup on the bedside table were not beyond their reach. Only saucers of water under the table legs kept them off the dining table. Valerie detested them at first, then learned to live with them, although she was never reconciled to their unnerving and sudden presence in the estate vehicles. On one occasion they discovered some food left overnight on a back seat and when Stuart opened the door in the morning it seemed the whole colony had assembled to remove it. Where they had come from and where they went was a mystery.

Stuart returned for lunch at one but was not good company. She tried sharing her experiences of the day with him but he had lived so long with the minutiae of daily life in the tropics that he no longer found them either noteworthy or interesting. After a light lunch, the day deteriorated into heat and boredom and the afternoons were endless. They both lay on the enormous bed, two islands of moist and clammy flesh, grateful for every fitful breeze which stirred the blinds. They avoided each other's touch as it brought only fresh effusions of perspiration. It was too hot to talk, even think, and only sleep brought any relief.

After Stuart had gone back onto the estate, Valerie tried to read, but it was difficult to find a body position in which one limb did not make sticky intrusion upon another, despite the use of the 'Dutch wife'. At six o'clock, as the sun lost its venom, she descended to the bathroom and let the tepid water in the Shanghai jar do its best to make her body fit for company once more. Then, with the mind restored to rational thought, she and Stuart shared the verandah for the hour before dinner with the first of the night's mosquitoes.

She came to look forward to this time, as the solitary sundowner Stuart allowed himself each evening inclined him to converse. At first, Valerie marvelled at her husband's restraint in regard to alcohol as it was a continuing weakness of many Europeans in the tropics, but she later discovered that after an initial brush with its effects and the damage it could do to a manager's efficiency and prospects, Stuart had decided to limit himself to one drink and one drink only a day, and never took it before the sun went down. It was another sign of his devotion to his career, for which no sacrifice appeared to be too great.

Under the relaxing influence of his one-and-only whisky Valerie found he could be encouraged to expand upon his day and she made a special effort as she knew how important it was to him. However, partly due to the fact that he had been used to keeping his own company for so many years and partly because he was unwilling to believe she was really interested, he found it difficult to tailor the day's events to her feminine understanding. Nevertheless, these occasions were amongst the relative few when her new life and her new husband, between them, allowed her to feel she was actually coming near to being a wife.

The only diversion during the day was an occasional storm or a sumatra as they were called. As is often the case in countries on or near the equator, it rained most days, giving lushness to the vegetation, and the rain usually came in the form of an hour-long downpour out of a leaden sky, perhaps for a week at three in the afternoon, the next at four, but very rarely before noon. At such times the torrent fell upon the cement apron around the bungalow with force enough to make the spray leap a foot from the ground, flooding the garden to within a step of the verandah and leaving the wooden building looking much like Noah's Ark after the biblical inundation. Once the sky had shed its contents, the sun would resume its sway, drawing up the vapour in curling wisps to fuel the next day's downpour.

Every so often, however, the rain arrived in a much more violent and destructive way, it being accompanied by a sudden and fierce wind which raged through the rubber trees and bore down upon the bungalow as if it had insults to avenge. Then, with the noise of an express train, it drove grey sheets of water through the window blinds and under the doors, sweeping the mats before them into a sodden mass. Valerie was excited by these demonstrations of nature's power, joining her excited laughter with that of Tambi and Cookie as they scrambled with their pails and cloths. The sumatra rarely lasted longer than ten minutes and was a catharsis for the day, purging the mind of lassitude and leaving everyone in the bungalow in better spirits, even Stuart.

Each week, Stuart sent the *kepala* into the nearby township of Kuala Lebir for their mail including precious letters from home. Then Valerie's homesickness was almost too sharp to bear, and was only partly alleviated by the long replies she made when she found herself on her own after dinner. This was the time Stuart liked to absorb himself in the newly arrived but out-of-date British newspapers and she resented how he seemed more interested in them than the snippets she read from her letters.

Often she was reduced to watching the *cicat* quarrelling on the ceiling or the smoke curling up from the mosquito coils, or simply sitting with her eyes closed and listening to the tock-tock bird, the nightjar, as he peppered the darkness outside with his volleys of monosyllabic calls. The Chinese, she had been told, often wagered considerable sums on the number of tocks in each salvo, and it was some consolation to her to know that others had as little to occupy their minds as she.

No wonder she found the *keng hwa* so exciting. The latter was perhaps the most spectacular of the many exotic plants which flourished in Malaya's hot climate and she had a range of them on the verandah – a location which put them at the tender mercy of the *tukang kebun* each morning, not to mention the depredations of the sumatras. Each plant grew a long slender stem once a year from the end of which emerged a solitary white flower of enormous size and beauty, and emitting a quite intoxicating fragrance. The bud began opening at dusk and by midnight it was at the height of its splendour, but by the following morning it lay limp and dying, reminding Valerie of a dying swan. There was something both noble and poignant in its brief glory.

Occasionally, on a Saturday, Valerie was able to persuade Stuart to go into Kuala Lebir, some twenty miles distant. The town itself was not of much interest to a European woman, a couple of provision shops with cold storage facilities where a few Western foods could be obtained, and a row of Indian dressmakers with brightly coloured rolls of local and Siamese cloths piled up on their counters and concrete floors. They opened directly onto the five-foot way and their proprietors sat on stools and solicited the women's custom.

The tailors, the *tukang jahit,* who sat at their antiquated machines in the back of the shops, were quick and efficient in making up their orders, but the materials creased badly and the dresses did not withstand the heavy pounding of the wash *amahs* for very long. It was as if there was a conspiracy by the tailors and the *amahs* between them to extract the wealth of the white man – or the white man's wife – and distribute it more equitably amongst their fellow countrymen. The wives enjoyed the bargaining, however, and it was not unusual to see one pursued down the covered way by a supplicant shopkeeper in a vain attempt to retrieve a lost sale. In such ways did the womenfolk while away the afternoon while their husbands, even on occasion Stuart, defied the sun on the club's golf course.

Apart from these infrequent diversions there was little to disturb the monotonous tenor of her week. The European club in Kuala Lebir was a difficult drive away and the estate did not employ a driver, or *syce* as they were called, as Stuart had never felt the need of one. He had little time for the social life of the Club and so never required someone to drive him home after a hard evening of consuming the planters' staple – whisky *ayers* (whisky and water) – the main purpose of which was to restore the body after the sweaty depletions of the day but which could so easily be indulged to the drinkers' detriment, both mental and physical.

As Valerie did not drive there was no point in her asking Stuart to buy a car but, as it happened, the life of the planters' wives at the Club was not greatly to her taste. She had never acquired the middle-class skills of golf or bridge although she did occasionally join in the odd game of tennis on those few occasions when Stuart had business in Kuala Lebir. She rather resented the fact that the other wives seemed reasonably content with their lives and she was very conscious of being outside their friendship circles, which were inevitably based on the social life which Stuart still refused to join. Grudgingly he went to the Christmas Eve dance one year although 'put in an appearance' might be more apt as he failed to get anywhere near the dance floor.

* * *

Valerie had been in Malaya about eighteen months when her world was transformed. 'Stuart,' she said after dinner one night. 'I think I am going to have a baby.'

He put his paper down and looked at her. It seemed as if the thought of parenthood had never occurred to him. 'Good Lord, when is it due?'

As usual, she found herself biting back a hurt reply at his matter of fact response. They had never discussed a family and she had not the slightest idea what his views on children were. They had never, together, been in the company of any, nor had the subject ever come up. Children played a relatively small part in the lives of Europeans in the tropics as they were either looked after by *amahs* or were at home in boarding schools. Nevertheless, it would have been nice if he had shown just a faint touch of enthusiasm or even solicitude.

'Oh, not for some time yet, probably not before August. Of course, I don't know for certain. I shall have to see the doctor.'

The following Saturday they went into Kuala Lebir where Valerie was examined by the doctor who was a consultant for Stuart's company. He was a Eurasian, a kindly man about fifty with a diffident manner and old-fashioned manners. He seemed in awe of Europeans but had bad news for her. She was not pregnant. It had been a false alarm. They went to the Club afterwards as Valerie felt in particular need of female company.

'My dear, I'm so sorry,' said one of the planters' wives when she heard Valerie's news. 'Never mind, there's plenty of time. A pity though as it would have been something to occupy your mind on that isolated estate of yours. How do you manage to keep sane? You really must make Stuart come to our next curry tiffin. The rest of us will be delighted to see you. You will give us all something new and different to talk about. God knows, we need it.'

'I don't think I shall get Stuart to budge on a Sunday,' Valerie replied hesitantly. 'He does so like his one complete day off to himself.'

'I know dear,' said her companion, 'mine is just the same. Men would be hermits if we let them but they must not be allowed to get away with it.' She was lying and Valerie knew it, Peter Stephenson was well known for his affability, but she appreciated the gesture.

To her surprise, however, Margo Stephenson persisted. 'Your husband is a workaholic I believe, or so I have heard. He needs to be made to unwind. I'll get Peter to have a word with him. He should not be allowed to keep you all to himself. I think he must be the jealous type.'

Valerie laughed but she was not amused. She was aware that Stuart was not popular with the other planters and that hurt her in a curious way. It seemed to cast doubt on her choice of husband, a choice she had already doubted herself, many times. Nevertheless, it did not stop her being resentful when others did the same.

But, much to Valerie's amazement, Stuart did agree to go to the Stephenson's tiffin although it meant getting up early one Sunday and making a long, hot drive. As Valerie knew, it was a considerable sacrifice on his part, perhaps the only time she could remember him doing anything just for her. He though, could see that Valerie had been badly affected by what she was beginning to see as the loss of her baby, and as he knew from dealing with the female tappers in the lines, sometimes a gesture of that sort did wonders for morale, and therefore productivity. To show her appreciation Valerie made sure she enjoyed herself. The other women seemed pleased to see her, their husbands even more so. It had been some time since Valerie had enjoyed the responsive company of a man.

Curry tiffins were an institution in the East although relatively unexciting affairs. Everyone congregated in the garden of the estate bungalow before a late luncheon, lounging in the shade of the frangipani trees, the women admiring the epiphytic orchids growing on their branches. The men stood in groups with their hands clasped round their *stengahs*, a measure of whisky in a tall glass with plenty of water and ice, and there were periodic arguments as to how they got their name. *Stengah* was short for *'satu tengah'*, Malay for 'one half', although whether this meant 'half whisky, half water' or only half a tot, or even half way up the glass, no one seemed to know for sure. The older, wiser planters barely coloured their water with the whisky, they had seen too many take it stronger, and then have to go home broken in health and spirits, sent either by their doctor or their Board of Directors.

The women rarely touched any alcohol but sat around in sun chairs with their fruit juices and cordials. The boys, some borrowed from nearby estates for the day and all dressed in white *'tutup'* jackets buttoned up to the neck despite the heat, moved unobtrusively around. No empty glass was put on the grass without being instantly refilled, no *stengah* was drained without it being immediately replaced. The guests delayed going into the bungalow to eat until three, the meal almost invariably being mounds of fragrant rice topped with curry, the various *sambals* surrounding and dropping off their plates, followed by cool, sweet *gula malacca*, a soothing mix of tapioca, coconut milk and molasses. After which, the men retired to the garden again with their beer to talk about the price of rubber while the women remained in the house to gossip about more domestic matters.

It was then that Valerie really caught up with the East, or at least, the European version of it. She heard about the latest scandals, the troubles they all endured with the servants, the problems of boarding schools for the children, the hardships of life in a climate which was unfit for the white man and purgatory for the white woman. Of the country and its native peoples, she heard nothing. What references were made to them were usually condescending, sometimes scathing, always derogatory – the indolence of the Malay, the acquisitiveness of the Chinaman, the duplicity of the Indian. Nevertheless, the day brought a much-needed element of normality into Valerie's existence, and the conversation and company were very welcome. As they drove home she resolved to exploit the breakthrough that had been made with Stuart.

'The Stephensons are very nice. Have you known them long?'

'Long enough,' said her husband.

'Don't you like them?'

'Margo talks too much. I've never had a great deal to do with Peter. He's not my type.'

'Have you not been to a tiffin before?'

'Years ago I went to a few, but it was always the same people there, talking about the same old things, and drinking more than was good for them and, as you know, I never touch scotch during the day. I felt out of place. Still do. Eventually I preferred to stay at home. Perhaps it might have been different had I lived a bit nearer.'

Driving in the East always brought out the worst in him. He was irritated by the apparent conviction of every living thing in the country that the roads had been built for their exclusive use – chickens, ducks, goats, cattle – there was no end to the domestic cavalcade – grazing, feeding, sleeping or just wandering aimlessly wherever their fancy took them. The locals even sat on it after dark, thinking the tarmac preferable, and certainly safer, than the grass verge, and when they walked or cycled on it they invariably did so in the middle. He supposed it was their experience of the jungle that made them think the centre of the path was safer than the edges. They seemed not to have grasped the fact that motor cars were infinitely more dangerous things than snakes or scorpions.

'We have been invited to the Chadwicks' next month. I would like to go.'

'You don't have this wretched drive home at the end of it.'

'Why don't we have a driver, what do you call them, a syce? I notice everyone else has. We seem to be the only ones without one. Why's that?'

'Never saw the need of one,' said Stuart gruffly, although he was feeling the need for one at that moment.

Diffidently, Valerie said, 'I could make good use of one. He could drive me into town, I often have something I need. I might also have to see the doctor from time to time and I know you find driving a chore.'

To her surprise, he agreed, and a month later, in time for the Chadwicks' tiffin, a driver was employed.

* * *

His name was Osman, a short, stocky Malay man with a wide grin and several gold teeth. He spoke very good English, explained by the fact that his mother had been an *amah* with a British family and he had been almost brought up with their children. Valerie took to him at once. He was almost the first Malay person she had anything to do with, the houseboy was Indian, the cook, Chinese. The first thing which struck her was his unfailing cheerfulness and good manners towards herself. It was not just the deference of a servant but the innate courtesy of his race, springing from his antecedents rather than his religion, and it was not very long before he became more of a companion than just her *syce*. She had heard it said in the club that Malay men were nature's gentlemen which was high praise indeed coming from her fellow countrymen, but it somehow fitted Osman.

Though a devout Muslim and therefore from a male-dominated society in which women traditionally played a subservient role, Osman had barely been a week in Valerie's service before she realised that he was far from being what she had been led to expect of a man raised in such a society. He was, in fact, very sympathetic and understanding, and also perceptive, particularly of her moods and feelings. In addition to these qualities he had an unassuming nature and so never stepped over the divide between them or attempted to take advantage of the familiarities which Valerie's unhappy marriage and her consequent need of consolation offered him. She was Mem, he was Osman, the *syce*, of humble and deferential status. This did not stop him being proud of his position, however, as the occupation of *syce* was regarded with much respect and envy in Malayan society, not only because it was relatively well paid but because it was also free from the taint of manual labour. Although he was occasionally used by Stuart, he was almost always at Valerie's disposal and seemed happy to fetch and carry for her, even occasionally in the house as well although, there, he took care not to stray onto Tambi's preserve.

As he was the only other English-speaking member of the household when Stuart was at work it was inevitable that his status advanced, gradually but steadily, from *syce* to companion and then to confidante In effect, he became a sounding-board for Valerie's frustrations, and they talked for hours while in the car together so that she very soon gave up sitting in the back seat as she noticed the other mems always did. When in the bungalow, however, Osman became a lot more reserved. On one occasion she persuaded him, very reluctantly and obviously against his better judgement, to sit on the verandah but she quickly discovered her mistake when she asked Tambi to bring them cold drinks. Osman leapt to his feet and retreated to the car, taking care to avoid Tambi's disapproving stare as he did so.

This social miscalculation did not prevent the incident from teaching Valerie something of the Malays' perspectives, in this instance how they regarded the British, the latest in a line of acquisitive foreigners who had settled in their country over the centuries in order to seek their fortunes or to save souls – from the Arab traders who had brought them Islam, to the Portuguese who were primarily looking for spices but were also anxious for converts to their Christian church. The most recent of them, however, the British, who had come to Malaya barely a century before, seemed more interested in the money they could make from the country's tin deposits and rubber trees than imparting any spiritual message although, inevitably, missions and missionaries followed in their wake. The rubber trees, *hevea brasiliensis*, had in fact been brought to Malaya by these mercantile newcomers, being unknown in the east before they had smuggled some seeds out of Brazil and set them to germinate in the similar climate of Singapore where they thrived. The resulting plantations had transformed the appearance of whole areas of his country, bringing work for all who wanted it and wealth to their owners.

But, like the previous foreigners, the British had immediately assumed a position of authority over them on a par with their sultans, and as the Malays revered their sultans so they felt obliged to look up to the British also. To drink as much as an orange juice in his house, therefore, or even to be there in an attitude of ease, was an unthinkable familiarity, especially for someone of Osman's background and temperament as he had a natural respect for those he regarded as his betters.

But this indulgence was not extended to Cookie's people, the Chinese, or to Tambi's fellow nationals, the Indians, both of whom in recent years had accompanied the white man to Malaya in such numbers as to put them, when numbered together, on a par with those of his own people. The Chinese had been lured by Malaya's tin deposits, the Indians imported and indentured by the British to work their mines and plantations. Such tasks had not been welcome to the Malays due to their dislike of menial drudgery, particularly in the service of others. The Malays were further discouraged from physical labour by their Muslim religion which taught them that the accumulation of undue wealth was an obstacle to their entry into the world to come. These twin disincentives to regular work had left them with economic ambitions only a little above the level of subsistence.

This was in contrast to the newcomers, both the Chinese and the Indians, whose industry and commercial skills – given free reign by what the Malays saw as the complacent rule of the British – were now threatening the Malays economically as well as numerically. As a result, it was not surprising that Osman, faced by the prospect of being supplanted in his own land, regarded both races as interlopers whose stay in his country should to be limited to what manual work was available for them, but who must not on any account be allowed to regard Malaya as their natural home, or be granted the same political rights and social privileges as himself.

As to the future when the white man came to leave their country and these differences needed to be resolved in order they should live together and govern themselves in peace and harmony, the Malays shrugged and declined to think about it. They had a phrase, *tid'apa*, meaning it was of no consequence – it could be left to the Almighty. Why concern themselves with something which was not likely to happen in their lifetime, Allah apparently having willed the British Empire to last for all eternity.

The coming of Osman lightened and enriched Valerie's day beyond measure, certainly more than she had ever expected, and she never ceased to congratulate herself on the good fortune his employment had brought. Now she never needed to be alone at any time during the day, nor did any part of it seem pointless, save for the evenings, as there was always someone to share her thoughts and her hopes, sympathise with her frustrations and irritations, or even to satisfy her curiosity about the country which was now her home.

She was especially pleased at the opportunity for the latter as, in contrast to many of her fellow countrymen, she found much to interest her in the various peoples and cultures around her and had always been surprised when her questions in the Club had always been met by just a look of indifference. Now, nothing she saw from the car on her trips to Kuala Lebir or driving around the estate, or even what she read in the *Straits Times*, remained without some sort of explanation, although she was struck at how basically indifferent and uncritical Osman could be at times about his own country and its history.

Much of this attitude could be laid at the door of his upbringing and schooling which were based upon the twin precepts of acceptance and obedience. It had been instilled into him from the cradle that to do, or be, otherwise was disrespectful in the eyes of his religion. Allah had ordained and Allah had provided, so it was not for his humble servant to seek to understand the purpose of it all, or worse, to call it into question. To query the ways of one's ancestors was an insult to their spirits as who was he to doubt what they had accepted? They had built their houses as had their forefathers, therefore it would be presumptuous of him not to do the same. They had planted their padi in the way of their elders, what made him think he could do better?

This unquestioning acceptance of tradition, which Valerie had often heard derided in the Club as being inimical to any sort of progress by the Malays, economic or otherwise, sometimes tempted Valerie to tease him, even at times to laugh at what she saw as the conservative ways of his countrymen. He though, rarely laughed in return, and she quickly realised that not every race shared the ability of her people to make fun of themselves or their way of life, especially if it was a woman who was assuming the liberty.

She, of course, well knew of the inferior status of women in Malay society but it took her some time to realise how difficult it must be, therefore, for her *syce* to manage and order his relationship with the white one who was his employer, particularly when she crossed the boundary of what he regarded was proper and polite as she did on one occasion when she compared his Muslim way of life with the more progressive one of the West. Immediately, however, she quickly realised she had stepped into that area of over-familiarity into which she should have known it was improper for her to stray and so had contravened what he considered were good manners, particularly in view of the constraints his position in her employ demanded. These same constraints prevented him from putting his resentment into words but his silence and his hurt expression made it obvious she had earned his rebuke, playful though her remark may have been. She thus came to understand how unfair she had been in leaving him to ensure the necessary and respectful distance between them, mistress and servant, was maintained, and she resolved to be more sensitive to the requirements of their relationship in the future.

Little did she know, however, how drastically that relationship was to be transformed.

So, despite occasional misunderstandings, Valerie gradually came to learn of the life and culture of the people in whose land she had come to live, and she found herself more and more drawn to its gentle cadences and peaceful ways, the nature and extent of which she had been completely unaware when she had first been confronted with the Malay world as it had appeared to her on the day she had first arrived in Kelantan. She also discovered that not the least of the virtues of Islam was the strong sense of family and community it fostered, while the Malay version of it, in particular, was refreshingly free of the religion's more extreme forms – the fundamentalism which over the centuries had periodically destabilised the Arab world and endangered the peace of Europe and Africa.

With her *syce* as her slightly puzzled tutor, she was even encouraged to practice some formal Malay and found it a far more sophisticated language than the bazaar patois spoken in the shops and by the boys in the Club. These lessons afforded Osman some amusement with just an occasional moment of doubt – he had never met a European before who had wanted to learn his language for no apparent reason, and he hoped it was not a reflection on his English, nor an indication that one day she might think of dispensing with his services. But such an eventuality was very far from Valerie's thoughts. In fact, quite the reverse – she was beginning to think that life in Malaya would be unimaginable without her *syce*, who providence – in the shape of her husband – had so fortuitously brought into her service.

* * *

The Mitchells were asked to a few more tiffins but as Stuart steadfastly refused to have one himself, the invitations tailed off until they ceased altogether. Valerie was embarrassed when she saw her European neighbours in the Club but they evinced no great resentment or surprise. Stuart's unsociability was known of old, they had wondered if marriage might mellow him but were not surprised it had failed to do so. Secretly, they felt sorry for her. Pretty thing. Could be a problem if she was let loose and neglected like that in the capital, Kuala Lumpur, with all those unattached men. What on earth had she seen in Stuart Mitchell?

About a year later Valerie's suspicions that she might be pregnant were justified although she did not tell Stuart until after it had been confirmed by her doctor. Stuart greeted the news in his usual matter-of-fact way and during the next few weeks he continued to show no visible enthusiasm for, or even signs that he was anticipating, the coming event. She hoped impending fatherhood might reveal a side of his character which had remained obdurately hidden during their marriage but, in this, she was disappointed. Stuart seemed to see the approaching birth as of no more significance than Christmas which, to him, was just another distracting intrusion into the routine of the estate.

Then, one morning, Valerie woke up to find herself bleeding heavily and she was rushed to the hospital in the state capital, Kota Bharu. Later that day she had a miscarriage – it was a boy with a suspicion of red hair like his father. Despite that, Stuart remained curiously unaffected. She knew children had never been an ambition in his life, nevertheless she hoped that his nearness to achieving fatherhood might have awakened some semblance of emotion on his part, but she should have known. Where feelings were supposed to reside in a man, Stuart seemed to have a void.

The Company paid for her confinement in a first-class ward but she was perturbed by her brief glimpses of the third-class, local ward. A huge room with the beds almost touching, a female relative sleeping beneath each patient's bed to provide the food and much of the nursing, the prescriptions dispensed by the inch – a squeeze of cream measured from the tube onto a banana leaf. Then there was the general lack of what was taken for granted in a Western hospital – basic washing and toilet facilities. She was thankful to return in one piece and without mishap to the estate.

* * *

Shortly afterwards, it was time for Stuart's home leave – it would be the first time Valerie had been back to Britain since her marriage. She was looking forward to it with an almost childish excitement. As they took the train on the newly completed line from Kota Bharu to Singapore she was moved to think back to her arrival in Malaya and the events which had followed it. It went through her mind that she might not see the country again as she was seriously considering staying in Britain whether Stuart liked it or not.

He was as indifferent as he had always been, except at night, and Valerie was finding these duties increasingly difficult to accept. What had originally been a resentment at what was being assumed without affection, had deepened into a near-revulsion at a ritual indignity she found humiliating. She was forced to admit that not only was she in a loveless marriage but one without any sort of meaning to it at all. There was no meeting of minds or interests, no shared activities or problems, no plans or mutual hopes for the future. She wondered if her husband would either be surprised or concerned if she failed to board the boat with him when they were due to return. She was convinced that only when he rolled towards her on their first night in bed back on the estate would he really be aware she wasn't there, and her absence be a deprivation for him.

However, when they got back to Scotland and she unburdened herself to her mother she received precious little sympathy. Her mother had not been very happy in her own marriage. As she said, somewhat cynically, to her daughter:

'Those five words "for better or for worse" are the Church's disclaimer in case your man turns out to be less than a bargain or below what you were led to expect – very much like you get in the big stores. In fact, I cannot see much difference between the marriage vows and the "no refunds given" on cheap lines.' She

paused, and then with some bitterness added: 'Except, of course –
the goods can last a lifetime.' It was no surprise to her, therefore, to
discover her daughter was finding her marriage partner wanting in
husbandly virtues, just as her own had been.

'What made you think you were going to be any different?' she
demanded. 'And though I said you were a fool to marry a man you
knew so little about, I doubt if he is any worse than all the others.
In fact it sounds as though he is probably a lot better. You say
he doesn't drink or gamble or chase after other women. Not like
mine who did all three, and could raise his fist to you if you dared
challenge him about it. You have a comfortable home. What more
do you want?'

It was true, many women had less and it was possible, of
course, that Stuart might mellow with age, that he might begin to
show a modicum of human sympathy or a glimmer of awareness
that others had feelings. To her surprise she found little pleasure in
the thought. She had almost ceased to care one way or the other.
So she was not particularly surprised or disappointed when her
mother was unable to offer anything that might lead her to hope for
a happier marriage in the future. Her only advice to her daughter
was stoical acceptance of the hand that life had dealt her, with the
hope that bairns would eventually come as a consolation prize in
what she saw as the lottery that was a married woman's life.

Her opinion of the male sex was simple and uncomplicated. A
few husbands, a precious few, turned out to be considerate partners,
while some others were little better than brutes or drank too much,
but most were as their mothers had made them – selfish, thoughtless
and self-indulgent. If enough of their wages escaped the clutches of
the local pub landlords to put food on the table and keep body and
soul together – then that was about as much as their wives could
reasonably expect. Of course, there was always the hope of a child,
but as Valerie reflected, bairns were her mother's answer to all of
life's disappointments. Unfortunately, it looked as though she might
not even have that consolation to look forward to, so there seemed

little point in prolonging her union in the hope it might improve. At last she had to accept – in true axiomatic fashion – that she had married in haste and was now repenting it in the years of empty leisure which had followed.

She seriously considered staying in Scotland at the end of their leave but all her friends had married, and she was not over-keen on being a gay divorcee in their midst. In any case, it did not require the wisdom of a sage to know that an attractive single woman circulating among their husbands would be about as welcome to those friends as a fox in a hen house.

As it happened, she was surprised to discover she felt little desire to stay on in Scotland anyway. After the initial excitement of seeing old friends and familiar places she felt out of place. The gap that her departure had made in the local scene had long since closed over. People seemed pleased to see her but gave no indication that she might have a part to play in their lives again. She also discovered that the routine of life in Britain was a lot more attractive from abroad than it was at first hand. Scotland was not as she had so fondly remembered it while listening to the tock-tock bird in the evenings on the estate.

The warmth of the hearth fire, the companionship of her family, the cheery greetings at the street corners, the friendly customers in the pub, the shops, the hair-dressers and theatres – they were all there, but whereas they had a touch of magic from afar, when they could be savoured every day they quickly became commonplace again. It was all most disappointing. As winter advanced and the date of their return to Malaya came ever nearer she found she had already made up her mind. She would return and pray for a child.

*   *   *

Nothing had changed during their leave at home. She slipped back into the old routines as if she had never been away. The months ground by and at the end of each one Valerie looked for evidence of impending motherhood – a fulfilment of her mother's words that: 'Your life will be your bairns,' but none came. At first she could not believe it as she had persuaded her husband to give up any form of contraception and to her relief he had acquiesced. They never discussed the question of a family, he just accepted the fact that she wanted one, without enthusiasm as usual but at least without demur.

On her part she had to accept that an inevitable consequence of her deciding on a family as refuge from her loveless marriage was her having to accept what the popular newspapers liked to describe in divorce cases as 'marital relations' although she noticed that when they talked of the same activity between the defaulting spouse and the co-respondent they often preferred the newly fashionable phrase of 'making love'. The irony of the difference was not lost on her as, night after night, she lay staring up at the black mass of the mosquito net after Stuart had gone to sleep. She wondered if making love had ever been a true description of their acts of sexual union.

What a strangely abstract term to describe what was essentially a physical act. It sounded like the purest Hollywood, the cheap culture and language of which had been readily accepted in the western world, and now, with the coming of cinemas to Malaya, were threatening to undermine the sturdier morals of the East. She could not help but wonder how many of the millions of acts of congress which took place every day in both the West and the East, was the making of love, or even the expressing of it for that matter, their main purpose? But perhaps she was becoming cynical – unhappy marriages did that to women. She, at least, had the curious consolation of knowing that for her, the act was for its natural purpose – procreation and the continuation of her species.

About half way through Valerie's second tour there was an incident on the estate that seemed minor at the time but which ultimately was to become of considerable importance in their lives due to the way it was handled by Stuart. It started when he knocked a tapper off his bicycle when driving back to the factory one morning. The man was not seriously hurt but his leg was badly cut and bruised and he had a dislocated shoulder. However, when Stuart helped him to his feet he realised he had been drinking. Although not drunk he had broken one of the rules of the Company by drinking during working hours and Stuart would have been within his rights to dismiss him on the spot, but as he had been with them for many years and was a good worker and as Stuart also felt partly responsible for the accident, he simply put him on half wages for the ten days he was off work.

Stuart thought that would be the end of the matter but for some reason, which he could not understand, his action caused resentment among the labour force. A deputation came to see him but Stuart, sensing the influence of a union, dismissed it out of hand, perhaps unwisely. This exacerbated the dispute and there were rebellious mutterings in the factory, even at muster. The *kepala* was worried.

Then, one morning, Stuart found a dozen of the best rubber trees had been slashed – their milky white sap seeping into the leaf-litter around them entrapping an impressive array of invertebrates including the one the tappers particularly feared – a giant centipede, a bite from which could kill a cat. The trees would not be of much use to the Company again. Slashing was standard practice when there was disaffection in the workforce. Despite much close questioning and dire threats, no one was prepared to break ranks and reveal the names of the miscreants and Stuart was forced to include the incident in his monthly report to the Managing Agents in Singapore. He was angry with himself as, if he had followed Company rules and dismissed the man, the whole incident would have been over and done with by now. In his view it was an example of what happened when managers were weak – they were taken advantage of by workers who had enough cunning to know that when a superior broke a rule he became vulnerable and could be exploited. It was not a mistake he had made before, and one he would certainly not make again.

The Managing Agency despatched a V.A. (Visiting Agent) to the estate – something of a humiliation for Stuart, but it alarmed the workers who thought the estate might be sold and so the matter was settled fairly quickly. The tapper was discharged but compensated with a trifling sum and honour was served. The Visiting Agent was a rather prim, austere man without a trace of humour and although Valerie welcomed the break in her domestic routine during the several days of his visit, he was hard-going. After Stuart had left for the factory on the day of his return to Singapore he sought to re-assure her by saying that Stuart's record with the company was still good. Then he said something quite out of character by referring to the incident in Stuart's past involving the girl in the weeding gang. After which, having immediately realised it must have happened long before Valerie had come to Malaya, he embarked on a long and clumsy explanation, plunging himself ever deeper into embarrassment, his discomfort becoming more painful by the minute, and he was visibly relieved when Kuala Lebir's only taxi came to pick him up, leaving Valerie to her thoughts.

She had heard stories about how the managers had coped with isolation in the old days but had sensibly dismissed them from her mind – there was no point in worrying about something that had happened before she had met Stuart. Being reminded of such things now was not welcome but left her curiously detached, as though she was hearing about a colleague of an acquaintance – someone who had nothing to do with her, although, as Valerie had to remind herself, Stuart was still the man she hoped would be the father of her children.

* * *

However, as each month passed there was still no sign that her great hopes in that direction were going to be realised. She tried expressing how she felt to Stuart but his expressions of sympathy and his recommendation of the need for her continued patience were made without conviction. He seemed not to care either way about a child and said as much when she pressed him. He muttered something about 'a family happening if it was meant to happen' and she supposed she would have to be content with the knowledge that while he did not welcome parenthood at least he was not opposed to it. But if he was apathetic about a baby he was certainly not in two minds about investigating the reasons why one had not come and he flatly refused to submit himself to any procedure that might establish whether he was the cause.

Valerie went to their doctor in Kuala Lebir who sent her to Kota Bharu for tests but there appeared to be no reason why she should not conceive. There the matter had to end although, for Valerie of course, it never ended. She gave almost all her thinking moments to it, until she reached a point when her mind would dwell on little else. One night they fell into one of those pointless arguments that come out of nothing in marriages in which there is a basic lack of affection or an underlying source of discord. It was about the merit of boarding schools of which, Valerie was not surprised to learn, Stuart was totally in favour.

'I went to boarding school when I was seven and it did not do me any harm.'

The irony of this simple sentence almost made her weep for him. It unerringly went to the core of why she so hated the idea of sending children away to school. How much she could have said about her husband's deficiencies of character, and yet she dare not as she knew there was not a solitary word she could say on the subject before their conversation would come to an immediate end. Stuart would have disappeared behind his newspaper in that infuriating, superior, humiliating, way of his, and that would have been that, today and for many days thereafter.

It was what happened whenever there was a disagreement between them, particularly if she had criticised him, or he thought she had criticised him. And this imbalance of personality, this lack of maturity, this want of warmth in his character, together with all his other emotional defects, she attributed, partially at least, to his having been sent to boarding school when he was too young to cope, and the thought of any child of hers going through the same experience and ending up like his or her father was heartbreaking. However, with the diminishing likelihood that she and Stuart would have children or that they would be living in Malaya even if they had, this was not a problem she was likely to face, but they continued to bicker about it – worrying at their divergent opinions like two bored dogs with a bone. After they had both lapsed into a resentful silence relieved only by a persistent tock-tock bird, it seemed to Valerie that yet another nail had been hammered into the coffin of their marriage. How many more would there be before the coffin was sealed and it was buried once and for all?

During her many hours with Osman around the estate and on shopping trips to Kuala Lebir or the Club Valerie had never said anything to him which might have diminished her husband in the eyes of his *syce* and she managed not to do so now, as she knew it was not only disloyal but damaging to the all-important image of those who regarded themselves as entitled to rule. Any overt sign of disharmony between the *tuans* and their mems might create doubts in the minds of the locals, then questions would be raised regarding their betters' moral superiority and therefore authority, inevitably leading on to reservations about their right to govern. But she found it quite impossible to keep her unhappiness from Osman and the reason for it, though she feared this unhappiness might, in itself, be interpreted as an implied criticism, a reproach of Stuart. If that was so, Osman gave no indication of being aware of it, but he was genuinely horrified at the idea of children being sent back to boarding school in Britain.

'What is the point of having children if you don't live with them, Mem?' he said in genuine puzzlement. Then he felt disloyal at having apparently criticised his employer. This was not what he was being paid for. He was sad, however, not only for his mistress, but for his master too, sad for the unhappiness which was obviously being visited upon them. The ways of the white man were indeed difficult to understand. These people came to his country leaving behind a land and a way of life which, according to what he had heard and had seen in the cinema, were much superior to his own. Then they had to suffer the tropical climate, the insects, the smells, the shortages of this and the lack of that, the home-sickness and goodness knows what else.

He knew this to be true because he had heard them say as much, many times. Then, to compound their misery, they were forced to part with the one thing in life that made it worthwhile, the most precious gifts that God could bestow, their children. Their lot was certainly not a happy one, and he grieved on their behalf. His brown eyes were so full of concern and his usually cheerful countenance took on such a woeful expression that it almost made Valerie laugh. She appreciated his sympathy, however, and the consolation of knowing that she was not the only adult in Kelantan who thought that separating oneself from one's children was not a natural thing to do, because, to her surprise, she found her views were not widely shared by her fellow expatriates.

At the Club one day she told Margo Stephenson about Stuart's opinion of boarding schools and no sooner had she started than she burst into tears. She had not cried before Osman, she could not cry before Stuart, but she had no qualms about doing so before her friend, and even thought she might have received some much-needed sympathy. But to her surprise, she found Margo agreeing with the heartless sentiments of her husband.

'It's the best thing for the children,' she said. 'They thrive out here at first, and will run around in the heat all day until they are about seven or eight but then they seem to go downhill. Everyone accepts they have to go to boarding school one day. Mine grew up thinking it was quite normal.'

'But don't you miss them?'

'Of course, we all miss them but,' and she echoed Stuart's

words, 'it's a fact of life out here, one of the things you have to put up with.'

But Valerie was more inclined to put Margo's cool acceptance of the necessity for boarding schools down to the fact that children cramped wives' lifestyle in the tropics, so much so, in fact, that their absence in Britain was far from being an unmitigated sorrow. Although there were *amahs* to shoulder the domestic work involved and there was never a need to find babysitters, children in Malaya could be a hindrance to the pleasurable killing of time. They wanted to go to the pool when it was pleasanter resting after lunch; it was not always possible to leave them in the clubhouse when there was a call for a fourth for golf, while games of bridge had sometimes to be interrupted while childish disputes were settled and other petty crises resolved.

So, there was much public distress on the quayside when the time came for their departure to the U.K., but also much private relief. Tears of outward grief perhaps, and every appearance of stoical resignation, but an inward hope that the old routines forged before the children made their appearance could now be resumed without undue distraction.

* * *

As each month passed with still no sign that a baby was on the way, Valerie became progressively more miserable and Stuart equally more irritated by her low spirits. He began to find her company depressing when he came in after a hard day. He tried to humour her in his gruff way but it failed to make any difference. It crossed his mind that now might be a good time for a real sacrifice on his part and he considered again the possibility of local leave in Penang or Singapore which they had talked about before but for which he had not found the need or the time since his earliest days as a planter. But whenever he tried to sort out a date it always seemed to coincide with a particularly busy period on the estate.

The truth was, of course, he did not really want to go as he always felt at such a loose end in either island city. He was not that fond of golf, and certainly not of drinking in bars – he felt conspicuous drinking fruit juice, especially in the company of strangers – and he certainly did not enjoy talking to them, and as the European clubs and hotel bars seemed full of tourists nowadays with only the odd planter on local leave, they had little attraction for him. As for shopping or going to the new picture-houses which were the only other activities open to the casual European visitor, he saw them much as he saw most holiday activities – just rather tedious ways of killing time. He had long exhausted the other attractions each island offered, such as the Haw Par Gardens in Singapore or the Snake Temple in Penang, a notorious tourist trap where live venomous pit vipers were kept and could be seen decorating the altar. Being nocturnal, they were sleepy enough during the day for the more adventurous of the tourists to be persuaded to have them draped round their necks to be photographed – after a suitable donation had been made to temple funds of course.

Such amusements having lost their savour, all that was left for him to do was play a round or two of golf in the cool of the morning and then lounge beside the club's swimming pool for the rest of the day, bored out of his mind. It wasn't much of a holiday to his way of thinking.

He would much rather be back on the estate where he felt he had a real purpose and where there always seemed something to do, either in the factory or the office or even around the estate. He was a firm believer in the old country saying he had once heard from his grandfather who had been a farmer in Ayrshire: 'There's nae fertiliser like the master's foot.'

As a boy he had been puzzled by it and what it had meant but since he had become a rubber planter he had tried to put it into practice. It never did any harm to be seen around the estate by the workers, and if he could manage it, when they least expected him. What he was quietly working towards this year was a significant boost in production in the hope it would wipe out the stain of the incident of the slashed rubber trees. He had heard other planters say local leave invariably had a harmful effect on daily latex returns as workers were never slow to take advantage of *tuan's* absence – it was the same the world over, and he could not bear the thought of production falling for even a day when it could be avoided.

Now, to Stuart's frustration, Valerie had started on again about holding a curry tiffin, returning overdue hospitality and giving her something to plan for and so forth. He thought he had scotched that idea years ago. It would be ridiculous giving his first tiffin after all these years. There would be endless difficulties – the bungalow, the garden, everything would need smartening up. The servants had no experience of entertaining, so they would not be able to cope. It would be a fiasco and give people even more cause to sneer at him behind his back. And all for what? Talking to people he could not give a damn about. They would not want to come anyway, probably half of them would not turn up, making it even more of a farce. Then he and Valerie would be invited back and the whole damn thing would start all over again.

He tried to put his foot down about a tiffin once and for all. But when he did so she became more upset than he could ever remember and disappeared into the spare bedroom. She did not even come out for dinner. She had never done that before even during the difficult time after the miscarriage. He had to tell Tambi that Mem was not well when they could both hear her crying. It was very awkward. His whole evening had been ruined. All he wanted was a little peace and quiet after a hard day on the estate, it was not too much to ask for, surely? Why did women always get so worked up and emotional about such little things as tiffins? The loss of a baby he could understand and so he had been very sympathetic about that, going out of his way to show he understood how she felt, but a tiffin?

The scene over the tiffin was the last straw for Valerie. It made up her mind, baby or no baby, she would bring the marriage to an end during their next home leave. She would tell Stuart that she could take no more, the charade of their marriage was over. In fact, she even toyed with the idea of asking him if she could go home now. She still had time to start again with someone else although the divorce would take a long time to come through when desertion was the only grounds upon which it could be granted. Perhaps she would give Stuart other reasons for divorcing her but it would be just like him not to take advantage of them.

Then something happened which completely altered her plans, and this was followed by another significant event – she suspected she was pregnant again. She waited until she was certain and then had it confirmed by her doctor, but she did not tell Stuart – she had to get it right this time, there must be no premature announcements followed by bitter disappointments. But her health blossomed, she never felt better and her doctor said he could see no reason why she should not go full term. Still she waited, making up her mind what to do; the direction of her life had changed, and changed in a radical way. There were many new things to consider. Finally, she acted.

*   *   *

Stuart was dumbfounded when he got back to the bungalow for breakfast to find his wife's note saying she was leaving him. She had not given the slightest indication of doing such a thing the previous evening although he had to admit, it had crossed his mind that she might decide not to come back to Malaya with him when their next leave ended. But to go and live in a native village with his *syce*! What on earth had possessed her? He was such an insignificant little man! Pleasant enough and a good driver but what was there about him to attract a European woman? The effrontery of it, to think he could help himself to an *orang puteh's* wife just like that and hope to get away with it. He felt betrayed. The two of them must have been conducting their affair right under his nose and yet he had not noticed a thing, nor had the servants presumably, because if they had known about it then he was sure Tambi would have alerted him. Tambi would have been as shocked and offended as he was, he was quite sure of that.

He furrowed his brow. Now he came to think of it, his wife had been much more cheerful lately. She had even let the matter of the tiffins drop, and had also stopped suggesting ways of improving their social life in other ways, much to his relief. It must have been because of this. Then there was that strange incident when she had, quite inexplicably, turned down the chance of going with him to Singapore for a few days. Now he knew why, and he felt angry at the deception and how they both must have been laughing at him.

At first, the matter-of-fact, almost casual, way in which the note was written had made him wonder if the whole thing was not a practical joke, but the *syce* was nowhere around and an apprehensive Tambi, confronted in the kitchen, confirmed Mem and Osman had left together. Then he thought she might have fallen victim to some dreadful eastern malady of the kind that occasionally drove locals to run *amok*, and that this had somehow turned her mind. There must be something to explain such an act of monumental folly. Had she any idea of what she had let herself in for? To contemplate sharing the life of a native, especially one of humble means, was beyond belief.

Finally, he fell to wondering if she was in the grip of some romantic delusion. If so, then a couple of weeks in a *kampung* would soon cure her of that. The novelty of trying to cope with living in a native house would soon wear off and then what would happen? There was no doubt in his mind. He was not going to have her back, there was not the slightest chance that she could come crawling back to Bukit Bintang. She might make a fool of herself but she was certainly not going to make a fool out of him. She had made her bed and she would have to lie on it, come what may.

Tambi brought in the coffee and scuttled back into the kitchen as fast as his legs could carry him. Well he knew what the contents of the note must be and well he knew also, his master's moods and uncertain temper. Stuart read the letter again and the part about having Osman's baby registered with him for the first time. So it was not just an impulse, a rush of blood. This adulterous affair had been going on for some time! Perhaps Ah Gan and Tambi had known about it after all and had been too frightened to say anything. But to have become pregnant! An affair could have been dealt with perhaps, hushed up, but when a baby was involved it was a very different matter. What had she been thinking of? Did it not occur to her to ask the fellow to take precautions? My God, she was worse than the tappers on the estate.

He walked out onto the verandah and stood, hands on the rail, looking down the estate road, which the runaway pair had taken not two hours before. It was almost as if he expected to see her standing there, waiting to see what effect her letter had had on him. His incredulity continued to grow. That any white woman could be so foolish beggared the imagination, but that it should be someone connected with him, his wife, was quite beyond endurance. To have let herself down in such a humiliating way, not to mention the disgrace she had brought to the estate, indeed the whole British community, was quite outside anything he had experienced or even heard of.

His indignation moved on to what the rest of the world would think. The opinions of his fellow Europeans did not bother him very greatly, he saw little of them anyway and their views were of no great consequence to him one way or another. It was the workers on the estate who concerned him the most. He saw them every day and he knew the importance of 'face' in their lives. He would go down drastically in their estimation, of that there could be little doubt. He knew the attitude they would take – henceforth he would be known as the husband who was unable to satisfy his wife or keep her under control. It would never happen in their households, of course, their fists or worse would see to that. Would it have any effect on discipline? Just let them try it, loss of face or no loss of face! He would soon show them that though he might not use his fists on his *wife* he knew what they were for.

But if only she had not gone off with a servant, it really was rubbing his nose in it. If it had been another planter, or one of the young princes of the Sultan – they rather fancied themselves with the European wives at times, or even a wealthy Chinese such as a *towkay*, it might not have been so bad. But someone who was not of her class, who had no money, no property, no prospects, his own driver, was truly mortifying.

For once he did not return to the factory immediately after his breakfast but sat and brooded on the verandah. It crossed his mind that he could perhaps make an attempt to bring his wife back before her desertion became generally known but he was not very sure where Osman lived and he would have to involve the local police, which would mean the affair would become common knowledge and so do more harm than good. In any case, there was the baby to consider. What could be done about that? But there would be repercussions, serious repercussions, there was no way they could be avoided. The Colonial authorities would not take this lying down. They would do their very best to get her sent home, he was quite sure of that. A British woman living in a native village with a Malay man of lowly birth and a baby would bring the whole administration into disrepute and would not be tolerated.

His thought about the baby prompted another. Of course, it was not a British child she was carrying, it was a Malay and that would really complicate the situation. The Malays were very proprietary about their own children, especially boys, and the British were most unwilling to involve themselves in such matters, in fact on any matter unless it was something of over-riding importance. Malays were normally very placid and easygoing but could be volatile particularly when they thought their religion had been slighted or their race insulted. It took only a small thing to set them off and then there could be civil disorder, even full-scale riots, resulting in the destruction of property and very unwelcome publicity for Britain in the world's press, the last thing the Administration would want as, like all Colonial governments, they were anxious to demonstrate the universal benevolence of their rule and the prosperity and happiness of their subjects.

On the other hand, sending Valerie home without her baby might create even worse publicity. The papers would be full of the callous attitude of heartless authority and not only those in Malaya but in Britain too. He could see the banner headlines in the popular British press now. There were likely to be all manner of problems ahead and although he would try to keep his head down and bury himself in his work he could not hope to evade all the unpleasantness. He supposed a summons to the British Adviser in Kota Bharu to confirm the facts would be his first indignity. Then, no doubt, he would have to listen to some lofty and pointed remarks about his wife's failure – and by implication his – to uphold the prestige of the administration. Windy speeches on the need to preserve British dignity was not at all to his taste, particularly after *his* had taken such a battering. He just hoped his employers in Singapore would show a bit more understanding of what had happened and the personal humiliation he was experiencing.

He also could not help remembering that this would be the third unfortunate incident on his file and coming so soon after the tree-slashing affair he wondered what the reaction of the Directors might be. He went back to the factory in the afternoon with a heavy heart.

* * *

That night the bungalow seemed quieter than he had ever remembered it. Valerie had never been a talker but just the occasional stir of her chair or the turning of a page in her book had indicated her presence and brought him all the companionship he needed. He had never had much time for idle chatter. As he had often said, because human beings had been given the power of speech there was no need for them to be exercising it all the time. He had always quite enjoyed silence, but silence in the company of others was very different to the enforced silence of solitude, and this was the first time he had been alone in the bungalow since those few days Valerie had been in hospital after her miscarriage. At that moment the only thing he could hear was the whirring of the cicadas and the occasional bark of a deer from the darkness under the rubber trees. The lack of human companionship had never bothered him in his early days as a planter but he was finding it surprisingly depressing at this moment.

He paced out onto the verandah several times and then back. A moth was battering itself against the glass of the oil lamp – a veritable storm of fluttering simply to achieve its own immolation in the flame. The ridiculous insect might well be his wife – eagerly going to what was bound to be her ruination in the Malay world. The commotion attracted the interest of a *cicat* and Stuart watched it stalk its demented prey for a few moments but lost interest when the lizard did the same. Having decided the hot glass made the chase too risky, it departed in search of an easier meal. There came the familiar sound of the tock-tock bird and he found himself counting the tocks and then waiting for another. Ye Gods, this is how it had been when he was a bachelor. The nightjar had quite amused him then, but the prospect of evening after evening with nothing to do but wait for the first tock did not bear thinking about. His future suddenly looked decidedly and unpleasantly empty.

All at once he became aware of a slight movement from the kitchen and a silent presence. It could not be Tambi – he had long retired to his room. Then he realised the *kepala* was standing in the shadows. Stuart's immediate reaction was one of surprise at the speed and efficiency of the estate's bush-telegraph system – it had certainly not wasted any time in catching up with his latest piece of news! His irritation at what seemed like an unwarranted intrusion upon his privacy was about to make him dismiss the headman with a curse when a vision of a pair of rounded thighs beneath a swathe of colourful cotton made him pause. Perhaps, just this once, it would help him take his mind off things. He directed a rapid volley of Tamil towards the waiting figure.

PART TWO

THE PLANTER'S WIFE

Looking back, Valerie was able to pinpoint the exact moment she realised life in Malaya was not just unimaginable without Osman, it was unthinkable and that she could not face the future without him, which meant – in accordance with the logic of such things – she must therefore be in love with him. It was when she and Stuart were returning to the estate from the Kuala Lebir Club one night in a tropical storm. The rain hurled itself against the windscreen of the car with such force that the single wiper was almost overwhelmed and struggled to provide even the briefest glimpses of the road ahead, while the deafening noise around them drove them all into little private worlds of their own. Giant swirls of water swept over the roof and along the windows in a ceaseless stream. Before many minutes, the rainwater running off the padi fields filled the ditches and spread across the road, making the wheels of the car slew alarmingly and propelling its passengers forward out of their seats.

Osman leaned over the steering wheel to peer at the watery world ahead of him and Valerie's attention was drawn to his glossy black hair spilling over his jacket collar. She had grown used to this view of him over the years and the sight never failed to reassure her. He was a good driver and enjoyed driving and, of course, this weather was normal for him. He would not be feeling awe, fear or even irritation while it had never occurred to him to rail at the fates. Whatever they chose to send him was accepted with the same unchanging good humour, and Valerie thought how indispensable he was to her.

It was depressing to think that he was now almost the only person in the whole country whose company she enjoyed and for whom she had an ounce of real feeling. There was no point even pretending she was still in a marriage any longer, she would have to bring it to an end during the next home leave, there seemed no point prolonging it. She should have done so during the last time she was in Britain when she would not have regretted leaving Osman so much. It was then she realised it would not be just a regret at leaving Osman – it would come near to breaking her heart, and the intensity of her feelings took her completely by surprise.

Unaware of this sudden elevation in his emotional status in the eyes of his mistress, Osman was as cheerful as ever but, then, he always seemed to find everything in life cheerful, even amusing. His face was perpetually creased in an infectious smile. He was enjoying his life as a *syce* and general amanuensis to this beautiful white woman who, oddly, seemed to prefer his company to that of the other mems in the club, although it meant that he was reduced to seeing his wife and children only once a week on his day off. A friend who was the taxi driver in Kuala Lebir collected him on Thursday evening and he was away until Saturday morning, giving him the whole of the Muslim Sabbath to attend the obligatory ceremonies in the local mosque, to catch up with his family responsibilities and listen to the latest gossip in his village.

Friday, on the other hand, was Valerie's low spot of the week. She was left with her own thoughts and to her own devices for the entire day. Walking on the estate had lost its novelty and so she had taken up gardening instead. She spent an hour or so every morning before the sun had any real power, fussing over her orchids of which she had made quite a collection, but thereafter time hung heavily.

She was in the garden with Osman one morning cutting some orchids for the house when something happened which, though seemingly minor at the time, was destined to cast a long and enduring shadow over both their futures. She was just about to cut a frond when it moved and she saw, at the last moment, that it was a small emerald-green snake. She gave a squeal and stepped back suddenly only to collide with Osman who was holding the flowers for her. She would have fallen had he not seized and steadied her and for a second or two he continued to support her as she strove to regain her balance. They both laughed, she more than he.

'Sorry, Mem,' he said, letting go of her arm at the first opportunity. He seemed ill at ease at the familiarity and Valerie realised it was the first time she had been aware of his touch. She felt guilt at having embarrassed him, though not nearly as guilty as she felt that evening when she found herself recalling the pleasure it had given her and trying to think of a way she could devise a similar mishap.

At the time, however, she had done her best to make light of it for his sake. 'Thank you, Osman,' she said, 'my saviour. I don't know what I would have done if you had not been there. It gave me quite a start. What sort of snake is it?'

Osman looked at the snake with an incurious eye. It was intent on resuming its place in the natural order of things by imitating a branch, and its identity was of the utmost indifference to him. He showed little interest in his country's flora and fauna and was mystified when others did so. It had amazed him, for example, when he had heard that some *tuans* actually studied animals and plants for a living. Was there no end to the white man's eccentricity?

'Shall I kill it, Mem?'

But Valerie did not want it killed, only its name. Osman was puzzled. Snakes were either poisonous or non-poisonous. The former were usually brightly coloured to let you know they were dangerous and so you killed them. You ignored the latter, unless they caused inconvenience, in which case you killed them too. Those whose toxicity was uncertain, you killed to be on the safe side. A dead snake could do no harm to anyone and what difference did one less snake make? The country was full of them. As to this one's name, he had not the faintest idea but he made one up as Valerie seemed to require it of him. These strange British mems , bothering themselves with matters which were totally unimportant – snakes, flowers, golf, card games. The important things, such as looking after their children and making their husbands happy, seemed not to concern them and so were left to others.

She was an attractive woman though, attractive enough to bring her husband plenty of envious glances at the Club and yet *Tuan*, strange man, seemed oblivious of his treasure. He had heard the other *syces* talk in lascivious terms about her and it had made him feel uncomfortable. Apart from offending his natural modesty, such talk aroused his proprietary feelings about her as an employee of her husband.

He also felt mortification on *Tuan's* behalf. If she had been his wife, he was certain he would not have allowed her to wear those revealing dresses. It was not right that other men should see the shape of her legs, or gaze into her bosom, himself included. At times he was positively embarrassed, even compromised. The incident with the snake was a case in point – it had put him closer to her than he had any right to be and he had seen more than was both seemly and proper. It was the same when she sat next to him in the car instead of in the back seat as mems were supposed to do. She failed to realise that Malay men were not used to dealing with such temptations. Several times he had had to pray to Allah for forgiveness for thoughts unbecoming to a Muslim.

However, the snake incident left a greater impression on Valerie than it did on Osman. She found her mind going back to her *syce* time and again in the succeeding days, and the nights too, as she lay on the enormous bed listening to the myriad sounds of Malaya's nocturnal wildlife after Stuart had gone to sleep. How was she going to face leaving him when she returned to Britain for good? Could she afford a chauffeur in Britain? She smiled ruefully. There was no way she would be able to afford a car, let alone a chauffeur, especially one with a family. She recalled his strength. Although he was small, he had no difficulty in taking her weight. She also remembered what she had felt at his touch and inwardly blushed.

She sighed and wondered how his wife, Minah, felt about him. Malay marriages were arranged, the couples themselves given little choice in the matter. The contracts were often made while they were still children, even babies, and a refusal to honour such agreements was to cause offence and bring disgrace to the parents. Love hardly seemed a consideration but, despite that, couples were expected to remain constant to each other and, compared to the amount of infidelity and promiscuity in most Western societies, the majority of them were. She had heard it said, however, that such correctness was not always because Muslim men wished to be faithful to their wives, it was just that there were very few opportunities in the villages for them to be otherwise, and even fewer for the women, for *kampung* life was very public while the *imams* were vigilance itself. But it was not only their religion which ensured their fidelity. Unfaithfulness on the part of a man brought particular shame to his parents as it reflected on their choice of his marriage partner. Moral derelictions, therefore, required much filial expiation and penance in the mosque.

The smallest fall from grace on the part of a wife, on the other hand, would almost inevitably lead to immediate divorce, or for a single woman, a life of degradation. The latter might end up as a taxi or *joget* girl in a dance hall if she was lucky, or, if her looks did not merit such good fortune, in a Chinese brothel. It said much for the virtue of Malay girls, though less for their beauty perhaps, that there was nearly always a shortage of such girls in the dance halls of the cities so that young men, suitably made up to look like hostesses, had to be recruited to take their place. Many a British serviceman in Singapore and Penang had discovered this curious deception to his embarrassment, not to mention disappointment, at the end of an evening of libidinous expectation.

Divorced wives could sometimes find themselves isolated from their families, rarely or only occasionally being able to see their children. Like planters' wives who sent their offspring to boarding school.

* * *

On the way to the Club the next day Valerie questioned Osman on his marriage. When did he first know he was to marry Minah, had he ever wanted to marry anyone else, what did they do together, what did they talk about, had he ever been in love? Did he love Minah? Osman felt acutely uncomfortable. Not only were these improper subjects to be discussing with a woman, any woman, he was at a loss for many of the answers.

He had never given a thought to such questions. As far as he was concerned, life consisted of duties, to his employers, to his family, to his community, to his religion, and these he accepted without question, one certainly was not given a choice in the matter. As for his feelings, they only came into it when these duties broke down. If it was a failure on his part then he would feel shame, if a man failed in his duty towards him then he would feel anger. He was somewhat doubtful about the sort of feelings Mem was talking about, they hardly seemed relevant to everyday life. Everyone knew that you deferred to your elders, honoured your parents, loved your children, and respected your wife. Valerie was silent for a while.

'That's the trouble Osman, I don't respect my husband.'

Osman was shocked both by the fact and the admission of it. It would have been different if she had said she did not love her husband. A Malay woman did not have to love her husband, not in the Western sense that is, the sense that Western singers were always on about on the wireless. Romantic love of that sort had no part to play in a Malay marriage. There was the courtly love of Malay legends and song although that had nothing to do with marriage either. Marriage was a serious business, far too serious to be left to the follies and the foibles of the young with their falling in love and being swept off their feet and their whirlwind romances.

He had seen such goings-on in American films. Marriages in the West, it seems, could be between people who had only just met, and so hardly knew each other, let alone their families. Nor did they often bother to find out anything about their new partner's background. No wonder there were so many divorces. The choice of a mate needed the wisdom and guidance of those who had a proper experience of life as there were so many important things to be taken into consideration when a partnership needed and was expected to last a lifetime. When the prospective mother or father of one's children was being chosen then surely the collective judgement of families was so much more reliable than mere romantic fancy?

It was not necessary therefore, for a Malay wife to love her husband – not in the way Hollywood portrayed it. But for a Malay wife not to respect her husband! Now that was a grave matter, and for a woman to admit as much, especially to a man, was quite shocking. Osman felt guilty at even hearing such a thing. Mem's admission meant Stuart had been dishonoured in his presence and he felt something needed to be said in defence of his allegedly errant master, if only to absolve himself from complicity in what he saw as a betrayal, almost a blasphemy, which, to make the offence seem even worse, had been uttered in *Tuan's* own car!

'Tuan is a good man. He loves his parents and respects his wife. He gives her a good home, she has everything she wants,' he said firmly, and then, as an afterthought and thinking it would please her, he added: 'And he doesn't chase after other women. Some syces say their tuans are very bad. They are always telling them to take them to the perempuan jalang.' Then, realising Valerie's Malay might not extend to such a subject, explained, 'Bachelor girls, the women who earn their living in the town.' It was awkward for him to use these expressions to any member of the opposite sex, but especially to a mem. To his surprise, Valerie was unimpressed.

'But I cannot talk to him, Osman, he never seems to understand how I feel. What does Minah do when she wants to talk about a problem?'

Osman was puzzled, the thought had never occurred to him. As far as he could remember, Minah had never expressed a desire for a heart-to-heart talk, and in any case, how would he know what women talked about when they were in the kitchen? A self-respecting Malay man would never allow himself to be seen there.

'She talks to my mother,' he said at last, and then, after an inspiration, 'To the other wives in the kampung.'

'But I have no other wives in the kampung, I only have you,' said Valerie sadly.

'What about the other mems . Can you not talk to them?'

'Not about these things, Osman. I'm afraid word would get around, there would be gossip. There are some things you can hardly tell even to a friend.'

Having at last broached the subject of her marriage to Osman, Valerie was inclined to return to it again and again. Osman was not a willing confidant but he hated to see her unhappy so he let her talk, his face mirroring her unhappiness; in any case, he had no other choice. He could offer little in return as he was quite at a loss how to advise a woman who no longer respected her husband or, apparently, wished to remain married to him.

He also felt very uneasy at the growing intimacy in her attitude towards him. He did not wittingly or willingly encourage it. In some respects it was even cause for some alarm. He had never heard of a European wife becoming romantically involved with a native, let alone with an employee, a servant. Many a planter had taken a woman from a neighbouring *kampung* and returned her there when circumstances made it necessary. These relationships were usually on a commercial basis, agreed to by the girl's family who all shared in the moderate wealth it brought. The girl involved might well find a husband later in the village, perhaps as a second wife to a widower. She would certainly be able to retain some sort of place in village society.

But it was very different for an Asian man, of that he was certain. He puzzled over what his mem was trying to do. She made no direct reference to a relationship between them but she was already more familiar than a woman in the village could ever be with a man without finding herself, indeed both of them, in the deepest trouble with the *imam*. To be found in any circumstances of intimacy with a member of the opposite sex who was not of one's family was to be guilty of the sin of *khalwat* which he had seen translated in the English-speaking newspapers as 'close proximity'. Nothing was ever specified, it did not have to be. Just to be near one another without the presence of a respectable third party to act as a chaperone was sufficient for the presumption that some form of immorality had taken place, or was about to take place. Even now, sitting as they were, would have been enough to compromise him in the eyes of the *imam* had it not been a necessary condition of his employment.

It was not the same for Europeans, they had different standards. He had seen things going on in the Club between memmems who were dancing with *tuans* who were not their husbands which would have scandalised his *kampung*. And the husbands took no notice, it seemed normal behaviour for them. Would they regard it as normal for their *syces* he wondered? He suspected not, but what was he to do? He was in a difficult position. To be even suspected of over-familiarity could cost him his job and also bring disgrace to his family. The *imam* at his local mosque was a powerful figure and his anger could be formidable. He might even find himself barred from worship. And a scandal of that sort would certainly prevent him getting another job with a European family with its relatively high pay.

He resolved to be as discouraging as he could. His mem's marriage was not a fit subject for them to discuss. He would listen as he was bound to do, but he would make no answer. If he did not give her any encouragement then what happened could not be laid at his door. It would be the will of Allah. But he could not deny that her physical charms were difficult to ignore, and any opportunity for *chumbu-chumbuan* with her would be a sore temptation. That fair skin, those sparkling eyes, that rounded softness which promised so much. Those unbecoming thoughts again! As the *imam* had said on many occasions, women were temptresses, always seeking to bewitch the unsuspecting male and lead him into evil ways. He would have to be on his guard every minute of the day he was with her, and belatedly, he made another supplication to Allah for forgiveness.

*   *   *

Some days later Valerie asked Osman to take her into Kuala Lebir. She lunched at the Club but there was a golf tournament in progress, the Club was crowded, and so they left for Bukit Bintang earlier than usual. Osman had been rather uncommunicative lately, just when she was in particular need of some sympathy, some soothing words. Talking in the car, even when she was sitting next to him and not in the back seat as she rarely was nowadays, was very unsatisfactory. For some reason he seemed always to be concentrating on the road and unable to say anything other than 'yes, Mem' and 'no, Mem'. They would have to find somewhere quiet where she could really give vent to her feelings or she did not know what she was going to do.

The previous evening had been the last straw. Stuart had been at his worst – curt, uncommunicative, unwilling to discuss how embarrassed she felt that no other European was ever invited to cross their threshold. The subject of tiffins had come up again, perhaps not wisely. As she had told him many times, tiffins were not difficult to arrange, she would have loved to host one, even after all these years, and she knew Margo and the other wives would have been pleased to help with the boys and anything else she needed.

In the end he put a copy of the *Planters' Journal* in front of his face and refused to say another word on the subject. She had only just managed to stop herself screaming at the top of her voice, and had she done so, she knew she would have gone on screaming and never stopped. It was not just the tiffins, it was everything, her loveless marriage, her pointless life on the estate and how it was being frittered away, her desperate longing for a baby. She had never been one to resort to hysterics to get her way with men – she could not remember ever needing to – but she wished she *had* screamed now, it would at least have shown Stuart how desperate she felt about everything. Instead, she had just gone into the spare bedroom and sobbed her frustrations into a pillow but with very little success as, even now, she felt as if her whole body was twisted into knots like an over-wound elastic band.

They reached the laterite road and Valerie asked Osman to turn on to a gravel track where she knew the tappers had finished collecting the latex. That part of the estate was usually clear in the afternoon apart from the maintenance workers and she knew they were doing very little at present due to the recent wet weather. She badly wanted them to have a proper talk, or was there something else? The question was suppressed before it could be properly asked, she only knew she would have to do something about the agonising tension that was twisting inside her. They stopped in the shade and Osman looked at her questioningly. Valerie asked him to raise the bonnet. If the car was seen by a stray worker, they at least would have an explanation for having stopped in such an out of the way place by pretending the car had broken down, although how she would explain them being in that part of the estate she had no idea. But they would not be here long, she only wanted a talk and for him to listen, a little warmth, some tenderness.

Osman returned to the car without looking at her. She gazed at him beseechingly but he sat staring fixedly through the windscreen.

'Osman, please look at me. You aren't driving now.'

The brown eyes in which she had always found such solace had never looked so troubled or less responsive. He looked away again immediately.

What was Mem doing? What had he seen in her look? No, it was not possible, yet she had asked him to stop in this little frequented part of the estate, surely not for just one of her talks about how she felt, how unhappy she was married to *Tuan*. There was something about the way she was sitting, the way she was looking at him, the message seemed unmistakable. Desperately he went over the *imam's* teaching. Never had there been a moment when it was more needed. But how difficult it was. European dress left so little to the imagination, there was so much flesh, so much shape to feed the senses, not to mention the scent European women always wore, which was a constant, insidious, threat to male resolution. Surely, Man's art and ingenuity had never been put to a more devilish use than when he had devised these enticing, almost irresistible, perfumes, so unlike anything in the *kampung*. And what was the purpose of all this subtlety and expertise? Astonishingly, it was just to bring about Man's own moral downfall! Madness. Were women not temptation enough in themselves?

He tried to remember the precise words of the *imam* when man was faced with a temptation of the flesh: 'According to the philosopher, nothing exists but thinking makes it so. Dismiss the thought and it ceases to exist, all desire will vanish.' Manfully, Osman tried to comply and did his best to banish all thoughts of the enticements sitting next to him. He concentrated his gaze through the windscreen, looking intently at the silver figurine on the raised bonnet as though he had never seen it in his life before, and then, in desperation, he examined the gravel path beyond it, but they did little to divert his seething imagination.

Valerie spoke to him again and he rashly turned his head. One half-glimpse of the shape of her thighs outlined through her flimsy dress and the thoughts returned, sending their messages more urgently than ever. It was strange, he had seen that sight a thousand times, why was it only now that it stirred these almost uncontrollable feelings? It was fine for the philosopher and his wisdom about the origins of male desire, but he had probably never been sitting as close to them as he was now, and had he ever seen such sights as his imagination was being tormented by at that moment? He closed his eyes and defied the rounded images to return. Then, steeling himself to keep his eyes away from her lap, he turned towards her again, only to be even more undermined by her soft throat and the swelling curve of her bosom. He felt ashamed of what Mem must be reading in his eyes.

Valerie continued to gaze at him and, as she watched, she saw the brown eyes soften with apparent sympathy and concern. She felt hers moisten and, on an impulse, she put her hand over his on the steering wheel. The touch of his fingers under hers was all she needed to open the floodgates of her feelings. She tried to lay her head on his chest only to find an arm in the way. Before he could move she had lifted it and slipped underneath. The next instant his arm was around her and she was shedding tears of relief. He did not protest, he seemed to find it quite natural. In contrast to Stuart who would have recoiled in contempt, a dismissive comment already on his lips. Osman's silent compassion released another wave of emotion in her.

He let her cry. He did not know what else to do. He had been bracing himself against her carnal presence, only to find himself being betrayed by these unexpected demands upon his sympathy. Valerie's softness and warmth began to spread, inexorably, into every corner of his body. They prompted an urgent question to the Western philosopher. Perhaps desire *could* be dismissed from the mind, but what was to be done when it found its way to a far more susceptible part of the body? He feared he could no more dismiss it from there than he could stop a runaway buffalo in a padi field. Frantically he began to mutter the *imam's* words over and over again under his breath.

Valerie nestled against him appreciatively. It was such a relief just to feel his warmth, his sheer physical presence – it was positively soaking up her unhappiness, absorbing her misery. What he was saying she was unable to hear, it was of no importance, his soothing voice was all she needed. Then, when she realised what she had done, the compromising position in which she had put herself, a sudden wave of guilt assailed her. She should not have exposed Osman to such embarrassment. She had gone too far, it was not fair of her to put him in this position. She had promised never to venture into that no-man's-land of mutual respect they had agreed upon months before, now she had not just invaded it but had leapt across it entirely, and so was now, conspicuously, where she clearly had no right to be. Only his wife was entitled to enter where she had intruded so brazenly. What must he be thinking?

But Osman was now beyond thought, he was totally in the realm of feeling, an irresistible feeling which was sweeping away the ancient, natural reserve between mistress and servant as well as the cultural and religious barriers that had inhibited relations between their two races for generations past. All were in the process of being replaced by one of the strongest feelings a man can have – the physical desire to make love to a woman.

Osman's excitement transmitted itself to Valerie and she instantly sought to give it release, but there was an obstacle – the restrictions of where they were sitting. Front seats of cars are no place for spontaneous love-making, unplanned or otherwise. Spur-of-the-moment lovers need to seize their moment. They were thus at the mercy of time and opportunity where any move meant delay, and delay could mean the loss of that precious charge of urgency, vital to a successful union. Embarrassment and reserve, never far away, could return as quickly as they had been banished. Valerie, however, was determined not to miss the chance and was moved to recklessness.

'Let's get into the back,' she whispered.

They both opened their doors, but as Valerie feared, when her feet touched the gravel path, her rashness disappeared and self-consciousness returned. It was as if her contact with the ground had earthed her ardour. What was she doing, giving herself to her Malay servant in this brazen way? She felt a wave of shame, and her passion left her as suddenly as it had come. She stood, one hand on the car door, immobilised by doubt.

For Osman too, the moment had been a crucial one. As he opened the door he also had been beset by uncertainty. Had he heard aright, had he interpreted her suggestion correctly, was this beautiful white woman about to give herself to him? He felt his desire, that uncontrollable force which had up to now been joyously sweeping away all his fears and reservations, suddenly desert him as dramatically as a storm wave rears back from a beach, leaving just abandoned pebbles rolling in its wake. It was as if the opening of the car doors had allowed his caged emotions to disperse into the branches of the rubber trees. Was it possible they could be summoned back again in the way a storm wave, having regained its strength from the sea, is able to throw itself once more upon the shore?

It was a crucial moment for them both but Valerie did not hesitate. Like a gambler risking all in a final throw, she stood up and, lifting her dress with one hand, with the other she deftly removed that item of underwear which she knew would obstruct their purpose. The effect was immediate. The baring of her body in the warm air filled her with a wave of feeling which was quite overwhelming. No medieval alchemist seeking to turn base metal into gold could have achieved a more miraculous transformation. In an instant, her simple need to be close to Osman had been replaced by a fierce desire for union with him. All her reservations, all her embarrassments disappeared. Now all she wanted to do was to show herself to him, to see and feel his excitement and take his body into hers. Her simple act of disrobing had transformed the planter's wife from a mere seeker of sympathy into a wanton without shame.

As she raised her dress, the sight of Valerie's pale body outlined momentarily against the trees released Osman's last uncertainty, his last inhibition, and the craving which he realised had been growing deep within him and which he had been suppressing for many months, gave way to an impelling demand.

They reached the back seat together and before embarrassment could return, he knelt and made love to her with a fierceness which was almost volcanic in its intensity and belied his gentle nature. His passion did not last long, he made no attempt to prolong it, as if he was aware their situation demanded only the briefest of unions. But he did not withdraw immediately but lay within her, prolonging the pleasure of the moment, as if he instinctively knew the therapy of their love-making would not be complete until her tortured feelings, ebbing slowly away like lava flowing gently down a mountainside, had finally come to rest. Valerie gazed through the car window, eyelids feathering the sunlight as it filtered through the branches of the rubber trees. For several priceless seconds she revelled in Osman's warmth, his scent, his maleness, as she felt it coursing its way, deliciously and all-pervading, into every inch of her body.

A sudden awareness of where they were broke the spell. Hurriedly Valerie sat upright and noticed, to her surprise, that Osman had made no attempt – or had no time – to remove any of his clothing. She was thus able to almost push him out onto the gravel path and he, responding to her urgency, half-ran to the car bonnet and slammed it down, the harsh sound echoing guiltily through the trees. Had they been seen? A thousand tappers could have been looking through the windows in that brief time they were together and they both would have been blissfully unaware of each one of them. The thought only added to Valerie's alarm and she shouted at Osman as he fumbled with the bonnet clips. She was desperate to get off the gravel path and onto the laterite road, back to their normal route, their normal routine. If they could achieve that without discovery, then their pleasure would have come without cost, and perhaps be there to enjoy again.

Their anxiety and haste served to fill that awkward time when they should have been seeking answers to all the many questions posed by their sudden and headlong surrender to passion. Even after they had turned onto the road to the bungalow and had been relieved to discover there were no suspicious eyes to speculate on their vehicle's unusual path, they were silent. And when they got back to the bungalow, they parted immediately, both still anxious to avoid explanations or recriminations. Time for those later.

* * *

And yet there never were. Not once did they manage to analyse the events of that day or to rationalise their new relationship. Perhaps it was impossible. Perhaps there were no words which could meet the situation, could express what had happened or what they felt. So, when they met the next day, he greeted her as if nothing had happened, and even when they were alone, she continued to be Mem and he continued to be Osman, her *syce*.

At first Valerie was astonished that Osman did not show some indication that the unbridgeable gap between them had been bridged, that he had known her as only his master could know her, so that, now, her orders to him must seem presumptuous, almost humiliating, and yet he did not. In neither word, gesture or deed did he betray any emotion or let her know his world had changed. It almost made her feel it had happened in a dream. It left her in control of their relationship but she did not wish to be in control. She had been in control too long, now she wanted something different. She wanted him to claim a lover's rights, rights which she was longing to bestow, and she also wanted him to acknowledge the obligations which came with those rights, and which she was even more desperate to enjoy.

Eagerly, each day, she looked for an indication that the afternoon in the rubber trees had meant something to him, had been in some small way at least, an expression of his feelings, but to her disappointment and frustration, there was none. No matter how hard she searched his face, how closely she examined everything he said, she could detect not the slightest indication that they were now more than they had ever been in their previous years together. In a thousand ways she made her conversation more personal, more intimate, but Osman did not once respond. Eventually, after several days, she could control herself no longer and put her hand on his arm as he got into the car.

'Your thoughts?' she asked, but Osman did not look at her. How could she understand his thoughts? She, no doubt, was concerned about their relationship, but what of his relationship with Allah? Was she concerned about that too? He had prayed to Allah for forgiveness, explained that he had been shamelessly tempted. Had she prayed also and asked for forgiveness for being the temptation? He had fought to the best of his ability but had succumbed. Had she fought as hard to preserve her marriage and her husband's honour? He had begged that the temptation of her body be removed, but there were no signs that she was willing to comply. Allah had been deaf to all his pleas; indeed, he seemed to be determined his servant's punishment should continue, for to his dismay, he still felt the lure of his mistress's body and the tormenting urges within his own, and he knew when the time came for this sorceress to renew her siren call, he would fail again.

Valerie was determined he should fail again, it seemed the only way to cut through the maddening reticence of her servant, but it had to be somewhere private where they could talk at leisure afterwards, and where she thought she could begin to fill the void that still existed between them. The following afternoon, after Stuart had left to go to the estate office, she slipped down the staircase into her bathroom and out through the outside door leading to the courtyard across from the *amah's* quarters where Osman, Ah Gan and Tambi had their rooms. Valerie had heard the houseboy in the kitchen and knew her way was clear for an hour at least, as Tambi always helped to prepare the evening meal before both he and Cookie retired for their afternoon rest. Even if they did return to their rooms early, she and Osman would be able to hear them coming, and as long as they were quiet as they passed the door, there would be little chance of their discovery.

Osman was asleep when she entered his room and lying in his night sarong, his head resting on his arm. As the floor was concrete, he preferred the iron bed to a mat. Valerie took off her dressing gown and lay beside him but he woke as soon as her knee touched the bed. His startled expression at her presence and his wide-eyed wonder at her nakedness gave her quiet amusement. They were able to exchange only a few whispers before their mutual desire overcame them and they made love with even more urgency than in the car, although Valerie insisted on him caressing her fully before the final union.

She found him reluctant to indulge in the sort of intimacy she had become accustomed to with European lovers, although she did not know whether this was the result of the taboos of a Malay or the inhibitions of their situation. He possessed all the traditional gentleness of his race, however, and his hands over her willing body were deeply satisfying, especially for someone who had been deprived of physical tenderness for so long. Nevertheless, he was unwilling to remove his sarong or allow her to touch him and, once again, he brought the act to swift fruition.

Perhaps it was the lack of privacy in Malay houses that enforced such a rigid functionalism in their sex, and also, apparently, passivity on the woman's part, as all her attempts to play an active role were firmly discouraged. But if Valerie thought their making love in private was going to lead to exchange of emotional intimacies also, she was disappointed. Perhaps it was subconscious guilt, or the need to listen for the other servants' approach, but they were unable to communicate in any way other than a murmur, and Valerie found stage whispers a most unsatisfactory way to conduct a long conversation, especially about anything as important as their new relationship. Instead, they lay briefly together listening to the crickets in the trees outside and the distant sounds of Ah Gan in the kitchen, before Valerie made her way back up the bathroom stairs.

Her visits to Osman's room became almost daily although she disliked its airlessness and the fierce reflected sunlight from its whitewashed walls. Despite her encouragement, his ways of making love continued to remain firmly rooted in his Malay traditions and it intrigued her that she had not yet seen him without his sarong. One afternoon she enticed him across the courtyard into the bathroom. She took a mischievous pleasure in disrobing before him, because she knew it excited him against his will, and she could not resist the tease. She saw how he looked at her, yet didn't look, like a schoolboy in front of a nude painting in an art gallery.

'I don't mind you looking, you know,' she said, and struck a provocative pose, but then regretted her thoughtless action because, as he turned his head away, she saw the mortification in his eyes. To a Malay, a naked woman was a flagrant immodesty, and although she knew also, from the state of his sarong, that she had excited him, she resolved to be more decorous in future. Like any sensuous woman she had always enjoyed arousing the men in her life, with the notable exception of her husband, but she knew it was going to have to be different with Osman.

She began to pour water over herself from the Shanghai jar and invited him to join her. He did so but, to her surprise and chagrin, still did not remove his sarong. She laughed aloud at the defeat of her stratagem. Of course, she should have known, native houses had no bathrooms, how often had she seen Malays bathing in a stream beside the road and always, of course, in their sarongs.

* * *

Despite their harmony in bed, Osman continued to be unwilling to indulge in any sort of physical intimacy at other times and any attempt by Valerie to hold hands or snatch a kiss in private moments were swiftly and expertly avoided. He seemed totally unwilling to disturb their normal mem–*syce* relationship. Valerie was frustrated and found the lack of emotional contact a strain. Perhaps it would be different if they could spend a night together in circumstances where they were not frightened of being overheard or seen and, quite unexpectedly, Stuart provided them with such an opportunity.

He was called to Singapore for a few days to attend a conference of United Estates' planters and he was utterly amazed at Valerie's decline of his invitation to accompany him. She had never been averse to such an occasion before, quite the reverse, she had always been keen to get off the estate and he had thought she would have jumped at the chance of a few days in relative civilisation. It would have been just the sort of thing she needed to lift her gloom, although, now he came to think of it, she had seemed a lot brighter in the last week or two. Even so, to say she could not leave her orchids at this particular time of year seemed rather odd. He had not realised orchids were so temperamental and did he not pay the *kebun* to look after them?

To Valerie, however, the opportunity was too good to miss and the absence of her husband was just what she was looking for. Her affection for Osman had deepened into an aching, physical love which had been an unexpected revelation to her after her years of mere friendship with him, and an exciting, fulfilling one after the heartbreaking years with Stuart. It was not surprising, therefore, that she was determined to seize any chance to indulge it. On the day Stuart left she was in such good spirits she was positively skittish with her husband, even kissed him goodbye, much to his astonishment.

That night she dined with a sense of anticipation that reminded her of some of the exciting events of her childhood – Christmas mornings, family holidays on Arran and birthday parties. It was by no means easy to rekindle such pure pleasure in adulthood and she revelled in it. After the servants had retired for the night she let Osman in through the bathroom door. He steadfastly refused to sleep in her bedroom, however. It was *Tuan's* room, *Tuan's* bed. He had taken his wife but he would not take his property, even for a night. Every fibre of his being rebelled at the thought. Valerie was exasperated but eventually compromised, and they slept in the spare room. As they sat on the bed, she asked him to take off his sarong just this once, but even though he obviously wished to please her he could not bring himself to do so. Valerie was sensible enough to let it pass but said with only the faint suggestion of a smile:

'But if you call me Mem once more when we are in bed I shall throw you out of the window.'

'Yes, Mem,' he said with his wide grin.

It was a cool night and Valerie savoured it to the full although, once again, Osman foiled her every attempt to lure him into Western ways of love-making. Afterwards, as Valerie pulled the sheet up around her she saw that he had almost immediately fallen asleep. The thought occurred to her that this was yet another of his ruses to keep her at bay but his regular breathing convinced her that he was truly sleeping. She looked at him fondly and was powerfully reminded of the words of one of the World War I poets she had read at school:

'Pillowed in silk and scented down, where love throbs out in blissful sleep.'

If only that was true. Her instinct told her that Osman's feelings were nowhere near as deep as hers but, at that moment, it really did not matter, her love was great enough for both of them and, surely, his must deepen. A breeze gently blew the blinds away from the wall and shafts of pure moonlight fell across the bed. Valerie had never felt so happy or so at peace. She glanced at Osman's sleeping form again and felt, at that moment, as if she would die of love. Then, on a sudden impulse, she slid her hand under his sarong and up his thigh. He stirred but did not wake.

Softly she cupped her hand around the wellsprings of her recent pleasure and took delight in their softness, so unlike the rest of a man which to her had always seemed so hard and unforgiving. Her questing fingers found, to her surprise, that he had been circumcised, but of course, and she smiled at this further lack of her perception, he was a Muslim. It reminded her of the incident of him bathing in a sarong. She had a lot to learn, loving a Malay. Osman stirred again and she withdrew her hand, but the tenderness she had felt remained. Such snatched moments of physical intimacy were all that she was ever likely to have with a Malay lover.

The blind flapped again and she felt a gentle wave of cool air. The moonlight which accompanied it filled the room but failed to penetrate the deep shadows. It was like her happiness, coming fleetingly and failing to fall into all the corners of her life. Her future, too, was likely to have even more dark places. She peered up into the shapeless mass of the mosquito net above her. It hung like the black cloud that was threatening her present happiness. She knew there were painful choices to be faced, fateful decisions to be made, and that they could not be postponed much longer. The chirruping cicadas, those ever-present choristers of the Malayan night, sang their song in the rubber trees outside the window. To have no awareness of the future, like them, was all she wished at that moment; either that, or the night should last forever.

* * *

About a month or so after Stuart's return from Singapore Valerie made a discovery which for some illogical reason astonished her but alarmed her even more – she was pregnant. She had got so used to not having to ensure her husband was not taking any precautions that it had not occurred to her to take them with Osman. Her first thought was an uncharitable one regarding Stuart – so their lack of a family was her husband's fault after all, just as she had suspected all along. Of course, it was possible the baby could be Stuart's as he had never failed to maintain his marital rights but she knew that it was almost certain to be Osman's. Any other possibility would defy logic.

In the days that followed she considered the implications. A planter's wife producing a child with a complexion a shade darker than the standard European white would create suspicions, whispers, questions and ultimately a scandal which, like a boil, would eventually have to be lanced and would be followed by all the messy consequences usually associated with that surgical procedure. She knew what would happen. The powers that be would close ranks and then embark upon a course of rewriting history like a communist regime. She could see the Board of Directors at an emergency board meeting in London, having suspended the secretary's minutes, shaking their heads around the table.

'Nasty business. What possessed the fellow to marry such a

woman? Not a word must get out of course, and he'll have to be replaced. A pity, because he was a good manager.'

The Mitchell family would be shipped back to the UK overnight. Stuart would not only lose his job, he would lose his identity. The company would replace him immediately, there would be no mention of it in the press and some sort of explanation would be entered into the company's records. He would become a non-person and everyone in the company would be sworn to silence and pretend they knew nothing about it.

In this, they would receive the utmost co-operation of the Colonial administration as it sought to preserve its image, an image which they regarded as the key to their authority. There had to be respect for the governors by the governed or the whole edifice could come tumbling down. When the British had arrived in the peninsula, authority had depended on a few gunboats and a battalion or two, but it was very different today. Prestige, wealth and just a hint of enough power to make the locals feel powerless but, vitally, also to feel secure in the protection it gave, all played their part but there had to be moral superiority as well, and how could that be maintained if the locals suspected the white man was subject to the same moral weaknesses as themselves? And if the white man was no better than they, then the locals might think they could do no worse – and this could lead them to believe they could well manage without him. And therein lay the seeds of self-determination which could quickly germinate, become seedlings of social unrest and flower into open rebellion, for as every farmer knew, a desire for freedom having once been implanted in the human mind, it was almost impossible to eradicate, like the tares which yearly took root amongst their corn.

Without doubt, one of the worst calamities which could befall the administration was a British woman taking a Malay man of humble birth to her bed. Nothing was more likely to induce illusions of moral, social and political equality amongst the *ra'ayat*, the masses, than a lowly native being admitted to the most sacred of the elite's temples. It was not just a crude question of colour. In fact, race hardly came into it. Someone of royal birth whatever his colour, a sultan for example, was quite acceptable.

This had already been demonstrated in a state in the south of the country where the Sultan had taken a married British woman, properly divorced, as his consort. Indeed, the European community had been rather amused by the fact that she had later been installed as Sultana. It was the Malays, oddly enough, and rather impudently in fact, who had been less than charmed by the arrangement. But a Malay of the servant class being allowed to enter the hallowed portals would not be tolerated for a moment and the offender would have to be banished. Rumours would circulate for a while naturally, but if silence was maintained, these would fade. Their very enormity would make them less likely to be believed. It was unfortunate for the husband, of course, but he would have a company pension, and he had really brought it on himself by marrying her in the first place.

What the loss of his job would do to Stuart Valerie could not bear to think, although she was more concerned about the certainty she would not be allowed back in Malaya and so would never see Osman again. An alternative plan would be to return to the UK and have an abortion, although whether Stuart would ever allow her to do so without telling him the truth she doubted, and in view of her hitherto desperate longing for a baby, how could she do anything else than tell him the truth of who the father was? That would mean he would refuse to pay for it and she would certainly not be able to find the money. In any case, she shrank in horror at the thought of an abortion as it would mean the death of Osman's child. Having waited so long for a baby, the mere idea of it appalled her. In which case, the solution was obvious – she was surprised she had not thought of it before – she would leave her husband and go to live with Osman as his second wife, and so keep the baby.

The more she thought about it the more she saw it as the perfect answer to all her problems. Initially it would cause an even greater scandal than having Osman's baby, of course, but the authorities would be able to do less about it. They were also less likely to involve Stuart, he might even be able to keep his job, but most importantly of all, she would have both her baby and Osman. She broke the news of her impending motherhood to him in the car that morning. Unexpectedly, he grinned.

'It will be a boy, Mem,' he said. Osman was not given to looking into the future or thinking of the implications of statements or events, not immediately anyway, but as Valerie outlined her plans and it dawned upon him that she thought he was the father, his face creased in concern, and then perplexity and finally alarm.

'Come to live with me,' he said anxiously, 'In the kampung? It cannot be Mem. You would hate it. No car, no bath, no cooker ... ' His mind struggled with what Valerie's next priority might be.

'Osman, I don't care about such things. I would have you, that's all I want. We would have each other. Things like cookers and cars don't mean a thing to me. My family don't have all those things back in Britain.'

She lied, but she could not bear him thinking Europeans were just shallow materialists or that the Malay way of life was, in any important way, inferior to theirs. Besides, she wanted to press on to the other, much bigger, obstacles to a white woman marrying a local and taking up residence in his village.

'Osman, I don't know if you would be able to get a job in the kampung or anywhere else ... ' Valerie paused. Where did locals work? She had never thought. 'But you would never be able to be a syce again, at least not for a European. They wouldn't have you.'

Osman considered this and reluctantly conceded the logic of it. He looked crestfallen. His job, and its pay, suited him well. The work was not onerous, it had prestige and relative security. He would have been prepared to make considerable sacrifices to keep it. He thought about the prospect of two wives and no job. Valerie continued.

'I know I would have to become a Muslim, of course. But

would there be any religious obstacle to us marrying? You do want to marry me don't you?' She had been rehearsing that question since their affair had started and had constantly looked for an opportunity to ask it. Her discovery she was pregnant had now made the question of crucial importance and she hoped she had not sounded too anxious.

'Yes, Mem,' said Osman, but with less conviction than Valerie might have hoped. In fact, it was almost as if she had merely asked him to close the car door. Was Mem really serious? Up to now it had almost been like a 'wonder what it would be like' game, the sort one played as a child. He began to think about the realities. A white woman in his *kampung*, living in his house, as his wife! Suddenly, a delightful picture was conjured up and he grinned at the prospect of showing off a mem as his wife, and a beautiful one at that. When he retired each night he would be the envy of the men of the village. He imagined their banter and what he would say in return. But she would definitely not be showing off her legs, that was certain. They, and everything else for that matter, would be well and truly hidden under a *baju kurong*. He was not going to have all the youths of the village eyeing what was his and his alone to see.

Then reality intervened and the picture dissolved. What was he thinking of? A white woman living in his little house by the river? What a nonsensical idea. It was about as practical as the Sultan coming to stay but with even more complications. What would the *imam* have to say about an infidel coming to live amongst them, even one who had embraced the faith? What would be his mother's reaction, or that of the village elders? Everyone would be scandalised. The whole thing was madness.

Valerie interrupted his thoughts with another question. 'What will Minah think?' Allah be praised. Minah, yes, another problem. It was customary to ask wife number one if a second wife was acceptable. It meant considerable sacrifices on her part, monetary and otherwise, and her acquiescence was necessary if a quiet life was to be ensured. Normally, it was polite to wait until the first wife was past child-bearing before wife number two was taken. It was no disgrace to her then if her husband wished to take another, younger wife. To do so while the first was still in the full bloom of her own youth and beauty was a discourtesy amounting almost to an insult, not only to her but to her family. Minah was still relatively young. Hopefully though, she, and indeed the whole *kampung*, would see that a mem, his mem, was different, that the usual considerations did not apply.

He remembered that she and Minah had already met when he had brought her to the bungalow one holiday and they seemed to get on well together but as a mem and her employee's wife. How different would be their new relationship as wives married to the same man? But even as his mind circled around the problem of having two wives, he knew how absurd the whole thing was. Insignificant men like him, with barely enough income to support one wife, did not take a second. This was what men of property did, the powers around the Sultan, the Sultan himself. Not a humble *syce*.

Osman did his best to explain the complexities of the situation to Valerie although he omitted to describe the subservient role which wife number two was expected to play in household affairs. She was third in line. Mother ruled, first wife had considerable authority, depending on the duration of the marriage and the number of her children, especially boys, but the second wife was often little more than the servant of both. But perhaps it would be different with a mem?

He suddenly felt weary and fell into a resigned silence. He could not go on contemplating such a problematical, uncertain future. It was all too much. Allah would have to decide. What was of more concern to him now was how much longer Allah would be making him pay for his transgressions, his yielding to the temptations of the flesh. He had known there would have to be a price to pay although, at one time, with the avoidance of any suspicions on Stuart's part, it looked as though they had got away with their madness amongst the rubber trees. Valerie had acted as if there was to be no account to be rendered, but deep down, he had not believed that was possible or even right, and he had not been really surprised at Valerie's announcement that she was pregnant.

It was Allah's judgement and he had been half-expecting something like this to happen, in fact it had almost been a relief when it *had* come. And had that been all, then it would not have been too bad. He would have lost his job but that would have been the end of the matter. But Mem deciding to come to live in his *kampung*! That was a different thing altogether. It was not only doubling his punishment, it was extending it for months, perhaps years. In fact, there might never be an end to the debts, moral as well as financial, he would incur. He sighed. There seemed precious little light at the end of his tunnel at the present moment.

But this mood did not last for long, in fact he even began to brighten. There was one hope he could cling to. Whatever the fates might have in store, they were not going to happen to him tomorrow. Perhaps, by tomorrow, Mem would see the foolishness of her plan and realise how impractical it was for a white woman to live in a Malay community. Yes, that would be it. Mem would come to her senses, find her own solution to their problems and leave him in peace. But whatever happened and whenever it happened, there was nothing he could do about it. It was out of his hands now. All he could do was hope that Allah would be merciful. He decided the matter did not require any further consideration on his part, at least not until Valerie mentioned it again, and perhaps, if Allah willed it, she never would. The world was not such a bad place after all. He could smile again.

*   *   *

Life in the bungalow continued as before. As Stuart and Valerie sat at dinner each evening she could not help marvelling at the normality of it all and then trying to visualise the impact her news would have on her little world. It was inevitably going to be a bombshell of the first magnitude as she was quite sure no one in the bungalow suspected a thing. Men, in contrast to women, were oblivious of those little signs which would have told them something unusual was happening around them. In fact, in her experience, men did not notice anything at all unless it was actually under their feet to trip over, but women were different. If there had been another woman in the house, a wash *amah* for example, she would not have felt so confident of keeping her secret, as women had a sixth sense about such things. They would have noticed the glances she must have directed towards Osman, the subtle changes in herself, the way she dressed, the little indications that she was so much happier despite her anxieties regarding her forthcoming life in a Malay village. Women in love can never conceal the fact from other women.

She tried to visualise the effect her elopement would have on the Club members in Kuala Lebir although it was not too difficult to picture the likely reaction there – first incredulity, then dismay at what they would see as a betrayal of the expatriate community, her countrymen, and finally contempt that she could lower herself in such a way. The women, in particular, would not forgive her. They would think she had demeaned them all by allowing herself to have become accessible to a man who should not have been allowed to feel a European woman was within his reach. In their eyes, Valerie's disloyalty had devalued them all. Now they could no longer pride themselves in being forbidden fruit. Not that one or two of them might not have been tempted at some time, but that was not the point. *She* had succumbed. Then there was her family back home. Valerie could hardly bear to think about home. She was cutting herself off from Glasgow forever – but she tried to banish any feelings of that sort – she was to have a new home and a new family, even a new country, and it was up to her to make a success of this drastic change in the direction of her life. There must be no regrets because, as she saw it, there was no practical alternative to what she planned to do.

She had made up her mind to leave without telling a soul, even Margo, perhaps especially Margo. She reasoned that only by maintaining absolute secrecy was she likely to be able to go through with it. She could not face long involved explanations with anyone, least of all Margo who had not an atom of romance in her, at least, not where the locals were concerned, and would probably think her mad.

She also thought it inevitable that her friend would let something slip one way or another, and once her secret was out the pressures on her to give up her plan would become intolerable. In fact, she felt sure that, between them, Stuart, the company and the colonial administration, not to mention the European community generally, would find a way of stopping her going. By slipping away quietly one morning she would avoid all that, and once living with Osman she hoped the powers-that-be would devote most of their efforts to minimising the scandal, even perhaps making it work, rather than giving it publicity by trying to make her return to Britain.

Naturally, she would have to leave a letter for Stuart and she spent some time deliberating over its contents. In the end she decided against a long letter of explanation as it would only turn into a tedious catalogue of complaints and justification. How could she condense ten years of neglect, heartache and humiliation into a letter short enough to meet a man of Stuart's limited patience? She could imagine him screwing the paper up and casting it aside long before he came to the end. Better a brief, dignified statement of intent with, she supposed, the news about the baby.

Her main worry was Osman. He had said little or nothing about the impact of their news in his house and village and, in fact, she wondered if he had said anything to his family at all. It would be just like a man to assume that things they disliked, or did not wish to deal with, would go away providing they were pushed to the back of the mind often and far enough, or even banished from thought altogether. Although, even as she had to admit, such an attitude could help sometimes. For example, she was certain there were going to be difficulties for her in the village but as she had no idea what form they might take, she was totally unable to make any provision for them, so there was no point in brooding on the matter and certainly no point in getting upset. She therefore pushed them all out of her mind, for, whatever the difficulties might turn out to be, there was no realistic alternative to her making the Malay village her future home.

At least Osman had said there would be space for her in the house. Hopefully, later, they could add a room which would be theirs, although that was more her suggestion than his. It was clear they were going to be cramped, with his mother, Minah and the two children all living on top of one other, but she was convinced that, despite it all, she was going to be happier there than she had been for almost all of her years on the estate. Although she would not have Osman entirely to herself, their relationship would at least be out in the open. It would be so much better than the furtive, underhand existence they were leading now which was beginning to take a toll of her nerves. It was quite a strain trying to ensure Tambi or Cookie did not get even a suspicion of what was going on. Once in the village she would be able to show Osman how much she truly loved him. She put his present sombre mood and his air of resignation down to the impending loss of his job, of which he was very proud. He had been a very good *syce*, even Stuart had never once complained about him.

One of the things she had to decide was what she should take with her. With the limited space in her new home it was obvious she could not take very much, and the ostentation of expensive property might create the wrong impression anyway. Most her clothes and all her cosmetics would have to be left behind, there was no point taking them, although she knew, when the time came, she would not be able to bear parting with her jewellery, modest as it was. Not that there would ever be an opportunity to wear it as Malay women, like Muslim women everywhere, were required to eschew personal finery. In future she would have to dress without any hint of Western ways. Make-up, for example, would be a grave error of judgement, but she would not want it any other way. She was determined to make a complete break and for that reason she spent little time sentimentalising over the rest of her personal property or worrying about all the other sacrifices she would have to make.

Osman's village, Batu Lima, was about sixty miles distant. Valerie rather wished it were more. She dreaded running into any of her former European acquaintances after her defection, particularly her husband. A sudden image of Stuart attempting to reclaim her by force almost threw her into a panic but, on reflection, she had to admit the possibility was rather remote. He would be angry rather than upset by her going and not greatly inconvenienced by it. It would be his pride rather than his feelings which would be hurt although he was certain to hate the inevitable publicity and public attention her desertion would cause. Apart from that, she could imagine his life on the estate continuing much as it always had done. After all, they had virtually no visitors, did not enjoy a social life together or have any mutual friends apart from the most casual – her husband's character had ensured that, and there was not one single activity which they shared, at least not in the daytime! She could even imagine Stuart's life slipping back into the same old routines that had existed before their marriage.

It was arranged that the taxi which took Osman to his village on his day off would collect them on the appointed day at about nine in the morning, when there would be no prospect of Stuart being anywhere near the bungalow. They would then be arriving in Batu Lima to begin their new life together at about the time Stuart would be returning for breakfast and discovering the envelope propped up on the table in the sitting room. Her only worry was getting Osman to decide on a date for their departure and then keeping to it. Twice there had been postponements for reasons which seemed to her to be rather lame. Was he testing her resolve?

*　*　*

Valerie toured the estate the day before she left. She was unable to say farewell to anyone, but she lingered long enough for the workers to remember her visit in the days after her going when they knew the significance of it. She wandered the paths between the trees and watched one of the weeding gangs cutting the grass verges. The girls whirled their long-handled blades in a ceaseless, rhythmic circle, high above their heads and then down within inches of their bare feet, leaving the grass trimmed as evenly as a lawn. It was said their eye was so sure and their hands so steady they could trim their toenails at the same time. A line of spring-footed carriers passed her on their way to the factory, the cans of latex strung on the long poles between them bouncing in unison with their step.

She glimpsed the scarlet figure of a woman tapper who was cleaning out the china cup on a rubber tree. The small cake of coagulated latex she retrieved was what had dripped into the cup since it had been emptied the previous day and it was riddled with leaf fragments and all manner of insects. Nevertheless, she placed it carefully in a bag on her back. Such pickings were her perks which she was able to sell to the company for a few cents a pound to be made into sheets of crepe rubber. Crepe was inferior to the processed rubber but when the price of the commodity was high on the world markets, its production was well worth the industry's time and expense. The woman stooped to pare the sloping scar in the bark and her bare breasts slipped below the loose fold of her *dupatta*. The sight must have raised the spirits of the bachelor planters in former years. Perhaps it still did – tales were always being told in the Club. The tapper moved on and Valerie paused by the tree which was already yielding its life-blood, the white latex welling up in the wound and beginning its long journey to the factories of the Western world.

All these sights had been commonplace in her daily routine but, suddenly, they held a particular import, a certain preciousness.

She came to the oldest part of the estate where the first trees had been planted. They were gnarled with age and their lower trunks were almost completely covered with the chevron-shaped scars made by a generation of tappers. They would have to be replaced by higher-yielding stock very soon, and she was sure her husband, with his usual efficiency, would already have the matter in hand. They were on the edge of the estate facing onto the jungle and so gave the impression they were the outermost limit of the civilised world which, in a sense, they were, and she felt a momentary qualm occasioned by the thought that the relative security they represented was what she was about to exchange for the less ordered world outside.

She wandered along a path in the adjoining jungle, the cool shade of which she had much enjoyed during her morning walks in her early days. The track had originally been made by wild elephants on their way to raiding the young rubber saplings when the plantation had first been established, and they had only been deterred by Stuart having trees felled across their path. Elephants will not cross a jumble of fallen timber for fear of breaking a leg. Fences, on the other hand, were less effective. Not only were they expensive, they could be leant upon with impunity and usually were. However, Valerie had not seen or heard of any elephants in this part of Kelantan for years and she could not remember when Stuart had last complained of the devastation they could cause which was considerable. If any succulent leaves were out of their reach, they simply uprooted the tree and browsed them that way.

The rainforest contained many other animals but none so destructive to a rubber plantation. The great majority of the fauna were nocturnal but, in any case, they shunned the jungle edges and therefore the rubber estates. Contrary to general perception, the floor of a tropical rainforest is almost devoid of thick vegetation as very little is able to grow under the shade of the canopy, it is only on its fringes can the sun generate the tangled growth that gives the jungle its reputation for impenetrability.

She was pleased to see there were still otters playing in the stream and, judging by the excited chatter and a rustling in the branches, monkeys were still foraging for their living in the trees above. At that moment, a straggle of *keluang* (fruit bats) which had been feeding on the fig tree the monkeys were seeking flapped indignantly into the air, having been driven from their evening meal. Meanwhile, a troupe of singing gibbons, dwellers in the highest tops and so rarely seen, but whose echoing calls she had often heard on her walks, chose that moment to treat her to a farewell serenade of their own.

She could not truthfully say she had been happy amongst them but they had been part of her life long enough for her to think she would miss them, for, without a doubt, she would never see them again.

* * *

As soon as Valerie heard Stuart leave the bungalow for muster, she got up and went down to Osman's room, but it was empty. Panic gripped her as her imagination, fed by the persistent doubts of the last few weeks, now raised the possibility that, at the last moment, Osman had lost his nerve and had abandoned her. Then she saw the car was missing which was puzzling as if he had returned to Batu Lima she knew he would never have taken Stuart's car. Then, with a stroke of intuition, she began to run down the track to the stream although it was barely light.

The chill air struck through her cotton housecoat and the stones bit at her bare feet but she barely noticed either. She reached the stream and there, as she had hoped and indeed expected, was Osman cleaning the car, bucket in hand. He was still in his night sarong, balancing on the car running board so that he could reach the centre of the roof with his brush – obviously determined not a square inch of shiny metal should be missed. She had seen him at the same task many times before but never had the sight filled her with such relief. Perhaps he was not creating an image to match the romantic events of the day but, to Valerie, that was not of the slightest consequence.

Osman, on the other hand, was clearly discomfited by her appearance, not because of what he was doing but why he was doing it. Valerie knew his reason at once. He was making the only restitution he could think of to his master, a final act of loyalty on a day of betrayal. She watched him for several moments until tears blurred the touching scene of penitential diligence before her. She did not dare to speak.

She retraced her steps trying to avoid the stones. As she went into the bathroom she saw Tambi emerge from his quarters. It would have been difficult for her to offer a convincing explanation for the mud on her feet and she made no attempt to do so. It did not matter. Nothing on the estate mattered any more.

Long before nine Valerie was on the verandah peering anxiously down the laterite road but it remained defiantly empty, then as she went into the hall to call the number of the solitary taxi in Kuala Lebir she heard the wheels on the gravel outside. She almost ran with her suitcase down the steps and saw that Osman was already in the car. Then she remembered the envelope. As she hurried back she met Tambi coming out of his room, looking questioningly at her. She turned from his gaze, placed the envelope on the dining room table and fled. Down the estate road along which she had come that first evening almost ten years before with so many hopes and expectations but also fears, past the sign which, despite its encroaching algae, still proclaimed BUKIT BINTANG ESTATE, and finally out onto the road to her new existence as a Malay wife.

PART THREE

THE MALAY VILLAGE

Valerie had much to think about on her journey into her new world, sitting on the back seat neatly covered with its drapes of batik, thoughtfully placed there by the driver to keep her bare and damp legs from the shiny upholstery. Osman joined them but sat in the front. Valerie felt a pang of disappointment. Having just entered his world she expected them to be together. Could he still have been acting as her *syce* perhaps, or maybe his companion, the taxi driver, was not yet aware of their true relationship and would have thought it odd if he had sat in the back with his employer. Then it occurred to Valerie there could have been a third reason. It might be that Osman was already treating her as if she was a Malay wife, and a Malay husband would, of course, disdain from sitting next to his wife in public. It further occurred to her that if that was so, then she was not even entitled to ask the reason because, as a Malay wife, she now had a subservient status to just about every male of her acquaintance. This meant she no longer had the right to speak to either man in the front seats as their equal, especially if it seemed as though she was questioning their motives.

As soon as she had got into the car that morning and stepped from an English into a Malay world, these two men had risen from being beneath her in the social hierarchy to a position of superiority over her. This represented a double demotion for her, as not only had she sacrificed her position as a wife, a mem, in a European society but had relegated herself to the subordinate position of a woman in a Malay one. From now on, in her new relationship with Osman, she would have to accept what would be a total role reversal. It was going to take considerable adjustment on her part to cope with the realities of this new status but she was determined not to ask for, or to expect, any concessions.

Her musings came to an abrupt end when she had to remind herself that, at that moment, she was very far from being a Malay wife and that there were a number of quite possibly significant hurdles to be overcome before she could regard herself as such. That being so, then almost certainly the reason Osman had placed himself in the front seat was that, to him, she was still a mem and to have sat anywhere else, therefore, would have been a presumption. It made her feel as if she was in some sort of limbo, halfway between the two roles of man and master – or in her case, woman and mistress – a feeling which was to become familiar to her in the next few weeks.

Osman and the driver talked all the way to their destination and never once did either of them acknowledge her presence. The driver was Chinese but spoke vernacular Malay almost as fluently as Osman. Valerie had acquired quite a vocabulary by now but, try as she might, she could not follow their conversation and she made a somewhat disconsolate figure sitting in the back, doubly excluded from their world. Had Osman told his friend of the situation between them or why she was travelling to his village? She listened for a mention of her name but it did not come.

She resolved to overcome the language barrier as quickly as possible, not only because of the isolation she would feel if she did not, but because a lack of Malay would diminish her status amongst the women of the village. Their acceptance was crucial if she was to become an accepted part of the Muslim society in which she hoped to live. But she could not expect to cross the cultural divide as if it was a state border. One might be able to acquire citizenship with a marriage, but a new social identity could take years, perhaps half a lifetime, to achieve.

They passed through Kuala Lebir and, fleetingly, she caught a glimpse of two familiar white faces talking on the five-foot way. She was relieved they failed to see her as that meant she did not have to make any responding wave. It was a gesture she rather wished to avoid. It would only have been a small deceit but any acknowledgement would have been like looking back, an indication she had not made a clean break with her previous life or hoped and expected to have a place in both societies. This was not her intention. If she ever came face to face with a European in the future they would both look the other way, of that she was quite certain. She most certainly would. She was happy that it should be so and she looked forward to the time when she could demonstrate the fact to Usman.

They passed into a part of Kelantan where Valerie had not been before although it looked very familiar, and she had to admit her adopted country had a certain uniformity about it. The jungle still flanked the road on both sides relieved only by one or two native rubber smallholdings which, not large or prosperous enough to justify a smoking shed, had to peg their white sheets of coagulated rubber out to dry like lines of washing. An odd coconut grove with the trees standing gaunt and headless where the rhinoceros beetle had done its destructive work helped to relieve the monotony and they also passed through the inevitable *kampungs* each with their ambling bullock carts and cyclists carrying impossible loads of one commodity or another.

One had such a large mound of grass tied to his carrier that it almost reached the ground, his laboured progress only emphasising the impression he was giving of a giant hairy snail. Another was transporting three wickerwork baskets piled one on top of the other, each containing a resigned-looking pig, while on the improvised seat of a third was sitting a woman holding a native umbrella made of lacquered paper and rattan, known as a *payong*, which was providing shade for both the rider and herself. The taxi went through a number of villages almost exactly similar to the ones she had seen on her first journey to Bukit Bintang. How differently she felt about them now that she knew she was about to live in one of them. Batu Lima would, almost certainly, look like all the others, but would have one vital difference – it would be hers.

In one little township some Malay boys were coming out of a religious school, a trim building with an asbestos roof. They were wearing their best clothes including a *songkok*, the peakless Malay head wear designed to allow the forehead to touch the ground during prayers. Valerie had always found small Malay boys quite irresistible, perhaps because they looked so neat – almost doll-like, and perfect miniatures of the men they were one day going to be, and she almost hugged herself with anticipation at the thought that she was carrying one inside her. Why was she so sure it was going to be a boy? Only because Osman said it was, she supposed, and his opinion was hardly one based on medical knowledge or experience. It was just that Malays, like most Asian men, always hoped for boys and what they hoped for, they expected to get. It was their nature.

The taxi pressed on relentlessly, a gleaming symbol of the modern world passing through what was still an ancient and traditional one. Very shortly, with her arrival in Batu Lima, she was going to see if a woman from the first could exist successfully, and happily, in the second.

* * *

Osman's village was about five miles outside the small town of Karang and was sited on a bend in a river some quarter of a mile from the road at the end of a track. They bounced over the latter in a cloud of dust, scattering chickens and skirting a small banana plantation before meandering through a grove of coconut trees. When they stopped there was a moment's awkwardness as Valerie fumbled in her purse to pay the driver and Osman waved her away. A Muslim wife did not demean her husband by performing such tasks, she should have known that. It was the reflex action of a mem which she instantly regretted but she did notice no money changed hands.

Immediately, a crowd gathered and Osman greeted them, it appeared to Valerie, somewhat awkwardly and with none of the warmth that she had expected – he was clearly not himself – although not one pair of eyes was looking at him, all were fixed upon her. Had they been warned of her arrival and the purpose of it? Valerie searched their faces for evidence of such pre-knowledge but without success, all she saw being expressions of wonder and curiosity at the sight of a white woman suddenly appearing in their midst. One thing was certain – she would have to accustom herself to being the centre of a group of onlookers for some time to come.

She looked about her. All of the houses were four to five feet off the ground and standing on piles either of timber or concrete, a sensible precaution against the risk of the monsoon floods to which the east coast was subject for part of the year, but while some were traditionally built with *attap* walls and a roof of thatch, others were made in the more modern style of locally cut timber under sheets of galvanised iron, and Valerie was relieved to see Osman advancing on one of these. She had always associated *attap* with spiders and worse. She had several times found a scorpion seeking refuge in the *attap* wall of the bathroom at Bukit Bintang when she went down for her morning 'shower' from the Shanghai jar.

Osman made no attempt to carry her case, which was so unlike him and it quite took her aback. Was he cross with her over her *faux pas* with the taxi driver? Or was it that he did not wish to be seen performing the duties of a servant of a woman, even a white one, in front of his fellow-villagers? In fact, he ignored her completely and went straight up the steps leading to a wide verandah enclosed by an ornate wooden railing, a space which Valerie was later to discover was not just an airy and roomy entrance porch to the house but also the traditional meeting place for Osman's friends and other male visitors – and so not a place where women should be seen taking their ease or even lingering.

She had never seen him so ill at ease and it occurred to her that if the villagers had not been forewarned of her arrival, might she also not be expected in the house? She recalled Osman's evasiveness on the subject on the estate. By now, his uneasiness had communicated itself to her and she looked nervously up at the building she was about to call home. Although its outside was no different to the countless others she had seen from the road over the years, she realised its interior would be as unfamiliar to her as if it had been on another planet. On two counts, therefore, she was stepping into the unknown. To add to her doubts about whether her arrival had been heralded or not, she was also at a loss to know how she was to address the woman she was about to meet – as her hostess or as a future mother-in-law? She took a deep breath and began to mount the wooden steps, slowed by having to hoist her suitcase up each in turn as best she could. Never had she been so uncertain or felt so acutely that she was at the mercy of events.

An old Malay woman appeared at the door leading onto the verandah. She smiled, revealing a row of gold teeth like her son, and Osman turned and said simply, 'My mother.' He did not mention her name or make any formal introduction and Valerie had to remind herself such niceties must be beyond anything he was used to. Why had she not sorted out things like names and titles long before, including the name the rest of the family should use for her? She had been unable to cure Osman of using Mem in their private moments on the estate but, surely, now she was on his territory, she could hope to see the end of the title which was so redolent of her old life, but she suspected that any such confirmation of her demotion in Malaya's social order would still be some way off.

Osman was unsmiling, covering his awkwardness by an off-hand manner. Valerie could see the unhappiness in his face and there was tension in everything he said or did and it was becoming increasingly clear to her he had done nothing to prepare either the village or his family for her visit, let alone the fact that this white woman had come with the intention of living permanently amongst them. Clearly he had been hoping she would change her mind and for the first time she began to understand the impact her coming to Batu Lima was going to make. But if her coming as a visitor was causing Osman this level of agitation, how was he going to cope when it was revealed she was to be his wife and was already carrying his child?

Had she been able to see into Osman's mind at that moment she would have had some sort of answer to her question, but it would have done nothing to allay her fears. Quite the reverse in fact, it would have caused her considerable alarm, as her former *syce* had been overwhelmed by what he was seeing as an irresistible tsunami of domestic difficulties.

Despite his air of detachment on the estate, he had in fact been watching with increasing anxiety the oncoming tidal wave of misfortune threatening his personal life, and today it had arrived to engulf him. He had been desperately hoping for a last-minute stay of execution and had twice been able to delay the fateful day by spurious excuses, but Allah had at last required him to face up to the consequences of his serial falls from grace on Bukit Bintang leading to his impregnation of his employer's wife. The reckoning was a considerable one – the loss of his job, the estrangement of his wife and children and, now, the humiliations of having a mem in his humble house for what promised to be a protracted visit, although he was still clinging to the diminishing hope that once she had experienced the facilities it offered she would see the impracticalities of her plan and depart.

But if she did not, and it was looking increasingly as though she was seeing her stay as a permanent one, then it would be only a matter of time before she announced to the village she was, or intended to be, his second wife, her swelling abdomen making it profanely obvious they had anticipated the event. What the consequences of the birth of their child would be were totally beyond his imagination. The disgrace of his family, the anger of the villagers, the horror of his parents who had arranged his marriage to Minah, and the outrage of the *imam* and the religious authorities, would be just the beginning of the many humiliations to come. He could think of no course of action which might either avert them or mitigate their effects. When, eventually, his personal Armageddon arrived he would have no alternative but to throw himself at the feet of Allah, beg for his forgiveness and hope his punishment and his miseries had come to an end.

* * *

The inside of the house was gloomy after the glare on the verandah but the wooden shutters, closed to exclude the heat, were admitting enough light for Valerie to see that the main living space was almost devoid of furniture save for some wicker baskets and what appeared to be an old desk of Western provenance. Where that had come from Valerie never did discover although she suspected it was from a previous employer of Osman's mother. The boarded floor had a scattering of woven mats but there was little else in the room. Her suitcase, when she put it down, looked as out of place and as obtrusive as a spaceship on the moon. Of Minah and the children there was no sign.

Around the door clustered a ring of brown faces all surveying her in silence. Osman beckoned her to sit down on a mat and his mother brought her a glass of coconut milk and then, to Valerie's surprise, disappeared into the back of the house. Osman sat cross-legged opposite her and smiled for the first time that day, not his usual wide grin but a subdued, apologetic half-smile which failed to get anywhere near his eyes. At last he felt he could put his feelings about having a white woman in his home into words:

'Not what you have been used to, Mem. I warned you. You will find things very different here.'

'Osman, we agreed you would not use that word Mem again. I knew the house would not be quite what I have been used to but I would rather be here a thousand times than on the estate. Where are Minah and the children?'

Osman looked even more uncomfortable. 'They have gone to her village for a while,' he said, not looking at her. Valerie said nothing, her uneasiness unallayed.

Osman then took her to the back of the house and she was surprised to find another room almost as large as the first but, once again, containing little furniture apart from more wicker baskets and a rough cupboard or two which were obviously used for storage; of tables and chairs there was no sign. On one side were some cubicles, they could hardly be described as rooms, separated by wooden walls extending little more than head high, one for each member of the household. The bedrooms, thought Valerie. She had been told there was virtually no privacy in Malay houses in the European sense of the word and here was confirmation of what she had previously concluded was the cause of Osman's conservative love-making and the reason he had been unable to respond to her uninhibited displays of affection.

A covered gangway to the rear, once again raised on piers, led to the kitchen where the main item was a wood-burning stove resting on a stone base. Conditions here were more primitive than Valerie had expected. There was obviously no running water in the house, the bathroom and toilet being two of a row of *attap* shelters running along the bank of the river about eighty yards distant which she had seen as they arrived. Valerie refused to allow herself to be despondent. This was to be her home and she was determined to make the best of it. Osman had made no attempt to bring her case into the back of the house – whether this was by oversight or design she did not know – and Valerie went to retrieve it. When she came back he was talking to his mother in rapid Malay.

Having been an *amah* for some years his mother spoke quite good English but when Valerie appeared Osman switched to a mixture of English and Malay although Valerie gained the impression that the Malay parts were more to keep her in ignorance than to enlighten his mother. At that moment he was explaining her presence and Valerie heard the phrase 'only for a while', presumably a reference to the length of her intended stay. He made no mention of what she thought was the accepted position, confirming her earlier suspicions, and making her even more certain that the fact that she was pregnant was still unknown as was the real reason for her coming to the house. Perhaps Osman thought she would not be able, or willing, to see her plan through. Clearly, he was underestimating her. Osman's failure to inform his mother or the villagers of her arrival was a disappointment but, in one way, had simplified things. The appearance of a British woman in their *kampung* without warning had obviously been a considerable surprise – and her suitcase, indicating she had not just come for the day, an even greater one. The present time did not, therefore, appear to be a particularly good time to announce she intended to make her stay permanent and this now determined how she should proceed.

Originally she had decided to make it clear from the outset that she expected to share the domestic chores as there seemed no better or quicker way to demonstrate she meant to pull her weight as a resident member of the household. She had speculated, however, as to what skills she possessed which would make a significant contribution to the task of running a *kampung* dwelling. She could hardly help prepare meals as her knowledge of Malay cooking was non-existent. As to the other chores which might be required she had no idea but she hoped that there would at least be *something* she could do otherwise she would find it hard to hold her head up in the village as the respect that all memmems enjoyed as wives of the colonial elite was hardly likely to survive the close familiarity of domestic life in a Malay house for very long. However, now she had the status of visitor, and a distinguished one at that, she was rather relieved she would not have to expose her domestic inadequacies to village scrutiny, at least not until after she had had the opportunity to look and learn.

She thought her first priority should be to establish a relationship with the old lady, who Osman informed her, was to be addressed as Puan Zainal. It was not easy. Her hostess's experience of white women had been confined to her duties as an *amah* and several times, to Valerie's dismay, she addressed her as Mem and Valerie had to insist she used her Christian name although it obviously required a very big effort on her hostess's part. Valerie imagined the experience must have been much as if she herself had been suddenly asked to address one of her old schoolteachers in the same way. On the plus side, Puan Zainal's reticence prevented her from asking Valerie the reason for her visit – although it must have been a burning question in the old lady's mind – for, at that moment, Valerie could think of no convincing answer.

She was told she could sleep in the cubicle usually used by Musa, Minah's son, so, quite obviously, there were no immediate plans for his or his mother's return. It would have been difficult to know who the cubicle belonged to as it was almost completely devoid of any furniture, apart from a sleeping mat and yet another basket into which Valerie put one or two of her things. It was quite obviously a substitute for a cupboard, but she left the remainder of her meagre belongings in the suitcase where they would be easier to access. There seemed nothing else to do to settle in.

The situation regarding Minah gave Valerie much food for thought as she could tell all was not as Osman would have her believe. She suspected Minah's absence was not just a social visit to her family diplomatically timed to avoid the embarrassment of having her husband's former employer as a guest. There was more than a suspicion in Valerie's mind that Minah suspected her husband was contemplating taking a second wife, who, in flagrant breach of decency, was already under her husband's roof. If that was so, then Minah probably knew the reason for her coming – her pregnancy. Valerie had several times impressed upon Osman the necessity of keeping Minah abreast of what was going on on Bukit Bintang but whether he had done so or not she did not know. The chances were that he had not, as he appeared to have taken a 'head-in-the-sand' attitude to all of his responsibilities regarding their affair. But if Minah *did* know, or at least had her suspicions, would she not have told Puan Zainal?

*　*　*

She now found she had to avail herself of the river facilities and Puan Zainal accompanied her though clearly embarrassed at what the riverine community had to offer in this respect, her former role as an *amah* making her all too aware of what her guest had been accustomed to. Even though it was such a short distance the old woman first donned the *selendang* or veil, a piece of material which she draped round her shoulders and head. It could be drawn over the lower part of her face when required, although, according to Puan Zainal, it was used more often to protect herself from the sun than any presumptuous eyes. Osman had warned Valerie Muslim women were expected to wear one in public and that it would be appreciated by the villagers if she did the same, at least around the *kampung*, although she later discovered the younger women rarely did so. There was no question of their going into Karang without it, however, although one or two of the bolder spirits, even there, sometimes dared to use it more as a means of covering their head than a concealment of their face. Although, in theory, such concealment was a religious requirement it was not rigidly enforced in Malaya, even in the east of the country which was stricter and more orthodox in its Islamic lifestyle than in the states on the west coast.

The interested onlookers who had gathered around the house on Valerie's arrival had drifted away but several children spotted them as they emerged and crowded around once more. They were met by some voluble Malay from Puan Zainal and they retreated obediently, still smiling shyly and showing no resentment at their correction.

Being free of an audience did little to reduce Valerie's feelings of self-consciousness, however, as she approached the little roofless shelter which served as a toilet. To her consternation she found it was actually a floating raft which had to be pulled ashore before she could open the *attap* door and step onto a small log platform with a gap made in the centre. Once her initial feeling of insecurity had been overcome she felt an irresistible desire to giggle. The swirling water almost under her feet made it appear as though it was she and the shelter which were moving and not the river. The effect was very similar to sitting in a train standing in a station and watching another one leave, so that when she opened the door she expected to be hundreds of yards upstream, and despite herself, she was quite surprised when she emerged to find she and the shelter were still safely moored to the bank and had not moved.

As she wandered back to the house, she was accompanied by a retinue of excited children as this time there was no Puan Zainal to chase them away, and they were all anxious to talk to her and finger the hem of her dress. Valerie assumed a British woman, and a dress, were something of novelties to them.

She took stock of her new circumstances. The house and its facilities were more spartan than she had expected but that mattered little to her. She was much more concerned about the obvious embarrassment her presence in the house was causing her hosts. How easy the phrase 'a second wife' seemed in abstract, but how sensitive and difficult it was in reality. Here she was, regarding herself as a second wife, but so far she had advanced no nearer to that status than temporary visitor in her prospective husband's home – there had been no marriage ceremony, nor even talk of one, despite her broaching the subject with Osman several times.

She was acutely aware of the ambiguity of her new position. Even in Britain it would have been unusual and it required no imagination at all to visualise the effect it would have on a strict Muslim community. How long could she continue living under the same roof as a man who was without his wife? Such a situation would clearly compromise everyone in the house and probably the village as well. There was, of course, an even more serious question to be asked – the ultimate one. What would be everyone's reaction when her pregnancy made itself evident and it became clear to all why Minah had vacated the house? Fortunately, the loose Malayan clothes she hoped she would soon be wearing would conceal it for a while but it was only a matter of time before the problem would have to be faced.

Unless, of course, she opted to move out of the village altogether until a ceremony could be arranged. Perhaps that was what must have been in Osman's mind when he had described her stay to his mother as 'only for a while'. She was reluctant to take this option, however. Not only because it represented failure but because she really could not afford to stay long enough in a hotel for all the impediments to her marriage to be removed, and she sensed that there would be many. She also suspected that once she was out of sight it would be all too easy for objections to her return to be raised and then endlessly prolonged. The Malays had a habit of avoiding what they did not like, and of postponing, rather than dealing, with problems to which they could see no obvious solution. If she remained in the village it would at least force everyone to start finding a way through the labyrinth.

Yet she was anxious not to offend the sensitivities of her Malay hosts and suspected that, in the case of Minah, she had already done so. Well she knew the importance of not upsetting a proud people by doing anything to demean them in the eyes of their fellow-villagers. She began to realise how selfish she had been in thinking she could take refuge from the storm that was inevitably about to assail her from all quarters, British as well as Malay, by placing herself in Osman's house and family. She would have to try to build up the foundation of trust which would be necessary if the problems which surely lay ahead were to be overcome. It was becoming increasingly obvious that, by leaving Bukit Bintang and coming to Batu Lima, she had merely exchanged one dark corner in her future for another.

*   *   *

Valerie then experienced the first truly Malayan afternoon of her life. Lacking the facilities of a European home, the simple house offered little in the way of amusement. Without electricity, there could be no wireless or telephone, or any of the normal domestic services, and even if there had been a newspaper she could not have read it, Arabic Malay, or Jawi as it was known, still being a mystery to her. Nor were there shops to visit, books to read, or, on this occasion at least, any neighbours with which to gossip, quite obviously the main leisure pursuit of the village.

Her time consisted almost entirely of watching Puan Zainal make an outfit of Malay clothes for her. Her request occasioned some surprise but, as Osman explained to his mother, their guest wished to discover if, despite their all-encompassing appearance, Malay clothes were cooler and more comfortable to wear in the tropics than European dress. So a sarong *kebaya*, an ankle-long gown with a close-fitting top which was the traditional dress of a Malay woman, and a *selendang*, were made, although Valerie had some difficulty in persuading the old lady she really intended to wear them.

As she watched, she was forced to sit on the floor, her legs tucked sideways beneath her, a position she was going to have to get used to during the times when she was not actually on her feet, including mealtimes. She found it made her back ache but she was also finding both the normal cross-legged position she remembered from her gym lessons at junior school, and the sitting-back-on-the-heels crouch which everyone in the East seemed to be able to maintain for hours, very uncomfortable after a few minutes, so she took every opportunity she could of getting up to walk around, stopping to look out of the shuttered windows at the *kampung* scene and the river beyond. She also missed the fan of her bedroom on the estate, native houses not being anything like as cool as Europeans had always assured her they were.

At the first signs of the swift Malayan sunset, Osman and his mother prepared themselves for the act of Muslim worship which regularly punctuated each day and so became very familiar to Valerie in the next few months. After the dutiful and careful washing of their hands and feet they both turned towards what everyone in the village accepted was the direction of Mecca, Osman in front, his mother in a position of respect behind, and together they performed the simple ceremony which involved a number of complete prostrations before Allah. Had it been at the local mosque, they would have had to worship separately, the sexes not being permitted to do so together in public.

Valerie was impressed by the solemnity of the proceedings and the devoutness of the worshippers and it gave her some food for thought. Although baptised, she had never been a regular church-goer since she had left her parents' home and saw herself, when she thought about it at all, as a neglectful or even a lapsed Christian, and so her forthcoming conversion to Islam would not involve any great change in her religious convictions. Nevertheless she felt uneasy at an apostasy which would be for the sake of convenience and not her beliefs. Eventually she satisfied her conscience by the thought she was not changing her God, if she had one, just the method by which she was worshipping Him.

After the ceremony, Puan Zainal began to prepare the evening meal and Valerie was able to see at close hand the native way of producing a fish curry, a dish which she was destined to get to know as thoroughly, and almost as frequently, as the Muslim act of worship. She had never shown much interest in the process before but after the relative tedium of the afternoon, it had its interesting moments. They ate, all three, in the back room which Valerie had already discovered was the domain of the ladies of the household.

To her surprise she found the meals were still eaten with the fingers – the Malays having a strong objection to forks and spoons – for as her hosts were quick to point out when Valerie raised the subject – into how many mouths had those implements already been placed during previous meals? Such hygiene considerations did not seem to worry Westerners but in the East a well-washed hand was preferred for conveying food to the mouth, as long as it was the right hand, of course, so Valerie quickly learned to lean upon her left during meals and thus avoid the cardinal sin of eating or passing anything to fellow diners with the hand which was associated with attending to bodily functions.

They each sat on a mat around a centre bowl of rice, eating from their own small dishes while adding curry and sauces as they chose. Afterwards she sat on the steps at the back of the house in the cool of the evening trying to talk to the village children in Malay. She felt they were likely to be good teachers in the days to come as they not only seemed to find her pronunciation of their language amusing – the Malay habit of shortening many words was proving particularly difficult for her to master – but were equally amused by their own attempts at hers.

After another trip to the river, an infinitely more hazardous operation in the dark than it had been in the afternoon, she retired to Musa's cubicle and her sleeping mat which, she was not surprised to discover, had none of the comfort of her bed at Bukit Bintang. Inevitably, her mind went back to the home she had left. Would Stuart be smoking and reading his paper after the evening meal as usual? What could a husband do after his wife had just left him except to carry on as before as best as he could? She was conscious of the severity of the blow she had delivered to his self-esteem and knew, though she had hitherto tended to minimise, the effect her desertion would have on him, how he would be in dread of the publicity when her affair became the talk of the clubs and bars of the peninsula. She was able to picture the pose of indifference he would inevitably adopt, but she knew that deep down he would feel the humiliation keenly, especially when dealing with the employees on his estate.

For the first time she felt a tinge of pity for him. He was going to experience a difficult and embarrassing time in the months ahead. He would not only have to endure unsolicited sympathy, prurient interest and the considerable indignities of a cuckolded husband, but also the boredom and isolation which she knew her coming to

Malaya had relieved. It was only a small consolation to her to think that he had helped to bring it on himself as, deep in her heart, she knew she could be far from proud of her own conduct during the last few months, as her mother would have been quick to point out. Her action that morning in leaving him would also be considered as both reckless and selfish by even the most fair-minded in the European community, and there were not likely to be many of those in evidence in the next few months. But, if any of them stopped to reflect for a moment, and as her experiences that day had borne out, none could possibly think that she had taken the easy way out of her predicament, as the next few months were likely to prove.

*   *   *

Valerie was not surprised Osman came nowhere near her that night although she lay awake for some time just in case, but then, how could a host share a guest's bedroom under his own roof? She did not sleep well. The mat on the board floor was going to take some getting used to and the sarong she had been given did little to protect her from the chill of the early hours.

She awoke at five and knew further sleep was impossible. Stiffly she got to her feet and fumbled for her toilet bag and towel. The house was in silence as she crept with great care to the back entrance. It was unlocked. Security, it appeared, was only a European necessity. It was almost dark and she had difficulty in keeping to the path. The grass was wet and the gravel painfully sharp. She realised she had forgotten her flip-flops just as she had the previous morning. Her flight down to the river on the estate in search of Osman had been made only twenty-four hours before and was only sixty miles away but it could have been in a different age and in another universe.

She had no idea which bath-house she should use but two looked as though they might be occupied so she picked one furthest away from these and gingerly opened the door. A clattering movement and a splash startled her but it was only a monitor lizard which had taken up overnight residence and was making good its escape. She was used to them as they had been a familiar sight in the stream on the estate although she had rarely needed to be in such close proximity to one. There were several steep steps edged with logs leading into the water and after discarding her sarong and throwing it over the wall of the shelter as evidence of occupation, she stepped into the slowly moving water up to her knees. It was colder than she had believed possible in the tropics and she gasped as she used her flannel to sluice it over herself. The contents of the Shanghai jar had never been as cold as this!

Only a couple of metres from the bank the river looked dark and forbidding and she thought vaguely of crocodiles and water-snakes as well as the large python she had once seen swimming in the river on Bukit Bintang. When she stopped splashing it was remarkably silent, the night sounds having ended, the day ones not yet begun. She heard, rather than saw, some fish breaking the surface of the water. She did not linger but hurriedly dried herself and, still trying to wriggle her damp body into her sarong, opened the door. She saw, too late, another early bather on the bank, a look of astonishment on his face. She fled past him towards the village, the roofs of which could now be clearly seen against a yellowing sky. She would have to adopt the Malay custom of bathing in her sarong in future or she would draw even more unwanted attention to herself.

*   *   *

Stuart made no attempt to go anywhere near the Club while he waited for the official reaction to the domestic calamity which had befallen him though, to his surprise, he heard nothing for several weeks, and he began to wonder if Valerie's desertion was to take its place among the world's numberless human events which evade record or public knowledge and so are destined to live only as long as those involved in them, after which they are lost to posterity and known only to the Almighty. But this, he thought, was highly unlikely. Somehow, by one means or the other, such news was bound to filter into the public domain and then begin to circulate in the forums where gossip was the normal bill of fare – the bars, the swimming pools, the smart dinner parties. There was very little the redoubtable wife of the British Adviser did not pick up on her social antennae for example, and once brought to the attention of officialdom the scandal would not be ignored.

The powers that be might be tempted to do so, of course, and it would be a huge slice of good fortune for him if they did, but he was not hopeful – expatriate tongues would surely wag, questions be asked, rumours grow in number and vulgarity and work their mischief. The Administration could not, would not, let that happen.

Meanwhile he tried to maintain his normal routine. Not a soul on the estate made any reference, direct or otherwise, to Valerie or her absence but these unnatural omissions told Stuart her departure must still be the major topic of discussion in the labour lines, no doubt with gleeful embellishments. Only when he began to hear the first casual mention of her name would he be able to assume the subject had been, if not forgotten, supplanted by more recent topics or events.

Then, just when he thought he was going to be lucky, he received a letter from the secretary to the British Adviser in the state capital, Kota Bharu, saying his political superior wished to see him at his earliest convenience, although there was no mention of the reason. The tone was casual but Stuart was not deceived. He decided to take a rare half-day off work. There was no point in delaying the inevitable and, in any case, he was keen to get it over with. He had to drive himself.

Kota Bharu, the capital of Kelantan, was the only town of any size in the state. Its name was one of the few that could be literally translated from Malay into English. Incongruously, it was 'Kota' – 'a Malay fort or castle' and 'Bharu' – 'new', and, like its English namesake, it was situated in the north east of the country, but there the similarity ended. Kota Bharu had no hinterland of mines or any industry at all to speak of. Since the British had absorbed Kelantan into its empire a quarter of a century before, rubber had been planted along the banks of its principal river following which other estates had spread inland, Bukit Bintang being an example, and there was also some logging and allied activity upstream, the produce of this development gaining access to the outside world via the town and its tiny port of Tumpat.

Kota Bharu was also the seat of the Sultan and the British Administration, but apart from these symbols of authority, it possessed little else of significance. Like the state as a whole, it drowsed quietly by the side of the South China Sea, content to be a backwater, and, until the railway came in 1931, was for all practical purposes, completely cut off from the rest of the country by land. Its citizens had few activities to occupy them apart from weaving, market gardening and fishing, and they were even deprived of the last of these during the monsoon season between November and March when strong winds from the north-east kept the boats on the beaches.

The Residency, home to the British Adviser who was the representative of His Britannic Majesty in the state, was situated next to the Resident Commissioner's Office and together they formed the heart-beat of the colonial administration in Kelantan. The British had become de facto rulers as recently as 1909, by treaty with Siam, only to find to their dismay that the State Treasury was almost empty. Soon afterwards, further financial misfortune overtook them in the form of the sharp opportunism of an expatriate Briton called Duff.

During the Siamese administration he had formed a company which had been granted substantial land concessions by the Sultan in the expectation that the commercial activity they generated would revive the state's revenues via taxation. Not only had this proved to be a vain hope, but Duff had heaped further impoverishment upon them in the form of two successful lawsuits. Ironically, these had come about as the result of a second commercial venture in which the state government had invested much expectation and even more capital.

It was a new railway through the jungle connecting Kelantan to the main trunk-line on the west coast running between Penang in the north and Singapore in the south, and had been almost twenty years in the building, but Duff found two most unusual ways to enrich himself at its expense. First, he brought a successful legal action against the state government for failing to take the railway across his land after its apparent previous promise to do so. Then, later, he won further damages for encroachment when the railway dared to cross another part of his concession without his prior authority.

From that time forward, Kelantan's finances had been in perpetual deficit and the Residency reflected the fact. No gleaming palace of white stone proclaiming colonial might and magnificence greeted Stuart as he drew up in his car. Instead he was confronted by a simple, single-storey building roofed with *attap*, not likely to impress visitors or strike awe and respect into the local peasantry as it was hardly more imposing than the latter's own dwellings, though more commodious. The 'thatched palace', as it was known, had long been the subject of patronising comment, not to say ridicule, among the citizens of the more prosperous states of the west coast. In an attempt to add a touch of dignity, the building had been surrounded by lawns and a fountain which, as Stuart approached, was being cleaned by a Tamil dressed in just a pair of faded shorts and a ragged square of cotton draped over his head as protection against the sun. His garb seemed depressingly in keeping with the edifice behind him.

Stuart knew the Adviser slightly, a civil servant who had been in the country even longer than himself – a tall, spare man with a pronounced stoop, his face betraying his years in the tropics and the many sundowners he had consumed. He had little imagination but was a competent, if slightly plodding, administrator. He was well known for a long-standing dislike of having to deal with the personal problems of his fellow nationals and his first waking thought that morning had been the interview before him. Not for the first time he had complained bitterly to his wife of the time-consuming burdens such duties imposed upon him. He had also included the High Commission in Kuala Lumpur, the capital, in his complaints – again, not for the first time.

He stood in his office under a gently moving fan which, with his increasing age, was becoming a necessity for him after about ten in the morning. Unfortunately, he could not position his desk directly beneath its slowly drifting blades as the downward draught blew his papers onto the floor or turned the pages of his files without his realising it so that he wrote memos in the wrong place, requiring him to copy them out again. Modern new conveniences such as fans could be very inconvenient at times!

While he waited for Stuart to arrive his mind went back to when he had first come to the country some thirty years before when there had been no electric fans, or wives either for that matter. Both were considered luxuries then. The function of the first had been performed by servants called punkah-wallahs who sat on the verandahs pulling ropes which, by setting ceiling curtains into languid motion, directed cooling breezes over those within. As a young cadet, he had often been sent out in the late evening to kick a punkah-wallah awake.

The role of the second luxury had been mainly filled by local girls who had been paid to provide the services of a wife, and sometimes a mother too. Such women kept the *tuans* on the estates sane and those in the towns out of the local brothels. Social and domestic life in the peninsula in those days had been conspicuously male but, at the same time, relatively simple. Electricity, however, had transformed everything. Living conditions had greatly improved and European wives could now contemplate dwelling in the tropics, and once installed, had not only insisted on surrounding themselves with a full range of domestic comforts, but a host of social complications as well.

European society in the country had become formal and governed by a strict order of rank and precedence. Racial snobberies were now commonplace and petty squabbles and domestic crises, like the one before him, an ever-recurring feature of his daily duties. He detested them, they not only made him feel uncomfortable, they were baffling, and he was greatly put out when he saw hitherto capable men reduced to administrative liabilities by the problems, emotional and sometimes financial, stemming from the frustrations of bored wives with too little to absorb their energies. Their companies, and needless to say, the Administration, were then required to resolve the domestic situations which resulted, the men usually having to be moved to positions elsewhere in the country or even replaced. On one occasion he had actually had one fellow openly weep in his office. Naturally, he was sent home, broken in mind and spirit, never to return. Taken all in all, he thought the coming of electricity, although a boon in many ways, had done little to improve the overall efficiency of the country's colonial service.

As Stuart was ushered in, he assumed what he hoped was a sympathetic expression. 'Sorry to hear of the trouble involving your wife,' he said.

Stuart noted that he had referred to Valerie as 'your wife' and not by her name although the Adviser had met her on several occasions. It was the start of the process of making her a non-person. He also managed to make it sound as though she had been involved in a fatal accident and Stuart could not help feeling how much simpler it would have been if she had. He assumed the B.A. had learned of the affair via his own wife, who was invariably referred to by all and sundry as 'the Lady Beatrice', like a ship, but the soubriquet was by no means to her displeasure. In fact, she revelled in her unofficial title and even more in the paramount position it gave her in local society, sparse as the latter was, and she ruled it with an imperious hand. No scrap of gossip ever eluded her for very long, enabling her to keep her husband well informed of all that was going on in his fiefdom.

Gossip normally bored him but he appreciated being made aware of those particular pieces of information vital to the smooth running of the Administration and therefore its prestige, and he agreed there could be none more important than the bombshell of the planter's wife who had absconded with her husband's *syce,* and he was grateful to the Lady Beatrice for her warning, although it had left him with an unpleasant task. In fact, it was probably the most awkward interview he had ever had to conduct since he had been appointed British Adviser in Kelantan. At the same time, he was extremely pleased his lady wife had heard about it before the High Commission in Kuala Lumpur enabling *him* to inform *them* of the matter. Such tiny triumphs made him appear as if he was on top of things.

'From what I hear it is going to be a deuced awkward business,' he continued. 'We are not quite sure the best way to proceed. We have sent wives home before, of course. That should not be a problem.'

This was said to reassure Stuart that there would be no lack of resolve on officialdom's part and that they also had powers to bring wayward wives to heel.

'There was that bank manager's wife in Perak who was accused of stealing in the bazaar, and then, of course, you know about Sharpe's wife who knocked down a Malay in KL. Killed him,' he added as if to confirm that expatriates' wives, though sometimes negligent, were at least thorough in what they did. 'I gather your wife has gone to live with this Malay chappie in his village?'

To the Adviser's discomfiture, Stuart said nothing but only nodded his head, and so he had to plough on. Unfortunately, at that moment he was not even sure his wife had got all her facts right, she was inclined to embellish things like this at times. A feminine trait he feared. Why didn't the fellow say something?

'This does make matters rather difficult. If he had been a Chinese or Indian things would have been a lot simpler. On the other hand the Islamic Council will not be at all pleased at a Muslim living *in flagrante*, as it were, with a non-Muslim and they will be sure to want her out as much as we do.'

He paused. This was becoming embarrassing. Just about everything he had said must be like a knife twisting in the man's wound. If only Mitchell would stop just sitting there and indicate how he was feeling and what he proposed to do. He decided on a question.

'Did you have no inkling of what was going on? No warning?'

Stuart broke his silence to indicate that the scandal had been a total surprise to him and that he felt let down by everyone concerned; not only by his wife and her lover, obviously, but by the other servants who, now he had time to think about it, he felt sure must have suspected *something* of what was going on, although they professed otherwise.

'I agree. Probably a case of the locals sticking together I would think. They always do. It's a bad show I must say. Quite unprecedented in my experience. It is going to reflect very badly on all of us and cause a lot of extra work I don't mind telling you. I suppose you will divorce her?'

Stuart confirmed that divorce was indeed his intention, and as soon as possible. He felt humiliated having to sit there and listen to Valerie being talked about as if she was an errant child. It was as if he had been summoned to his daughter's boarding school to be told she had been involved in some nefarious activity or other and was being expelled. Furthermore, the headmaster, though trying to sound sympathetic was making little effort to conceal his conviction that you, as her parent, were responsible, not only for the girl's behaviour but for him having to make a lengthy and time-consuming report to the school governors as a result. Privately, Stuart did not give a fig for the extra work Valerie might be giving the Administration. Sorting the matter out would give *them* something to do for once as they did little enough in his view. They had a soft life compared to planters. *They* were certainly not up at five every morning.

The Adviser sensed he may have struck a false note and cast around to say something which might ease Stuart's mortification and lit upon a reason to justify, rather than condemn, Valerie's conduct.

'Of course, this is no country for a white woman. There is basically nothing to occupy them. The one thing they need, children, we pack off to the UK. No wonder some of them get bored, don't know what to do, and look for a little excitement.'

But as he spoke he realised that having first appeared to be critical he was now sounding patronising. Valerie's behaviour was inexcusable and nothing he could say would make it look any better. She could hardly have chosen a more public way to humiliate her husband. Whatever had he done to make her inflict this on him? With his own *syce* too. He tried to be reassuring.

'Now you have confirmed the main facts, we will let the religious authorities have the details and then leave it to the Malays. They will be able to put a lot of pressure on the man you know. I should think he will very soon be extremely sorry he ever got mixed up with a white woman. Your wife should be on a boat within a fortnight or three weeks. I assume you will defray the cost of her passage home?'

However, to his surprise and embarrassment, Stuart expressed himself unwilling to be involved in any further expenditure on behalf of his wife, and suggested, none too tactfully, that if the Administration wished to see the back of her, they would have to do it at their expense and not his.

For a moment the B.A. considered contesting the point. As everyone knew, Kelantan was always in an acute state of financial embarrassment and so it was certain the State Treasury would be unwilling to bear even part of the expense of sending Mrs Mitchell home, regardless of the case for it which he, personally, would be willing to make. As for the other sources of official funds – he pictured a buff file shuffling between himself, the High Commission in K.L. and the Secretariat in Singapore and then back again, getting fatter by the day but no nearer to a decision on how Mrs M.'s passage home could be paid for out of official funds, or even nearer to finding how such a decision might be reached. There was always that thorny problem of setting a precedent.

Then he had an inspiration – perhaps Mitchell's company would be prepared to help, they must be as much mortified by the whole business as the Administration. He must remember to make the point in his report and then suggest the High Commission write to the company. That statement of the obvious would rile them, as well he knew, they being perfectly aware that persuading the business community to take responsibility for their employees in such matters as these came very much within their province. It also gave him more than a little satisfaction to think he was giving them something to do for once. They really had no idea of the burden he was required to shoulder with just the skeleton staff his state revenues allowed, whereas they had far more secretaries than they needed. What with the social attractions of the capital as well, no wonder K.L. was such a popular posting.

Stuart got up to leave and the Adviser breathed a sigh of relief. He had managed to avoid what he had most dreaded – having to listen to the grisly details of a disintegrating marriage and then been required to sympathise with its unhappy victim – a task completely beyond his capacity. The prospect had quite ruined his breakfast. But, he had to admit, the Lady Beatrice would be disappointed as she was looking forward to his summary of the interview over dinner. There was precious little to relieve the daily tedium in this corner of the peninsula.

'We'll let you know of any developments. I assume you will not want to make any further contact with her again,' he said.

As Stuart walked down the corridor he wondered if he should have mentioned the fact that Valerie was pregnant but dismissed the thought. He had been through quite enough for one day.

*　*　*

For Valerie, each day that passed in Batu Lima varied but little from the first. She put herself out endlessly for Puan Zainal and the old lady – she was not particularly old but the ravages of the tropical sun had made her appear so – became increasingly confident in her company. As an ex-*amah* she had felt intimidated by Valerie's presence at first but slowly she began to sense, if, as a mother, she had not seen straight away, the affection in which her son was held by her guest. She was now suspecting Osman had not acquainted her with the real position and that Valerie was going to be considerably more than a casual visitor. She was also beginning to sense, perhaps, what was under Valerie's *baju* and was viewing the prospect of presiding over a household containing two wives, particularly one in which the second wife was a former mem and pregnant, with considerable misgivings.

Second marriages amongst Malays of humble birth were relatively rare and fraught with difficulties. Normally, a husband who took a second wife would possess the wealth to be able to provide a separate home, or at least quarters, for her in order to avoid what were bound to be difficulties, but this would be impossible for Osman, and so Minah would have to be persuaded to live under the same roof with a second wife who, though lower than she in the domestic hierarchy, was clearly her social superior.

The complex web of rights and privileges to which the first wife was entitled was bound to impose considerable strains in a house of this size so it was not surprising Puan Zainal was not looking forward to the months ahead. She clung to the hope that her guest would have second thoughts about wanting to share their home. Why such a beautiful white woman should choose a Malay lifestyle when she could have been living in the lap of luxury back in her Western world she could not begin to comprehend. However, she saw it as no business of hers to persuade her to go, in fact it would have been a grave breach of Malay etiquette to try to do so.

As for the implications of her presence in the village Puan Zainal hardly dared to think. Officially, Valerie's status was a visitor – albeit a very unusual one. But the situation was already seriously flouting Malay custom in that no woman who was not a relative could reside under the same roof as a man, particularly a man who was without the company of his wife. The only way this could be regularised would be the man taking the woman as his second wife but in Malay society a prospective second wife was subject to all manner of restrictions and conventions. She would not be allowed in her future husband's company without a male relative present, even meeting him at all would be irregular, and she would certainly not be permitted to be in daily proximity with him under the same roof.

Puan Zainal decided the only way she could reconcile these conventions was to hope they would be seen as not having to apply to a special guest like Valerie. In her mind, however, it left her in a quandary as to how she should treat her – with deference as a guest or authority as a prospective daughter-in-law, and she ended up by doing something in between. In this she was helped by Valerie's anxious desire to do everything that was asked of her.

Of the problems facing her hostess, Valerie remained in relative ignorance as Osman refused to be drawn on the matter. It seemed to her that at times her former *syce* was living in a world of his own and had been from the moment she had come to live in Batu Lima. She was unable to get him to focus on anything to do with the baby or the problems which were likely to arise when its arrival became obvious. Nor did he seem capable of offering his mother any comfort in her troubles with the villagers. On some days he gave the impression his mind was in a complete tailspin with barely one coherent thought following another and he certainly had no suggestions as to how they might avoid the impending disaster facing them.

It did not even seem to occur to him to try to persuade Valerie to reconsider her decision to come and live amongst them, although had he attempted this obvious way out of their situation, she would have almost certainly refused, as although she was very conscious of her obligations as a guest in the Zainal household, she had the baby to consider. As she saw it, Osman's son – she was persisting with her view that it was a boy she was carrying – had the right to be born in his father's house. In any case, she was as constant as ever in her conviction that once they had married all would be well. She was also equally convinced that once she had left Batu Lima, circumstances and various interests would conspire to prevent her from ever returning.

All that Osman seemed able to do was to reiterate his belief that everything which had happened to bring them to this state of affairs, and whatever dramatic events remained in the future, were all manifestations of the will of Allah and so had to be endured with as much grace as they could muster. The only consolation he could offer was that one day their nightmare would surely come to an end and when Allah considered that time had arrived, he would reveal his intentions for each and every one of them. Meanwhile, as Allah's faithful servants, it was their duty to wait as patiently as possible for that blessed moment to materialise, as any attempt to resist their destiny or seek to alter it in any way, was not only unthinkable, it was a sin.

Meanwhile, to his personal sorrow, all his normal pleasures in the village had ceased to exist. None of his male friends came to gossip on his verandah in the evenings, nor did he feel welcome on theirs. It was almost as if Valerie had thrown up a barrier between them. He felt the loss keenly as he had always enjoyed the company of his peers.

* * *

If Puan Zainal was perplexed as to what attitude she should take towards Valerie, so was the whole village including its *penghulu*, the elderly headman. They had no idea what the true situation was – European news and gossip of that sort took time to filter down to the villages, if it ever did, so they were left to make up their own minds. Had she been a Malay there would have been no doubt, she would have been banished immediately, but as she was a mem, they were forced to conclude, like Puan Zainal, that normal considerations did not apply.

The arrangement was without precedent in their experience, but they were happy to take their lead from the *penghulu*. He, like them, appeared to have accepted her as a temporary visitor who was exempt from the normal conventions because she was one of the ruling class, on a par with the Sultan, of whom he was extremely respectful. Indeed, he was secretly rather beginning to think the presence of such a distinguished and beautiful visitor in his otherwise unremarkable village might be a mark of some special favour, perhaps even an honour of some description, although in what way he was at a loss to imagine.

By and large the villagers kept their distance from the household and merely exchanged token greetings when they met. This was a hardship for Puan Zainal as the companionship of the villagers was her main comfort and their gossip her chief entertainment. Nevertheless, for the sake of her son, she bore it all with dignity.

The other women avoided Valerie when they could, and looked the other way when a meeting proved impossible, although the boldest began to nod and smile as the weeks went by. Eventually Valerie was encouraged enough to take the household washing down to the river – the length of her stay in the village having enabled her to claim this task from Puan Zainal as a visitor's perquisite. Her first appearance occasioned much amusement but she took care not to intrude upon the women's presence, keeping well apart from the circle and her gaze averted. She was pleased to do this as her laundry skills, though better than those required for the other domestic tasks she occasionally undertook, were not yet good enough to bear comparison with those of the villagers. In any case, language was still a problem. Valerie was learning very quickly but when Osman and his mother or indeed the villagers spoke in the vernacular she could barely understand more than a phrase or two.

Osman was out most of each day looking for a job but he returned one evening with something like his old grin much in evidence. His friend the taxi driver had persuaded the Chinese owner of a fleet of taxis to rent him a vehicle on a daily basis. This was an unusual concession to a Malay whose reputation for hard and regular work was not the equal of a Chinese. The rent was high but Osman was thankful for the chance of earning some money again. Valerie had brought a few hundred dollars with her, all she had been able to glean without arousing Stuart's suspicions in her last few months on the estate, but Osman declined them, shyly but firmly. Osman's job meant he and Valerie now saw very little of one another as he worked into the small hours of every morning and had to be out again promptly the next day. He came home in the afternoons but spent most of the time sleeping in his cubicle.

One afternoon, however, he came home with an item of news. His friend, the Karang taxi driver, had met a worker from Bukit Bintang who had told him that Stuart was ill with malaria and there was a new manager running the estate. At first Valerie was sceptical – Stuart was never ill – and she wondered if the report was just a clumsy attempt at a reconciliation on Stuart's part, unlikely as that sounded. Reflection convinced her, however, that she was mistaken as it would be quite unlike Stuart to use a native for a message of a personal nature, although what means he would have used of contacting her if such a thought had entered his head she could not think. She was also quite certain that while she was carrying Osman's child any sort of approach on his part was not only out of the question, it was unthinkable.

Several weeks later there was a another report, this time that Stuart was back on the estate, but in the words of the tapper 'without his *panas hati*' – his anger. From which she deduced he had either not fully recovered from his ordeal or the malaria had in some way mellowed him. She heard no more and, in fact, she forgot about it. The incident had left her unmoved.

If anything, Osman was more affected by it than she was, as he still seemed to be feeling the guilt of a *musuh dalam selimut* – an enemy under the blanket.

As a consequence of the circumstances in which they were forced to live, Osman was unable, or perhaps he was unwilling, to demonstrate any physical affection for her. They also exchanged very few confidences, and he made no attempt to visit her at night. In fact, their relationship became little more than that of what they were supposed to be – host and honoured guest. Meanwhile, underneath her loose Malay *baju*, the baby grew apace, and Valerie began to feel more and more self-conscious during her daily baths in the river. The time was fast approaching when her status as a temporary guest would need to be redefined and the facts of her pregnancy made public. The situation was on the brink of having to be resolved when, as so often happens, it resolved itself, although Osman preferred to regard it as Allah, at long last, revealing his long-awaited plans for his faithful servants.

* * *

The *penghulu* called at the house one morning and Puan Zainal met him on the verandah. He had received a message from the Sultan's Office to say that a secretary would be coming to the village the next day to see Osman, and also, probably, Valerie. Osman was petrified at the news. He was aware of the danger of his situation, knew of the wrath of the Islamic Council, the guardians of Muslim law, if his relationship with Valerie, a Christian, should be revealed. The next morning he and Valerie went to the *penghulu's* house. Valerie was seen into the back room where she was left silently to herself, the *penghulu's* wife who spoke no English, gazing shyly at her, two unmarried daughters keeping out of sight. Osman talked with the *penghulu* on the verandah, both of them ill at ease.

At eleven, some time after it was due, a shiny car came bouncing down the track driven by a *syce* in impeccable native dress. The Secretary himself, surprisingly, was in Western clothes, immaculately tailored trousers, cream shirt and highly polished black shoes, an over-large wristwatch with an elaborate gold bracelet hanging loosely from a wrist which was as narrow as a girl's. He was marvellously slim and neat, with a toothbrush moustache and pomaded black hair. He looked much more out of place in the Malay village than Valerie. He talked briefly with Osman and the *penghulu* before asking that Valerie be brought out to see him.

'Good morning, Puan Mitchell,' he said very deliberately and with a sideways look at the *penghulu*. Then, as the headman showed some surprise at her title, said in rapid Malay, 'Yes, Mrs Mitchell is married to the manager of the Bukit Bintang Estate at Kuala Lebir.'

The Secretary meant business. He turned to Valerie and, speaking in faultless English, said, 'May I ask your purpose in coming to live in Batu Lima? You realise how unusual such an action is by a white woman.'

Valerie decided that caution might be wise until she discovered the purpose of his visit.

'I no longer wished to live with my husband and Osman was prepared to put me up … give me somewhere to stay.' She rephrased the colloquial expression for his benefit, although it did not seem as though that was necessary. Her answer seemed lame and unconvincing but she was unwilling to say more until she discovered how much he knew and what attitude he was going to take.

The Secretary regarded her carefully for a moment. His confident manner was making it increasingly evident that he was in full possession of all the facts.

'That does seem a very strange thing to do Mrs Mitchell. Most women in your position would seek the company of their own people and return to their own country. Would not the explanation more likely be that you have,' and he paused seeking the right words in English, 'formed a special friendship with Osman? That you and Osman have an adulterous relationship in fact?'

He turned to the *penghulu* and translated what he had said into Malay. Osman hung his head like a small boy, while the *penghulu* looked from the Secretary to Valerie with ever-mounting alarm. His mouth, which was almost toothless, opened and closed several times as he sought words to meet the gravity of the situation, and this made the sunlight glint on his grey stubble. He was facing twin calamities. This prestigious guest, of whose presence in his *kampung* he had been secretly rather proud, was it seems, not a guest at all, but a scarlet woman ensnaring a Son of the Faith, and what was more, she had been working her wicked ways under his very nose.

From being an ornament in the community she had, at a stroke, become an alarming liability. The village was thus shamed and he had been shamed with it. Inevitably his own role in the affair would now be questioned. Why had he not made it clear to Puan Zainal that an unaccompanied Christian woman living in the *kampung* was not acceptable? Why had he not ascertained the reason for the delay in Minah's return? The authorities would see these omissions as a gross dereliction of his duties towards both his religion and his village, and they could have the most serious consequences for him. Suddenly finding his voice, he began to call upon Allah to be merciful.

'I have come to Batu Lima as I wish to be Osman's wife,' said Valerie firmly without taking her eyes from Osman's face. Her heart went out to him. He was so clearly wretched and she was acutely aware of her own responsibility for his plight. For the first time she allowed the word 'seduction' to enter her thoughts. She knew this would be how every white woman in the Malayan peninsula would regard her behaviour, and even she was not particularly proud of how she had lured Osman into the back seat of the car on that fateful afternoon amongst the rubber trees. But could an irresistible effusion of love ever be seduction?

The Secretary smiled. 'And you are both in a position to marry?' he asked. 'Surely you are still married to Mr Mitchell. Osman is married and has two children. He does not have permission from the *kadi* to take a second wife.' The *kadi* was a judge who was responsible for the administration of Muslim law in the state and a figure of importance and influence.

Valerie was determined not to capitulate. 'I thought Muslim men could have more than one wife.'

The Secretary smiled again. He clearly thought he was dealing with someone quite ignorant of the ways of his country and who needed to be instructed like a child.

'Mrs Mitchell,' he said, and his precise manner seemed to accentuate his condescension. 'You are a Christian. Under our law a Muslim is not allowed to marry a Christian.'

'But I am a Muslim, I have given up my religion, I consider myself to be one of you.'

The Secretary raised his eyebrows. He turned to Osman. 'Is this so? Has the *kadi* accepted Mrs Mitchell into the Faith?'

Osman shook his head miserably.

'Mrs Mitchell. I do not wish to prolong this discussion longer than is necessary. The British authorities are angry at what you have done. They believe you have acted shamefully. You have disgraced your husband and brought dishonour to your people. They are taking immediate steps to return you to Britain. The Sultan also is very displeased. He wishes you to end your association with his Muslim subject and leave Batu Lima at once.'

Valerie listened to this speech in mounting horror. All she had hoped and worked for was breaking up around her with quite bewildering speed. Perhaps she had been naïve, but she was surprised to be receiving this treatment from the Malay authorities. She had thought they would have been pleased at the prospect of gaining a convert to their religion, particularly a Christian convert, and far from adopting this attitude, she had hoped they might have given her some support against what she had expected would be the arbitrary treatment of the colonial administration. Now it looked as though she was without a supporter in the world. She felt her resolve begin to crumble. But, just as she was about to admit defeat, she remembered her condition. What was to become of her child?

'But I'm having Osman's baby. What am I to do? The baby is the reason I am here.' Her simple words were said with such feeling that they almost sounded like a cry of distress.

If she had said she was the daughter of the Caliph of Baghdad her statement could not have had a greater impact or a more dramatic effect. The Secretary's face registered first surprise and then concern and his confident manner vanished completely. For several moments he was at a complete loss. If Valerie had not been so upset she would have been able to take pleasure at what had clearly been a deadly thrust.

It did not seem to occur to him to seek confirmation of Valerie's statement, to doubt her word or even to question the paternity of her baby, he just stood transfixed by the dilemma into which he had been suddenly plunged. What had been, a moment before, a comparatively simple problem with an obvious and straightforward solution, had now become an issue of considerable complexity. No longer were they just ridding themselves of a troublesome British woman, they were abandoning a baby, a Malay baby, a Muslim, to an alien faith. The whole thing was far beyond a mere secretary's competence to deal with. It was a matter for a much higher authority. He turned to Osman.

'You said nothing of this,' he said sharply and, then, to the *penghulu*, he released a stream of Malay, which made its recipient assume a look of abject misery. Within a minute he was back in his car and waving away what was obviously a desperate plea from the headman as to what he should do. If the dust from the wheels of his departing vehicle had been a genie's smoke, he could hardly have disappeared more rapidly.

* * *

The days that followed the visit of the Sultan's secretary were heartbreaking for Valerie. Puan Zainal did not speak to her at all, in fact, hardly looked at her, and when she did she could see the hurt in her eyes. What she and Osman had to put up with in the *kampung* became clear the next time she took the family's washing down to the river. The wives used an area of rock a few hundred yards downstream of the toilets. It was not very hygienic to Valerie's mind but the rocks were as indispensable to the Malay way of washing clothes as a washing board and a mangle were in the Western world. Their method was not very subtle. After soaking and lathering the clothes with a piece of soap, it was battered against the rocks, rinsed, wrung out and thrown back in the basket or, if the weather was fine, laid out on the rocks to dry. Valerie had done the family washing quite a few times before and the women, while not actually talking to her which was difficult as none of them spoke any English, usually smiled or made as if they expected her to join them. Until then, she had been content to be on the fringe of the group.

This day, however, there was no smiled greeting. They did not even turn their heads in her direction. What spare room there was, was quickly taken by them shifting their baskets sideways. Valerie sat on the bank and waited. Eventually a couple left, still not glancing in her direction. Valerie took their place and began washing. The other women were silent, a marked difference to the chatter of other days. For some reason, the daily washing was always a happy occasion when the women laughed and joked with one another. In fact, the beating of the rocks with the wet clothes seemed to trigger amusement amounting almost to mirth. Now, not a word was exchanged and Valerie began to find the silence intimidating.

She became uneasy, then flustered and a *baju* she was beating flew out of her hands and landed on another woman's washing. Without a moment's hesitation, or comment, the woman flicked it into the river where it began floating away. Valerie leaped up, a remonstrance on her lips, but she bit it back. She ran round the rocks to retrieve the garment, which was already beginning to drift downstream. Maddeningly, it kept its distance from the bank and Valerie was forced to follow it down as it was deflected from one obstruction to another.

It was not expensive but she had no intention of going back to the house without it. It must have been ten minutes before she was able to get a stick and draw it to the bank and, by then, she was out of sight of the rocks. When she returned the women had gone but she found her washing had been strewn over the bank and deliberately trampled into the mud. It must have taken some time and trouble to do. Her basket too, was full of dirt. Angry and hurt she looked around for those responsible but the riverbank was deserted. There was not a villager to be seen, not even a child. It was surprising how deserted the village could look when it wanted to be.

She made no mention of it when at last she returned to the house with the washing as clean as she could make it. She felt as tired and dispirited as never before. Clearly the villagers had made up their mind about her and, in all fairness, she could not blame them. In their eyes she must have been an affront to their decency. She had used her privileged position to tempt Osman and then compounded her sin by coming to live amongst them. This had implicated them all in her brazen behaviour, and by so doing, dishonoured their village. Now, not even the children would come to talk to her in the evenings.

*　*　*

She tackled Osman about it one day when he returned from his morning work in the taxi. His eyes, once always alive with merriment, were now dull and listless and it was obvious he was suffering as only a good Muslim is bound to do when Allah shows his displeasure in such an obvious way. There was still no sign of

Minah and it was clear it was more than just resentment that was keeping her away. Osman may have gained one wife but he had also lost another and, with her, his two children. It had not only been a disproportionate exchange but one that had brought him much unhappiness and anxiety.

Common sense told Valerie how much he must be regretting the events at Bukit Bintang leading to her decision to come and live with him. She could see now how very selfish it had been of her. She had automatically assumed that because she had wanted to be with him, he must feel the same way about her and therefore the best thing for them both was to be together. That may have been in the best romantic traditions of Western society but it was certainly not in accordance with convention here. In fact it had been the very worst solution for Osman and she had not had the sensitivity or imagination to see it. She had not just been lacking in perception, but in her understanding of Malay culture. In any other Muslim country less gentle and courteous than Malaya, she would not have been allowed to impose her problem and her solution to it upon them.

It was this innate courtesy which had been partly responsible, at least, for Osman meekly accepting her decision to come to the village. He must have considered refusing her or to at least done his best to make her reconsider her decision when the consequences of her coming became painfully obvious, but this apparent incivility would have been alien to his natural good manners and had clearly weighed more heavily with him than the dread of what he knew would happen.

Nevertheless, it would be very ungracious of her to apportion any of the blame to him or to the Malay villagers generally. His misgivings at her original suggestion should have been obvious to her – particularly his evasiveness and lack of positive responses to her questions. She remembered the two occasions when he had deferred their elopement, but only now did she realise what he was trying to tell her. At the time she had been too full of her own problems on Bukit Bintang to realise she was about to create even more intractable ones in Batu Lima. But this was hindsight, it was easy to forget how confident she had been that she could overcome all the difficulties and, also, what the alternatives had been. Perhaps, in the end, it was a case of East and West failing to understand the nature of their differences. Kipling was right, there was little common ground between them.

Her regrets did not end there, however. It was becoming increasingly evident that, even if they had been able to marry, their life together would never have been as she had visualised it in the first heady days of their affair at Bukit Bintang. The gap in their attitudes towards love and marriage was far larger than she had anticipated. Western women had been conditioned to thinking love could conquer all, they failed to realise the different role romantic love played in the lives of other races. Malay men were not solely conditioned to feeling affection of that sort for their wives. They also married to raise a family and to fulfil their filial duty to their parents. They had frequently never seen, let alone spoken to, the girl they were expected to marry until the actual wedding day. That they came to love them later was often true, but it was the love which came from sharing a life together and raising children, from enjoying a myriad of shared experiences and coming to appreciate each other's qualities, it had little to do with the romantic notions so popular in the West.

It had also been an unpleasant surprise to Valerie to discover that second marriages among ordinary people were almost unknown. No other man in the village, not even the *penghulu*, had a second wife, and for a man in Osman's circumstances to even contemplate such a step had obviously been regarded as presumptuous on his part and so resented by the villagers.

Reluctantly, Valerie came to the conclusion there was really only one thing she could do and that was to leave. Seizing a moment when Puan Zainal had gone into the kitchen she suggested to Osman that she should do so.

He did not say anything, he did not have to, his answer was in every line of his face. His life had been in turmoil for months, his mind beset day after day with problems to which he could find no solution. He had never seriously considered refusing his mem's suggestion that she come to his home. From the moment when Valerie had tempted him into the back of her car and then again later when she had come down to his room day after day offering her blandishments, he felt he had neither the right, and certainly not the will, to resist her in any way. It was as if his failure to overcome his weakness for her had taken away his ability to stand up to her, or think for himself.

For the same reason, he had never seriously considered asking her to leave the *kampung* although he knew there was no other realistic way out of their difficulties. Even to express an opinion on the subject would have been, in his eyes, a liberty and a grave breach of manners, and even now, when she had suggested she should go, he could still not say anything, as his agreement might imply she had been wrong in the first place. Nevertheless, although he could control his tongue, he had no power over his eyes and they answered Valerie's question unequivocally.

Valerie was hurt but not surprised, and she was practical enough to see that if she had to leave, it was relatively immaterial what his feelings were for her as it was the end of her dream anyway. But how about their baby? If it had not been for the baby she would have already been on a boat headed for Britain, the Sultan's secretary and the British authorities between them, would have seen to that, but then, if she had not been pregnant, she would not have been in Batu Lima in the first place. The baby had not only been the cause of their predicament, it was now the obstacle to its solution. What was to become of the child they had created and which she had once hoped was going to be the symbol of the union of their two races and cultures?

Would Osman reject their child also? It had been her experience that babies, even their own, touched nothing elemental in many

British men, in fact, in some cases, it was quite the reverse, a child conceived in an extramarital affair often aroused resentment, occasionally something even worse. Osman, on the other hand, was not a man from the West, he was a member of a race who regarded children as a blessing, a gift from God, a justification of their place on earth.

What was more, Malay men were not socially conditioned to distance themselves from their children in the same way as were men in the West. On the contrary, it was not unusual for them to be as tender with them as their womenfolk. They could often be seen dandling them in all-male groups by the side of the road in the cool of the evening. Consorting in public with their wives in a similar manner, on the other hand, was a different matter entirely. It was not only considered socially unacceptable but beneath their male dignity, almost indecent in fact. A sexual kiss, for example was a private affair, the sight of which was not to be imposed on the public as it often was in the West. Children on the other hand were exhibited with affection and pride. Valerie had often imagined Osman sitting with theirs in a similar way. She could remember how he had been with the European children at the Club. Surely he would not turn his back on his own now?

She looked longingly at him as he sat on the mat opposite her, his head bowed by the burden of all their problems, a veritable picture of dejection. How she yearned to touch him, put her arms around him, bridge the gulf that had grown up between them, perhaps also, to feel once again the physical charge that had thrilled her so often in the weeks before they had left the estate. But had she tried she knew she would have been rebuffed, and though such a rebuff might only have been for convention's sake, it would have been even harder to bear than the gulf that now separated them.

'Osman, what shall we do about our baby?'

Again, Osman had no reply. How could he? To him it was not his baby and he had never thought of it as such. Malay children were born in Malay villages, to brown-skinned women, not to white women even in the brown man's world. Try as he might, every time Mem had referred to 'our baby' he had to make an effort to stop himself from saying 'your baby' or even 'Tuan's baby'. He had no proprietary feelings about the swelling under Valerie's *baju*. In his mind, the baby was simply the cause of all his problems, the reason his world had been turned upside down, whereas she seemed to think it was something special, a consummation of their love. He had never been brought up to regard babies in that way.

Children were the result of a pleasurable gratification in marriage and were a natural bounty, proof of God's blessing, like the harvest. You acquired a wife, and not unlike a piece of land, you tilled it conscientiously as any good farmer should, then, in God's good time, the babies came forth, just like the padi, to enrich the family and provide for one's old age. Babies had nothing to do with a sentimental longing for a woman or an indulgence in romantic love. And when a baby came as the result of a profane act of lust with another man's wife on the back seat of a car, it was a judgement. He was dreading what her confinement might bring forth, what further retribution Allah might yet have in store for him.

Yet Malay men loved their children dearly so he had tried to imagine how he would feel when he held the baby in his arms for the first time. Unfortunately, try as he might, it did nothing to arouse his paternal feelings, for although he knew he was the father, he saw it with Valerie's blue eyes and white skin, not his dark eyes and brown skin, and he knew he would never be able to regard a white-skinned child as his. It would always be a stranger, someone from a far-off land, nothing to do with him. Putting all that into words was beyond him, however, even in his own tongue, let alone hers. So how could he answer her? Perversely, all he could think of was 'Keep the baby as a memento of your Malayan affair, my compliments.' But that sort of reply, from someone who, contrary to what many of other faiths believed, had been nurtured by a religion which had an innate respect for women, if not their political and social rights, was unacceptably ill-mannered, and so he maintained his silence – the meaning of which was all too clear to Valerie.

It was a bitter moment that she had not expected. In fact, it was so unexpected she could barely believe it. Perhaps he would feel differently when the child was born? It was difficult, after all, to have an emotional response to a bulge under a floppy garment. The father had no means of feeling a baby grow and kick, twist and turn, its lifeblood in his veins. It could have no identity for him at the present moment. It would be different when he saw it, held it in his arms for the first time. But where would she be when the baby was born? She might be oceans away, far beyond the reach of a late blossoming of fatherly feeling on his part.

All at once, she felt a flash of irritation at Osman's failure to respond to her questions, to understand and discuss the problem, his inability or unwillingness to reassure her. It was the first time she could remember feeling angry with him.

'Osman, what am I to do? You must have some idea,' she demanded impatiently.

He was puzzled how she could be in such doubt. There was only one realistic course of action for Mem to take and that was for her to return to Britain to be amongst her own people. That was assuming, of course, that the British Government were prepared to pay the cost of her sea passage, as he would certainly not be able to afford it, not on his meagre earnings from the taxi. The only sea passage he could ever hope to aspire to was the Haj, the pilgrimage to Mecca in his old age, and now he had lost his job as a *syce*, even that might prove to be beyond his means. Perhaps that was to be his punishment – Allah deciding he was unfit to take part in the crowning experience of a Muslim's life.

Not for the first time he felt a wave of bitterness at what had happened to him on Bukit Bintang. Normally, he accepted misfortune as the will of Allah, and he was also well aware of his own part in his downfall. He knew he had been given many opportunities to avoid his fate in his last few weeks on the estate and he had spurned them all. Each time he had heard Valerie's footsteps on the bathroom stair he could, and should, have summoned his resolve and brought their affair to an end, but he had weakened every time. But what chance had he? Few Muslim men can have had their will so severely and regularly tested by such temptation as he had to face day after day, and he could not but help feeling some resentment towards the woman who had been responsible for it.

He knew self-righteousness was a sin but was he not right to blame her? Was the baby not her fault? Islam was quite clear on the matter – the sexuality of a woman, that is her ability to provoke desire in men and so help to perpetuate the human race, had its purpose in life – but it had to be exercised within marriage and marriage only, and any indulgence of it outside that God-given institution must therefore be a sin. This was why a woman's body, once she had ceased to be a child, even if necessary her face, had to be properly covered at all times, and seen by no other man than her husband. It was also why the many and varied ways in which women were exploited in the Western world, and the equal number of ways in which they, themselves, allowed themselves to be exploited – even connived in their involvement – were profanities in the eyes of his religion.

And there could be no better example of such a profanity than how Valerie had used her body to ensnare him on the estate. The way she had behaved had been more brazen than anything he had seen in the picture-houses in Kota Bharu, or in dances at the Kuala Lebir Club, or even in the magazines, filched from the drawers of their masters, which some of the other *syces* had furtively passed from hand to hand as they waited outside the Club for those dances to end. Few pictures in those magazines were more shameful than the images he had seen time and time again in his little room in the servants' quarters of the estate bungalow.

He remembered also, with guilt and shame, the particular occasion when Valerie had flaunted her body, completely unclothed, in *Tuan's* bathroom. There could be no other explanation for her behaviour than that she was, as the *imam* would have been quick to point out had he known, the devil in human shape, sent to lure him from the path of virtue. But, he had to admit, she was also quite the most beautiful, the most beguiling, the most exciting devil that it had ever been a Muslim man's misfortune to meet, or was ever likely to meet. She had been temptation and guilt, pleasure and despair, heaven and hell, in one totally irresistible combination.

But wickedness, in whatever its forms, had to be punished and perhaps Valerie's punishment was at hand. Once back in Britain, Mem would have to bear the stigma of the baby's colour whatever it turned out to be, just as he had had to accept what had happened to him during the last few months and what the Muslim authorities might even be preparing for him at that moment.

But why trouble oneself with such things when their futures, his, Valerie's and the baby's, had already been settled. *All* their destinies were set in stone from which there could be no escape. Their lives were running as if on the railway tracks the British had taken so much time and money to lay down in his country.

'Mem, I don't know. It is in Allah's hands. Allah will decide.'

* * *

Valerie got nothing more from him and so she made up her mind, or perhaps Allah had already made it up for her, that she would leave the village and return to Britain as soon as the Administration could make the necessary arrangements, a decision which Osman, in his usual way, accepted without comment, but with profound relief.

It was the same stoicism that also enabled him to accept, with equal equanimity, the consequences of another visit, this time unannounced, by the Sultan's secretary on the morning after Valerie had made her decision. Once again, Osman and Valerie were summoned to the *penghulu's* house a short time after they had seen the familiar car bump its way through the *kampung*. The Secretary, trim, spotless and girlish as before, assumed he was bringing glad tidings and smiled accordingly. He came straight to the purpose of his visit.

'The Sultan wishes that Osman bin Zainal marries Mrs Mitchell immediately. He considers the present domestic situation in which Mrs Mitchell is residing under the same roof as one of his subjects as highly undesirable. In view of the unusual circumstances surrounding this case, the normal ceremonies will not be followed. The *kadi* will ensure that the marriage is properly conducted at his office in Karang on Friday.'

Valerie was the first to recover from her surprise. 'But what about the fact that I am a Christian and married already?'

The Secretary seemed surprised at the question and treated it with his usual air of condescension. 'Your statement when we last met that you were already a Muslim is regarded as sufficient evidence that you are willing to convert to Islam. The *kadi* will satisfy himself before the ceremony on Friday that you are a practising Muslim and are familiar with the rudiments of the Koran. As for the fact that you are already married, on your marriage to a Malay you will automatically become a citizen of this country and, therefore, no longer subject to British law and, as a Muslim, no longer a member of the Church of England. Your marriage in Britain will simply not exist any more. I believe you have a word for it in English – the marriage will have been annulled.'

The Secretary took his departure in a much more dignified manner than before and a bewildered Osman and a delighted Valerie were left standing on the *penghulu's* verandah, the owner giving fervent thanks to Allah for having bestowed his mercy on his humble servant by heeding his prayers and so, apparently, absolving him from blame. Valerie was beside herself. It was as if her former reservations had never existed – she was to be married to Osman. Who could doubt she would make him happy? It seemed, after all, she had been right to come to Batu Lima. In accordance with all the very best traditions of Western romance, she had demonstrated that love had the power to conquer the world. Indeed, she had shown it could do more than that – it could even solve the problems created by interracial marriages and, by its sheer emotional force, defeat the subtleties of Islam. There was nothing it could not do.

Puan Zainal looked pleased when they told her although she was not at all sure why. In her view it seemed as though one problem had simply been exchanged for several others, and the first one came when Osman received a message that Minah and the children would be returning to the house as soon as the marriage had taken place. It had been the Sultan's express wish, equal to a command, that they did so. Valerie offered prayers to Allah for the first time that evening at sundown in the sole company of Puan Zainal, it not being considered proper that she and Osman pray together before the marriage ceremony, even in the privacy of their own home.

Valerie now immersed herself in a study of the main beliefs and practices of the Mohammedan religion and never was there a more dutiful student. Hers was not just the zeal of the proselyte, but of one who was pursuing her dearest wish and ambition, albeit for altogether ulterior reasons. For each of the remaining days of the week an *imam*, specially sent by the *kadi*, gave her instruction in the Koran. Her enthusiasm was somewhat dampened, however, by the fact that the instruction seemed to consist almost entirely of repeating, after him, lengthy passages from its scriptures. Islamic teaching seemed to be based on rote learning and little else. There were no interpretative discourses and her questions about doctrine were met, first, by blank stares and then, by looks of disapproval from the *imam*. No one questioned the sacred text, least of all a woman. It was the Word of God as handed down to the Prophet and was therefore the perfect revelation. Obedience and submission were the watchwords, not debate and the resolution of doubts.

To her regret, Valerie was unable to read the Holy Book for herself as she found it was in Jawi, the Arabic form of Malay, her only experience of the written word being in the Romanised form of the language. Despite that, she was able to acquire a good working knowledge of the rites and duties of her new religion although she was already well acquainted with its five obligations – the Pillars of the Faith. But privately – and she had the sense to keep the thought to herself – she was left with the distinct impression that the religious education of a Muslim woman was not regarded as being anything like as important as that of a man. Now she came to think of it – she had only ever seen little boys coming out of the religious schools, never little girls.

*   *   *

After Osman returned from the mosque on Friday, they set out for Karang in the taxi, accompanied by a very apprehensive *penghulu*. He had spent an uncomfortable fortnight in between the two visits by the Sultan's secretary, although the satisfactory outcome of the second had encouraged him to hope that the religious authorities had overlooked his administrative failings. However, a last-minute instruction from the *kadi* that he attend the marriage ceremony had renewed his fears, and he was in an acute state of agitation wondering if he would still be holding the honoured position of headman of Batu Lima on his return.

Meanwhile, he had decided to have as little to do with Valerie as possible. The rapid changes in her person coming so rapidly one after the other, the first from honoured guest to scarlet woman and then to prospective Muslim matron, had convinced him that she represented a substantial threat, not only to his position as *penghulu*, but to the very safety of his person. It was a firm belief among his people that when the moon was full, certain of his countrymen could undergo a remarkable transformation – they could assume the form and features of a tiger, an animal of more than usual ferocity and with a reputation for levelling scores with those for whom it bore a grudge.

The existence of were-tigers was a long-held superstition in Malaya, but for him it was more than just a superstition – he personally knew it to be true. As a boy, he remembered a story his father had told him of a certain Mat Salleh, a man living in a neighbouring village about whom there had long been concerns as he hailed from Korinchi in Sumatra, a district of the East Indies well known for its were-tigers.

One night his father had been roused from his sleeping mat by the terrified bellows of his buffalo. The animal was being attacked by a tiger but, with the assistance of the villagers, he had managed to drive it off, one of the men even managing to spear the snarling animal in a hind leg. It had fled, but the villagers dared not pursue it in the dark. The next morning, however, they were able to follow the trail of blood and it was leading them very clearly in the direction of Mat Salleh's village before it started to rain and the bloodstains were washed away. When they reached the village to warn the inhabitants of the presence of a wounded tiger in their locality they found Mat Salleh was confined to his house. His wife had come to the door and said her husband could not walk as a recent wound in his thigh was too painful. No one believed her story that he had burnt it on his kitchen stove two days before.

Was that not proof enough of the existence of were-tigers? In his official capacity as *penghulu*, he was required to pour cold water on all such stories, but he knew better. As a result, ever since the second visit of the Sultan's secretary when his village had been told to welcome her into their fold he had been harbouring doubts about Valerie – this extraordinary white woman who not only possessed an impressive ability to change her character but also a suspicious determination to marry one of his flock. He therefore had no desire to place himself anywhere within her vicinity, either now or at any time in the future, in case she decided to transform herself yet again – this time from Muslim matron to striped feline of the female gender, and as far as he knew, a tigress was no less dangerous an animal than the male of the species. The anxious headman recalled yet again how he had treated Valerie after the first visit of the Sultan's secretary – he had rather conspicuously ignored her – and he was fearful she might remember his neglect. Were-tigers were known for their long memories.

Puan Zainal did not accompany them, nor anyone else from the village. The *penghulu* was as uncertain of the form and content of the ceremony as was Osman. Neither had ever heard of a marriage by the *kadi*, who was a most senior and respected, even slightly intimidating figure, in the Muslim hierarchy. Village marriages were usually conducted before an *imam* and were complicated, protracted affairs with the bride's family playing a large part but, as Valerie did not have a family, such a ceremony was out of the question. Normally, also, large numbers of villagers attended local weddings as both witnesses and celebrants, but this function was going to be discharged by the *penghulu* alone as representative of the villagers, together with the Sultan's secretary.

The proceedings were a distinct disappointment to Valerie. They were conducted by the *kadi* who sat in a leather chair in his office throughout and questioned her on her knowledge of the Koran, questions which were distinctly unchallenging and to which Valerie was able to give entirely satisfactory answers. Both the *kadi* and the Secretary were in traditional Malay dress making the latter look altogether more distinguished than on his visits to the *kampung*. In fact, Valerie thought him quite handsome, though perhaps her revised opinion of his looks may have had more to do with her new-found regard for Malay authority than for his new, more traditional appearance.

Most of what was said was in Malay, but the Secretary expertly translated the proceedings into English, on some occasions quite needlessly as Valerie's Malay had improved considerably in the last few months. She was waiting for a declaration of marriage at some stage during the questioning but it did not come and when the ceremony was over and it was obvious they were about to leave, she enquired as to when the marriage was due to be declared, only to be assured that it had taken place and that she was, indeed, now married to Osman and that her title henceforward would be Che

Osman bin Zainal.

The wedding group emerged onto the five-foot way in the glare of the midday sun. The Secretary departed after speaking briefly to Osman. Valerie would have liked to know what he had said but knew that to ask him was more than she dared do in public. As they returned to the taxi she remembered to fall into step several paces behind her husband. This would be her place whenever they appeared in public in the future, no strolling arm in arm as in the West. Despite an almost complete lack of form and atmosphere in the ceremony, Valerie felt content. She had got what she wanted, she was married to Osman, and she chose to dismiss from her mind the one-sided conversation she had had with him on the day before the Secretary's second visit. She had seen the look in his eyes when she had suggested she leave and she did not wish to recall or to dwell on it.

She had persuaded herself things would be different now. Like many of her sex, she was capable of a considerable degree of wishful thinking in such matters, and she had managed to convince herself that his apparent wish that she should leave the village had been the result of the pressure they were both under, and not due to any lack of feeling on his part. Neither of them referred to the conversation subsequently, Valerie because she did not wish to broach a subject which brought her such unhappiness, Osman because it was in his upbringing and culture to accept whatever life sent him, and at this moment it was sending him a beautiful white woman as a second wife, an arrangement which had been the direct wish of the Sultan. Like most Malays, Osman was nothing if not deferential to his superiors, and therefore respectful of their decisions, however difficult they might be to carry out or what personal burden they might involve. How all the problems created by his second marriage were going to be resolved, he had no idea but, then, it was not his concern any more. The decision he should marry Valerie had been taken by the Sultan so it was Allah's will, in which case Allah would have to decide.

It was customary for Malay weddings to be accompanied by music followed by feasting and the playing of various sports by the young male guests, their female counterparts having already been set apart behind curtains elsewhere in the building, but there were no such celebrations in Batu Lima when the newlyweds returned. Osman's brother, who lived in a neighbouring *kampung*, called with token gifts of food but no one else. Although there had been no overt hostility from the villagers since the Secretary's second visit, it was still too early for their easy association with this most recent and unlikely addition to their village's population. Osman spent the rest of the day building a sleeping cubicle for Valerie as Musa would be reclaiming his when Minah returned with her family. Any hopes that Valerie had of sharing her wedding night with her new husband were dashed by Puan Zainal who, in the most roundabout way possible, gave her to understand that Malay husbands did not share their wives' company during their pregnancies. Valerie never ceased to wonder at Malay conservatism regarding sexual matters.

*   *   *

The following day Osman went to collect Minah and the children in his taxi and Valerie waited for their return with some trepidation. The last time she had seen them was when they had come to Bukit Bintang to visit Osman almost a year before. Minah was a shy girl but she and Valerie had got on well, while the children had been an absolute delight, exhibiting the impeccable manners of their race and an innate respect for their betters – or whomever they perceived as their betters. Since then, however, Valerie had stolen Minah's husband, the father of her children, and had taken her place, if only temporarily, in the matrimonial home, as well as bringing notoriety to them all. Now, she and they were going to have to share both husband and home in a relationship that was going to be markedly different to the one that had existed the last time they had met. In fact, they might almost be strangers meeting for the first time.

Although polygamy amongst the ordinary people, the *ra'ayat*, was now fairly rare, when it did occur the first wife had the option of declaring *talak*, divorce, for herself and also to be given some share of the family property, although Minah's return suggested this was not a course of action she was considering. Despite what Valerie had heard, the precise reasons for her return were not clear. Whether Minah had always wished to come back but had been prevented by convention, or was doing so now only as the result of official pressure, and whether this was with or without the approval of either one or both families, were only a few of a number of possibilities in Valerie's mind. Osman, if he knew, showed no willingness to share the information.

The meeting between the wives, when it came, was formal but polite and Valerie could hope for nothing more. She felt strangely free of any emotion, only a strong desire to make the arrangement work, while Minah's face and manner showed neither her thoughts nor her feelings. There was certainly no sign of the resentment Valerie thought she herself might have been feeling if she had been in her position. If the two were to live amicably side-by-side in one room, the start was as good as could be expected.

If Minah and Osman recommenced their old intimacy they took pains to conceal it from her. In any case Valerie made it her business not to notice any sign, and certainly no sound, of it. In small ways, however, Minah was seen to take preference over Valerie in their domestic roles. Valerie was expected to do the more menial tasks about the house, Minah took precedence at mealtimes and she sat next to Puan Zainal. When there was something to buy in Karang it was always Minah who went with Osman in the taxi. Osman had explained that her status as the mother of his children entitled her to these privileges and Valerie was happy enough to accept them.

She was puzzled why she did not feel any jealousy. Perhaps it was because she had come very close to losing Osman completely that she was now content to share him. Whether she would feel the same after the birth of her baby when, hopefully, their relationship would become more intimate again, remained to be seen, but there was no point dwelling on it. As Malay philosophy would have it, 'What was to be, will be.' The children were a pleasure to Valerie and treated her as they had done on their visit to Bukit Bintang. The other children of the village became frequent visitors again and re-assumed their old friendly interest in her, although their mothers still kept their distance. The incident of the *baju* in the river was still too fresh in everyone's minds.

* * *

A few days later the family shared in a village festivity. A *wayang kulit* was being staged as part of the celebrations to mark the wedding of one of the sons of a village elder in a distant part of Kelantan. A *wayang kulit* was a shadow play performed by a professional puppeteer known as a *dalang*. The shadows of the leather puppets were projected onto a screen, in this case a large white sheet, by means of a strong lamp. The stories they depicted were from Malay legends and were accompanied by dialogue, which was also supplied by the *dalang*. Most of the stories were well known to the audience who joined in enthusiastically.

The whole performance reminded Valerie of a combination of a Punch and Judy show and the finger shadows they used to amuse themselves with as children at Christmas. A small generator produced the power for the lamp and the coloured lights erected for the occasion created a festive atmosphere made even more enjoyable by a musical accompaniment provided by a visiting group of Malay instrumentalists.

Valerie's grasp of Malay was now sufficient for her to pick up the sense of the stories without difficulty and she found herself joining in with the merriment of the women and children around her. She gazed round at the excited faces lit up from the stage, and then at the tops of the palm trees outlined against the starlit sky and the swarms of enormous atlas moths larger than soup plates, fluttering vainly against the lamps, and was content. At last she felt as though she was achieving what she had set out to do – make the giant step from a Western culture to an Eastern one. It needed only one final act of integration – the birth of her child.

Birth in a Malay *kampung*, a rural community, at this time was hardly different from what it had always been. Modern medical science had hardly filtered into the towns despite the coming of the British, which on the west coast had been barely sixty years before, on the east coast less than half of that. In rural communities, things had changed but little, childbirth being an everyday event which the women were expected to undergo without fuss or ceremony, using whatever knowledge and expertise had been accumulated in the community over the centuries. No male was ever permitted to attend the confinement, certainly not the husband and there were no doctors of any sort available, qualified or unqualified.

The one with the highest expertise was the *bomoh*, the medicine-man, who remained in the background performing his ancient rites and rituals to ensure the house remained free of evil spirits. The only skills and experience at Valerie's disposal were supplied by the older matrons of the village. If anything went wrong and the mother or the baby died it was considered to be Allah's will, and if the services of the local hospital had to be called upon and the patient survived, then that was Allah's will also. Valerie surveyed the lack of sterilised facilities with some misgivings but knew she had to take her chances with what the village could provide, the slightest hint of reluctance would destroy the image she had been at such pains to create.

She felt the first contractions at midday and they developed with alacrity making it appear likely that the birth would take place during the ensuing night. This was not considered auspicious as, to the Malays, a child delivered during the hours of darkness was much more susceptible to the baleful influence of the spirits. Indeed, it seemed to Valerie that there was more energy expended in protecting her from demons than from infection. Food was placed by the doorway to divert those spirits who might try to make a conventional entry into her cubicle, and there was a deafening banging of kitchen utensils at intervals during the night to frighten away those who had either secreted themselves underneath the house or were attempting to gain access to it from the roof. Finally, a precious tiger's claw was pressed into her palm for her to hold for the duration of the delivery.

At four in the morning Valerie finally gave birth to a baby boy and he was placed in her arms. By the light of the smoky oil lamps, which lit the cubicle, she gazed at last upon the face of her long-awaited child. But instead of the hoped-for dark skin of Osman, she saw the fair skin of her own people. Instead of the round head of a typical Malay, there were the unmistakably long features of a European. What little could be seen of the hair in the half-light, had a distinctly reddish hue rather than black. Without a shadow of a doubt, this was not the progeny of a mixed marriage, a child destined to unite their two races, British and Malay, and so bind her future with that of Osman's. To her horror and disbelief, Valerie saw that she had given birth, not to Osman's son, but to Stuart's.

PART FOUR

THE OUTCAST

The events of the next few days, as far as Valerie could later remember them, were the worst experiences of her life. She refused to have anything to do with the baby and, in her waking moments, was distraught, partly in grief at her savage disappointment but also in distress as a postnatal infection took hold. As she had feared, she lacked the villagers' natural immunity to the routine bacteria of the riverine settlement and, within hours, her life was in serious danger. What was originally thought to be simply an invasion of evil spirits turned to alarm as Valerie's temperature soared and she became delirious. Osman rushed her to the local hospital in Karang and for several days there was concern for her safety.

On the fourth day the fever passed and Valerie awoke to find Minah at her bedside. As Valerie remembered from her previous stay in hospital, relatives were an indispensable part of the nursing in a common ward, and it seemed Minah had accepted these duties without demur. She found the role of auxiliary nurse easier than that of senior wife, a position she had not sought and which had always made her feel uncomfortable. What she was doing now was more in accordance with the natural order of things.

That evening, after the reality of her position had filtered into Valerie's consciousness, she placed her hand on Minah's arm.

'I cannot tell you how I feel, how desperately sorry I am for what has happened. What has become of the baby?'

Minah's reply was almost inaudible. 'It is in Batu Lima. Puan Zainal is looking after it.' Valerie paused before she forced herself to ask what was uppermost in her mind. 'What of Osman? What must he be thinking of me?'

But it was not a question Minah felt herself capable of answering and she was silent.

'I know I have wronged both you and Osman and I bitterly regret it, but I loved him, Minah, I really loved him, and I was certain the baby was his.' She was dismayed as she realised she had used the past tense but, in her heart, she knew that Osman was likely to have been lost to her forever, and her next words demonstrated the fact. 'As soon as I am well enough I will go. I promise you that.'

Once again the other woman made no reply. Like all Malay women, Minah had been schooled to keep her feelings in check and her opinions to herself, but she could not prevent the relief she felt showing on her face. She had no idea what had possessed this mem to think that she could come and live in a Malay village. And for what reason? A totally inexplicable obsession with her husband. Minah loved Osman dearly, but it was the love of custom and familiarity, she had never felt any overwhelming passion for him. He was, in many ways, a very ordinary man, hardly worth giving up a world of luxury and privilege for, and certainly not one to make a beautiful woman lose her head.

She had lost her head once as a girl, not over Osman, but for Kumar, the heart-throb in an Indian film. She had pretended to swoon in her cinema seat and her teenage friends had half carried her out, laughing and giggling, and she had revelled in being teased about him for months. She had even had the courage to put a picture of him, cut from a newspaper, on her bedroom wall until her father had seen it and made her take it down. But Osman as a heart-throb? She thought he had been jesting when he told her of what had been going on at Bukit Bintang, and when he had said that Mem was coming to live with them in the *kampung* she had been amazed, then frightened. She thought *Tuan* would come and take Mem back by force and she had feared for Osman's safety.

Her father had made her return to his house until the authorities had dealt with the problem which they said would take only take a week or two. But it had gone on for months and she had missed Osman, and so had the children. He was a good husband and an even better father, and they had all welcomed the Sultan's command they should return. As far as she was concerned, half a husband was better than none. Then had come the shock of the baby's birth, followed by a quite unprecedented anger throughout the village. Mem did not know it yet but she had no choice but to leave and to take the baby with her. What Puan Zainal was having to put up with looking after him was more than any woman could be expected to endure. Still she sat and said nothing, but the thoughts on her face had been read by Valerie.

'I know I should not have come to the village, but it is easy to be wise after the event. I really thought I could make it work, you know. It was the baby, if it had not been for the baby everything would have been all right, I know it would. What is to become of him? You know he isn't Osman's don't you?'

Minah nodded. How could she not know? The whole *kampung* was in ferment over the fact. But to her, the arrival of *Tuan's* baby was the one good thing that had happened, the first sign that Allah considered they had suffered enough, the one redeeming event in a sorry saga of human weakness and stupidity. Now she and Osman could be left in peace to put their lives together again. It was difficult to feel too much sympathy for this European woman. It was unfortunate her British husband had turned out so badly, but he had been her choice after all, and she could not help making a comparison with her own marriage. Osman had been chosen for her and she was content with him. Mem had been free to select her husband and he was a disappointment. As Malay girls were often told, freedom to choose meant freedom to make mistakes also. Perhaps her countrywomen were not as badly off as Europeans liked to claim, after all.

'What will you do, Mem?' she said at last. She had not used the title once in Batu Lima but now she said it deliberately. She could not have signified more plainly that, in her view, Valerie's venture into the Malay world was at an end.

'There is only one thing I can do, Minah, I suppose, and that is to go back to Britain. What will happen after that I cannot think. But I would like to see Osman one last time.'

Minah already knew Osman's thoughts on the likelihood of that happening but she kept them to herself. Her husband would have to deal with the problem of his second wife in his own way. She dutifully delivered Valerie's message, however, when Osman called to pick her up that evening although he declined to go into the hospital to see her, as she suspected he would. Nor did he do so early the next morning when he returned Minah with Valerie's meals for the day.

Minah continued to perform her nursing functions while Valerie regained her strength. The patient was determined to leave hospital just as soon as she was able, as a European in a Malayan ward was a distinct embarrassment to all concerned and Minah's duties on her behalf were only serving to magnify them. So, although feeling far from well, Valerie discharged herself and, in the absence of any clear idea of what she should do next, took a room in a cheap Chinese hotel nearby. It was her introduction to the real Malaya – the world as the majority of the locals knew and were obliged to live it – as it was becoming abundantly clear that from now on she was going to have to cope outside the economic and social cocoon that was her former home, the *kampung*. The few hundred dollars she had brought with her from Bukit Bintang, and which Osman had refused, were now her only protection against what the world might have in store for her, but at least they would give her a few days to come to terms with recent events and decide on her best course of action.

* * *

The hotel proprietor was a squat Chinese dressed in the usual white singlet and blue shorts, his wooden clogs clinging precariously to his feet by odd scraps of frayed rope tacked to the soles. To proclaim his race's abandonment of the servile pigtail, he had cropped his hair, which added a touch of truculence to his stocky figure. Blue veins bulged from his hairless calves and there was a large mole on his chin from which was growing a single, grotesquely long hair. It mesmerised Valerie and drew her gaze irresistibly.

He was doubtful about letting a room to an unaccompanied Malay woman. He knew from experience that such women were usually *joget* or taxi girls earning their living in a dance-hall or brothel and any hotel providing them accommodation quickly found itself under the scrutiny of the local mosque. He was about to turn her away when he noticed she was not Malay at all, but more likely Eurasian, at least as much as he could see of her face behind her *selendang*. Doubtless her profession was the same but she would be of no interest to the mosque, and so he turned to show her up to a room. As he climbed the stairs he gave his nasal passages a lengthy clearance, making it seem to Valerie like an expression of disapproval.

The room was not much larger than the bed, which was its only major item of furniture. Its slatted boards were covered by a thin canvas mattress and patched sheets, barely concealed by a thin red coverlet, which looked as if it had started life, many years before, on a table in a British roadside café. On a shelf in the bed-head was the only concession the room made to an ornament – a forlorn-looking palm tree made of Bakelite with a cluster of coconuts of pink stone, from one of which clung a monkey made of painted raffia. Apart from the bed, there was only a small table under a curtain-less window of louvred shutters.

The one bathroom in the hotel, on the ground floor, was of a type with which Valerie was by now familiar. It had blue mosaic-tiled walls and a cement floor, which sloped down to a drain in one corner. In the opposite corner was a half-filled quarter-round sink, also blue-tiled. It had obviously not been emptied or cleaned for months and so the sides were providing a colourful backdrop to a foot or so of greenish water which, she noticed, had become the home of a rich variety of aquatic life. A zinc hand basin, from which hung a broken wooden handle tied with string, had been provided for any guest willing to share the water with its inhabitants.

She lay on the red coverlet during the heat of the day, hoping in vain for the sound of Osman enquiring for her below, before, in the early evening, she found a Malay café similar to the one she remembered seeing from the lorry the day she was driven to Bukit Bintang for the first time. Even the white, stone-topped table from which she ate her fish curry appeared to be the same. Although it had been ten years before, the vivid novelty of that journey enabled her to recall almost every scene. To her they had seemed like the exotic pictures on the curtains of a pantomime stage, two-dimensional and unreal. Now, however, the curtains had been pulled back and this two-dimensional Malay world revealed for her in all its three-dimensional reality, in fact it was almost more real to her than the European one she had left.

She now felt she could walk and talk, think and behave, almost as well as if she had been born in the country, and few of its smells, tastes and sounds were unfamiliar to her. Gratifyingly, once she had got used to the Spartan conditions of the village, she found she had missed the comforts of her former existence far less than she had expected, its boredoms and frustrations less still. The simplicity of *kampung* life, isolated as it was from the petty vanities and animosities of the European world, had proved to be an unexpected bonus for her, while its timelessness and lack of materialism had given her a peace of mind she had not experienced before.

She ascribed this surprising outcome to her venture into the Malay world from being forced to live so close to nature, which she had found, to her surprise, to be most refreshing after the artificiality of her existence on the estate. The river, in particular, had made a deep impression upon her. Though home to dangerous creatures, it was the bountiful companion of the villagers throughout the year and served them in a variety of ways, although they feared its moods and never failed to give it their respect, particularly during the monsoon season.

She would never forget its sparkling reflections in the morning, its cooling influence during the heat of the day or the mystery of its dark depths at dusk, a time which she had particularly enjoyed sitting by its side and watching the sun slip behind the banana trees on the far bank. The unhurried pace of the eddying water seemed to mirror the rhythm of village life, leaving her feeling more in tune with the world than she had ever been on Bukit Bintang. In truth, her daily routine in the *kampung*, involving domestic chores as it often did, had been far more satisfying than the idle one on the estate where much of her time had seemed pointless. Only her concerns about her acceptance by the villagers and the baby's birth had prevented her happiness from being complete.

To her surprise, she had found the restrictions of a woman in a Muslim society not nearly as irksome as she had expected. They had seemed quite natural in the village and she had only become aware of them in the towns. The village was a Muslim citadel where its culture was unchallenged, but in the towns the Malays were being exposed to the many influences of an increasingly Western and secular world. As a result, it was not surprising the mosque was anxious to maintain its authority in every way it could and insistent on Muslim custom being observed wherever and whenever it was possible – and correspondingly resentful when it was breached. She could feel the need of its protection at that moment, as she suddenly became aware of the stares of her fellow-patrons, male to the last one. As a woman on her own, she knew the significance of the looks and the queries in their minds and so she left the café and strolled along the five-foot way. Sensibly she took care to cover her face with her *selendang*, knowing this would be sufficient to deter presumptuous glances. It was curious how a single woman shopping was acceptable, one eating in a café was not.

She was about to move on when a taxi drew up beside her. She felt a moment's exasperation before she realised it was Osman and she was just able to contain her excitement sufficiently to remember not to get into the front seat with him as she had so often done on the estate, before the car was nosing its way through the throng and she was gazing, as of old, at the familiar black hair curling over his collar. She sought for something to say which would make him turn with the old familiar grin also, but the words just would not come, and the more she tried the harder it became until, in desperation, and more to break the silence than anything else, she said something quite banal.

'Osman, I'm so so sorry for what has happened.'

It was spoken like a schoolgirl's apology for missing a first date.

'That's all right, Mem,' he said, in return, and he made it sound as if she had just excused herself for keeping him waiting for a few minutes in the car as in the old days. He used Mem in the same old way too but, although there was no hint of reproach in his voice, she was not deceived. There was no forgiveness, no wiping clean of any slate. His staring through the windscreen and failure to turn to look at her as he spoke, told her that all too plainly. There was to be no return to the past. Obviously, all that was to be settled now was the future of the baby.

It appeared he had already divorced her in the simple little ceremony in which the husband said the one Malay word *talak*, meaning divorce, three times and he now assumed she would be aware of this fact in the quaint way *kampung* Malays had of thinking that decisions, even conversations, held in the anonymity of their homes would reach the ears of those who needed to know without any real attempt on their part to make them public. It was just taken for granted that everyone would become privy to them. Perhaps in small *kampung* communities they always did.

But when Valerie learned they were no longer married she was strangely unmoved, it was irrelevant now, although she did seem to remember hearing that the wife had the right to be present when the divorce ceremony was performed. That, however, was in the past – she had other matters on her mind now, but first there was something she just had to know. She leaned forward and put her hand on his shoulder.

'Osman, there is something I need to say. I know we are no longer man and wife but I still love you. You know that, don't you? Do you still care for me?'

Osman's heart sank. This was the one thing he had dreaded – an inquest, a picking over of the painful events of a broken relationship. British women had a preoccupation with the past and never missed an opportunity for an autopsy if they could find one. He could remember the mems chatting amongst themselves when he had been playing with their children as a boy during the time his mother had been an *amah*. They never seemed to talk about the important things that were happening in the world such as the padi harvest or the price of *nasi* in the market, it was always about something which had happened in their little world such as what someone had said or done at the club or even, Allah be merciful, what another woman was wearing. When there was a quarrel amongst the children they always had to get to the bottom of it, no matter how long it took them. How did it happen? Who started it and why? It was a strange obsession with the inconsequential, the minutiae of life.

He had not noticed the same pointless curiosity in British men but, then, he had never been allowed into the bar at the club. However, they *did* spend a lot of time and energy on some very unimportant things, such as something they called sport and, in particular, the various ways of hitting a small ball into a hole almost as small, and then going out in the heat of the day to demonstrate them! For what earthly purpose? Having to plough a padi field under the pitiless eye of the *matahari*, the sun, was bad enough as any farmer knew, but at least that was unavoidable.

Women had a similar obsession with their feelings and, what was worse, yours. They were always wanting to know if you loved them and then, if so, how much? This endless raking over the ashes of love and life, it wasn't healthy. It had been Mem talking about her feelings for *Tuan*, or her lack of them, and his for her that had got them into this mess in the first place. Going over the past was pointless as it had nothing to do with the future. What was to be would be. There was only one thing to be settled now and that was the baby. Then it would be *selamat jalan*, goodbye. So he remained silent.

'Osman, come back to my hotel where we can talk properly.'

'Mem, we cannot. I dare not. Osman has work to do. He has a family waiting for him.' It was almost the first time he had forgotten the English syntax and referred to himself in the third person. Valerie could hear the tension in his voice. He turned to face her for the first time. They could not delay talking about the one thing still to be decided.

'Mem. What about your baby, *Tuan's* baby?'

'What is happening to him now?'

'Minah and my mother, they are looking after him, but Mem, it isn't right. People in the village ... ' He stopped, clearly unhappy.

'Have they been talking? What have they been saying?'

'They say your illness was caused by evil spirits. They say you should not have come to the *kampung* bringing your baby with you. They think your baby has the devil in him. They even say ... I do not know what you call it Mem but we call it *ilmu sihir*.'

Valerie was familiar with the expression. 'Witchcraft!' She was incredulous.

'It is not good, Mem. You have to take him away. He cannot stay any longer in the village.' Valerie buried her face in her hands. This was the last straw. All the love, all the tenderness she had felt for Osman, and they were now calling it witchcraft. To think that these people, her people, amongst whom she had been happily expecting to spend the rest of her life just a short while before, could believe such nonsense. They suddenly seemed as remote and strange to her as the natives she remembered in her geography books at school, staring solemnly at the camera, their children half-hiding shyly behind them.

But she could imagine it all. The gossip whenever the women got together, the portents recollected in hindsight, the angry denials of those accused of her friendship. Then would come the anguish of those who imagined they had fallen under her evil influence, perhaps while they had been doing their washing next to her by the river, or having spoken to her at some village function. Once they were convinced they had been cursed then the other villagers would feed on their misery, first by whispers, then by accusations and finally by ostracism.

The *penghulu* would have to bring in the *bomoh*, the medicine man, with his rituals and his incantations. Old friendships would be broken, new enmities begun, and, for the most vulnerable, their health would decline as strange illnesses took hold, while the endless wrangling would leave the whole village cursing Valerie's name. But her main concerns were for Osman. Poor Osman. He would never be free of her now. He had brought the witch to live amongst them so everything that went wrong in the village would be laid at his door; every animal that died, every crop that failed, even every storm that damaged a roof, would be his fault and would never be forgotten.

She suddenly felt a terrible anger, senseless and irrational, but no less strong for its lack of reason, and it centred on the object she perceived was responsible for it all – the baby. Ever since he had been conceived there had been one calamity after another and he had been at the heart of them all. If it had not been for him she would still be on the estate enjoying Osman, and if he had not turned out to be Stuart's son she would have been living happily in Batu Lima. Now, on top of everything else, he had turned the villagers against her.

A wave of loathing towards the child swept over her. No wonder the villagers saw him as evil. He was evil. It was as if Stuart had infected her and then, while incubating the disease, she had taken it to Batu Lima where it had then erupted like a plague. Not only had her chance of happiness with Osman been destroyed, but the lives of all those around him had been blighted, and finally, this poison had been released amongst the villagers. He must be, as they said, the devil's child. Would that the villagers had taken their vengeance upon him, left him in the jungle or abandoned him to the river, anything rather than that she should have him.

'Osman, I can't. I just can't. I don't want him.'

'Mem, you must. The child is yours. Show me your hotel and I will fetch him. He cannot stay in the *kampung* any longer.'

Valerie could see that Osman was desperate. He was a man distraught, and the knowledge that she had brought him to this only added to her despair and her resentment towards the baby.

'I will come with you,' she said dully.

'No, Mem,' Osman's reply was almost fierce. 'Better you stay at the hotel. Don't come near the *kampung*.'

* * *

Osman left her standing in front of her hotel and the distress caused by their conversation made her momentarily oblivious of the scene before her. Then she became aware of the bright lights of the hotel sign shining on the oily water in the monsoon drain at her feet, the reversed letters of its name, THE NIRVANA, reflecting incongruously on the stagnant surface, although its Buddhist connotation of everlasting peace and harmony was lost on Valerie at that moment. The hotel café, open to the five-foot way, was ablaze with light. Over the counter at the back was a row of featherless ducks, smoked a rich brown, and hanging by their necks like trophies on a gamekeeper's gibbet. Below them was the cook, the tapping of his clogs on the cement floor sounding a counterpoint to the ladle in his wok from which was issuing billowing clouds of steam. A few patrons, one group playing mahjong, were scattered around the tables, their conversation breaking periodically into shouts of laughter. The café could have been in China, except, as usual, there were no women to be seen.

Rather than face the men's curious stares to get to her room, Valerie walked along the five-foot way. Despite the late hour, most of the shophouses were still open, their occupants busy. A bicycle repair shop had strewn its frames and wheels across the path and a young Chinese boy, barely six years old, squatted amongst them, absorbed in assembling a chain. She picked her way around him and was rewarded with a shy smile. She wandered down a side street and then another and came out by the river, its surface looking black and impenetrable below the bridge. There were few people about but, despite the late hour, she knew she was perfectly safe. Crimes against women were relatively unknown in the country. Her problems were from within, not without. She dreaded the prospect of having a child thrust upon her care. She felt dangerously near total despair, hardly capable of being responsible for herself, let alone a baby.

She got back to her hotel long before Osman returned and waited miserably in the road. A lorry brushed past her, the driver staring in wonderment at her motionless figure; a trishaw rider stopped enquiringly but Valerie gave no indication that she had even seen him. Not until a familiar taxi drew up did she stir. Minah was in the back holding a bundle and, without getting out, she just opened the car door and handed it to her. Osman came round the car with another bundle and she took it awkwardly under her other arm.

'Goodbye, Mem,' he said and Minah gave a brief wave. Then they were gone, a haze of heavy blue diesel fumes hanging in the air. The moment had a brutal brevity to it mocking her and all that had gone before. Careless now of the interest she was causing, she walked mechanically through the café and up to her room, placing the bundles on the bed without even glancing at them. She sat beside them in utter misery, the raffia monkey on his Bakelite palm tree gazing at her questioningly. How long she remained there she did not know but she was aroused by a protest from the larger bundle, which quickly grew into a wail. Valerie fumbled in the other but found nothing with which she could satisfy infant hunger, there was not even a comforter. Inexorably, the wailing increased and Valerie looked helplessly at its source. A head was barely visible, there was a squirming lower down. Try as she might she could not bring herself to pick him up. She looked at her watch, it was nearly one in the morning.

At that moment there was a bang on the wall and a shout in a tongue she did not recognise. The baby's crying seemed to gather strength alarmingly, reaching up to the ceiling, reverberating around the walls, magnifying itself as it went. There was a knock at the door. Wearily Valerie opened it and the mole and its sprouting hair once again transfixed her. The proprietor spoke in colloquial Malay, which Valerie could not catch above the crying. Its meaning hardly needed translation, however, as there was no mistaking what she was being told to do. She asked for some milk, '*susu*' in Malay, but the Mole was just as unable to hear or comprehend as she had been, and as she said the word over and over again, its sibilance began to sound ever more ridiculous. There was a renewed banging on the wall and, in desperation, she snatched up the offending bundles, pushed past the aggrieved figure of the hotel proprietor and fled down the stairs.

The sudden movement quietened the baby and she passed through the café in relative silence, the heads of the mahjong players raised in query. Once in the road the crying re-started. Where was she to go, what could she do? She was unable to think coherently, the world around her just a jumble of sound and colour. Then, as if a switch had been abruptly flicked off in her brain or the latter had run into an obstruction, her mind seemed to cease functioning and, as in an after-death experience, she was gazing down upon herself, or at least her body, which, unaware it was without any means of guidance, was continuing on its own.

She had become an unwilling spectator of a chilling scene which began to unfold before her – that of a robotic woman, obviously without sense or sensation, questing first one way and then that, but with no idea of where she was or what she was doing. Clearly, the wretched woman was in desperate need of assistance – a danger both to herself and those around her and certainly to the baby she still held in her arms. But the onlooker, despite being desperate to help, could only continue to watch as though in that frightening, catatonic, 'locked-in' state – able to see the world but unable to communicate with it in any way.

All at once, the demented figure started along the five-foot way – but surely this was in the direction of the bridge over the river? What might she want there? Horrified, it dawned on the helpless watcher it could only to be to rid herself of her hateful burden and so bring the remorseless, ceaseless crying to an end, yet she was still unable to intervene. The figure began to run and turned a corner, and then another, blundering against obstructions, dashing into the road, tripping, her loose *kebaya* flapping. Breathless, she slowed to a walk, then stopped. This was not the way to the river she had followed earlier that evening, she must have taken a wrong turning. She tried to retrace her steps but nowhere was familiar. She was lost, not knowing which way to turn. She leant against a pillar of the five-foot way and began to sob, her breath coming in painful gasps. The bundles which, hitherto, she had miraculously kept in her grasp, slid to the ground.

At that moment a taxi stopped and with a joyous shout the pathetic figure recognised it. 'Osman!' Immediately, mind and body became one again and she was overcome with relief and joy. She had not been abandoned after all, Osman had come to take them home. The tales of black magic were no more and she was not a witch – she could go back to the village with her baby.

But it was not Osman. Instead, she was gazing into the enquiring face of a young Chinese taxi driver.

'You want a taxi?'

Of all the things she wanted at that moment a taxi seemed to be the last. But, then, why not? Her feeling of hopelessness had returned so what quicker way to get to the river? Without a word she picked up her bundles and got into the back seat.

'Where to?' asked the driver. Valerie was about to say the river when she hesitated. Sitting in these familiar surroundings and facing a matter-of-fact young man waiting for her instructions, asking for the river seemed ridiculous. How could she ask to be taken to the river at that time of night – just so that she could drop her bundle over the parapet like a bag of rubbish? The engine was running, the driver turned the meter flag over. She hesitated.

He asked again. 'Where to?'

Having given up the idea of the river, Valerie could think of nowhere else. Should she tell him her story and leave it to him? It would have to be full of lies as he must know Osman. But what were a few lies compared to the bundle she had been about to sacrifice? She hesitated again.

Then, unexpectedly, the taxi driver gave a short laugh, not of amusement but of comprehension. He knew the problem. His sister had had a baby out of wedlock. His father had turned her out of the house too. She had been at her wits end, had not known where to go or what to do. But he knew the answer. As a taxi driver, it had not been the first time he had been faced with the problem of a homeless girl and an illegitimate baby, and he told Valerie so.

'You want the orphanage,' he said.

Valerie stared at him. 'The orphanage?'

'The Kota convent orphanage in Kota Bharu.'

Kota Bharu was the state capital about twenty miles distant.

Of course, why had she not thought of that? She knew of these orphanages which could be found throughout the country and which were run by a Catholic order. They tried to cope with the never-ending flood of waifs, Chinese mostly, which were being constantly abandoned.

'How much to Kota Bharu?' she asked. She realised she had rushed out of the hotel without her purse. But, then, how much money did one need to throw a baby into a river?

'Ten dollar,' he replied without hesitation. Like all of his race, he had no time for the needless plural. 'You got the money?'

'Yes, well no, but I can get it.' The thought of an unguarded purse in an unlocked hotel room flashed through her mind and she did not feel as confident as she sounded.

'We'll get it first,' said the taxi driver with the decisiveness of someone who had been in this situation before.

Valerie named her hotel and the taxi driver expressed his surprise with a tonal acknowledgement, which was as far as he would allow his curiosity to go. She was not Chinese and she did not sound Malay. Eurasian perhaps?

Valerie's purse was where she had left it. The baby, who had been quiet in the taxi, started to wail again, and the Mole met her on the stairs. Unexpectedly, he spoke to her in English. He had obviously discovered who she was.

'I get you milk,' he said, and he was as good as his word, disappearing into the rear of the building and bringing out a full baby's bottle almost immediately. It would seem that, following her sudden departure, her previous high-decibel call for *susu* had been understood and acted upon. Valerie thanked him profusely. She was feeling especially vulnerable to any act of kindness. 'I'll be back,' she said over her shoulder.

She sat in the back of the taxi and tried to summon up the will to feed the baby but, to her relief, she found he had gone back to sleep. She put him on the seat beside her. The hatred she had felt for him earlier that evening had been replaced by indifference. In fact, she was surprised to discover she was devoid of almost any feelings at all. The problem of what to do with the baby had been solved and so, as far as she was concerned, that was the end of the matter. He had become just another piece of baggage, superfluous to requirements, no longer needing her attention and so not worthy of her notice. All that was required now was the final act of handing him over at the orphanage.

Her hysteria having passed, she felt remarkably calm. It was astonishing how her state of utter despair had been dispelled by the simple suggestion of a total stranger. Why on earth could she not have thought of an orphanage instead of losing her head and having all those wild ideas about the river? She gazed through the windscreen and watched the road disappearing, inexorably, beneath the bonnet of the car. On every bend the headlights swept across the grey trunks of rubber trees or the tangled greenery of the jungle. The taxi seemed invincible, omnipotent, a super-charged behemoth equal to any challenge to her well-being, protecting her from the hateful world around her and everything in it. A growing feeling of peace and security gradually spread over her and she longed for her journey to go on and on without end. She even began to feel a little light-headed, as if she was just starting to succumb to the first happy influence of alcohol.

When they arrived in Kota Bharu the streets were deserted but the driver had been there before and knew the way without directions. Oddly, it had not occurred to her that the orphanage might be closed but when the taxi drew up she saw immediately that not only were the gates firmly shut but there were no lights showing. Her feeling of anti-climax was profound and it was as much as she could do to leave the security of the taxi. She looked up and down the street helplessly and was just about to get back into car when the driver joined her and indicated a concrete shelter nearby.

It bore a notice in Romanised Malay, Tamil and a Chinese script and Valerie had no difficulty in translating the first language – it was instructions to those who had come to abandon a baby. Inside the shelter she found a wicker cradle and a bottle containing what appeared to be a juice. It made leaving her charge simplicity itself. No awkward questions, no lies, no embarrassing explanations. She placed the baby, who was still asleep, in the cradle and lowered the lid. She did not hesitate, she did not stop to question what she was doing, she did not even feel obliged to say a word of farewell or give him a second glance. She was simply solving a problem, one which had seemed insurmountable barely an hour before. And how easy the solution. But only possible in a tropical climate, the benevolence of which meant that even the coldest night could not be a threat to a man, woman or child or, as in this case, an abandoned baby, unfortunate enough to find themselves homeless.

* * *

They returned to Karang in silence and Valerie sat without moving. Her experiences that evening had left her drained. Even her eyes were still and unmoving, fixed on the road ahead in a sightless stare. She paid the taxi driver his ten dollars and then, after the taxi had gone, realised she was locked out of the hotel. A burly Sikh lay on a *charpoy*, his flimsy bed – a wooden frame loosely strung with rope – which he had placed so that it straddled across the five-foot way in front of the hotel as a bar to unwanted visitors, but it was not until Valerie had passed up and down several times did he bother to rouse himself. He was the *jaga*, the night watchman, ready to lay down his life in the defence of the hotel and its occupants in the finest fighting traditions of his Punjabi ancestors – providing he was awake. She motioned with her eyes towards the hotel, which, at that moment, was giving every indication that its entire clientele was in the state of blessed repose proclaimed by its name. Even the mahjong players had gone.

The *jaga* got up, went up to the door set in the shuttered partition in front of the café and hammered on it with his flattened palm. After a few minutes the Mole appeared, still dressed in his blue shorts and white singlet. His face betrayed neither irritation nor surprise. He let her in and accepted the bottle without a word. Valerie was pleased she had remembered to empty it into the monsoon drain beforehand. She wanted him to feel he had helped. She groped up the stairs, into her room and fell onto the bed. Its hard resisting boards were like a reproach, but a reproach for what? For abandoning her son to strangers? She had simply solved a problem, nothing more. She had not given the matter a moment's thought since, her mind already pre-occupied with the future, and inevitably, with Osman.

She had to face the probability that she had seen him for the last time and that fact and the manner of their parting were already causing her the most acute distress. By tomorrow he would also know what she had done with the baby. The taxi driver must have guessed who she was by now and was bound to give a blow-by-blow account of his trip to Kota Bharu the next time they were on the taxi rank together. What would Osman think of her giving up her own flesh and blood, and a boy too. That would be compounding her crime in his eyes as Malays would never abandon their children unless it was to save their lives. But had she not done it to save the life of the child? It was a question to which she did not have an answer, or was it, perhaps, she was unwilling to search for one? She was just relieved the baby and his fate were no longer her responsibility.

She shuddered when she thought about the events of that night but the details were already becoming difficult to pick out in her mind. She was completely unable to recall anything in between the time she had left the hotel and finding herself in a taxi, while even what happened at the orphanage was as if she was seeing it through the falling waters of a mountain torrent which parted only fleetingly. Partial pictures came and then were broken up before she had time to focus on them and, worryingly, despite many attempts, she could form no firm idea of how she had come to be in the taxi. The more she tried, the thicker and more urgent came the images of rubber trees and jungle. Obviously, her mind which had come dangerously close to giving way completely earlier in the evening, was already beginning to suppress memories of things it did not wish to know or recall.

She swung her legs off the bed and went to the window. Someone had closed the shutters while she was out and the room had become unbearably stuffy. She leant out over the street. She could just see the end of the *charpoy* and the *jaga's* feet – he had obviously resumed his duties and was busy laying down again, not his life in the defence of the hotel, but his ample body and a turbaned head on his bare bed of wood and sisal. There was a breeze, it might be the beginning of a sumatra with its accompanying storm. It would bring a welcome relief as the day had been stifling.

She remembered the night she had spent in the bungalow on the estate with Osman when Stuart had been in Singapore. She had been supremely happy then although she knew it could not last, but if only she could have foreseen a little of the future. How differently she would have acted and how much misery could have been avoided. The unhappiness of her mother to whom she had written without reply, the misery of Osman and all his family, the embarrassment, shame even, of those in Malaya who had formerly had some regard for her. The emotional damage had been incalculable to so many people, making the last six months a total disaster. Even her life with Osman in Batu Lima had been a disappointment as they had not shared more than a brief moment or two of affection since they had left Bukit Bintang.

She then tried to turn her thoughts to what she should do next, but no matter which path she contemplated, her future seemed full of dark corners.

*　*　*

Valerie woke late having had a restless night but not due to the boards – after her mat on the floor in Batu Lima the bed was by no means uncomfortable – but her dreams had been troubled by wild and disturbing images which really made no sense to her at all, but mercifully faded almost before her eyes had a chance to take in the significance of the unfamiliar wall facing her, and certainly before her sleep-befuddled brain had solved the mystery of how she had come to be in a strange room with just a raffia monkey for company. But, within a second or two of wakefulness, her thoughts had turned to Osman. Her first idea was a wild plan by which, without the encumbrance of the baby, she might return to the village and resume her life with him, but she immediately saw how impossible that would be. The realisation then dawned that today, therefore, was the first day of a whole lifetime without him and, at that moment, the separation seemed to have all the finality and pain of death.

But before she began to feel sorry for herself she slipped downstairs to the bathroom and forced herself to intrude upon the aquatic wildlife in the sink. The door, without a lock or even a catch, swung aimlessly, offering as much privacy as the swing doors of a Wild West saloon, but she flung her sarong over it in the way she had done by the river – she had never got used to the Malay habit of bathing in it although that was obviously how users of the bathroom were expected to preserve their modesty – and made as much noise as she could to deter any guests who might feel brave enough to face the freshwater invertebrates. The water itself was cool and refreshing, and after all, what harm was there in a few mosquito larvae? She had bathed in far worse in the river at Batu Lima no doubt.

She was unable to face either a breakfast or the first of the mahjong players in the café. Instead, she bought some fruit in the market and wandered out of the town centre. She gazed into every taxi she saw, half hoping to see Osman but dreading the rebuff, the heartbreak, if she did.

Without realising where she was going, she found herself crossing the bridge where she had been the day before. She saw, with a shock, that the water under the bridge was barely two feet deep. Of course, she had forgotten, there had been very little rain recently. But why did the sight give her a feeling of horror? What was it about the parapet that, when she was about to lean over it, made her recoil in fear?

Beneath her, on the edge of the shallows, a bullock-cart driver was scrubbing his animals with a broom. They stood impassively, enjoying their treat and flicking their ears against the flies, while the cart, forsaken, sat back on its own two wheels which had the effect of pointing its single shaft to the sky. Its twin yoke at the end made it look remarkably like a double-sided gibbet. For some unexplained reason, the sight made her quail, as if it had touched a disturbing reminder of something in her past. Lower down the river were some *dhobis*, dark-skinned figures beating white shirts against a wooden frame. It looked an unworthy way to treat garments that might soon be appearing at an important dinner, or a prestigious civic function, on the backs of local dignitaries. *Towkays* perhaps, Chinese businessmen, who, even now, were looking forward to their evening of bonhomie and *yam sengs,* oblivious of the ignominious and very public treatment of their personal property.

Valerie peeled a mangosteen and let the purple shell drop into the water where it drifted away in the slowly eddying current while she contemplated her future. She really had no alternative but to return to her own country. Trying to recover a place in the British community in Malaya would be as pointless as it was foolish. There was almost no role for a white woman in the tropics save as an accessory to her husband, and any who attempted to assume one would quickly fall foul of the colonial authorities. To them, unattached females were social and moral liabilities as there was no way they could earn their own living acceptable in the eyes of the Administration. There would always be a man, or men, selfishly or malevolently taking advantage of them in one way or another, be it paramour, protector or pimp, and there was no more humiliating spectacle in the East than a white woman at the mercy of a predatory male – of whatever race or colour.

A number of White Russian émigrés, fugitives from the Russian Revolution of 1917, had scandalised the 1920s by their behaviour and the embarrassment to the authorities had been prolonged for years as they had no homeland to which they could be repatriated. For that reason, if no other, Valerie could reasonably hope for some official assistance to get home, and this was best sought in

Singapore.

Not once did she give a thought to the baby she had abandoned.

* * *

The quickest and most convenient method of long-distance travel for local Malayans, and which was surprisingly inexpensive, was taking a seat with four or so other members of the public in a taxi, but for obvious reasons Valerie decided against going to the market place. She was longing to see Osman again but not in public, not in front of his fellow taxi drivers. Instead, she left it to the Mole who, for fifty cents, ensured that a vehicle appeared in front of the hotel at nine the next morning and, diplomatically, made sure the driver was not the one who had taken her to the orphanage or her ex-husband.

How he knew who her ex-husband was she had no idea but by now she was growing used to the locals' extraordinarily efficient intelligence system. They seemed to know more about the affairs of Europeans than even the Europeans themselves, but this, she had been told, was because they made it their business to know, and were willing to liaise with each other and share every piece of information they could find before turning it to their advantage, financial or otherwise.

For instance, at dinner one evening, a husband might remark to his wife that it was about time they moved house, only for the latter to find herself accosted by a complete stranger in the market place the next morning, saying he knew of a fine property to rent which would suit her and her husband admirably. It was uncanny, until one realised that little of what was said or went on in a house was not overheard or seen by one or other of the servants and the information immediately passed on to whoever was most likely to profit. The intelligence network spread everywhere and involved everyone – from those with whom dealings had been done in the past to those with whom dealings might conceivably be done in the future – the boys in the club, local shopkeepers and hairdressers, mechanics in the garage or even taxi drivers. The locals' grapevines were endless in their ramifications.

Valerie spent the next four hours in the company of two Chinese youths, an elderly Tamil and a Sikh matron. None was even slightly curious why a British woman was dressed in Malay clothes and had chosen to travel with them although the Sikh woman, a retired geography teacher, showed a keen interest in Britain and asked a number of questions of what it was like to live there as well as expressing a long-held desire to see it. Their reticence sprang from a combination of natural good manners and a respect for their colonial seigneurs.

The journey was long and tedious, relieved only by a stop in a road-side café for a thick, black, locally grown coffee, and they all taking the opportunity of availing themselves of the cafe's toilet – a hole in the floor of a shabby cubicle which, in the baking heat, was advertising its facilities at a hundred paces, saving any necessity for a sign. Valerie thought wistfully of the floating platform on the river at Batu Lima. They arrived in Kuala Lumpur by midday and within an hour Valerie was on her way to Singapore in another vehicle, accompanied by a further assortment of local citizens.

A useful advantage of this long-distance taxi service was that it also delivered each passenger to his or her own address. Valerie did not know Singapore very well and asked the driver for somewhere to stay that was *'kurang mahal'*, less costly. He already had a good idea what her likely destination might be as he had seen, almost immediately, she was British, but her native dress and her mode of travel had told him, equally quickly, that it would almost certainly not be the *Raffles* or the *Hotel d'Europe* she was seeking, and he was intrigued. In fact, he had spent the three hours on the road from K.L. listening for any comment that might have explained the mystery. Valerie, however, had said little, apparently pre-occupied with her thoughts. Nevertheless, nothing would have persuaded him to probe for details. Malayan taxi drivers, in contrast to their

New York or London counterparts, knew the value of silence and when to hold their tongues.

Once in the city, he headed for a cheap hotel in the dockland area and delivered her to a run-down dwelling in the Tanjong Pagar Road. Two generations before, it may have had a British merchant trader as its owner but it had since gone steadily down in the world. It was not the sort of establishment which European women would normally expect to patronise but in view of the fact that Valerie had to make her meagre funds last as long as possible, she was perfectly satisfied. It was more than a 'star' or two above the one she had just left in Karang and had an atmosphere of faded colonialism, which rather appealed to her.

That evening she ate modestly at a rattan table in a dining room facing onto a tiny inner courtyard with a single papaya tree growing in the centre – perhaps planted by the original owner of the property – and the thought moved Valerie to enliven her solitary meal by summoning a tableau or two from the dwelling's past: *guests arriving in their rickshaws and gharries; servants padding silently over the marble floors bearing sweetmeats and curries; bats hawking the coconut oil lamps around the walls; flaming torches lighting the sky as the guests departed.* Ghosts such as these kept her company until her coffee was served.

The hotel provided for a mixed clientele, the better-off members of which would just be able to aspire to European society but only to its lower reaches. The only examples present that evening were the Danish captain and first mate of a local trading steamer who talked noisily, drank copious quantities of tiger beer and laughed a great deal. Valerie felt very conspicuous in her Malay attire but her fellow diners hardly gave her a glance.

* * *

The following morning she phoned the Colonial Secretariat's office and was given an appointment for late that afternoon. Her transformation back into a European could no longer be delayed and that morning she went to the leading store in Singapore, Robinson's, where she spent more of her precious dollars on a cheap summer dress and a hat. She just had to have a hat as she had got used to the *selendang*. She had disposed of her former European clothes to Puan Zainal who had been pleased to have them, presumably because she knew how to dispose of them to her advantage. What she had received for them was, no doubt, a great deal less than Valerie had to pay for their replacement in one of the only two European stores in the city.

The face of the Chinese girl who served her was impassive but Valerie knew she must have been highly intrigued by the circumstances in which a European woman dressed as a Malay was buying a dress, and Valerie caught a glimpse of her in a mirror eyeing her with interest. Their eyes met briefly and the girl looked away in alarm. She knew how such an intrusion could mean the loss of her job and she avoided further eye contact when Valerie came to pay for the dress. Valerie was well aware, and deplored, how important a complaint from a British woman would be regarded in the eyes of the management of a store in a Crown Colony like Singapore, and tried to re-assure the girl with a smile. A job such as hers would be prized, and its loss to a family with no other income a serious misfortune.

Valerie toyed with the idea of leaving her Malay clothes in the fitting room, thought better of it and put them in her bag. She would dispose of them later. Her purchases looked little enough, but the tropics required nothing more. It was an ideal climate if one was homeless and thus required to live on the streets, as all even a European woman needed was a light dress, shoes, perhaps stockings, a handbag and, of course, a hat, with an umbrella as an optional accessory, it being far too hot for a raincoat or an outer garment of any kind. A local woman, on the other hand, would require only the first of these or its equivalent in native garb.

Local and European women faced very different expenses

in other ways as well, and not only because their lifestyles were different. Overcharging mems was a way of life for the locals in the colonies although it was sturdily resisted, and so there would be no cheap living for Valerie now she had to pay European rates for everything. It started immediately she left Robinson's. The trishaw which had taken her to Raffles Square had cost forty cents, but she was unable to get the rider who took her to the Colonial Secretariat in Government House in the afternoon to accept anything less than double that for a shorter journey.

*　*　*

Valerie was dropped before an imposing Colonial style building set on a slight rise in its own grounds on the edge of the business quarter of the city. It had formerly been the island residence of one of the most Europeanised of the Malay sultans and was designed to impress the Sultan's subjects. Its change of ownership had done nothing to diminish its grandeur. She mounted the steps and was directed by a handsome, almost pretty, Malay youth in immaculate local dress to an airy vestibule, which had formerly been part of the main reception area. It was as cool as a cavern despite the heat outside, and the fan that turned languidly thirty feet above hardly seemed necessary.

She sat on a chintz cushion in a rattan chair and listened to the drone of a mechanical grass-cutter outside. She had watched it criss-crossing the sweeping lawns as her trishaw had laboured up the path, and from a distance it had looked like a tiny boat on a sea of grass. As she approached she could see it was being guided by a Tamil who, every so often, had stopped to tinker with the engine. On each such occasion he had removed the piece of cloth which was doing its modest best to protect his head from the sun and wiped his hands on it before rewinding it round his head again with great care.

Valerie could not but contrast the scene with the ones she

had been so familiar with recently. It was the same country but different worlds. She doubted if more than a tiny fraction of the inhabitants of Karang had ever been to Singapore, and so remained in woeful ignorance of the magnificence of the Empire under whose protection they spent their days.

The secretary who came to collect her and show her to his office looked absurdly young. This was obviously his first appointment and he could hardly have been in Singapore for more than a few months. Certainly not long enough for him to have heard about the notorious planter's wife who had deserted her husband and gone to live with a native in a *kampung*, or 'gone native' as the local idiom termed it. This would make the task before her a lot simpler.

Valerie had decided she would use her original married name as it would cause less confusion and be less likely to be queried, so the young secretary began by saying 'How nice to see you, Mrs Mitchell,' and he meant it. Despite her cheap dress, she could not help radiating allure and the young secretary was missing the girlfriend he had left behind in Britain. In fact, although he would not have cared to admit it, he was feeling quite homesick for London. He was already bored with his large bachelor boarding house and its rowdy, all-male inhabitants off the Orchard Road and even more with Singapore.

The novelty of the East had worn off and he was beginning to count the months to his first home leave. It was female company he missed the most. There appeared to be no single white girls in Singapore and the local ones he had seen had been inaccessible so far and he was at a loss to know where to meet them. It was not the accepted thing for young members of the Malayan Civil Service to be seen in the local amusement parks such as Happy World, and he did not have the nerve to try the seamier haunts of the city. The lecture he had attended in London on the perils of certain Eastern maladies, not to mention the pictures that had accompanied it, had made a considerable impression on him.

In any case, the local girls looked all alike – black hair, brown skins and small breasts. He preferred the softer, paler shades and the fuller figures himself, and Valerie had immediately reminded him of the girls he used to watch, as unobtrusively as possible, sitting on the grass in St. James's Park at lunch times during the summer. Back home, watching girls sunbathe had been one of his favourite pastimes and it was strange that with so much sun, so many girls, and so much grass, it was never a sight seen in Singapore. Apparently it was not just female modesty in a society where the Muslim influence was strong, but the fact that a suntan on a girl was the mark of the labouring class and so not favoured by the young men. So much of the East seemed the reverse of things in Britain.

He feasted his eyes on Valerie. Had he been a little older he might have noticed she was not of the generation that sunbathed in St. James's Park, might have spotted a few deepening lines here and there, the fingers roughened by work and stained by native cooking; might have seen that her dress was so cheap that only a soldier's wife in Singapore would have dared to wear it. But he was young and very impressionable, so only saw how cool and fresh she looked.

Valerie had resolved to be frank about her predicament and the causes of it, but now she hesitated to relate in detail the events of the last six months. What did this young cub know of the domestic and social realities of a planter's wife buried on a rubber estate in the tropics without children? On the other hand, she was being left in no doubt of her ability to awaken his deepest interest. What then, might be her best approach?

'I have had a serious domestic dispute with my husband and he has turned me out without a penny,' she began and smiled at the Victorian overtones in her statement, and the young secretary smiled also. He felt quite bucked. A lady in distress, the idea appealed to him. What an opportunity. 'I therefore find myself in a very embarrassing situation,' she said. 'Mainly because I need financial help and have no one to turn to.'

She was in need of an advance too! This was getting better and better. He could hardly have devised a more promising set of circumstances himself. Unfortunately, he was in much the same state himself, his newly acquired roadster, parked unobtrusively at the rear of the Secretariat, having proved to be a more than reckless extravagance. It looked as though he was not going to be able to take advantage of this unexpected opportunity of earning his visitor's everlasting gratitude.

'What I have come to ask is whether there is any way the Colonial Government could assist my passage home because I cannot possibly afford the fare in my present circumstances. It is a loan I am asking for of course.'

Even the young secretary was not deceived by that, but it was polite of her to say so. There was a problem, however. In his limited experience of the East, European women were never destitute, and therefore never in need of ex-gratia payments from official funds. The latter were for merchant seamen who had missed their ships and were beginning to make nuisances of themselves in waterfront bars, or tourists who had either lost their luggage or had their money stolen. That did not mean she could not qualify, of course. On the contrary, there surely could not be a more deserving case than hers. A helpless, vulnerable woman with no one to turn to must be in the first category of entitlement. After all, what were the funds there for? If a drunken matelot qualified, then surely must this delightful reminder of home.

The secretary's next question was a simple one, in fact it was hardly a question at all, just a simple statement needing corroboration but it had a most unexpected and dramatic effect. 'I assume there are no children involved. I gather you and your husband have no children.'

'No,' but as Valerie uttered the word, the secretary's office froze around her. It was as if she had just touched a live electric wire which, without warning, had caused all her senses to come to a full stop, a state of paralysis from which she found herself being released but only gradually, by degrees, and without sensible thought or coherent speech. 'I mean yes ... no ... I have no ...' Then, to the Secretary's astonishment this poised representative of the British Colonial ruling class seemed to crumple before him. Her shoulders slumped, she buried her face in her hands and she began to cry, softly but inexorably.

'I'm sorry to have distressed you Mrs Mitchell. *Do* you have children?' But he got no reply. Eagerly he assured her that His Majesty's Government would assist her return to Britain, would be happy to assist, would see it as its positive duty to assist, and, naturally, provide the maximum amount allowable and with the minimum amount of embarrassment to herself. But she appeared oblivious to everything he said and after a long two minutes during which there was nothing to be heard but her muffled sobbing and the noise of a fan, Valerie rose and left the room, too distressed to notice his embarrassment but not enough to be unaware of her own.

By the time she had returned to the vestibule she had recovered herself a little but felt too mortified to try to resume her interview with the secretary, apart from which she had been completely devastated by the revelation prompted by his question. Then to add to her dismay, she realised she had not asked the trishaw to wait. Now she would have to walk back into town. She started down the winding path that snaked its way through the sea of grass. The Tamil gardener was crouched by his machine nearby, cloth in hand, but his declined head and diffident smile in acknowledgement of her passing went unheeded as the myriad implications of the realisation triggered by the young secretary's simple enquiry filled her mind to the exclusion of everything else.

Unnoticed also was the afternoon glare of a tropical sun beating down upon a newly bought hat, the protective qualities of which the British pioneers of a century earlier would have considered as being totally inadequate as a means of protecting the head of a white woman intent on anything as foolhardy as venturing outdoors at noon. As the whole of the medical world seemed to agree at the time, a temperate head was quite unable to resist the depredations of an equatorial sun at such an hour. The pioneers, therefore, would have been in no doubt that without what they considered to be the most indispensable part of a white man's tropical kit, the solar topee, Valerie's walk through the park that afternoon would have been her last. Fortunately, Valerie was oblivious of the solar obsessions of her colonial predecessors, or any other threat to her safety for that matter, her only concern at that moment being to gather her scattered thoughts and her shredded feelings.

She had known that the emotional stress she had suffered as a result of the events which followed Osman handing over the baby had led to her suffering some form of amnesia, as to this day she had been unable to remember certain things that had happened that night. But it was now equally clear that coming so quickly after the circumstances of the birth itself, those events had also caused a degree of mental disorientation to the point where she had lost the ability to make logical connections or foresee the consequences of many of her actions.

Even so, it was difficult to understand how she could have achieved motherhood, a status to which she had aspired for so long, without it leaving at least some trace on her memory or her consciousness. The mental trauma of that night must have been considerable for it to have had such a drastic effect, yet it taken just a simple question from a complete stranger to reverse the process and make her see the awful things that had happened after she had been handed the baby. She actually had a child – and she repeated the words slowly over and over again as if, even now, she could hardly believe it. Yet, it seemed, she had discarded him like a worthless bag of household rubbish. The baby she had carried within her, bearing so many of her hopes and longings and whose arrival she had looked forward to with so much anticipation, had been left like a pauper's child by the side of the road.

It was difficult to grasp the enormity of what she had done.

She, the one person in the world who should have been his stoutest defender, his greatest protector, had been the one to desert him in his hour of need. A perfect stranger would have done more and a beast of the field no less. What was worse, she had not had a pang of conscience or had given a single thought to the child's existence after she had closed the lid of the crib outside the orphanage and got back into the taxi.

Every minute that had elapsed since then had compounded her crime. To think – at that very moment a baby of hers was laying in an unknown cot in an unfamiliar building in a strange town and in a country which was not his own. He had no name and no identity, and was being looked after by strangers speaking a foreign tongue. He was almost as far away from the two people who had brought him into the world as he could possibly be, one of them understandably so, as he was unaware of his existence, the other uncaring whether he lived or died. And whereas the ignorance of the first gave him an excuse, there was no such saving grace for the other. What she had done had been unforgivable and it could hardly be explained by the heartbreak of his birth and the subsequent despair that had followed – she had had more than enough time to recover from both and have come to her senses and realise her responsibilities. Guilt was hardly the word to describe her feelings at that moment – it was something more akin to self-loathing.

By now she was almost back at the gates to Government House – imposing in their lofty eminence but never seen at their best by the local citizenry as they were permanently left open in order to demonstrate, in theory at least, the democratic accessibility of their rulers, and still her thoughts were racing and tumbling. What would be the reaction of friends and family when they realised what she had done? What would her mother say when she discovered she had a grandson without a name? What would be Stuart's reaction? Would he try to take him from her? Could he take him from her? Had the orphanage even found him? In the space of a few seconds the direction of her life and every one of her plans had changed out of all recognition. She just had to get back to Kota Bharu at the first opportunity and start finding answers to these questions. What a good job she had kept her Malayan clothes.

As she was about to pass through the gates, she suddenly became aware of a sporty red car drawing up at her side and a familiar voice saying:

'I didn't realise you had no transport. Can I drop you anywhere?'

It was the young secretary, looking a little self-conscious as he leant across the car to speak to her.

Despite some irritation at having her train of thought broken, she answered politely, as who can resist an eager puppy? He hardly looked old enough to have left school. The sun on his hair was emphasising its youthful lustre and he still had Britain's cool climate bloom upon his cheek. But, apart from not wishing to spurn his friendly gesture, she was also glad of the opportunity to put her recent lapse of good manners behind her and it was her desire to rectify this transgression which tempted her to suppose he might enjoy having his leg pulled, gently, especially by a woman.

'You finish early,' she said. 'They don't overwork you in the Secretariat, do they?'

'Oh we get away promptly most days unless there is a panic on. I was just coming down the stairs and noticed you were having to walk. It's very hot in Singapore at this time of day,' he added unnecessarily.

He lied. He had watched her leave from his office window, had swept the contents of the top of his desk into a drawer and muttered to his colleagues that he was late for an appointment, before nearly breaking his neck to retrieve his car. Then he had accelerated down the drive with enough speed and noise to frighten the Tamil gardener half out of his wits. Apart from anything else, he was genuinely concerned that he might have been the cause of her distress and he hoped she would now see his concern as justifying his renewal of their acquaintance. 'I was also worried,' he said. 'You seemed so upset when you left.'

Valerie smiled her appreciation and assured him she was fine. 'I don't have anywhere in particular to go,' she said. 'Raffles Place will do.'

'Would you like to come to the Club for a drink?'

Valerie hesitated. It was the one thing she had made up her mind not to do for lots of reasons. It was not a lifestyle she was very keen to take up again, the company of her fellow nationals could be mutually embarrassing, and, in any case, she was anxious to avoid any unnecessary demands on her dwindling reserve of dollars. On the other hand, a small drink would not do any harm she supposed. It was most unlikely there would be anyone there who would know her and she had nothing else to do. She was also amused by the young secretary. He was so obviously smitten by her. It was some time since she had been in the company of a man who was.

*   *   *

How different the city of Singapore looked from a car than from a trishaw, and how different she found the ride – to enjoy the security of merging with the traffic and not to suffer the insecurity of being a constant obstacle to it; to revel in being a passenger in a powerful machine and not the self-conscious burden of a labouring coolie in a vehicle looking like the pointless survivor of a bygone age. She had never ridden in a trishaw without, in a curious way, being made to feel guilty. The whole experience seemed to her like an indictment of Western decadence, she lolling indolently, the rider struggling as if his life depended on it. The car was a similar condemnation of course, this time of Western wealth and possessions, but as it was also an example of how ingenious the West could be, it left her without a feeling of self-reproach.

And after what had happened in Karang, how familiar, and comforting too, was the Club and all its trappings of the white man's power. The young secretary stopped in front of a large building from which emerged a Sikh porter in a magnificent red turban and matching cummerbund who opened the car door with a bow. She walked up the steps and into the spacious entrance. No one knew her, she was a total stranger, and yet she was immediately accepted, her character unknown and her credit unchecked. Because of the colour of her face, it was assumed she was of the ruling elite, rich, or at least married to one who was. They did not doubt, or resent, for a moment that she was entitled to give them orders commanding the finest service they could provide.

These were the benefits, the privileges, of the system. It was also part of the same system that those who failed to keep to the rules, to meet the standards, had to be excluded. The select could not feel select unless there were others who could be denied their privileges, and Valerie was very conscious at that moment that she deserved to be among that unhappy band, as, if it was known who she was and what she had done, her welcome might not have been so warm.

The young secretary bustled in and ushered her into the bar. He was still tickled at how easy it was in the East to entertain a lady. There was always an obedient doorman waiting and a deferential boy to do one's bidding. There was never a struggle to catch the eye of the barman, or the tedium of a table having to be booked. The irritation of having a waiter constantly hovering to be bribed was quite unknown, as was the humiliation of his subtle contempt when a cheap wine was all that one could afford. Commands could be given with a flick of the fingers, complaints made with the pleasing certainty they would be acted upon. There was not even the necessity to ponder the size of the tip for the simple reason that tipping was forbidden, indeed, risked the dismissal of the beneficiary, so that even meanness became a virtue.

All this and there was no reckoning of accounts until the end of the month. Unfortunately, the young secretary had not yet come to terms with the sense of power it all conferred and, when he ordered the drinks, his cry of Boy was just that little bit too loud. Valerie had to look away. It was painful for her to think of Osman being treated like that. But then, it was painful to think of Osman at all in these surroundings.

They wandered out onto the verandah overlooking the pool. 'You know,' Valerie said, 'I don't even know your name.'

'Milburn,' he said, 'Peter Milburn,' and he silently cursed his social ineptitude in having failed to introduce himself. Why had he not done it at the Secretariat? So much for the image he hoped he was presenting.

'And I'm Valerie, but of course, you know.'

He played the concerned card again. 'I hope I wasn't the cause of you being so upset in the Secretariat.'

Valerie assured him he had just triggered a painful memory and apologised for her loss of control, which he could not possibly have foreseen, and then they talked casually of her years in the East, of her life up-country in a Malaya that he hardly knew at all, having served exclusively in Singapore. He tried to ask some intelligent questions but only accentuated his ignorance. In fact she openly laughed at his idea that everyone in Kelantan travelled by elephant, and he was quite put out until he saw heads turn, and he was able to persuade himself that the club members were noting that the new boy Milburn from the Secretariat was, quite clearly, amusing his very attractive companion. She asked him how he liked his job and his reactions to the island. She was beginning to feel as if she was entertaining a friend her son had brought home from boarding school and who was all anxious to please and on his best behaviour and so laughing at almost everything she said. Valerie knew he was going to invite her to dinner and had made up her mind to refuse but, as she suspected, he would not take no for an answer.

'I'm afraid,' she said, 'I will be totally unable to return your hospitality.'

This only added to the young secretary's pleasure. Valerie was as near to a damsel in distress as he was ever likely to meet in Singapore. He knew he could ill afford to treat anyone to an expensive dinner, but that was a problem for the end of the month, not now, not until the brown envelope bulging with chits appeared in his pigeon hole and, in any case, Valerie let him off lightly. He watched her covertly over his menu.

There was no denying she was a damned attractive woman although, and he could see it now, not nearly as young as he had imagined that afternoon. He could not help wondering if she was the sort who went for younger men, the type who enjoyed initiating the uninitiated into the finer points of mutual pleasure. He would be a most willing pupil. The late-night, gin-induced stories of the conquests of his companions in the boarding-house mess had excluded him for too long. It would be nice to be able to contribute one or two of his own for a change.

He had earlier noted her nicely turned ankles and shapely legs, with just a hint of strength, something which had always appealed to him. There was also no lack of feminine contours elsewhere which the dress, though cheap and now looking more than a little crumpled, did nothing to conceal. They were half way through the entrée when a couple walked past them who he had not seen in the Club before. There were a lot of out-station members in Singapore at certain times of the year. The fellow looked a typical planter, sallow skin, hair thinned from always being under headgear of some kind, eyes tired from too many early mornings. As the woman passed their table she stopped and looked as though she was going to speak, thought better of it and quickly passed on. When they reached their own table she spoke animatedly to her husband, clearly of Valerie, as his eyes were momentarily turned towards her, before being, rather obviously, made to look away again by his wife. 'Friends of yours?' he enquired.

'Hardly,' said Valerie, 'but I know them, knew them might be more accurate perhaps.'

She said no more and the secretary sensed it was better not to pursue the matter. Valerie was quiet for a while as she got over the surprise of meeting, of all people, the Stephensons, and face to face at that. Why couldn't it have been across a room where they each, she was sure, would have pretended not to have seen the other. It had to happen some time she supposed. At least, there would be something for Margo to regale at the Club when she returned.

'But, my dear, yes of course it was her, I would know her anywhere wouldn't I? Cheap dress, looked very impoverished, and with a young fellow not half her age. From the Secretariat by the look of him. Poor Valerie. I wonder what has happened to her Malay?' They were always pitifully short of news in Kuala Lebir. That piece should keep the Club going for weeks.

It was natural that over the meal the conversation should turn to the reason for her visit to the Secretariat that afternoon. At first Valerie was cautious in how much she told her host but she was increasingly coming to realise the plight she was in. The delayed shock which had caused the reaction to her abandonment of the baby and which had led to her terminating her request for assistance so summarily that afternoon had left her in a spot. She knew she would have to renew her application at some time in the immediate future as she was in an even greater need of funds now there was the baby to consider. In the end she decided to take Milburn into her total confidence – she was beginning to feel the need for a sympathetic shoulder in any case, as the events of the last couple of weeks were beginning to take their toll.

He was, as might have been expected, anxious to provide all the sympathy she needed, and just as anxious to assure her of his devoted assistance in whatever course of action she chose to take and, naturally, the assistance of the Colonial Secretariat as well. He managed to give the impression the entire resources of His Majesty's Imperial Government in Singapore had been placed there just for her convenience. In fact, as the wine began to have its effect, he made it seem as if the full majesty of the entire British Empire in the East was poised – just waiting to do her bidding. All that was needed was for her to crook her finger and it would rise up, resplendent in all its pomp and pageantry, and with fifes playing and drums beating, come marching over the distant horizon to her assistance.

Not only were his assurances almost without end, he was over-brimming with good intentions – to speak to his superior almost before that colonial luminary had emerged from his taxi the next morning; to take the first administrative steps to secure her passage home; to enlist the services of their legal department to ensure the baby's release from the orphanage, and finally to phone her to let her know of the progress he had made on each and every front – and all before his first iced drink of the morning had made a glistening wet ring upon his desk. Valerie smiled her thanks and hoped her face was not betraying the scepticism she was feeling; or her mischievous thought that male intentions had never been flagged more obviously.

*   *   *

They went for a drive after dinner. Valerie was not very familiar with Singapore and it could have been a pleasant way to see it if the secretary had not put the hood of the car down and driven faster than was wise or polite. Valerie gently remonstrated once or twice but it only made him worse. She sighed inwardly. He was very young, of course, but why did he have to show off so obviously? These young men seemed to revel in frightening their female companions. Had she been younger she might have gratified him with a squeal or two. Instead, she just quietly hoped he would not hit anything or anyone.

The thought of a native child – such as one of the group she had chatted with on the back steps in Batu Lima – being thrown, broken and bleeding, into a monsoon drain filled her with unspeakable horror. An incident in a novel she had once read suddenly filled her mind – of a French nobleman contemptuously tossing a coin into the road to pay for the funeral of a child his reckless coach had just consigned to oblivion. Even to think of the *ancien régime* of France in the same context as the colonial authorities of the

Straits Settlements was far-fetched in the extreme of course, as well she knew but, at that moment, she was finding being one of the privileged elite of the British Raj not to her taste; in fact it was downright embarrassing. To banish her disagreeable thoughts she tried to remember the book in which the incident of the pauper child had taken place and decided it must have been *A Tale of Two Cities*.

They drove down the Orchard and Stamford roads, turning into Beach Road past the Raffles Hotel and then on into China Town. The secretary could not have pointed out the two contrasts of the East more graphically or given Valerie a more vivid demonstration of how easy it was to slip from one into the other. Would that she had found it personally to be so simple.

They bowled back into the city, over Elgin Bridge and along South Bridge Road into Keppel Road, the wind swirling Valerie's hair around her face as she turned to gaze at the winking lights of the myriad ships in the harbour. How grieved she would have been if she had just had an expensive perm – there were a few advantages in being poor. Eventually they ended up at Pasir Panjang where they stopped to admire the view.

The secretary wondered if this might be the right time to put his arm around her but thought better of it. He had been told to look for a signal on these occasions and that older women knew just when and how to send them. That was all very well, but did he know how to spot them? As far as he could see, she had not made one yet. He wondered in what form it would take, it would be a tragedy to miss it. Would it be as a word or a gesture? He wished he had listened a little better to the tips of his friends in the mess. Still, they had all said you would know one when it came. Rather nice in a way, relieved of having to make the first move and risk a rebuff. On the other hand, just think of the contempt she would be feeling if he had already missed a string of them. He leaned a little closer and made sure he kept her in sideways view as they gazed out to sea.

The stars were bright, the moon made a dancing, shaft of pale light across the water. Ye Gods, there would never be a better time for a signal than this, but it did not come.

He dropped her back to her hotel. Valerie noted his astonishment at both its dingy exterior and its run-down surroundings. It would be nice to think they had added strength to her application but the decision was not in his hands, as well she knew. If it had been, might she not have got out of the car so quickly when she sensed he was about to do something rash? Might she also not have been so unwilling to offer the encouragement that he was clearly looking for when they were at Pasir Panjang? She was sure he had been going to make a pass at her but, to her surprise, he had failed to do so. There seemed to be something holding him back.

She was thankful for his forbearance as it would have put her in a predicament. The last thing she wanted to do was to offend him, for obvious reasons, and it was always a pity when one's dinner host forced one into a rebuff. It was difficult not to make it seem like ingratitude, even bad manners, but in her present circumstances she knew it would have been the most sensible thing to do. Something, however, told her she would not be seeing him again.

* * *

He had promised to phone the next day but she was not surprised the call failed to materialise. Nor did she hear the day after that. The next day she received a message to go to the Secretariat for another interview but it was not from Milburn, nor did she feel he would be the one she would see. However, she was glad she did not have to wait any longer as she was getting worried – her carefully husbanded funds were beginning to run low and soon she would be destitute. It was difficult for a European woman in Singapore to occupy herself without spending money.

She was fortunate to discover the Botanical Gardens. They were a godsend as they were free to enter and yet were an acceptable place for a white woman, even on her own, to be seen. She was genuinely interested in the displays of flowers, especially the orchids. She recalled her efforts to cultivate them on Bukit Bintang a little wistfully. The monkeys provided some amusement unless they suspected you had something to eat when they became nuisances, sometimes quite spiteful nuisances, but there were a number of quiet seats tucked here and there, and so always one or two in the shade where a white woman could sit unobtrusively and read a book without arousing the curiosity of the locals.

Her second visit to the Secretariat was in sharp contrast to the first, in fact, it could not have been worse. She was collected from the vestibule, not by young Milburn, but by a much more senior figure. He was balding and with a ginger moustache. She could see immediately he was an old Malaya hand, wise to the ways of the white man in the East, and to the white woman too, no doubt. He had a superior, discouragingly brusque, manner and Valerie sensed he would be neither friendly nor particularly sympathetic to her plight.

'I saw Peter Milburn before,' she said as he led the way upstairs to his office. He did not have to be told. He'd nearly had a fit when Milburn told him what he proposed. What was the Colonial Office sending them out nowadays? They were not only wet behind the ears – there was precious little between them either. He blamed the cinema, filling young fellows' minds with romantic nonsense. It was lucky Milburn had come to him with the problem before going to the Treasury Department. He seemed to have lost his judgement completely and now he'd seen the woman he was beginning to see why. He had told him to leave the file in his in-tray for him to deal with, and then sent the young puppy off with his tail between his legs.

'Yes I know, Milburn is out today. You will have to do with me I'm afraid.'

He invited her to sit down while he shuffled a clutch of papers before him.

'Mrs Mitchell, I understand you have asked if we can assist you to return to Britain. This is most irregular you know. It is not His Majesty's Government's responsibility to provide funds to ferry their nationals, or ex-nationals,' he corrected himself hastily, 'around the world.'

They both knew his statement to be untrue, but, then, he had not really said that at all. He had merely provided the official terminology for: 'Members of this exclusive club of ours cannot expect H.M.G. to solve their problems for them. One of the conditions of membership is that personal emergencies are dealt with privately. Only those Britons who have no pretensions to membership can expect official assistance, and a request for it is, in itself, proof of being unfit to be a member.'

'But my husband has cut me off without a penny,' she protested. 'What else am I to do?' The senior man thought for a moment before he replied. He had been briefed by his opposite number in Kuala Lumpur who, in turn, had been brought up to date by the Kelantan Adviser, so he was well acquainted with what he considered to be the somewhat sordid facts of the case, but he did not wish to be discourteous in alluding to them. It was vital that he choose his words with the greatest care, in fact the whole case required the most delicate handling. As he had been told, but was also well aware, there could be repercussions, serious repercussions, especially if the Malay authorities felt their rights were being infringed in any way.

It was indeed fortunate he had been alerted to it in time. Mrs Mitchell, or perhaps he should say, the former Mrs Mitchell, was something of a cause célèbre in the country. The High Commission in K.L. was quite certain she was now a Malayan citizen and the Malays did not take kindly to any interference with their people. Clearly she had tired of her native life and now wanted to return to civilisation, but this would only make the Malays even more sensitive about the issue. National prestige, or face as it was more vulgarly called, was at stake. There had also been mention of a baby, in fact K.L. had said that they had been told quite categorically that, as Mrs Mitchell was pregnant by her Malay husband, there could be no question of her return to the U.K. He noticed she had had her baby, yet she had made no mention of it. Did this mean she was expecting H.M.G. to get them both home? If the Malays suspected that, there would be, literally, the very devil to pay. There was no conceivable way the Secretariat could help her.

And to think that all this had been left in Milburn's hands! Apart from everything else, he was relieved Milburn had not discovered she had been co-habiting with a local. Not only was such an indelicate fact not suitable for one so new to the East, but he also feared the effect it might have had on that young man's febrile imagination. He was becoming a little concerned about Milburn. He was aware that the sudden, almost complete, deprivation of white women's company had an unsettling effect on young cadets posted to the Straits Settlements for the first time, especially those with, how could he describe it, a sociable nature, and Peter Milburn was a prime example. That young man had a dangerously sociable nature. It was something the Colonial Office did not take account of in their selection procedures or in their postings. He must make a mention of it in his next report on recruitment and training.

In a manner that he hoped would appear sympathetic but firm, but only made him sound rather pompous, the senior man said: 'Since you made your application we contacted your husband, your former husband, who tells us you left him of your own accord. He does not feel he is obliged to accept any financial responsibility for you, nor does he feel inclined to come to your aid.'

'I was not asking for his help,' said Valerie hotly. 'I was asking for yours.'

Perhaps it was going to be necessary to refer to the scandalous business in Kelantan after all. Could she be imagining they had not heard of it? She really did have a nerve in expecting them to bail her out after what she had done in abandoning her British husband and going off with a native in that unseemly way, and without a thought for the consequences.

'I suggest this is a matter for your new, er, Malay husband,' and he hesitated just long enough over the word husband to cause Valerie irritation. 'As far as we can determine the legal position, it would seem you are no longer the direct responsibility of His Majesty's Government. When you married a citizen of this country you effectively put yourself beyond its reach and obligation. You are not a British national any more, and although we are mindful of your plight, we do feel you should now look to your existing husband.'

He thought he had put that rather well, diplomatically, even kindly, but with no hint of the real reason why they were not going to touch her even with the longest barge pole at their disposal. He had not been a civil servant for thirty years for nothing.

'But he is in no position to help me at all as you can imagine,' said Valerie.

The senior man spread his hands. 'And neither are we I'm afraid,' he said with finality.

Valerie considered how much she dared tell him of the change in her circumstances during the last few weeks. Obviously, Milburn had said nothing about her being banished from the village and the baby having been left in the orphanage. Indeed, he had appeared not to have mentioned the baby at all, and like the rest of the European community, her interviewer was probably unaware of it, but she suddenly felt a shaft of guilt about what she had done that night. Perhaps she had committed a criminal offence, it certainly did not seem a very Christian thing to have done, leaving a European child to be reared in a Third World country. She also wondered what good telling them could do. It might make them feel even less like helping her. It certainly did not show her in a very good light, so all she said was:

'Have you any advice as to what I can do?'

'Have you no relatives in the U.K. who could help?' he asked.

'None,' said Valerie grimly. 'None whatsoever. I shall walk out of here with no money, no hope of acquiring any and with no one to turn to.'

She said the last with some bitterness and the senior man felt uneasy. Not on her behalf but on his. One of the imponderables in this case was what was going to happen to Valerie now. Well he knew the dangers of the situation. As he had said to Milburn, there could be repercussions, and one of them was the social implications of an unattached and penniless British woman at loose in Singapore. But before the senior man was tempted to make a concession, Valerie lost the opportunity by saying, with a desperation that almost sounded frivolous: 'I suppose you don't know of a job going, do you? Anything considered. I've had plenty of practice washing-up lately.'

The question was too near the senior man's thoughts for comfort. 'Surely, dear lady, things cannot be as bad as that. Something will turn up.'

He wondered if he dared broach the subject of why she had left her Malay husband but decided against it. Thankfully, it was no concern of his. He could not imagine what life in a *kampung* must be like. It could not be much, he imagined, if she would rather face washing up in some hotel rather than go back to it.

The senior man got up. There seemed no point in prolonging the interview any further. As he watched Valerie's departing back he had the uncomfortable feeling that the British authorities had not heard the last of her.

Disconsolately Valerie walked down the curving staircase. What a waste of time the last three days had been but what was worse, what a waste of her steadily depleting funds. She was now almost desperate. She glanced out of a rear window and glimpsed a familiar red car standing in the shade of a clump of Casuarina trees. She thought sadly of the owner. Had he been warned against her or had he just decided she was too risky to pursue further?

This time she had asked the trishaw to wait. The rider looked up expectantly as she climbed in. There was a pause and then she said wearily 'The Botanical Gardens,' with a sigh. It was too late in the day to try for a taxi back to Kota Bharu.

The Singapore sun shone as mercilessly as it had done four days before but she no longer had the recent revelation of her motherhood to distract her thoughts, and she began to feel the heat acutely. The glare beat onto the tarmac of the asphalt path and was radiated back again, to find itself trapped beneath the awning of the trishaw, making its occupant feel as uncomfortable as if she was standing in an over-heated kitchen on a hot day in Britain and had just opened the oven door. Meanwhile, she had the feeling two pairs of eyes were watching her, both perhaps a little guiltily, from two different office windows behind her.

But what could she expect, she had broken the rules of the Club. Now, to all its members she was an outcast – too embarrassing to know, even by the most impressionable ones of the opposite sex, let alone the worldly wise ones whose task it was to administer the Empire. It hardly seemed possible, but somehow she had managed to have herself excluded by both the Malayan societies she had known – the brown one she had hoped to join and the white one she had rashly left. It was quite an achievement and had left her in a difficult situation.

If it was not for the fact that her head was full of hopes of regaining possession of the baby – she would have been feeling really quite desperate as she was fast running out of ideas of which way to turn.

PART FIVE

THE ORPHANAGE

The first thing Valerie did in the morning was to hail a trishaw to take her to a goldsmith's where she hoped to raise some sorely needed dollars by selling the last of her liquid assets – her jewellery, most of which contained at least some gold even if the stones themselves were of little value – her social life on Bukit Bintang had made few demands on the worth and ostentation of her personal accessories. She deliberately wore her European dress – it would not do to give the impression she might be fencing stolen goods.

As she was well aware, the odd European *might* just stoop to such a thing but the locals themselves would never think them capable of it, an illusion assiduously fostered by the Colonial Government in the interests of its precious image. The authorities rarely missed an opportunity of demonstrating that although the British would always remain committed to the rule of law – it was the much-respected cornerstone of their constitution after all – in reality the expatriate community had no need of the legal restraints it imposed. Laws were there to ensure social order and good governance and so were primarily for the natives, they had no more relevance to the governing class than school rules had to teachers.

That did mean, of course, that any expatriate who did anything which might require him, or even her, to make an embarrassing appearance before a magistrate, had to be whisked back to Britain as quickly and as unobtrusively as possible. On one occasion, for example, a soldier's wife in Singapore, suspected of trying to sell her favours in Bugis Street – a notorious haunt for British sailors – found herself on the next passenger boat home, her husband with her. Not all such situations could be resolved so easily, however, as when a British headmaster's wife murdered her unfaithful lover in K.L. one Sunday evening in 1911 and so had to be taken to the city's jail in a blaze of embarrassing publicity, the authorities were presented with a situation which no amount of evasion or guile could conceal. They therefore made a virtue out of a necessity and self-righteously demanded the death penalty.

Valerie had briefly considered giving the authorities grounds to return *her* to Britain for some transgression or other but a strict Scottish upbringing prevented her from taking the idea very seriously. A little shoplifting in Robinson's would have almost certainly done the trick but risked a criminal conviction back in the U.K., which would have been hardly fair on her family, while she just did not have the nerve for a gesture such as a dramatic appearance at the annual Governor's Ball dressed as the day she was born and with a rose between her teeth, although it probably would have been just as effective.

She did her best to bargain with the proprietor, a solemn Chinese man who kept his eye-glass in place and his gaze firmly fixed on the jewellery the entire time he was talking to her which made her feel as if the conversation was taking place on the telephone. Surprisingly, he seemed entirely without interest in the Chinese sport of haggling, and hardly budged at all from his original valuation. She therefore received less than she hoped and, at the last moment, she took her wedding ring back although she was quite unable to explain why, even to herself. It may have been because she was upset at the value the goldsmith had put on it – he making the point several times there was no second-hand value in wedding rings – but it was more likely because of his unresponsive attitude. It could hardly have been for sentimental reasons. Later, however, she had cause to be extremely thankful for her spontaneous action, just as she was going to be for keeping her Malayan clothes, only for a different reason.

* * *

She felt some European-style irritation at the delay in the departure of the taxi from Singapore later that morning when they had to wait for one of the passengers to complete her visit to the market. That was typical of the East – three waited for one, without haste from the one or a trace of impatience from the other three – except for her. Time seemed to have no meaning for so many Malayans.

It was another long, tedious journey back to Kota Bharu and they did not arrive until after dark. Her driver's first stop was the taxi rank to see if he could find passengers for his intended return south the next day, there being a notice board nearby on which prospective travellers could register their required destinations. This was Osman territory but her ex-husband was nowhere to be seen, nor did he arrive during the time her driver chatted, seemingly endlessly, to the other taxi owners who were idling their time away until the evening trade began. His absence could have been deliberate because, although she had been in the Kelantan capital for only the briefest of time, she did not doubt she had been recognised and the intelligence flashed to him by a bush telegraph which she had discovered on other occasions was never less than extremely well-informed about the affairs, even the movements, of the expatriate community. After a wait which she endured with mounting impatience, her driver took her onto the convent orphanage which was on the outskirts of the town for, despite his long drive that day, he was obliged to deliver her to its door.

They drew up outside the orphanage well after the sun had gone down. Valerie knew she was about to place herself at the mercy of the world from which she had just been excluded because, although the convent was run by a Catholic order, it functioned within the civil system, which was dominated by the mosque. The colonial regime kept a very circumspect distance from the latter, especially here on the remoter, less-developed east coast where the influence of the British administration was less sure.

One of the reasons it was so uncertain was that during the war there had been an alarming wave of anti-British feeling in

Kelantan following Muslim Turkey's entry into the conflict on Germany's side. Such feeling had diminished somewhat in the years since and expatriates could now command most things by virtue of their money or their colonial authority, but they still had no real influence over the mosque, be it on the west coast or the east coast, and Valerie suspected that her British nationality would have no leverage in her quest for the baby if the Muslim authorities decided otherwise. Her hope was that the latter would not have to be involved at all – after all, what interest would, or should, they have in a British child in a Christian orphanage?

The gates of the orphanage were shut and looked much the same as on the night she had left the baby. The crib was in its usual place nearby and Valerie looked at it with a mixture of guilt and regret. If it had not been conveniently available would she have kept the baby? It would have made her life very difficult at the time, even perhaps impossible in the highly charged state she was in, but how much simpler now? That desperate night was still hazy in her mind and she could not recall any of the events before her journey in the taxi and certainly none of her thoughts. Some pictures came to her as in a half-remembered dream, disjointed and with no logical sequence, with just the odd one or two standing out – a bridge, running as if for her life, and for some reason, a bottle of milk. She particularly remembered the bottle of milk and pouring it away – the whiteness against the grime of the drain was as vivid an impression in her memory now as it had made at the time. Such a waste, and why on earth had she done it?

She rang the bell and the taxi driver looked questioningly at her. 'Tunggu,' she said, instead of 'wait', the Malay coming automatically despite her wish and intention to be a European. The door remained closed so Valerie rang again, more insistently, but it was still some time before it was opened and then by only a few inches, the gap being filled by the worried face of a nun. Valerie asked for the Mother Superior only to be told the convent was not open to visitors after dark. Valerie was about to say she was certainly not a visitor, but a prospective parent, when she thought better of it. It was a most peculiar time to be seeking adoption. She briefly considered making a heart-rending appeal based on the fact that she had just come all the way from Singapore, but thought better of that too. Having elicited an assurance she could see the Mother Superior in the morning, she turned away. What difference did one more night make? Hopefully, she and her son would have a lifetime to share together, but she longed to see him. This was the baby she had looked forward to with so much joy and anticipation but who, shamefully, she could not even picture in her mind despite her frequent attempts to do so.

She decided to stay at the Rest House in Kota Bharu rather than try one of the cheap Chinese hotels she had noticed near the taxi rank which did not look very inviting, in fact not so very different to the one she had used in Karang. Rest Houses were government-financed hostels for the use of visiting officials, but as they were also available to the ordinary public – when there were vacancies as the officials had precedence – they were a godsend for Britons seeking reasonable accommodation in out-of-the way parts of the country. In fact, there were no realistic alternatives in such places as European-standard hotels, generally speaking, could only be found in the main towns and holiday areas where there were enough expatriates and tourists to make them financially viable.

Now she was officially a European again, she would have to live like one, and government Rest Houses were a happy compromise for the provident traveller, offering an acceptable level of accommodation at a moderate expense. She was determined to make the most of her last few dollars for, as her mother liked to say when financial hardship threatened, they were the only things between her and the workhouse or, in her present circumstances – and in the absence of a workhouse – a desperate plea for assistance to anyone who would listen.

The money also represented a considerable sacrifice on her part as she had been more than sentimentally attached to her jewellery for all its relative lack of value, as almost every item reminded her of some aspect of her former life in Scotland, a period she was now inclined to view through that hazy gloss of memory which eliminates the unpleasant and leaves only an unrealistic glow. However, if the proceeds from its sale enabled her to reclaim the baby, the deal she had made with the goldsmith in Singapore would be beyond price. What would happen to her when her last dollar had gone, she dared not think. But then, the whole of her future did not bear thinking about – it was so uncertain and full of difficulties. But, at the present moment, the only thing she felt able to focus on was the recovery of her son. The need to achieve that objective was pushing everything else into the background and she found it almost impossible to believe that less than a week before she had not even been conscious of his existence.

* * *

The next day, with the sun barely above the treetops, Valerie was, once more, before the convent door. This time she was greeted with a smile and led through a covered way into a sunlit courtyard in the centre of which was a bed of canna lilies of quite breathtaking colour and radiance, their red and yellow flags so vivid against the shadow of the covered way behind them, that they almost demanded a painter's palette, and Valerie paused in wonder, quite overcome. The nun waited patiently for her with a smile – the lilies were their pride and joy – and then stopped by the open door of a high-ceilinged office.

There was no fan and a broad beam of sunlight streamed through the open shutters to fall across a littered desk at which sat an elderly woman in a black habit. She looked up and smiled and her face, which would have graced a woman half her age, shone with a serenity Valerie thought sublime. With the sun catching the still youthful blush on her cheeks, she seemed to have all the aura and sanctity of a religious icon. Convinced that this saintly creature must also be blessed with a god-given intuition, and so would know the exact purpose of her visit, Valerie waited for the Mother Superior to say:

'Welcome my child. I presume you have come for the little Moses you left us in the rushes. Here he is, safe and well. Take him and God be with you.'

Instead, after indicating that Valerie was to sit, she sat there, still with that beatific smile, waiting for Valerie to collect herself.

'I have come because I, we, my husband and I are hoping, are considering, I mean we would like to adopt a baby. I am told you have many orphans here. Is adoption possible?'

It was nothing like what she had intended to say. In fact it was so garbled as to be embarrassing. She had originally made up her mind to tell the truth and lay proprietorial claim to her baby, but under the gaze of the Mother Superior she changed her mind. It would have been indecent to subject the divine figure before her to such a tale of human folly and weakness as she had to tell. Even to talk of adoption seemed impertinent. How could anyone presume to take a child from the care of such an embodiment of saintliness and obvious self-sacrifice? Valerie suddenly felt ashamed of the extravagance of the cheap Singapore dress she was wearing.

'Oh yes, adoption is very possible. We are always looking for good homes for our babies. May I ask your nationality? I assume you are British?' Her accent betrayed her Irish origins. Valerie's hopes rose.

'Yes,' she said eagerly, 'I, we, are British, does that make a difference?'

'Indeed so,' said the Mother Superior, regarding Valerie intently. 'It creates difficulties.'

Valerie was dismayed. 'Difficulties? What sort of difficulties?'

'To all intents and purposes you are a foreigner here. Don't forget these babies are Malayan nationals and there is a reluctance on the part of the authorities to let their children out of the country when the time comes for you to return to Britain. There are likely to be many formalities.'

Valerie was crestfallen. She had expected some administrative difficulties, there always were in cases like these wherever you were but she had hoped there might be official relief in a Third World country that they would now have one less hungry mouth to feed. After all, the country was full of children, not all well fed, what difference would one less make, especially as he was not really theirs? The question made her thoughts turn to her more immediate preoccupation. Her son was here, maybe just the other side of that wall. She must find a way of seeing him.

'May I see around? I have never been in an orphanage before, in Britain or here.'

'Of course, would you like to go now?'

Valerie could hardly contain her impatience and stood up immediately. The Mother Superior understood her eagerness. Any prospective mother would be naturally anxious to see the children from amongst whom might come the most precious thing in her life, and to know what her feelings might be when she saw him, or her, for the first time.

She led the way into an inner courtyard where various adult women and young girls were at work washing clothes and preparing food.

'You seem to have plenty of helpers,' said Valerie.

'Hardly helpers in the sense you mean, I'm afraid. These are our girls who have never found homes. They are our orphans just like all the others. We have them all ages you see. But I expect you are thinking of a baby?'

Valerie indicated that she was. So, they had difficulty in finding parents. Surely, that should help, they must be pleased to have someone, even a European applicant, who was keen to take one off their hands? She followed the Mother Superior into what seemed to be a nursery where a large number of female helpers were supervising an even larger group of children. Valerie strained to see any fair skin amongst the assortment of browns and blacks. There was none but she did notice that a number were either mentally or physically handicapped. Then she noticed something else which, to her, was more disturbing. Every one of the children seemed to be female, there was not a male child to be seen.

'They're all girls,' she almost blurted out.

The Mother Superior looked at her keenly. 'Oh yes,' she said, 'that has always been so. Girls are not valued as highly as boys in Asian society, especially amongst the Chinese. There is the cost of their dowries and, of course, they cannot support their parents financially in their old age like the boys can and do. They are often considered expendable here. In fact, a girl born at night during one of the years of the Chinese cycle is thought to bring the whole family bad luck so can often be left for us to look after. We always have a surge of babies during that year. Still, better that we should have them than what used to happen before there were Christian orphanages to look after them, when they might be just left out on a mountainside to die.'

But Valerie was not really listening, she was thinking of the implications of the Mother Superior's first statement. If girls were unpopular, presumably it was easier to place boys and being fewer of them, there might be a waiting list. Then another thought struck her. Perhaps her son had already been promised or even given to someone else? 'Do you ever get boys?' she asked with some trepidation.

'We get very few boys. Boys are prized everywhere in the East, though we do get an occasional one when poor parents cannot cope with a large family. Plus a few who are illegitimate of course. Were you thinking of a boy?'

'Very much so,' said Valerie, her spirits sinking. 'Have you no boys at all?'

'Only one or two and they, I'm afraid, are usually handicapped in some way.'

Valerie's heart nearly stopped. Her baby handicapped? How could that be? It was true she had not really examined him properly, in fact had hardly bothered to glance at him at all, either in the village or afterwards. On the other hand, Minah had not said anything about a disability. But could that have been why the villagers had turned against him so savagely? Had he borne some blemish or deformity that marked him out and which they might have considered to be evidence that the devil had claimed him? Such attitudes were common in some societies and not unknown in hers until recently. Why had she not thought to ask Osman or Minah?

She suddenly felt sick with apprehension. Was this to be her punishment? Osman had often said there had to be a price to pay for giving in to temptation. That her son might have a physical deformity made her feel even more guilty at having abandoned him.

Then another thought struck her, which was even more disturbing. If he was handicapped might she not have the courage to accept him as her own and thus have to endure the humiliation of leaving him where he was, so adding herself to the list of those who had used the orphanage as a convenient means of avoiding one of life's most crushing burdens? She had heard it said that caring for a handicapped child was very rewarding, but whereas that might be true for those saintly women who had the inner reserves of strength needed when suddenly faced by a life-changing challenge of that magnitude, not everyone was made of such clay.

She was very unsure of herself. Could she force herself to cope with a situation like that when she knew there was no need to – when there was an institution at hand ready to relieve her of the responsibility? Perhaps now was the time she should leave the orphanage before she had to face such an agonising choice. But that would mean abandoning the child she had longed for, not to mention how she would feel about herself when she next looked in a mirror – or, for that matter, had to face her mother. Fateful words came back to her: 'You can always hope that bairns will come as a compensation in the lottery that is a married woman's life.'

But her mother had made no mention that the bairns might be handicapped and live long enough to bring heartbreaking problems.

Inevitably there would be a time when you might not either be there, or perhaps able, to look after them. All children were a risk as to how they turned out when they grew up, it was a possibility all parents had to face, but those with severe handicaps posed extra and particular worries of their own. What sort of compensation in the lottery of life was a child who could not look after itself as an adult?

They retraced their steps to the office and Valerie sat miserably in her chair, her mind in turmoil. She had come into the orphanage with such high hopes, now she felt utterly cast down. A helper came in with a fruit drink and smiled shyly at her. It was of a cheap local type, homemade probably – no Frazer & Neave soft drinks bottled in Singapore here! Although the orphanage and all its children and helpers looked clean and wholesome, it was quite obvious that money was short. A liberal donation would obviously be expected of her, adoption or no adoption, and that would be a problem in the light of her current financial situation, but how trivial was a shortage of money compared to the problem of having a son who was handicapped? Shortage of money was temporary, physical handicap permanent, as was the feeling of guilt at having brought a damaged child into the world. Paid assistance could help relieve the burden but not the worry and responsibility for a twenty-four hour commitment. Money might perform wonders for the rich but it could do little to relieve their sorrowing for a damaged child and nothing at all for the child itself.

'I'm sorry you have your heart set on a boy,' said the Mother Superior. 'I thought you might know that was the position.'

Valerie mumbled something about her husband wanting a boy. The Mother Superior had said boys were prized everywhere in the East. She had never thought of a boy being a valuable possession before. To think how cheaply and easily they came to so many people, even poor people who frequently did not want them or found them a financial burden. But a handicapped boy? It was difficult to think of a handicapped child as a possession at all. In time perhaps – when his character and personality, and therefore his welfare, became dear to you – but not now. She knew she had little to be proud of in such thoughts but the possibility that her longed-for child might not be the perfect specimen she had always assumed he would be – as every prospective parent assumed their child would be – was difficult to come to terms with at that moment.

The Mother Superior, unaware of the impact her simple statement had made upon her listener, broke into her thoughts. 'Of course, men always want a son. But there is an added problem in the case of a foreign national wishing to adopt a boy. The authorities never, or very rarely, give permission for a boy to be taken out of the country. A girl yes, but not often a boy.'

Valerie's misery was now complete. She felt like crying out: 'But he's mine. I gave him to you. Where is he? What have you done with him?' Instead, she just looked dejectedly at the serene figure opposite her.

'I can see you are very disappointed. There are other orphanages in the country you know. There are several in K.L. The question of adoption is also different depending upon the racial origin of the child. The Malay authorities would never allow one of their own out of the country but in the case of an Indian, also a Chinese, they might. There would not be the same pressure with the other races, although it would depend on the circumstances of course.'

Valerie noticed she made no mention of European, or even Eurasian babies. What a mistake she had made in trying for adoption first. It now made the truth doubly difficult. She would have liked time to think out a new approach but another thought had occurred to her. Perhaps the baby had not arrived in the orphanage at all. Maybe he had been taken from the crib before the morning. Boys were popular, she had been told that, maybe the taxi driver had alerted someone. As soon as he had seen her carrying the baby he might have had the idea of making some money for himself. But then she remembered he had not asked about her charge, had shown no interest in whether he had been boy or girl.

She must pull herself together, but her inability to discover anything of her baby's fate was shredding her nerves. She cursed her own indifference, her lack of concern in the days after she had left him. Despite being in obvious shock after the trauma of that awful evening, surely she could at least have rung the convent orphanage the morning after to make sure he had been found safely. Why on earth had it not occurred to her? Valerie could contain herself no longer. She leaned forward.

'Do you ever get any European babies, or Eurasian perhaps?' she asked.

'Ah, a European baby, now that would be something unusual wouldn't it? What European family or woman would leave their child in an Asian orphanage?' Her smile made Valerie even more certain she was omnipotent, that she could see all and knew all. Had she already suspected the truth and was reproaching her? Inviting her, in short, to condemn her own crime? But the Mother Superior went on as blithely as before, unaware of the unwitting aspersion she had cast upon her visitor, and this, in turn, covered Valerie in some private confusion. To even think this saintly being could stoop to such a stratagem, or consider anyone so base!

'And only the odd Eurasian, and not one of those for a great number of years. There was a time when they were not unusual but not in my time. That was before there were very many European wives out here.'

The Mother Superior sat back a little in her chair, almost as if she wished to take a renewed look at her visitor. Valerie was now quite certain this epitome of Christian virtue had either detected something was amiss and was waiting for her to confess, or possessed the power to see into her mind.

'There was a rumour that a European baby had been brought into your orphanage about a week ago. I had hoped I might see him this morning and, I must confess, it was him I had in mind for adoption.' She stopped.

The Mother Superior was no longer smiling. For someone who

had appeared to possess a universal benevolence, even a divine spirituality, she could look quite forbidding. It was several seconds before she replied.

'Mrs Mitchell,' she said slowly and deliberately, 'I think you have not been totally frank with me. I think you ought to tell me the whole story.'

'But cannot you at least say whether you have him or not. I must know that. Please put my mind at rest.'

At last, all was clear to the Mother Superior. She was talking to the mother of her latest charge. Compassion for the weak and needy was prominent amongst her many Christian virtues and she now felt overwhelming pity for the poor woman in front of her who, it was now becoming increasingly obvious, was yet another who had fallen victim to male selfishness and an indulgence in their physical passions – the Mother Superior had been a martyr to them ever since she had come to Malaya in search of a mission. This woman, as almost invariably happened in cases like this, had obviously been through a most harrowing experience. Though well accustomed to human misery and misfortune, she was moved by the picture of absolute wretchedness before her.

'All is well Mrs Mitchell I assure you. We *did* have a baby brought in some days ago, or I should say, left in our night-crib outside. We were uncertain of his race. We thought he might be Eurasian, it is not always obvious with newborn babies. Whatever he was, we suspected a sad story.'

Valerie was quite overcome. 'He was mine, that baby was mine,' and through her tears, she cried out: 'Where is he? What has happened to him? Is he all right?' She twisted her hands in her anguish.

'He is safe and well I promise you. A most bonny little boy.' The Mother Superior half-turned and motioned away a small group of women and girls who had collected outside, drawn by the sounds of Valerie's distress, and were hovering around the doorway. 'Now tell me how you came to leave him with us.'

Valerie told her story as best she could. It was not how she had rehearsed it when she had considered this course of action in the taxi the previous day. She lost her thread and restarted sentences, thinking to omit certain things and then realising she was not making sense and having to go back and explain them. She tried to avoid the more unseemly parts, not to save her own feelings, but those of her listener, who surely cannot have heard such a sordid tale before.

Valerie was surprised how shallow her conduct sounded especially when it was reduced to the bare facts and then looked at in hindsight after events had betrayed them. It was even worse when she attempted to justify what she had done, especially in this bright and normal office and before this positive personification of purity. At one stage the Mother Superior fingered her crucifix as if she was summoning protection against the evil spirits which might have been alerted by this tale of wickedness and be lurking expectantly, in the dark corners of the room, awaiting their chance. How dreadful this litany of unbridled behaviour must be sounding to a woman who had clearly never experienced a feeling in which she could not rejoice, or felt an urge which she could not immediately control. At last, Valerie stumbled to the end.

'Can I see him?' she implored.

The Mother Superior went to the door and issued instructions in rapid Malay. There was a minute while Valerie tried to stop herself crying and the Mother Superior chose to concern herself with something in the covered way outside. Then a bundle was borne into the room and placed gently in her arms. A head protruded above a worn shawl and a tiny face stared sleepily at her. Valerie was quite overcome, certainly too overcome to see if he did indeed possess all his fingers and toes or consciously note if his appearance suggested a suitable name when she held him for the first time.

To think she had abandoned this delightful bundle or, far, far worse, contemplated doing away with it. Had she really considered doing such a thing? Could she have actually done it if the moment had arrived? There was a partial lifting in the swirling mists which always seemed to be surrounding her memories of that night. Ceaseless crying, fleeting images of crowded streets and her just running and running, as if her life depended on it, rose up in her mind as if to accuse her. Would she ever be able to forgive herself for what she had done, or worse, what she might have done, during those terrible hours after she had been handed her own child?

'Is he all right?' she asked at length. 'I mean does he have anything wrong with him?'

'He is fine,' said the Mother Superior. 'Eats well and lets you know in no uncertain terms if he thinks you are late with his food. It is his feeding time now, incidentally,' and she motioned to the girl to remove him. Valerie's heart was so full and her relief at the discovery that he was safe and sound so overwhelming that she failed to comprehend fully that that her right of ownership had been far from established.

'Can I have him?' and then, when she saw the look on the Mother Superior's face, 'Don't you believe my story?'

Of course I believe you Mrs Mitchell. I am sure no one could have made up such a story as you have just told me. But I'm afraid I cannot let you take him away just like that. I have to get the approval of my superiors and then there is the question of the father's wishes. Are we sure who is the father?'

Only the Mother Superior could have asked the question without it sounding like a moral aspersion, or making its recipient feel a deep tremor of shame.

'My husband of course.'

'But which husband?'

Valerie was momentarily confused. 'My British husband of …'

The sentence was left unfinished as Valerie realised what questions were bound to follow. Was Stuart still her husband? Would he acknowledge it was his baby? She had no idea what Stuart had done in the last six months since she had last had contact with him, apart from the report that he had contracted malaria.

She had assumed he had taken the obvious step and dissolved the marriage. How would that affect the custody issue? Might there be a legal battle to decide custody, in which case how would her claim be affected by her abandoning him? But it appeared as though the Mother Superior, by some divine ability, had been able to follow the train of her thoughts, and having seen that Valerie was beginning to realise all the implications of her uncertain marital status, had decided to proceed to a matter which she regarded as more important.

'Does he know?' she asked.

Valerie had to admit that he did not.

'His views will have to be sought,' said the Mother Superior. 'He has rights in this matter although, I greatly fear, he may first have to establish his paternity. In the eyes of the Muslim law under which you placed yourself when you went through with your Malay marriage, the child will probably be regarded as being your Malay husband's.'

'We are divorced,' said Valerie.

'Are you sure of that? In any case it will not affect the rights of the father over his son.'

'But it isn't his son. He wanted nothing to do with it. That is why he turned me out.'

'I'm afraid that is something else we shall have to establish. You have to admit, Mrs Mitchell, it is a very tangled story and an even more tangled situation. There seems to be an awful lot which needs to be sorted out before custody can be decided.'

The Mother Superior indicated she had devoted as much time as she could spare on this particular problem and hoped that Valerie would excuse her. She consoled her, however, by an assurance that she could see the baby whenever she liked and delivered the statement with another of the smiles that had so unnerved Valerie when she arrived. No one who witnessed them could ever doubt she was about God's business.

* * *

There seemed nothing for Valerie to do except return to the Rest House. She lay on her bed in the stifling heat of the afternoon listening to the clamour of a heavy storm on the roof. The rain mirrored her spirits. What had appeared relatively simple before this morning was now very complicated indeed. As she saw it, she had given birth to a baby. She had loaned him to an orphanage. Now she wanted him back. Osman certainly did not want him and Stuart had been indifferent when there had been the possibility he could become a father on earlier occasions, so he would definitely not want a child born at a time when she was another man's wife. Yet she was desperate for him.

The solution seemed perfectly simple to her. Instead, there was all this talk of nationality, establishing paternity, divorce, who was married to whom, and that was before the problems of dealing with the Malay authorities. It was going to be both long-winded and expensive, the last things she needed or could afford. Why could the orphanage not just hand him back as if the last week had never happened? Surely the child's paternity was her problem, not theirs?

She went down to dinner. She was the only one in the dining room. Afterwards she sat in the sitting room with her coffee. Rest Houses were popular with Europeans as they were so cheap, but, if they were not located in a holiday area, they were often left empty for long periods while they waited for the visit of the next government official. The rooms became fusty, the staff lazy and uncaring. When there was only a solitary guest in residence, as in her case, they had a particularly depressing air.

On a sudden impulse, Valerie went up to her room, took her Malay clothes from the bottom of her suitcase, put them on and slipped out into the darkness. She not only wanted to clear her mind but her interview with the Mother Superior that morning had given her another reason.

She had a lengthy walk into the town centre. The heavy storm that afternoon had left the road strewn with leaves and small branches. She skirted several large puddles and, as she stepped sideways round one, she collided with a venerable Chinese on a bicycle. He laughed and said something in Malay, which she did not catch. He had no idea he was talking to a white woman. It had been so easy to slip from one racial identity into another. It was not just the change of clothes or the discarding of her high heels. She found she had immediately adopted the typical Malay stroll in which the knee straightened at the beginning of each stride. It had been an automatic reflex as she had come down the steps of the Rest House. A brisk European pace was inappropriate in the heat and humidity of the tropics, but in any case, time had little meaning here and so undue haste, except in an emergency, was pointless. Indeed, unnecessary exertion of any kind attracted only scorn. As the Malay proverb went: *Bergalah ke hilir, tertawa buaya* – 'pole downstream and the crocodiles laugh'.

As she had slowed to a stroll she found her thoughts slowing too, as if her whole being was adjusting to the more tranquil ethos of the East and already she felt some of the tensions created by her visit that morning draining away. It was the same with the irritations of the previous day, they now seemed quite absurd. She had chafed to get to the orphanage although common sense should have told her that she could not possibly arrive until after dark when it would be closed. The others in the taxi with whom she had shared her frustrations had simply smiled their 'what will be, will be' smiles and looked at her as a mother might an impatient child. The Malays were the same when it came to the material things of life. They looked down on wealth and the ostentation it encouraged, making Westerners look down on them because of it. Yet, as she had seen, it was the Muslim who was living at peace with the world, the Christian fretting because he could not wait to change it. Who was the happier? Who was more attune with this life or preparing himself the better for the one to come?

She had seen the two societies, Muslim and Christian, at first hand and felt the attractions of both – simplicity and acceptance in the one, progress and aspiration in the other, but at that moment the pull of the former was proving almost irresistible. This was not the first time the act of wrapping a sarong around herself and pulling on a *baju* had enabled her to feel the spirituality of the East and so it was no surprise to her that, at that moment, she felt a longing for her former *kampung* home – indeed, to her surprise she found she was actually feeling homesick for Batu Lima. Before she had even reached the centre of the town, in her mind she was walking back from the river on one of those bright sunlit mornings for which the Malayan climate was noted, her washing piled high in a basket on her head, laughing with the village women, a contented, native wife. After her frustrations in the taxi the day before when she had felt such impatience with Malayan attitudes she was beginning to feel there must be two different sides to her character or perhaps she had a split personality. If so, she was being left in no doubt as to which one was in possession of her at that moment.

The chief reason for her choosing to go for a walk that evening had been the hope of seeing Osman although she realised that the likelihood of an encounter on the off-chance was remote. Whenever she was in Kota Bharu she got the feeling she was being watched by dozens of pairs of eyes as if she was Alice in the enchanted wood of Wonderland. Could it be that, once again, despite the darkness, she had been recognised and Osman warned?

Nevertheless she made her way to the taxi rank near the market and, despite herself, felt more than just a tremor of excitement. Just to be near where she knew Osman might be was enough to rekindle her old feelings. Although she had easily reassumed the European way of life she knew she would just as easily give it up again if Osman would have her back. But, of course, she knew he would never accept the baby and she would never consider giving the baby up, assuming she was eventually given custody of course. It was amazing how abruptly the priorities in her life had changed. The recovery of her child was now her one ambition. It meant everything to her, and she was prepared to make any sacrifice to achieve it. Holding him that morning, brief though their contact had been, had been a defining moment for her. In the short space of a week, the baby and his future had gone from being almost the most inconsequential thing in her life to the one she would give almost anything for.

Osman's taxi was nowhere in evidence and Valerie sat at a nearby café table and waited. No one bothered with her apart from a dog with a hairless rump, which gave a cursory sniff at her sandals before wandering off. With a composure born of her new-found purpose in life, she was happy to wait – Osman had to return to the taxi rank at some time or another.

A group of Chinese youths, laughing and bantering with each other, came and sat at an adjoining table and the proprietor emerged to greet them. He obviously knew them and joined in their chatter. Valerie did not understand their dialect but every so often there was a phrase of Malay thrown in from which she learned that one of the young men was shortly to be married. The proprietor went to the back of the café and swiftly reappeared with a tray of dishes containing a variety of sauces and condiments. He quickly and deftly distributed them around the table and, still laughing and speaking volubly, retired again to prepare their meal. He had not glanced in her direction. He seemed to assume a solitary Malay woman would not be a customer. Or had he recognised her too?

At that moment Valerie became aware of a taxi drawing up and a familiar figure getting out of it. He also, apparently, knew the party and came up to talk to them. As he did so his eyes strayed in her direction and he stopped. Valerie got up and without a word, went to the taxi, got in and closed the door. Osman followed and, without giving her as much as a glance, got into the driver's seat. He neither turned round nor spoke before starting the engine and driving swiftly down a turning. He was obviously disturbed at her presence and he did not speak until they reached a quieter area. He left the engine running.

In a voice full of tension, he said, 'Mem, what are you doing here?'

'Osman, I had to see you again ...'

'It is finished Mem, it is all over. You should not have come.'

'Osman please. Listen to me. I have not come to cause you any trouble. I have made enough as it is, I know that, and you have no idea how miserable it makes me.'

Osman had still not looked at her apart from a furtive glance in the mirror. Now he turned and Valerie could see how upset he was. Even during their worst days in Batu Lima he had never looked like this. Of former pleasure and respect there was not the smallest sign, and the cheerful countenance on which she had once so much depended was now creased in a combination of resentment and anxiety. She had not thought her reappearance would be welcome, but she had not expected a reaction quite like this. Anyone unacquainted with them or their past might have thought it one born of enmity.

How she longed for a flash of the old Osman – one of his usual greetings, perhaps, after he had brought the car round to the bungalow in the morning and before he asked her what her plans were for the day. His arrival then had made the prospect of even an ordinary day seem exciting, his company enough to give the most commonplace a magic of its own, while the dreariest activity had become a pleasure when he had been there to share it. It was what had convinced her she was in love with him. What would she not give now for just one of those infectious grins, and what would she not sacrifice for the chance to return, even for an hour, to the blissful, carefree days following that unforgettable afternoon among the rubber trees? But all she received was a rough reply.

'We must not be seen here. It isn't right,' he said.

'Osman, I am your wife.'

'No, Mem. You forget. I divorced you, you are no longer my wife. Talak. Talak. Talak.' and Osman repeated the Malay words which signified their separation as if to reassure himself, and to emphasise to Valerie the degree of finality he felt. Despite her good intentions she felt her eyes smarten.

'Please, Osman. Don't make me cry. I loved you so much.'

He stared at her in the rear mirror. How often, in the past, had her tears moved him, moved him to sympathy and much more. He remembered the day in the car among the rubber trees. It had been her calls on his compassion then which had brought about his downfall. But he was determined that things were going to be different now. For the first time since he had known her, he had made up his mind to put his feelings into words. For too long he had allowed himself to be carried along by her wishes and by her needs and had ignored his own, and it had been this weakness on his part which had been the root of all their trouble. He just could not let her ruin everything again. There were signs that things were at last returning to normal in the *kampung*, he was making a reasonable living from his taxi, he was getting on his feet again. Even the talk of witchcraft was diminishing. If she had come tonight hoping to persuade him to have her back she was about to be swiftly disillusioned. The time had come for him to put his foot down.

But when he spoke his feelings got in the way of his words. Instead of a reasonable explanation of why she was unable to come back to live in the village again, there was just a jumble of accusations.

'You say you loved me but good wives love their husbands, not other women's husbands,' he said heatedly. 'We shouldn't have done what we did, Mem, and in *Tuan's* house. It was 'jahat', it was wrong, it was evil.' In his agitation the odd Malay word welled up before the English. 'You should not have come to my kampung. You angered the *hantu*, the spirits, and they are still angry. Today my friends still do not speak to me, my mother is unhappy and Minah is alone in the village, all because of you.'

He was exaggerating but it was better he let his former wife know there was no question of her coming back to the village. 'I helped you when you wanted help but what did you do for me? You brought me shame, do you know that? You should not have come to my house, Mem, and when you did ...' his voice faltered as he sought the English words, 'and when you did, you brought *Tuan's* baby. Do you know what the other men are saying in the *kampung*?'

He stopped. He had suddenly realised that he could never actually repeat what the men in the village were saying about her, not to any woman, and certainly not to the one who was the object of their ribaldry and spite. To his relief, she did not ask. In fact, she failed to make any sort of reply at all, she just seemed to disintegrate behind him.

Valerie had bowed her head and buried her face in her hands. It was as if each word was a blow beating her down. She knew Osman had every reason to be bitter but she had hoped it would never have to be spelt out, and particularly not by him. He had suffered, it was true, but it could have turned out so differently if only the fates had been kinder. If the baby had been his, then their love affair would have been seen as two people bold and brave enough to defy the conventions of their two communities in order to be together. How often had cinema audiences, in the East as well as the West, thrilled to such a story? But instead of a Hollywood happy ending, there was only this ugly wrangle. Life was so unfair, just one small thing and everything had been turned upside down and good had been, literally, turned into evil.

She raised her face from her hands and rested her head against the back of the seat and closed her eyes. It was as if the world at that moment was too difficult to bear. 'We just did not have a chance,' she said. 'We were so unlucky.'

The remark did nothing to appease Osman. 'There is no such thing as luck,' he said angrily. That was one of the white man's silliest explanations. They were always going on about bad luck and good luck as though fate was a straw in the wind waiting to be picked up by whoever came along. The future was *Allah's*. What was to come in this world was in his hands. If Allah was merciful, life was good. If he chose not to show his mercy, then life could be hard. But it was Allah's will. It was not bad luck.

'That's not true. It could just as easily have been your baby.'

Osman was outraged. 'It was *Tuan's* baby because that was what Allah willed, because that was what was right,' and he raised his voice.

Valerie was quite alarmed, she had never seen him like this before. Her sweet, gentle Osman looked anything but sweet and gentle at that moment. And every bit of his unhappiness had been of her doing. It was like a knife twisting inside her, magnifying her guilt.

'But if he had been yours, we would have been happy. I would have made you happy.'

'We would never have been happy. We did not deserve to be happy. How could we expect to be happy after what we did? You say you loved me and yet you brought me *nasib celaka*, misfortune,' he said heatedly. 'What we did in *Tuan's* house was wrong and you coming to my house was wrong. What happened after that was bound to happen. And Mem, what I did, you made me do.'

'I know it must seem to you as though I set out to make you do wrong but it was not like that at all. I loved you and you cannot control love. I did not have any idea how bad it would be for you when I came to your house. You never said a word to me about how difficult my presence would be for you in the village. I had no warning. Nor did I know the baby was Stuart's. Do you think I would have come had I known? You must believe that. And you must believe I loved you, loved you with all my heart. How can love be wrong?'

'Yes, Mem, love can be wrong if it makes you do wrong things. We had duties, both of us, me to my family and you to yours. If we had remembered them Allah might not have punished us. Instead, your love made us forget those duties, and that was where love is wrong."

It was a second or two before she could answer. 'I thought you loved me too.'

'It was the love that a man has for any woman, it was not the love a man has for just one woman,' he said bitterly. 'And it made me forget I had a duty to you as my Mem, and also to *Tuan*, and that was very bad. You both had been good to me and I tried to remember my duty to you in the car that afternoon on the estate. And what about your duty to me? A mem should not have done what you did to me. Did you try to resist the devil, Mem? I tried, but I was not strong enough, but it was you who made me weak.' His anger and despair seemed to fill the car.

There was a silence between them broken by only a half-word from Valerie as she attempted another answer but which she then thought better of and left unsaid. The time for words had passed, words seemed only to make things worse. Those happy days on Bukit Bintang when Osman had been so full of life and she had first realised she was in love with him seemed so very far away. She knew when she had discovered she was pregnant there would be problems but never did she think things would turn out like this. She had lost everything – her position in colonial society, the respect of friends, perhaps also that of her family at home. She had also lost Osman, and it looked as though she might even lose the baby. If it was all her fault as Osman claimed, she had certainly been punished for it.

She could not deny she had been selfish as well as foolish, justifying her actions all the time by the belief that she loved him. And she *had* loved him, loved him with all her heart, still did, but this should have told her that what she was doing was the worst thing possible for him. She should have let him go back to his life in the village without her when she knew she was pregnant. At least one of them might then have found some happiness, which was what he deserved, deserved so much more than she had any right to hope or expect for herself.

She had many things to reproach herself for, but perhaps the most serious and obvious had been allowing herself to become pregnant. That monumental piece of thoughtlessness or carelessness whichever it was – it certainly had not been any dark plan on her part – had been the catalyst for everything that had followed. Deciding Osman was the father had been both reasonable and understandable, but her logic in assuming that what was then the best solution for them all, including Stuart, was to be together in Batu Lima, was neither.

She had deceived herself. It would have been far more sensible for her to have returned to Scotland and faced the consequences of her condition, although this was perhaps with the benefit of hindsight. Thus her wrong decision to follow the dictates of her heart had compounded her failure to ensure Osman was taking precautions, and thereafter all of them – including of course the baby – had been caught up in a remorseless chain of events. From the moment she had made the decision to go and live in Batu Lima their fate had all the inevitability of a Greek tragedy.

Her thoughts brought her back to the reason she had come into Kota Bharu that evening – to try to enlist Osman's help in persuading the Mother Superior to release the baby. She had no worries that he would want him back – whatever the Malay authorities might think – the last thing he would want would be to see the cause of all his misfortune back in his house in the village even if the whole of officialdom were to regard him as a Malay, and if he could only say as much to the Mother Superior that might at least be one hurdle surmounted. She would have to be careful, however, as she had never seen Osman in such a volatile mood. She wanted to avoid the pain of another outburst if she possibly could.

'I know now that we must never see each other again and I promise that I shall leave Malaya forever very soon and so leave you in peace, but there is one thing I must do before I go and that is get my baby back from the orphanage. At the present moment the orphanage will not let me have him. Under Muslim law the baby is yours, they say he is Malay, and I need you to state that you are not the father and that you do not want him. All you have to do is say that he is not your baby and that he is not a Malay.'

Osman swung round to look at her again and for the first time she heard the words she had said to herself so many times since she had been brought back to reality in Singapore when Milburn asked her if she had any children. 'Why did you put your baby in the orphanage, Mem, your own baby? I could not believe that when I heard it. The baby you had always said you wanted so badly and which you talked about so much. Why did you do it? No one in my kampung would have done such a thing. How many Malay babies did you see in the orphanage? Tell me that.'

'Osman, I wasn't well. You turned me out of the village. There was all that talk of my being a witch. I didn't know what I was doing. When you and Minah left me that night did you not realise the state I was in? I had to take him to the orphanage, I just could not think of anything else to do. But I did not expect the orphanage to say he was a Malay when I went back for him, and that he was yours and I could not have him unless you agreed.'

But Osman had stopped listening or, if he was, he had not understood what she was saying. She could see the confusion and the desperation in his eyes. Clearly he was near breaking point. What was Mem saying, that the baby was Malay? That the baby was his? Were they saying he had to have the baby back? That would be worse than having Mem back. There was no knowing what would happen if he took the baby back to the *kampung*. He was seized with panic.

'The baby isn't mine. We both know that. I want nothing more to do with the baby.' His voice suddenly rose to an unnatural pitch. 'And I want nothing more to do with you.'

In his agitation he forgot the engine was running. He got out of the car with the starting handle in his hand, but, as he tried to use it, the revolving engine jerked it from his hand and into the air, hitting him on the forearm before clattering to the ground. Valerie got out of the car in alarm but he pushed past her, his face a picture of pain and anger, and before she realised what he was doing, he was back behind the wheel. She tried to follow him but he slammed the car door.

'Osman, listen to me. We both know what you say is true but under Muslim law I cannot take the baby. They won't let me have him unless you say he isn't yours and you give him up.'

But Osman was past listening. It was too late for reason. He let the clutch in and began to reverse the car. Valerie grabbed the door handle and was pulled across the road, stumbling as she did so. She made one, last, desperate plea.

'Osman, listen please. Don't let us part like this. I need you to say the baby isn't yours. You must do that or we will never be free.'

But she was talking to thin air. He had let the clutch in again and Valerie was left standing in the middle of the road as the taxi disappeared behind the clutter of a roadside stall. Under the curious gaze of a couple of late-night diners, she wept, not just tears of frustration at the failure of her objective that evening, but tears of sorrow that their final parting had been so full of rancour. It was, quite obviously, the last time she would see the man with whom she had hoped to spend the rest of her life.

Her Malayan affair had ended in heartbreak as, indeed, had so many affairs of the heart since the world began, including some with fewer obstacles to overcome than she had faced. As was not unusual when love affairs ended, harsh words had taken the place of endearments, accusations exchanged instead of promises, passion been turned to anger and dislike, or worse. Where feelings are involved these extremes are never far apart.

Unfortunately, women in love cannot always see that whereas the emotion spells fulfilment for them, it does not always do the same for men, even men brought up in the Western traditions of romantic love, and Osman was a whole world away from being that. In her innermost heart she had known, or should have known, that marriage to him could not have been as she would have wished, that too many compromises would have had to be made, but like many women before her, she had thought her love would be enough for them both and would make up for the things she must have known the union would lack – the approval of his family and friends, the compatibility of their religions and their cultures, not to mention common interests, education and social background.

Above all, she should have realised that just as men from her own country cannot always comprehend the demands love makes on them or live up to the expectations women have of it, still less, then, might one from an Eastern culture to whom the idea of romance as a basis for marriage was not only unfamiliar and baffling, but alien. Valerie should have foreseen the consequences of trying to make a life with a man from such a different world as Osman's. There were just too many obstacles. Her Malayan affair was bound to have ended in tears, and inevitably, her tears. Love, not for the first time, had made a woman see only what she wanted to see.

She wandered along the five-foot way, conscious but uncaring she was the object of every curious pair of eyes she passed. That her precious memories of Osman would now be seen through a prism of bitterness was bad enough, and his refusal to help her get the baby back promised further problems in the future, but what was more heart-breaking than either was the realisation that despite what had just happened, and despite how he now clearly felt about her and what their marriage had meant to him, her feelings were as deep as ever.

* * *

Valerie found herself back in the market place which, having been cleared of traders, was now crowded with eating stalls of all descriptions. The scene was a Malaya in miniature and despite her unhappiness, she could not help lingering, drawn by its vitality and almost infinite variety. Gradually she found it beginning to exert the same magic as it had when she had wandered into one while strolling with Stuart the day they had landed in Singapore all those years ago. The *pasar malams,* the night markets, were famous throughout the East and tourists found the cocktail of the three races, Malay, Chinese and Indian, together with their respective cuisines, almost irresistible.

Nearly every stall was a handcart as comprehensively equipped as a café – a charcoal cooker, piles of rice-patterned dishes and spoons, condiments and sauces, glass containers of coloured drinks, mounds of local vegetables, meats and noodles waiting to be cooked, tins of splintered ice and cooking oil, in fact everything an oriental restaurateur might need. There was even a rack of stools for the customers to sit on and a can of hot water simmering to wash the dirty dishes. It was café and kitchen, scullery and larder all in one, a masterpiece of ingenious improvisation which could provide a tasty meal for any of its customers in just a few minutes and for as trifling a sum as twenty cents.

However, the two main races, Chinese and Malay, each tended to patronise their own, due to major differences in their feelings about the pig, a culinary delicacy to one, religious anathema to the other. It was the same with the satay, so beloved of visitors from the West. The vendors, crouching over their smoking burners, were basting their skewers of meat with an oil which, as it dripped into the sizzling charcoal, was sending its odours into every corner of the market, rendering any advertisement for their wares superfluous, but the Hindus would not touch the beef and the Malays, of course, the pork.

The Chinese, on the other hand, were willing to eat just about anything, be it furred, fish or fowl, and cared little whether it crept or crawled, slithered or flew, swam in the sea or swung in the trees, and were quite indifferent to it being cooked, cured, pickled or preserved, or if taste and circumstances so required – it was served to them raw. As a Chinese once gleefully said to her: 'We eat everything on four legs except the table we eat it from.' Their catholic tastes sprang from the periodic famines they had endured during many long millennia of peasant life in China.

Valerie's bruised feelings were beginning to ache a little less and her crushed spirits showing signs of returning to normal, and she now rather regretted dining in the Rest House. She would have enjoyed letting her nose choose her meal and then merging with the other diners in the market, as she was not only familiar with all the foods but knew how to consume them like a local, handling chopsticks as if to the manner born. And did she also not know how to bargain with the vendors as if she had been one of them? She knew the rates they could not accept if they were to earn a living and what was a reasonable return for their labour, and they knew she knew, despite her nationality. She did not have to shrug and pretend to go elsewhere. She surveyed the busy scene and felt at one with it. How ironic, then, that her association with it was coming to an end, as the scene with Osman had shown only too well.

By the time she had walked back to the Rest House the unhappiness of the evening was beginning to fade into just another bad memory. Her meeting with Osman had been upsetting, it was true, but really, it had not changed anything, nor had she learned anything she had not already known. She had not seriously thought that whatever Osman was prepared to say to the Mother Superior or the authorities would have made any significant difference to the situation with the baby. She sensed a lot more than just his paternity was going to be involved in the course of her attempt to get him back and that the orphanage was going to be a lot more difficult to deal with than she had originally thought.

She could see it was at the mercy of a religious council more than happy to make use of the nuns' devotion to their cause but less happy to make any reciprocal gesture of its own. The very presence of Christian charities in their land was a condemnation of their Muslim society, the success they achieved proof of the effectiveness of a faith Muslims despised. Religious pride and obligation, therefore, were inextricably bound up in her quest and, as she had discovered before and seemed about to discover again, obligation breeds its own special brand of ingratitude.

It was becoming increasingly certain that any chance of success Valerie might be able to achieve with the Malayan authorities would almost certainly depend on what pressure she could persuade the British Administration to place on them. The colonial administration in Singapore could not, or would not, help her as she had discovered to her disappointment, but she was much more hopeful about the similar one in Malaya, as she and her problem must surely be one they saw as their responsibility. How could they ignore the fate of her baby, a British baby? It seemed totally absurd that the British Administration in a British territory could sit back and see a British woman deprived of her own child by the capricious will of a subject people. But whatever her countrymen were or were not prepared to do for her, of one thing she was certain – the Administration was her last hope.

Her walk had awakened many regrets and, she was forced to admit, had had a fruitless outcome, but there was no point in dwelling on it. At least she had achieved one thing – she knew exactly what her next step must be if she was going to find a way through the tangled web in which she found herself.

PART SIX

THE ADMINISTRATION

The next day, Valerie became a European once more and used the train to get to Kuala Lumpur, although to her surprise, she discovered there was no direct line to the Malayan capital from the east coast except by going far north into Thailand as far as Haadyai and thence to Penang, or alternatively by a long detour to the south, both routes taking the best part of two days. Either would further deplete her reserve of Straits dollars, and she opted for the northern route, possibly because she suddenly realised that though she had lived for ten years only a few miles from the Thai border she had never so much as set eyes on it, let alone cross it. But when the time came, she discovered that the Thai jungle was much the same as Malaya's, although she was interested to see that the Thai locomotives ran on wood instead of coal, great piles of logs that had obviously been cut straight out of the forest bordering the track.

The Malayan railway system, however, was more conventionally fuelled. Built by the British and used mainly by them, although not to the exclusion of the other races, they had to cater for so few passengers that there were only two trains a day running between Penang and Singapore, but this leisurely timetable gave Valerie some necessary time to herself. She needed to think like a European again so that she might better withstand the condescension and, possibly, the hectoring treatment she thought might be in store for her at the hands of her compatriots. Dressing like a Malay made her too often think like one and if this then led to her behaving like one as well, it would make her too docile and subservient when faced by the lofty attitude and superior manner of the typical colonial administrator.

Kuala Lumpur was the home of the British High Commission which, though subordinate to the Colonial Secretariat in Singapore, was the nerve centre of British Malaya north of the Johore Causeway which was the land bridge joining Singapore to the rest of the Peninsula. The precise nature of Britain's rule of the country was far from straightforward, however, as the haphazard and piecemeal way in which her possessions in this part of the world had been acquired had resulted in some distinct variations in the way they were governed.

Britain's imperial presence began in the eighteenth century with the establishment of the colony of the Straits Settlements, which comprised Singapore and two of the eleven Malayan states, namely Penang and Malacca. Colonies were expensive to govern and so, when there was the opportunity to acquire a further four states in the centre of the Peninsula during the last quarter of the nineteenth century, they were made protected territories. Protectorates were much cheaper to run as the burden and much of the expense of government was left to the local rulers – under supervision from Britain of course – but the four Federated Malay States, as they came to be called, prospered. As a result, when four further states in the north of the country, including Kelantan, came within the sphere of British influence in 1909, they were also given the status of protected territories, the task of overseeing them on behalf of the Crown being entrusted to an official known as a British Adviser.

Meanwhile, the most southerly state, Johore, had somehow managed to attach itself to this expanding area of pink, although no one seemed to know exactly how or why. The result was a mishmash of the first order especially as each territory, apart from those in the Straits Settlements, also had an independent Malay ruler allied to the British Crown by treaty. To the outsider, it was quite unfathomable, a typical and devious confection of 'perfidious Albion' – as the world, including her rivals in the scramble for empire liked to refer to Britain. Very few of the expatriates in Malaya could understand or explain it, least of all Valerie.

In particular, she had never fully understood why the British Crown's chief representative in the protected states of Malaya was a High Commissioner and not a Governor General as in Singapore. However, whatever they were called, they both represented British authority as far as she was concerned and she hoped a British baby in a Malayan orphanage would be of more concern to the former than her penniless state in Singapore had been to the latter. Her attempt to persuade the Secretariat to provide her with the means of getting home had come to nothing, although that had been partly her fault, but her present request was very different. Surely, officialdom in K.L. would see her plight as a matter affecting imperial prestige?

The High Commissioner who resided in an imposing dwelling called Carcosa set symbolically high on a bluff overlooking the European quarter, was there to look after British interests after all, despite the fact, in this case, they only came in the modest shape of a three week old baby. But more importantly, no public money would be at stake. Nothing was better calculated to bring out the worst in a British official abroad, or perhaps anywhere, than when he had to draft a memo to his Treasury authorising a grant from public funds. The dreaded concept of precedence always seemed to get in the way and prove insurmountable. She phoned from the Rest House and was given an appointment for the following afternoon.

*   *   *

Kuala Lumpur itself was a relatively undistinguished city and it had an even less distinguished past. Only seventy years before, it had been a jumbled collection of *atap* houses straggling around the confluence of two rivers, the Gombak and the Klang. Both had regularly flooded when the monsoon rains came each December so that the surrounding countryside was little more than a swamp until the site was drained by the British after they chose it to be the capital of the state of Selangor. In 1886, twenty or so miles of railway were hacked through the jungle to link it to the coast, the elderly Sultan being invited to ride in one of the coaches on the inaugural train, pronouncing it to be the best bullock cart in which it had ever been his good fortune to ride.

A township quickly developed as the local Chinese tin miners, who until then had spent most of their time bickering amongst themselves, were prodded into concerted action by a redoubtable new Capitan China – leader of the Chinese community – called Yap Ah Loy, who set them to build a sprawling mass of shophouses of local brick and tile. But the biggest boost to K.L.'s development had come when it was chosen in the 1890s as the capital of the newly formed Federated Malay States comprised of the first set of four states to be made protectorates, and an even brisker building boom ensued. Much of the old centre was cleared away and a new administrative complex, complete with post office and railway offices, was erected in a style of architecture imported from the Middle East described at the time as 'mock-Moorish'.

Curiously, this was by no means in keeping with what was being built elsewhere in the country but it created what the colonial authorities hoped was a suitably Muslim ambience for their prestigious new showpiece situated at the heart of their Malayan possessions. With its onion domes, pointed arches and white stucco it made an impressive back-drop to what quickly became a modern bustling city with a population growing steadily with each passing year. Under the guiding hand of an enterprising town council, curiously called the Sanitary Board, an airport was added together with an impressive new railway station, and these helped to make K.L. the second city of the peninsula by the 1930s. Only Singapore could surpass it in the grandeur of its administrative buildings or the range of commercial opportunities it was offering a growing number of business enterprises from the West. Already, however, there were signs of the teeming traffic and the polluted air that were later to make its streets a misery to walk in.

* * *

The Secretary who received Valerie in the High Commission was a large man with a moon-like face who perspired immoderately and was forced to mop himself endlessly with a large handkerchief. To Valerie he made a striking contrast to the senior man in Singapore who had been one of those fleshless men who never seemed to perspire at all. She waited patiently while, somewhat glumly, he leafed through the file in front of him. It was surprisingly fat in view of its short life, but what was worse to his weary and cynical eye, was that it showed promise of becoming even fatter in the immediate future.

He remembered the case well as he had had to deal with it, had initiated the buff file in fact and, as a result, his spidery handwriting adorned the front. He had been forewarned by the British Adviser in Kelantan of the impending scandal, and it had then fallen to him to brief his exasperated colleague in the north of what their official policy towards the problem should be preparatory to him conducting his painful interview with the deserted husband soon after his wife had left him. He recalled the amusement he had felt at the B.A.'s obvious discomfiture at what lay before him. The affair of the planter's wife running off with her *syce* had been a burning topic in the High Commission and his Club, and indeed his own household at the time, and had even occupied several discreet paragraphs in the Straits Times before the editor had been advised it was better to let the matter drop. He found the cuttings in the file, together with the original memo he had received from the High Commissioner when the scandal broke.

He gave a quick glance at the notes added by the colleagues he had consulted regarding precedents, one of which included a summary of the unfortunate case involving a secretary's wife and the American consul back in '05. No one in the High Commission wanted reminding of that! He noticed the letter from the British Adviser in Kelantan complaining about having to do what he considered to be the task of the High Commission, and so causing him to neglect his own responsibilities, which he seemed to think should be confined to looking after Britain's relations with the Sultan. He had decided the letter did not merit a reply, partly because it had also contained a rather impudent reminder of *their* own duties, but also because it really was only yet another complaint about him having to give up his valuable time to deal with the personal affairs of his fellow expatriates, his distaste for which was well known to the High Commission and the source of some wry humour therein.

There was also a copy of another letter, this time to the chairman of the planter's parent company, United Estates, whose reply had irritated the High Commissioner as it showed the Company had decided more or less to wash its hands of the whole affair – saw no reason why it should involve itself in any expenses on behalf of its employee's wife it seemed – presumably because, he assumed, it intended to write Mrs Mitchell out of its records and into oblivion. This course of action was obviously more for the sake of its own reputation than that of its employee or the Commission, and the H.C. had taken a very dim view of it. In his opinion some of these commercial firms were inclined to distance themselves from matters like these far too quickly. In fact, when it suited them they could be most uncooperative, taking a head-in-the-sand attitude towards the problems of running an empire – keen to have a well-governed and peaceful country in order to maximise their profits, but failing to do their bit to keep the flag waving when the need arose.

He took his handkerchief out of his pocket and began to pass it from hand to hand. He had long been noted for the habit. It kept his palms dry, and when they were dry he felt just that degree or two cooler. It also helped him to think. Every so often he deftly folded the white square of cotton bearing his monogrammed initials in royal blue, one of a dozen of which had been a birthday gift from his wife, and which, that very morning, had been carefully laundered and ironed by his wash *amah*. He then made it into a neat, rounded pad before applying it to his forehead in a series of dabs. This ritual was then followed by another of his well-known mannerisms – that of opening it out again with a flourish in order to bring relief to the other parts of his face. During the course of the day all twelve of the squares, having each made their own vital contribution to the efficient running of His Majesty's British High Commission, found themselves back in his briefcase for the attention of his wash *amah* again when her master arrived home.

Despite a lifetime in the tropics his body had been quite unable to adjust to the country's humidity and temperature. 'It's as if I was born without a thermostat,' he used to say to anyone who cared to sympathise. He presumed the problem would plague him until the time came when he could retire to his home in a rural backwater of Worcestershire, where he hoped the invigorating effect of a temperate climate would enable him to revive his passion for fox-hunting. Malaya was too hot to chase anything. Shooting snipe was the nearest it got to a field-sport although the more idiotic of his countrymen chose to make spectacles of themselves in their free time chasing balls of varying sizes on the *padang* in the centre of the city. He noticed, to his satisfaction, it made them perspire even more than he.

What did Mrs Mitchell want now he wondered? Money to get home presumably just as she had in Singapore. He re-read the letter he had just received from his opposite number in the Singapore Secretariat following her visit to him the previous week. He noted his colleague's concern, a concern that he now shared. An attractive white woman without adequate means of support in a British territory was a potential hazard as well as a likely embarrassment to the Administration. It appeared she had terminated her first interview in Singapore in some distress but had applied again for a grant almost immediately, which had been refused. He idly wondered what she had been doing for the last few days.

He raised his glistening countenance towards his visitor and contemplated her for several seconds before he spoke. It was true what his colleague had said, she was a woman who was bound to attract a great deal of attention in what was still a predominantly male society, and a lot pleasanter to look at than her husband he would imagine. He had heard he was a cold fish whereas Mrs Mitchell was, undoubtedly, a real femme fatale, at least as far as he was able to judge. What had she seen in Mitchell he wondered, and then to have allowed herself to be buried in the Kelantan jungle, of all places. It was just asking for trouble. But to go off with her chauffeur, that was unfeeling to say the least. Were there not enough spare European males around in Malaya if she had just wanted a fling?

Valerie resented the Secretary's gaze. She was used to being ogled by men she was meeting for the first time but she particularly bridled under his scrutiny as she thought she saw disdain as well as a trace of male superiority, not to mention a liberal measure of the usual ill-disguised lechery. She knew his type – the sort of man who was titillated by talking about sexual matters with women but was almost certainly without the nerve or capacity to try the real thing for himself. She just hoped he did not address her as 'my dear lady' or she might not be responsible for the consequences.

'As I understand it,' he began, 'you are having difficulty in getting back to the U.K. as you have left your Malay, ah, husband, and your former British husband has declined to assist you.' Valerie had considered what she was going to say on her journey south and had decided total frankness was likely to be the best option and so she brought him up to date with all the developments in her personal affairs and with her current problem. The secretary, despite himself, listened attentively. He had forgotten there was a child involved somewhere. Now he came to think of it, he did remember a phone call from the British Adviser one morning with the surprising news that the Sultan of Kelantan had changed his mind and approved the marriage between Mrs Mitchell and his subject. The Adviser had not known why at the time, but, in a later phone call said the *Mentri Besar*, the Chief Minister, had informed him it was because Mrs Mitchell was pregnant which was a complete surprise to him because Mitchell himself had not mentioned it in his interview. Neither phone call had been recorded in the file, which had been very remiss of him.

What he also remembered was how the High Commissioner had, as a result of the Sultan of Kelantan getting involved, washed his hands of the whole business or, to put it more accurately, dropped it like the hot potato it undoubtedly was. A British woman living with a local was an embarrassment to the Administration it was true, but not one worth upsetting the Sultan for. If the state ruler approved of the arrangement then the only thing that could be done was to sweep the whole affair under the carpet in the best civil service tradition, hopefully to be forgotten, as indeed he thought had happened.

Now, it seemed to have surfaced again as Mrs Mitchell was saying the baby, who she originally thought was her Malay paramour's was, in fact, her husband's. This was an extraordinary development and would certainly renew interest in her case at the Club. It was not often that in the course of his work he acquired information that would enable him to command the attention of his wife over the dinner table, but he would need to know more of the details in order to satisfy what he knew would be her inevitable curiosity. She particularly enjoyed not only being the first with a piece of gossip in the Club but also to be able to assure her listeners as to its official status, and therefore its reliability. The greater the number of background facts he could discover, discreetly relayed of course, the more impact the news would make around her bridge table, and the happier she would be.

'You say this child is your British husband's?' He corrected himself. 'Your former husband's. Do we have proof of this?'

In remarkable contrast to the Mother Superior, he unfortunately managed to make the question sound extremely offensive, a reflection not only on her morals but also her veracity. Valerie had to make a conscious effort to avoid a tart reply. As she had suspected, she was just going to have to put up with much condescension from high places if she was to recover her child.

'He is obviously a European baby. He looks European. He has his father's pale skin and red hair. Anyone who saw him would be in no doubt at all.'

The Secretary drew his handkerchief across his brow for the umpteenth time that day but it brought only momentary relief. Although not long after midday, there were already dark patches under the arms of his jacket which he sought to conceal by keeping his arms as close to his side as possible but this stratagem only caused him to perspire the more. His hair lay plastered firmly to his skull, while his neck seemed in endless, moist conflict with his collar. How he yearned for a crisp British December morning, the local peasantry gathered around the village green, eager hounds milling, his breath condensing in pleasing clouds around his stirrup cup. He began to pass his handkerchief from palm to palm with increasing frequency, but while he was in the process of relieving one, the other moistened.

Meanwhile he considered the implications of Valerie's last answer. Perhaps there had been some rum goings on at the estate bungalow. The French had a name for it, didn't they, but then they would. What was it? Ménage à trois? He could not believe it. That may have been fine for Paris but not in Malaya, especially not in rural Kelantan. He must not let his imagination run away with him. He phrased his next question carefully.

'From this, I assume you were expecting the baby before you left the matrimonial home?'

'Yes, obviously.'

'But you thought your Malay lover was the father?'

'Yes.'

The Secretary was beginning to regain his scepticism. What Mrs Mitchell was asking him to believe was that she was having a normal relationship with her husband almost up to the time she left him. It was true that the B.A. had reported the man looked devastated at their interview, but, really, this was too much to believe. There must be another explanation. He began to think Mrs Mitchell might be playing a dangerous game. She was a cool customer and no mistake. He felt he needed to probe the matter a little deeper.

'You must excuse my asking, Mrs Mitchell, but in a case of this sort, a marriage breaking up, the husband and wife usually cease to have anything more to do with each other. I am referring to marital relations, that sort of thing. Is that not so?'

'I ceased having marital relations with my husband,' said Valerie bitterly, 'but he did not cease having them with me.'

The Secretary shifted uneasily in his chair and decided to drop the subject. Although not without its *frissons*, he felt he might be getting out of his depth.

'And you say your Malay husband turned you out when he saw the baby wasn't his?'

'Yes.'

'Then, it seems, you took him to an orphanage. Wasn't that rather an unusual thing to do with your own child Mrs Mitchell?'

'I was in no position to look after him. I had no clothes, nothing for him. I could not think of anything else to do. I had been ill after his birth and I was desperate'

'So, when your Malay husband gave him to you, did he not give you the things you had got ready for him, what is it called, his layette?'

'No, not really. It isn't like that in a Malay village.'

'But you didn't ask for them?'

'No,' said Valerie with some vehemence. She was not only annoyed at this inquisition but alarmed, as, if her account was going to be doubted by the High Commission, their assistance was not likely to be forthcoming.

The Secretary surveyed his sopping handkerchief with a morose air. He could see Valerie's irritation and concern. He shifted his ample rear in its chair once again in an unsuccessful effort to bring some relief to the dampness he was feeling there. 'I'm sorry to be questioning you so closely,' he said, 'but I am trying to understand what is a most remarkable story. Now you say the orphanage will not give the baby back to you. What arrangement did you make with them when you left him with them?'

Valerie hesitated. She had omitted the precise details of how the orphanage had come into the possession of the baby but, as it seemed the Secretary was determined to get to the bottom of everything, she decided to be perfectly frank. It might help to remove some of the doubts he was obviously feeling.

'Extraordinary,' he said. 'You will pardon me saying so I hope, but it is almost in the best traditions of Victorian melodrama. A baby being left on a doorstep so to speak.' And he repeated himself. 'Extraordinary.'

Valerie did not pardon him but resisted the temptation to say so.

He went on. 'But if the baby looks as European as you say, I cannot see how they can withhold him from you, once they have established your credentials of course.'

Valerie was delighted to hear it but had to confess that the orphanage was not convinced the baby had a European father, and was also expressing concern that Osman might have some rights regarding him.

'I see,' said the Secretary. So they were as unbelieving as he was beginning to be. He was doubting Valerie's story more and more, but he did his best not to let his voice reveal the fact. 'There could be a problem there, I'm afraid. The Malays are very touchy where their rights are concerned. But what does your British husband … former British husband … say about the situation?'

Rather wearily, Valerie had to admit, as she had to the Mother Superior, that Stuart did not know.

'He doesn't know!' The Secretary's incredulity at her answer was genuine. 'You mean, your husband has a child he knows nothing of? A child several weeks old? Don't you think you ought to inform him at once?'

Valerie was beginning to see the justice of the statement. On her way to Kuala Lumpur the previous day she had had plenty of time to come to the same conclusion – that she could no longer delay telling Stuart that he was a father. Apart from anything else, it was possible he might be willing to provide some much-needed support in her efforts to gain custody of what was his own flesh and blood after all.

The Secretary became brisk and business-like. He had heard the *peon* in the corridor with the first cold drink of the afternoon. 'I really do not think the High Commission can do anything or can reasonably be expected to do anything, until we have heard Mr Mitchell's views on the matter. I also think you should be seeking legal advice. There seems little doubt to me that before this whole thing is over you will need to be legally represented. Meanwhile I will consult with the High Commissioner to see what a British Protectorate's responsibilities are in a case of disputed custody involving a British national and a Malay. As I see it at the present moment, I think that it will turn out to be a purely private matter in which we are unable to intervene. In short, it is a matter for the courts, not for the Administration.'

Valerie left. She therefore did not see the Secretary take up his pen, almost before she had closed the door. And, it was just as well for her peace of mind, that she did not see what he wrote in the file before him. After giving a summary of their conversation he added:

(1) 'Strongly suspect Mrs M. has become disillusioned with life in a Malay village and is trying to return to the U.K., taking her Malay child with her. Reasons for these suspicions:

(2) Took nothing with her when she left Batu Lima. This could indicate, contrary to what she says, she left without her Malay husband's approval.

(3) As a consequence, she had to leave child at local orphanage.

(4) This orphanage now refuses to release child on grounds he may have a native father.

(5) Has made no attempt to inform, as she claims, the real

father, Mitchell. This would surely be the first thing she would do if he *was* the father.

(6) Made no mention of a baby in interview in Singapore when official funds were requested to enable her to return to the U.K.. It would seem that she hoped to get him out of the country without our knowledge. The orphanage seems to be as doubtful as I am at present that Mrs M. is being totally frank. I feel she may be concealing some elements of the truth.'

*   *   *

Valerie was not often given to anger and bitterness but she felt them now. Never had she thought that her claim to her own child could end in this ridiculous fashion. And to think she had held the baby in her arms that night at the hotel in Karang and the world could not have cared less what happened to him. But then, at that moment, neither could she. If only she could go back in time and start again. She had all that she effectively wanted then, apart from Osman of course. Osman. That was why she had acted so inanely. She had been beside herself at the thought of losing Osman and to get him back had been her only consideration. The baby, then, had just seemed to be an obstacle to that end, nothing more, and certainly not a substitute for a lost husband. Now she had lost them both.

She wandered out of the High Commission, down the hill and into the town, by which time the heat had added to her misery. She gazed across the Padang, the neat and orderly expanse of grass in the centre of K.L. which had been reserved by the European pioneers during the first days of the town's development, in order that the future grandees of the British Protectorate could perform their ancient rites of rugby and cricket, to the wonder and mystification of the locals.

She pondered the term British Protectorate. The very word Protectorate had a hollow ring about it as far as she was concerned, as it was doing very little to protect her interests or those of her baby. And as for the grandees themselves, they no doubt considered themselves far too important to be bothered about the future of a small child, even though he might be as British as they.

It was that word British which most concerned her. What did it mean? Was it really true that, regardless of his native blood, her son was a Malay simply because he was born in Malaya and his parents were Malayan citizens at the time? Legally that may have been correct but was hardly logical as there must be a difference between being Malayan and being a Malay, and of course, his biological father was not a Malay at all, but British. She could accept the idea that when she had turned her back on her own people and embraced Malayan citizenship she had effectively deprived herself of the rights of British nationality, but how could she have done that for her baby as well? He must still be British – in fact at least, if not in theory – if his father was a British citizen. She was beginning to see the justice of the High Commission Secretary's remark that 'it is a matter for the courts'.

On the other hand, why should the British authorities show any interest in him when even his own father did not? Or presumably would not when he eventually learnt of his existence. If only she could *prove* he was Stuart's, but that did not seem possible, even his red hair was not scientific proof. Meanwhile, she had to face up to the unpalatable fact that when she had abandoned her place in European society, she had not only effectively cut herself off from its respect and concern but, it seemed, its desire to involve itself in her affairs and its willingness to ensure she was not the victim of injustice.

On the far side of the *padang* was the Selangor Club, known for as long as anyone could remember as the Spotted Dog, the origin of its unusual name being the subject of much late-night talk in its bar during which various theories were passed back and forth ranging from an early pioneer and his Dalmatian dog sitting on its verandah, to the democratic curiosity that, from the day it opened, the Club had accepted all races as members. Its prominent position and its black and white façade made it one of the most familiar buildings in the capital. It was the popular haunt of most of the expatriate personnel in K.L., although its great rival, the Lake Club, flattered itself on having the very top people amongst its exclusive membership.

Valerie had been in the Dog with Stuart a number of times and was well aware that at about this hour in the afternoon, civil servants, doctors, bank managers and the like were beginning to congregate at the bar, unwinding after what they regarded as the pressures of the day. Somewhere amongst them at that moment, probably sipping a gin *pahit,* as the locals termed their bitters, was a clever lawyer who might have the answer to her problem, but how long would it take him to find it, and at what cost? And even then, he might fail. With all the vested interests of Malaya ranged against him, she had to face the possibility that even that avenue of approach might be an expensive waste of time. She was becoming increasingly convinced of the hopelessness of her cause, and her one overriding thought at that moment was to see her baby again before it was too late, and she desperately resisted the idea that it might be for the last time.

Dusk was beginning to gather – it was when sundowners became the order of the day for the expatriates. Time was hanging fire for Valerie. She had no wish to run the gauntlet of expatriate opinion in the Spotted Dog, or the Lake Club for that matter. Neither expected their members to pay with cash, it was true, the risk of embezzlement by staff being too great, and so payment for drinks and food was by the famous chit system, signed receipts which had to be redeemed at the end of the month. The proper procedure for out-station members like herself was for bills to be sent back to their own club and settled there, which in her case would be the Kuala Lebir Club. Only men could be full members, however, and be held responsible for, and settle, accounts. Wives had only associate rights through their husbands, and whether she was still married to Stuart or not, he would be hardly willing to pay her bills.

She had a little smile at the thought of the expression on his face if the secretary at the Kuala Lebir Club handed him a pile of chits run up in her name at the Spotted Dog! Tempting, but not possible unfortunately, as it was ages since she had seen her club membership card. With no thought she might ever have need of it again, it had been lost somewhere on her travels, or more likely it had been left with her other possessions on the estate. But the whole system was a further example of the way expatriate women were deprived of any official status except through their husbands. Once they had severed their connection with their spouses, wives were non-persons, and unless they had a private income, had to be satisfied with a civic status similar to that of ex-convicts, vagabonds and beggars. Which was the very reason she had hoped the British Administration would have seen the need to help her.

Valerie could see that the High Commission Secretary was almost certainly right on another matter – the time was fast approaching when lawyers would have to be involved in her case, and she might already have taken that step if she had had the money, but she was unwilling to seek the services of a solicitor until all other avenues had been explored. Maybe it was her sensible Scottish upbringing, but she did not see the sense in paying a lawyer to do something she could well do herself, and if the first thing to be done was to inform Stuart, then who better to do it than herself? The only question was, how could it best be done?

Her first thought was to use the same means as a solicitor – by letter, but she could just imagine Stuart recognising her handwriting and tearing it up unread. Perhaps she could type 'Important news within – do not destroy' on the outside but she had no faith that would work either. And then, how long would it take him to answer, if he answered at all? Meanwhile she would have to hang around and watch her money being frittered away in cheap hotels or the Rest House.

She was becoming seriously worried about money. She knew

one or two European couples in K.L. socially but was most reluctant to embarrass or compromise them by availing herself of their hospitality. In any case, she was still unsure how her old friends and acquaintances felt about her desertion of Stuart and leaving Bukit Bintang in the way she had. But with those avenues closed, there was no practical alternative to seeing her last dollars disappearing while she waited for Stuart to reply, if he did. And how would she occupy herself in K.L. meanwhile, cut off as she was from European Clubs by her destitute status?

She could not window-shop indefinitely in the only two European stores available in the city. Apart from which, there was always the risk she would run into an acquaintance while she was doing so. In fact a meeting with someone who would recognise her would be almost a racing certainty, as there was precious little for a European woman to do, even in the Malayan capital, than to follow the eternal daily triangle – club, golf course and the shops, the two main ones principally, the restaurants of which served as more than adequate substitutes for the Dog as venues to exchange gossip – at least during shopping hours.

The only real alternative to these was the public gardens. Unfortunately, the ones in K.L., known as the Lake Gardens, had neither the variety nor the interest of the Botanical Gardens in Singapore, although they had the advantage of being relatively little used by Europeans which made it less likely she would encounter those she wished to avoid. A few young Malay families strolled in the Gardens in the evenings and at weekends, the men often in European dress to indicate their modish lifestyle and holding the children's hands, the women in a *baju kurong*, a step or two behind. They liked to wander around the large central lake, quaintly called Sydney after the wife of the first British High Commissioner. Otherwise the Gardens were mostly deserted, rather dull and, during the day, extremely hot.

Then she had an inspiration, a really startling idea, the sort of idea which initially appears quite nonsensical but which grows steadily in the mind until it appears so obvious you cannot understand why you had not thought of it before. She remembered the same thing happening when she was pondering what she should do after she discovered she was having, as she thought, Osman's baby. If she was going to have to contact Stuart, then there might just be a way of getting the baby back from the orphanage that would not involve solicitors, the High Commission or anyone else. The problem she faced was a Mitchell problem whichever way one looked at it, so it was up to a Mitchell – in the form of herself – to provide the solution. She had just such a solution in mind.

However, there was a snag, one Mitchell acting on her own was one too few for what would be involved. If her solution was to have a successful outcome it would need Stuart's help and that would mean her doing something she would have considered unthinkable until that very minute – she would have to make an unannounced visit to Bukit Bintang. It would need to be unannounced as a prior warning to Stuart by letter or telephone might result in him refusing to see her and so defeat her purpose, especially if he was in one of his uncooperative moods and, given the circumstances, he was likely to be. In any case, as she had already decided, writing to him would be a waste of time as he would recognise her handwriting. Apart from which, a letter would not be much use anyway as it would not convey more than just a bare outline of her plan and so be unlikely to convince Stuart it would work. And he needed to be convinced as his co-operation would be very much needed if her plan was to succeed – she could not carry it out on her own.

The casual mention by the senior man in the Singapore Secretariat that they had made contact with Stuart told her he must still be in residence on the estate and so while she still had enough money to avail herself of public transport she resolved to make the visit as soon as she could arrange it. A return to Bukit Bintang might not be the wisest way of letting Stuart knew he was a father, but it was certainly the surest. And once she had convinced him that he had a son, she could then hope to begin the much harder task of persuading him that fatherhood brought duties and responsibilities which, in his case, would have to be engaged immediately if they were to solve the problem facing them. Two reasons then, why she had to risk a face-to-face confrontation with her former British husband. It was not an event she was looking forward to, and she had serious doubts of its success, but she had no alternative if she was to recover her baby.

* * *

Four o'clock the following Sunday afternoon found a taxi turning onto a familiar red laterite road. It was a visit the vehicle's anxious occupant could not have envisaged at any time and in any circumstances only a week before.

Nothing on the estate seemed to have changed but, after little more than six months, she could hardly have expected otherwise. Rubber estates changed very little over the course of generations, let alone months. Trees in one section might be felled and replaced with grafted seedlings, or if the price of rubber went up, a further section of jungle might be cleared and planted out, but nothing more. Once or twice in recent years, when the price of rubber had dropped alarmingly, a few plantations had been taken out of production, or in one case when things had become particularly bad, a whole estate had been converted to the coming crop, oil-palm, the price and the demand for which seemed to be forever on the increase.

Had the circumstances been different she would have enjoyed coming back. She had always enjoyed the rubber trees and the peace they conveyed. Like all trees on or near the equator, not all of them lost their leaves at the same time, so there were always some in summer foliage and the constant greenery was a pleasant aspect of the unchanging character of the climate. She remembered how, when she was fresh out from Britain, their measured rows had created a reassuring sense of order and security in what, to her, had seemed an otherwise rather turbulent country. With its sudden storms, untamed jungle, reputedly lethal wildlife, strange and unfamiliar diseases not to mention its people pre-occupied with the spirit world despite the influence of several centuries of Islam, Malaya had rather intimidated her. Bukit Bintang then had seemed like an island of civilisation, a haven of safety, in an otherwise vast ocean of primeval rain forest, much as a military fort in the Wild West of America must have seemed to the frontiersmen.

How differently she felt about the country now. Over the years she had come to respect rather than fear the forest and its native animals – the dangers of which, in her view, were always being grossly exaggerated in travel books anyway, not to mention the popular press. From time to time the newspapers liked to retell stories such as the occasion in 1912 when a tiger was found under the billiard table of the Raffles Hotel in Singapore, while omitting to mention the much more prosaic fact that it had escaped from a nearby circus and a gung-ho hunter had taken it into his head, disgracefully, to shoot the terrified animal before it could be recaptured.

It was true that the existence of tigers and crocodiles in the wild had troubled the minds of some of the early European pioneers who had come to Malaya almost a century earlier, and several of their memoirs had contained the odd hair-raising incident or two, but those days had long gone – she had not even as much as caught a glimpse of a single specimen of either animal in the wild in almost ten years in the country, or could remember meeting anyone who had for that matter. In fact, to see a tiger at all outside a zoo nowadays was enough to warrant a mention in the *Straits Times,* and if a crocodile was ever spotted it almost invariably proved to be an escapee from a farm where they were being bred to make handbags for mems and shoes for *tuans.*

As for the smaller terrors such as snakes, scorpions and poisonous centipedes – they were encountered from time to time, it was true, but common prudence such as tapping one's shoes out in the morning and avoiding walking through long grass in flip-flops, was all that was needed to avoid most of the dangers. Unless, of course, it was a python which crossed one's path. One needed to be very wary of pythons. Even a ten-foot specimen could be more than a match for a man, let alone a fully grown adult, the largest of which were long enough to stretch from one side of a road to the other with something to spare. Wild pigs and deer of almost any size, swallowed whole, were their standard prey, but if the records were to be believed, one had never taken a human being, although there had been rumours of a 14-year old boy in Sumatra. There were always stories in the press about pythons, one of which Valerie particularly remembered as it showed that although people had been fortunate in their encounters with the reptiles in the past, their livestock and pets had not always fared so well.

A Chinese smallholder was astonished one morning to find the chain which had been tethering his guard dog the day before, was now trailing from the mouth of a twenty-four foot specimen which, following its canine meal, found itself prevented from returning to the jungle by the chain and so had been forced to take its customary post-prandial nap at the scene of its crime. Although pythons have the ability to regurgitate meals that do not agree with them, this animal had neglected to do so which meant the smallholder had little difficulty in despatching it. Needless to say, when the snake was opened up the dog was dead but would have been anyway before it was swallowed, as pythons suffocate their prey by constriction prior to eating them.

As far as poisonous snakes were concerned, Valerie had heard it said that fewer Malays died of snakebite each year than from falling coconuts, and tappers feared hornets far more than the biggest poisonous snake – the king cobra, lethal though the latter might be. Perhaps the most feared creatures, however, and justifiably so as they must have caused more human deaths than all the other animals in the country put together, were the mosquitoes as they could carry a silent and unseen killer – disease.

As for the people, what more could be said? Their simple,

unhurried lifestyle had charmed her without question, her only reservation being the way they allowed the spirit world to dominate their lives – their reaction to her baby's birth still fresh in her mind. It was unfair to describe the medicine-man, the *bomoh*, as a witchdoctor but the power he exerted over the minds of the people was deeply unsettling to a westerner. She had heard stories told in the *kampung* that had horrified her, not because she gave them any credence, but because she had seen the seriousness with which they were regarded by the villagers. She knew superstitions persisted in her own country despite almost two thousand years of Christian culture but for the majority of rural Malays, the myths and legends of their forefathers were real. Perhaps urbanisation and economic progress would bring them enlightenment as it had largely done in Britain.

* * *

Valerie sat well back in the seat of the taxi and averted her face from the stray walkers and cyclists so as to avoid the risk of being recognised. When they were still several hundred yards from the bungalow she stopped the taxi and paid the driver, making him turn around on the narrow track. She did not wish to be heard. As she approached the bungalow she skirted the patches of loose gravel, determined to make as unobtrusive an approach as possible. She really had no idea why. All she knew was that her increasing anxiety demanded it. Well she knew Stuart's quick temper and the likely effect her humiliation of him would have had.

More than six months had elapsed since her going, time enough for the fury in a normal person to have abated, but not in Stuart. Those six months would merely have given his resentment time to feed upon itself and thus make him even more unpredictable. There had, of course, been the reports that he had suffered an attack of malaria and had been at death's door. Then she had heard he had been replaced as manager, and later came the news he had returned to the estate but was not the man he once had been. These reports were little better than rumours and rumours, of course, were always prone to exaggeration. Now they just added to the uncertainty of the reception she would receive.

But why did she wish to arrive unobserved? That was something she could not explain even to herself. Perhaps she wanted to retain the option of sneaking away again if her nerve failed her, or to at least to be able to delay a decision until the last moment. She was not physically afraid of Stuart as he had never once been violent towards her – it was his manner which was so intimidating, as it had always made her appear small and of no importance. Not once in their marriage had she felt her opinion was in any way of interest or of value to him.

His attitude was all part of his determination to exclude the world and everyone in it and this insularity had first struck her as unnatural as early as the Bay of Biscay during her first voyage out to Malaya with him. It was as if he had deliberately grown an outer shell, like a crustacean, in order to protect himself – but from what and why? She had never discovered, but she could not deny it was the impression of inner strength which this aloofness gave him that was what she had originally found so attractive. Most women were drawn to male strength because of the protection it promised them but, as she all too soon discovered, she had never been able to call on that strength and enjoy the security it should have provided. Quite the reverse in fact, it had always seemed like a barrier keeping her at bay rather than a shield protecting her from those without.

It was this hard and unforgiving exterior which was at the heart of her problem with Stuart, as it had never allowed her to feel part of him. Not once had she been permitted even a glimpse of his inner self which would have done so much to make her feel she was being a wife and not just a concubine, or a real friend rather than just a casual companion who happened to be sharing his house and table. She could have forgiven him his other faults if he had ever shown he had needed her, but that need had never existed, or if it had, it had never been expressed. Not once. She could not remember discussing with him any problem or any worry he may have had during their entire ten years together.

He had not even shared the day-to-day frustrations of running the estate in any meaningful way. She remembered trying to coax him to talk about his work during their sundowners on the verandah before dinner. The incident of the slashed rubber trees, for example, had moved him to little more than exasperation, never doubts, or at least not any he was prepared to admit to her. It was as if he feared giving her the impression he could not cope. She had therefore remained a permanent outsider, a stranger in her own marriage.

* * *

It was an anti-climax when she finally stood in front of the bungalow steps as there was no one to be seen and the sitting room was as deserted as the verandah, most of her cherished pot plants having gone. No Tambi appeared from the back as he usually did on the arrival of a visitor, which was not surprising, she supposed, in view of her silent approach. Nevertheless, she was pleased she had not disturbed him and this could have been the explanation as to why she had been so secretive – she had wanted to ensure that her meeting with Stuart was in private for fear of what his reaction might be. She could endure what he might say, or even do, as long as it was not in front of the servants. Perhaps it was that colonial preoccupation with image making itself felt again.

Feeling relieved, but at a loss to know what to do next, she sat on one of the wicker chairs that she could remember buying soon after she first arrived from Britain. She could also remember making the cushions for them. She looked around the room. As on the estate, nothing much had changed. Like many men, Stuart was mostly indifferent to his domestic surroundings and there was an air of neglect about everything. It was still a room, but hardly even the partial home she had made it. In some ways it looked very much as it had been when she had first arrived on the estate ten years before.

She must have been sitting quietly for several minutes before there was a noise from the kitchen and Tambi suddenly appeared. His exclamation of 'Mem!' and ensuing high-decibel greetings were enough to waken the dead and, within seconds, Stuart opened his bedroom door. He had a sarong tied loosely around him and he had obviously been asleep. It was also equally obvious he had not shaved – clearly, this was just another Sunday on the estate. For a moment he stared incredulously at her, and then his face darkened.

'What the hell are you doing here? You've got a nerve showing your face here again.'

Out of the corner of her eye Valerie saw Tambi retreat into the kitchen.

'Stuart, we have to talk.'

'Talk! Talk! I never wish to talk, or to say another word to you as long as I live.'

'Stuart, you need to know, you have to know. You are the father of a baby boy, a lovely baby boy. Stuart, we have a child at last.'

Valerie had rehearsed in the taxi how she would deliver the news and imagined the various ways in which it was likely to be received, but none of them was remotely like the one she was about to witness. Stuart's response to the other occasions when the prospect of parenthood had loomed in their marriage had wavered between acceptance and indifference, with never a glimmer of enthusiasm or even moderate pride, but that was before he had endured the last six months – before he had been forced to come to terms with a renewal of his bachelor isolation and his growing awareness of a future without aim or meaning.

At first he thought getting used to Valerie's absence would be just a question of adjustment, the re-establishment of old routines, but that had proved to be wishful thinking. Eventually he was forced to accept he was suffering from what could only be described as plain old-fashioned loneliness – but in one of its most acute forms, the beginning of which had probably been the reason he had been driven to seek a wife in the first place. His renewed sessions with the estate girls had been a big disappointment – their listless company leaving him with an emptiness, which only served to accentuate his loneliness. It seemed as if he was being reproached for some failure on his part but what it could be puzzled him for some time.

The *kepala* had recruited the young tappers in his usual way and, as always, they had offered him their services, as unenthusiastically but also as unstintingly, as before, and at first he had found their company did much to while away some of the tedious hours of darkness. As always too, the converse between them had remained minimal. The girls all looked and sounded exactly the same to him. There was not a single one with whom he felt inclined to share a thought, a moment of affection perhaps, or even a kind word. In short, the nature of their traffic had been as it had always been in the old days when he had been simply looking for female companions, as opposed to female companionship. But, in the last few months he had gradually become aware something was lacking and although the purely sexual aspect of the arrangement still suited him, there was a vacuum at the heart of it which either had not been there or he had not detected before, and which he could neither understand nor identify.

Until it occurred to him it was because he could not really care a fig for any of the girls or feel a trace of emotional involvement with them during their so-called lovemaking, and this seemed to be the cause of the problem, as for the first time in his life he was finding himself in need of something more than just physical contact – he was wanting emotional contact as well. He was wanting a girl – any of the girls – to show just a spark of interest in him or his affairs, not out of curiosity but because he was something more in their lives than simply being an employer or a provider of a few extra dollars for services rendered.

Then it struck him that this meant he was asking more from them than, hitherto, he had ever offered them. And that was the key.

All his life he had been relatively indifferent to people – showing as little interest in their affairs as he assumed they had in his. It was not that he was uncaring of others' welfare. Where they were of use to him he was as solicitous as he needed to be but that was as far as it went. Now it was becoming increasingly clear to him human relationships were based on more than just mutual need, and he was very much feeling the lack of what a truly affectionate liaison can bring. Thus the words love and affection not only entered his personal lexicon for the first time – he was beginning to understand their meaning.

After this unexpected revelation about himself, he was not surprised to discover the reason why his sessions with the girls were making his growing sense of isolation more acute but, identifying the problem was one thing, knowing what to do about it, quite another. He had long thought any undue familiarity with the staff was bad for discipline, and so he had not sought or encouraged it. Never once had he learnt a name or expressed a preference for any particular girl, nor did he feel able – for the same reasons – to do so now. But it was this mutual indifference, he realised, which was at the root of the emptiness he felt every time he took a young tapper to his bed. As a result, the frequency of his requests to the *kepala* tailed off, much to the latter's puzzlement. His faithful headman had done his best to re-invigorate the interest of his employer by recruiting some fresh young girls but without success. Eventually the *kepala* put it down to the fact that *tuan* was getting old, his fires not burning as brightly as they had twenty years before when he had first come into his master's service. The *kepala* understood – he knew the problem well.

Briefly Stuart thought of a local mistress. Not one of the tappers, of course, that would make things even more difficult, she would have to come from elsewhere, but as he had discovered before his marriage to Valerie, the time when such arrangements were acceptable for planters was long past.

Inevitably, therefore, Stuart's mind went back to his marriage and his relationship with his wife – surprisingly, he still thought of her in the present rather than the past tense – and he pondered why she had preferred a life in a Malay village to the comforts of a planter's bungalow. Could it have been because she had derived as little from their relationship as he was doing now from the girls? For the first time in his life he saw his lack of natural warmth as a failing and he cursed it, cursed it as roundly as he would have done a clubbed foot or a withered arm or any other congenital infirmity. He realised it had been as big a handicap in his life as anything physical, and had been ever since he could remember.

*   *   *

Then had come another blow. He had always enjoyed the rudest of health and took pride in never having missed muster for even a single morning, but one day he returned from supervising the latex-weighing in the factory and, to Cookie and Tambi's surprise, declined lunch and retired to his bedroom. He had a headache and, to his own amazement, slept until the following morning, after which he felt better. But two days later, the fever returned in a more pronounced form and then, after another two days, it struck again but this time with a terrible malignancy. His temperature soared and his head throbbed with a severity that threatened to separate it from his body, which, paradoxically, felt ice-cold.

He called Tambi for blankets but they did nothing to stop his almost cataclysmic shivering, and after the fever had passed the bedsheets were soaked with sweat. He knew the signs, in fact to an old Malaya hand they were unmistakeable – he had malaria, a mosquito-borne disease difficult for the authorities to control outside the towns. He kept some quinine somewhere in the bungalow against such an occurrence but the tiny bottle could not be found – perhaps Valerie would have known where it was – and so a taxi was summoned to take him to the hospital in Kota Bharu. And not before time, as he was told the next attack could have been his last.

Malaria was a notifiable disease, and so both the State Health Department and his company had to be informed. The latter sent a relief manager to the estate and when he was discharged from hospital he was – to his mortification – despatched to recuperate in the company's own bungalow in the temperate air of Fraser's Hill, a holiday resort for colonial civil servants, situated in the jungle-clad mountains of the Federated Malay State of Pahang. It had been established by the Government for those of its employees who had been unable to get back to Britain for home leave during the Great War, although Government being Government, it was not completed until the mid-twenties although the amenities it offered consisted of little more than a golf course and a few tennis courts and bungalows.

However, as he could have told his doctors, civil servants and their families on vacation were not his idea of congenial companions and they certainly did not provide him with recreational therapy, and after six days of listening to their constant complaints about the privations of life in Singapore, he discharged himself and returned to Bukit Bintang, a sadder if not wiser man, lacking his former energy and considerably more given to introspection. His red hair had begun to turn an iron grey from his ordeal – not at the hands of the querulous civil servants in Fraser's Hill although they had tested him sorely, but from the proboscis of the mosquito which had infected him. His brush with mortality made him think increasingly of his future, and not only because he knew the malarial parasite would henceforth be his life-long companion.

* * *

His loneliness had then developed into a deeper malaise. For the first time in his life he had begun to have visions, dispiriting visions, of what his retirement might bring after the mainspring of his existence – the production of ever more rubber in Malaya, had come to an end. What would there be worth doing back in Scotland when there were was no estate to supervise, no tappers to bully, no monthly returns to pore over? What would replace the rubber seedlings, which he had always taken such pleasure in seeing grow year by year, into productive trees yielding their precious latex in ever increasing quantities? Without something to watch over and take pride in during his retirement, there would be nothing to give a purpose to the passage of time and his passing days.

It came as not a total surprise, therefore, when he found himself thinking wistfully of the company Osman was keeping and these thoughts had only occasionally been interspersed with bouts of anger born of his wounded pride and a sense of betrayal, and even these had gradually diminished in intensity as the months passed. He had hardly been able to believe it, but he had found himself putting off, time and again, the divorce proceedings he had initially promised himself.

During the long evenings after the servants had retired and he had pushed to one side the folder containing the sheaf of papers bearing the tables, graphs and forecasts he liked to draw up for the future of the estate – the formulation of which had never failed to keep him well entertained in the past but which were now beginning to lose their savour – his thoughts turned more and more to Valerie. It was some time, however, before he realised it was more than just her presence he was missing, it was her companionship, and this realisation was eventually followed by the admission, grudging perhaps at first, that his lack of feeling may have been partly responsible, at least, for her desertion. At last, he came to the conclusion that if missing someone was the same as loving them then he had loved Valerie, still did, in his own way. The revelation came as a shock as he had always thought the emotion beyond him, or as he once thought, beneath him.

Having cut himself off almost entirely from European company – he could not bear the thought of what he was certain everyone was saying behind his back – he had heard nothing of what had happened to Valerie since the day she had left. Had he swallowed his pride and gone to the Kuala Lebir Club he would have discovered that the members – thanks to information supplied by Margo – were well aware that the rural idyll which their erstwhile friend had contrived for herself in Batu Lima had apparently come to an end, much to their satisfaction and just as they had prophesied. They deplored the whole business of the planter's wife going native, so much so, they did not mention the subject any more. Had Stuart heard Margo's news or even known how the other club members felt, he might have been pleasantly surprised although he would probably have found their sympathy just as hard to bear as their pity.

So, it was entirely out of the blue, when only recently he had received a letter from the Colonial Secretariat in Singapore, asking if he was prepared to help his wife financially in her attempt to return home.

The letter had surprised him for several reasons, not least because there had been no mention of a child and he felt sure the baby Valerie had been expecting must have been born by now. Nor had there been any reference to Osman, and he wondered if his prediction of the elopement ending in disaster had come to pass. This last thought had induced just a brief moment of gratification which had probably been the reason why he had replied to the letter with a flash of the old Stuart – although he wondered if his pride would have prevented him from making any other response anyway – but his unnecessarily acerbic reply saying that he had washed his hands of his wife's affairs had left him wondering if he had done the right thing, the thing he really wanted to do, and he had pondered for days afterwards if he should have written a second letter rescinding the first.

It would not have been easy as such a letter would have been tantamount to an admission he had been at fault for her leaving him – an acknowledgement of failure he had never made in his life before – and it proved a step too far now. But deep down, after some deep reflection and even more soul-searching, he had regretted not taking the first tentative step towards a possible rapprochement with his wife.

So, although Valerie's appearance in the bungalow had been a complete surprise to him, now he had had time to adjust to it, it was by no means an unwelcome one.

In the late afternoon sun slanting across the room Valerie looked as attractive and inviting as ever. There had been an understandable flash of rekindled anger, of course, when he had first seen her – that was understandable in the circumstances – but it had been almost instantly dispelled by her bombshell that he was a father, his reaction to which had taken him completely by surprise. It was so utterly unexpected, but before it could be fully comprehended and assimilated, there had to be confirmation of the fact. After all, from what he had heard, impending fatherhood was the last thing he should have been expecting as he was sure it was the *syce* who had been the prospective father. How could the baby be his? But perhaps he had not heard correctly as Valerie appeared to be alone. Where was the child? Might there be some mistake?

'What do you mean, I am the father of a baby boy. I don't understand. Can you be sure? You said you were having the *syce's* baby, how do you know it is mine?'

Step by step Valerie went over the events of the last few weeks, omitting only those parts where she had felt an overwhelming desire to renew her relationship with Osman, but making no attempt to disguise the circumstances of how the baby had come to be left at the orphanage. This catalogue of failings on her part which in the past might have been met by derision by the old Stuart, now elicited, to Valerie's amazement, what could only be described as concern and sympathy although perhaps not quite on the scale which might have been expected of a normal husband, or even a former husband for that matter. But for a man like Stuart it was a revelation, and was probably as far as a man with his emotional limitations could go towards an understanding of the weaknesses of others.

Valerie regretted she could spare so little time to explore its implications, to appreciate its novelty and confirm what, if she had not known Stuart of old, very much looked – as she recounted her story of trial and tribulation – remarkably like solicitude written in almost every line of his face, but she had to forgo the pleasure of that experience and proceed to the account of her interview with the secretary in the High Commission.

His reaction to the events in K.L. was more predictable and, indeed, was what Valerie had fervently been praying for when she had made up her mind to return to the estate. Stuart's indignation at what he regarded as the unfeeling attitude of the orphanage quickly turned to anger when he heard of the unreasonable rejection of her plea for assistance from the British High Commission. Valerie knew Stuart's opinion of the colonial administration had always been one bordering on contempt and his views on Muslim sensitivities, little better. Officials who sat at desks assuming they knew better than those who were required to live in the real world with all its attendant risks and problems, had always earned his scorn, and so it was not surprising he was now deeply resenting the way those two monoliths of officialdom, the Islamic Council and the British High Commission, seemed intent, between them, on depriving him of his new-found status of fatherhood. So, as Valerie was not altogether surprised – but certainly very pleased – to see, he was more than just exasperated by her story, he was showing every indication of being extremely annoyed.

However, Valerie was mistaken as Stuart's thoughts and feelings at that moment were not quite what she was imagining them to be. The anger he had felt at the injustices she had described had quickly receded and was being replaced by what could only be described as a state of total disbelief and astonishment at what was happening that afternoon. It was becoming increasingly obvious that something like a miracle was in the process of unfolding on Bukit Bintang, this ordinary, run-of-the-mill estate on what had, up to now, been a totally hum-drum Sunday. Perhaps it was not a miracle in the biblical sense but it *was* in every other, as he was being brought face to face with a major turning point in his life, and it was leaving him with emotions which he could remember having felt only once before – when, equally without warning, he had found himself laying at the bottom of a muddy trench one afternoon in 1915, the victim of a German sniper's bullet and in fear of his mortal existence.

Today's events, perhaps, were not likely to be as dramatic in their consequences as that afternoon in Flanders but they promised to be just as life changing. Less than an hour earlier, he had been unaware he had become a father or that he possessed any parental feelings either for that matter, and had he been asked, he would have said that both were of the utmost indifference to him. Now – and he could scarcely credit it – a few simple words informing him he had a son had not only radically altered his thinking on the subject – and crystallised his feelings about Valerie at the same time incidentally – but had also given him a remarkable opportunity to remedy a lifetime of error and failure, thereby transforming his entire future. He could hardly believe it but he actually had a son! And he might still have a beautiful wife as well, and the combination of the two promised a brand new start to his life, completely banishing the depressing picture he had been conjuring up in his mind during these last few months as he contemplated his impending retirement.

What else could it be than a miracle? An afternoon which had begun in the same way as countless other Sunday afternoons on the estate – a lonely siesta followed by an even lonelier, solitary meal – had been magically transformed so that he was no longer faced with a career with little meaning and a retirement with even less, but one blessed with a rich promise in both.

And it was not ending there, for no sooner had this wholly delightful prospect been revealed to him than a cloud had gathered to obscure it in the form of a threat, not only to his newly acquired son, but to the bright new future he hoped would be centred on that son – unless, it seemed, he was prepared to act with despatch and determination. That was of little worry or concern to him, however, as a failure to respond to those twin imperatives had never been amongst his failings. In fact he was relishing the challenge, as it meant he could now also be a man with a mission – a role in life which had always appealed to him, perhaps because it would give him an opportunity to go to war with the world with a proper sense of purpose rather than just a lifelong grievance. He would no longer be just an estate manager adding more and more bales to the world's stockpile of rubber, but a crusader with a cause – and that cause? To rescue a helpless child – his child as it happened – from a perverse and arbitrary authority, and surely a man could have no worthier an objective than that?

So it was in a flush of real exultation he was able to inform Valerie that he would not only do precisely what she thought was necessary to redress the injustice facing the Mitchell family, he would positively relish doing it. Moreover, he hoped, by assisting with her plan, he would not only be able to demonstrate his regret for the past but also his desire to begin the long journey to personal restitution which, not unreasonably, he thought would now be expected of him.

*   *   *

Valerie had been delighted to see and hear Stuart's reaction to her saga of rejection but it was his reaction to the news he was a father which delighted her the more, as his indifference would have written *finis* to the plan she had in mind. She had always known she could arouse her husband's resentment by what he thought was a sleight to his person, real or imagined but, realistically, the most she had expected from him after her account of her interview with the High Commission was an indignant protest or two and a verbal condemnation of crass officialdom generally. But his joint response to the news of the baby and the threat he might lose him almost before he had time to adjust to his arrival, had far exceeded her most optimistic expectations as they appeared to have unleashed a veritable tiger in him. Or perhaps, there was another carnivore whose public image could provide her with a more fitting metaphor, as without a word of exaggeration what she had just heard and witnessed had been nothing less than what might have been expected from a she-bear deprived of cubs.

Clearly, what she had to do now was to provide this personification of offended fatherhood with a means of converting his anger into a practical course of concrete action, and she outlined to her husband the plan she had devised to recover their son.

However, before she did so, she realised she had not yet fully assured herself he *was* still her husband, for although everything Stuart had said since her arrival had given her the growing impression he had not divorced her, it had not been confirmed, and her feelings when she discovered she had not been cast off by both her spouses in the space of little more than a month came as a relief bordering on gratitude. Amazingly, she was still a wife – or at least she ought to be, as according to her reasoning, after having been divorced by her second husband she must still be married to the first, assuming the unusual circumstances of her second marriage had not automatically put an end to the first.

The Sultan's Secretary had assured her that her marriage to Osman would immediately annul the one to Stuart, and if that was true, then surely the reverse must be true also. Her divorce from Osman should have annulled the original annulment, and in the absence of any divorce proceedings by Stuart, she must therefore, still be married to him. In other words all her marital comings and goings should have brought her back to square one. And, if all these suppositions were correct, she must still be a British citizen, as the renewal of her marriage to Stuart must have had the effect of making her British again. Not only did she find this fact reassuring but she suspected the problems she and Stuart were about to encounter might be just that little less intractable if they were still legally married and of the same nationality.

Just as astonishing as Stuart's reaction to the news he was a father was his demonstration that, somehow or from somewhere, he had acquired some human sympathies in the period since she had left him. She had long given up hope of ever finding any finer feelings in her husband as she had become convinced they had, by some biological quirk, been omitted from his genes at conception. But now, it seems, he could be prey to doubts, worries, even anxieties, just like everyone else, and this could only make him a far nicer human being. In fact, it already had. It was ironic. Throughout their marriage she had sought to discover, or to instil, these human qualities in him but in vain, whereas during their separation he had acquired or uncovered them in liberal measure. Six months of her absence, it seems, had done far more to advance him along the road to humanity than ten years of her company.

* * *

Valerie and Stuart talked long into the night in a way she could not remember ever having done before, and, after the generator had been switched off, their heart-to-heart exchange continued by the light of an oil lamp. Fortunately, neither wished to dwell on the failings of their earlier life together, they were too many, and what was the point? Self-justification, blame, resentments, accusations and counter-accusations, had no bearing on the present, they needed to be consigned to the past and left there and, thankfully, both were now prepared to do so. All talk must be of the future – the immediate future and then, hopefully, beyond.

Stuart seemed reluctant to bring their new-found empathy to an end, and for one awful moment Valerie thought he was going to suggest it did so in the bedroom. The success of her visit had disarmed her but not to that extent. It was far too early for a re-consummation of their marriage, even if that event was ever to come to pass. But she was grateful for his reaction to her visit and said as much. His delight from his discovery he was a father and his almost pathetic need for human company, even affection, had touched her in a way she found difficult to put into words but she managed to leave him in no doubt of her surprise, and her joy, at the transformation. This was a new Stuart and, remembering her heart-breaking years with him, it had been marvellous to behold. And miraculous in its effects too, as for the first time since her marriage to him, she was not feeling she was a stranger in their relationship. Not only did she need his help, but quite obviously he needed hers too, possibly even more so.

That night, difficult as it was to believe, she found herself a guest in her own spare bedroom and she could not but help recall the last occasion when she had occupied it – and with whom. The blinds still stirred in the gentle breeze just as she remembered they had done that night. So much had happened since, and as she had expected, most of it had brought great unhappiness. Since the baby had been born, she had suffered one set-back after another but the events of that day, totally unexpected as they had been, had at last seen a reversal of her fortunes, and for the first time in a long time she could see a possible end to her troubles.

After once seeing Stuart as the cause of her problems and then, at best, an irrelevance to them, it now seemed as though he might prove to be their solution. And the thought of Stuart as an ally was already proving a comfort. Almost for the first time since she had married him she was feeling the benefit of that inner strength and determination which had first attracted her to him.

But perhaps the most improbable thing of all was that he had not divorced her. She could still hardly believe it. Could it possibly be that despite everything that had happened during their marriage and all the appearances to the contrary, she had married a fond *paterfamilias after all* but one whose self-image had not allowed him to behave as such? Or was it just a case of a man needing a few more of life's hard knocks and a little more time than most, to reveal to the world and perhaps to himself, he was not the rough and rugged individual he thought he was – or he would have liked to be? Either way, his metamorphosis into a more than passable human being had been almost as miraculous as Paul's conversion on the road to Damascus.

She had a sudden thought and despite the lateness of the hour she got out of bed and began rummaging in the simple contents of her bag. As she slipped her wedding ring back on her finger she marvelled at the sixth sense that had made her keep it. If she was going to be Mrs Mitchell again she ought, in fact she needed, to look the part.

* * *

The next morning Stuart drove her to Kota Bharu and she bought what she thought she would need if her plan that afternoon met with success. Afterwards, they went on to the orphanage. It looked as quiet and deserted as ever, few would have suspected the hive of devoted industry within. She rang the bell but as soon as the door was opened Valerie knew something was wrong. The welcome was muted, there was a slight hesitation before she was invited to follow. When she got to the door of the Mother Superior's office the radiant smile was only brief before she was asked to sit down. There was no immediate call to fetch the baby. Valerie's heart sank. She instinctively knew what had happened and her worst fears were immediately confirmed.

'Mrs Mitchell, I'm afraid I have some bad news for you. My superiors have said that on no account must you be allowed to see the baby.'

Significantly, the Mother Superior did not use the term 'your baby'.

'There can be no question of adoption in this case. I know how you must feel and I am very sorry but it is quite out of my hands."

Valerie quailed within but was outwardly calm. She then saw that this might not be the response most likely to gain her ends and she allowed her face to register what she felt.

'But why? I thought that, once they knew the facts, all would be well.'

'It seems they do not think you are a suitable parent.'

'Suitable parent! But I am his real parent. Surely I cannot be more suitable than that?'

The Mother Superior was more than uncomfortable; in fact, for someone with an inner peace and composure, she looked remarkably troubled. 'Mrs Mitchell, please try to see things from my position. We are a Christian charity working in a Muslim country. They really do not want us here but suffer us because they know we are able to help alleviate social evils, which are quite beyond their means. We dare not upset the religious authorities, no one can. Not even the colonial government.' She added hurriedly, anticipating the next comment on Valerie's lips.

'I really cannot believe this is happening. I am a British woman who simply wants to reclaim her own child from a Christian convent in a civilised country where Britain is the apparent ruler, and I cannot do so. You do believe I am the baby's mother don't you?'

The Mother Superior was beginning to look a little distressed.

'It really does not matter what I think,' she said. 'I simply have to do what I am told, and, yesterday, two officials from Kota Bharu came to see me to remind me of the terms under which our mission operates. The matter has been decided at very high levels.'

'They have no right to keep my baby, no right at all. If I had known that perfect strangers of another faith could deprive me of my own child how differently I would have acted that night.' She felt a momentary pang of conscience at a statement that was hardly in accordance with the facts, especially when she recalled what her original solution to her problem might have been. Any deviation from the truth, however small, seemed a particular sacrilege in the presence of the paragon who faced her, and Valerie felt enough guilt to bring a flush to her cheeks.

If the Mother Superior recalled the events the night the baby was left in the outside crib, she gave no indication of it made and made no comment other than 'They say he is a Muslim child whoever his parents are,' she said gently, but firmly. 'I do so wish I could say or do something which might help to ease the pain you must be feeling. I know this may sound inadequate, just as prayer is inadequate if you do not have faith yourself, but I have prayed each night for you ever since you came here, and I will continue to do so. Sometimes God's purpose is difficult for we mortals to understand.'

There was a pause. Valerie looked steadily at the Mother Superior who, in her turn, was supposing her visitor was coming to terms with the decision and the younger woman's reply appeared to confirm this. 'Can I see him for one last time?' she asked.

The Mother Superior visibly relaxed. Mrs Mitchell was sensibly accepting the inevitable and had made a perfectly natural request, one she had anticipated. Although instructions had been given that the mother should not be allowed to see her baby again under any circumstances, the Mother Superior had already decided that this was an edict that could be overridden by the dictates of Christian charity. One last time was not too much to ask, and then the whole wretched business would be over and this poor woman could start coming to terms with her loss. Within a minute, which suggested her plea and the Mother Superior's reaction to it had been anticipated, the baby was brought in. Valerie rose to her feet. She had decided that it was better to assume she could walk around the orphanage with him and enjoy a private moment, rather than to risk asking for permission and it being refused.

She moved to the door and the Mother Superior half rose from her chair with an arm raised, as if to stop her, thought better of it and sat down again. Instead she motioned to the girl who had brought the baby in to accompany her. Valerie stepped into the courtyard and deliberately turned into another, an inner one – away from the entrance. She could feel the adrenalin beginning to pump inside her although she felt remarkably calm in herself, even detached.

The difficult part was over, all she had to do now was act

perfectly naturally. That was easier said than done, however. She kept wanting to look up to see if she was being watched but that, she knew, would be fatal because, once she had aroused their slightest suspicion there would be no second opportunity. They obviously had not the slightest inkling of what was in her mind, otherwise they would not have let her hold him, let alone carry him around, and so all she had to do now was to convey the impression she had accepted the situation. She had to look relaxed, appear delighted to be holding him, smile, then smile again. Whatever she did, she must not look tense. A couple of times she stopped and cuddled him, acting as she hoped a normal mother might in the circumstances. Of all her actions that day, this one made her feel the most deceitful.

An overwhelming desire to just rush along the covered way, open the door and be gone, filled her. But still she waited. The longer she delayed, the more their attention might be diverted and so give her that yard or two extra start which she thought she would need. But if she delayed too long the Mother Superior might come to find her and bring the visit to an end. No, she would not do that, surely not cut short the last time a mother was going to see her son, the Mother Superior of all people would never consider doing something like that! Nevertheless this tour must seem increasingly suspicious, after all, what point was it serving other than prolonging, as they supposed, her heartbreak?

She moved to another room, then another. She could not say what was she waiting for, after all she had what she wanted. Stuart must be getting hot in the car outside. Was she hoping for a distraction on the part of her companion? She had to ensure she had a second or two start in order to gain those precious few yards that would make all the difference between success and failure. She moved to yet another room, then back again to the inner courtyard, which took her that little bit nearer to the entrance.

At that moment her companion turned away to speak to a helper. Valerie was alone. She began walking along the covered way towards the Mother Superior's office as if she was taking him back, and then, quickening her stride, she went straight past the doorway, into the outer courtyard and round the canna lilies, still magnificent in all their glory and unaware they were almost certainly witnessing the only crime ever likely to be committed in their presence, turned the corner and reached the door. She fumbled with the catch, opened it and was through, just as she heard a shout behind her.

She was in the bright sun running across the square, Stuart was standing by the car. 'Get in, get in,' she shouted, but he was already doing so. She ran across the road, fell into the back seat and the car, after an agonising lurch and a cough, drew rapidly away.

It had been even easier than she thought possible. She chose that moment to look back, and caught a glimpse of a black-robed figure frozen in the doorway. It was only then she began to feel sorry for the Mother Superior. Never would her qualities of goodness and benevolence and her Christian virtues of faith and charity be more severely tested than they would be in the next few weeks.

* * *

They returned to Bukit Bintang and awaited events but nothing happened. Was this it? Were there to be no repercussions? Stuart, meanwhile, was a revelation. No first-time father could have been more lost in wonder at the miracle of birth or more solicitous in his care for its embodiment. Valerie was amazed and impressed in equal measure. Tambi and Cookie, even the *kepala,* took their turns in the admiring circle around the youngest Mitchell with Stuart standing by, playing the part of the proud and protective father to the manner born. Valerie would not have believed it if she had not witnessed it with her own eyes. Perhaps it was the few wisps of red hair on the baby's head that had induced this onrush of paternal pride – no new father could have been presented with more obvious proof that his blood-line had been perpetuated.

On the third morning after their return from the orphanage the phone went. It was the British Adviser's private secretary with a request – although couched more in the tones of a command – that Stuart come to Kota Bharu with the utmost urgency.

That morning saw Stuart once more entering the portals of the *atap* Residency. The elderly occupier was visibly agitated and standing where he could derive the maximum benefit of the fan.

'I had a most uncomfortable interview with the Sultan yesterday,' he said, before Stuart even had a chance to sit down. 'Just what has been going on? I am informed that your wife removed a child from the Kota convent orphanage in Kota Bharu three days ago, assisted by yourself. A Malay child I believe, a baby born to your wife and her Malay husband but a few weeks ago.'

Stuart intervened with some heat. 'I must correct you there. It definitely was not a Malay child. It was my son, my own flesh and blood who my wife had left at the orphanage following his birth, she having been turned out of his house by her so-called Malay husband.'

The B.A. did his best to assimilate this new and very different version of events. 'That is not what I heard,' he said. 'Let me get this straight. Your wife, ex-wife, eloped with your *syce* I believe. Later I was told she was expecting a baby by him. Now you tell me this baby is not your servant's but yours?'

'That is it precisely,' said Stuart. 'And this orphanage refused to give the child back to my wife, his mother. On what grounds I cannot imagine. She was treated disgracefully. So we took him back and I consider that we were both within our rights to do so.'

'Not according to the Mentri Besar, a very difficult gentleman as I expect you know, and later I heard the same thing from the Sultan. Both insist he is a Malay baby and that the rights of his father – his name is Osman I believe – have been flouted. They regard this as a very serious lack of good faith on our part, apart from it being a breech of the terms under which the British administer this state.'

'What do you mean – the terms under which we administer this state?'

'Mr Mitchell, Kelantan is not a British Colony, it does not

belong to the British Crown whatever you may have thought. It is only what is called a protectorate. Despite your long stay here, perhaps you are not totally familiar with the way a British protectorate works. It is not the same as in Singapore, which is part of the Colony of the Straits Settlements. The constitutional status of the Malayan states is very different. When the British first came to the mainland in the 1870s their only objective was to establish stable government so that trade and mining could flourish. We did not annex the country, we came with the consent of the rulers – the sultans – and that is still the position today.'

The B.A., for the first time that day and despite the urgency of the occasion, was beginning to feel a little more at ease both with himself and the situation. He was certainly not enjoying the interview – indeed, he had faced the prospect of it that morning with his usual mixture of irritation and trepidation – but explaining the constitutional position of Britain in the Malay States was another matter. He felt he was performing the role for which he had been appointed; apart from which it was a subject dear to his heart and one in which he considered himself something of an authority.

'We are here in accordance with the terms of a treaty which was drawn up between the Sultan, his council and the British Crown. Broadly speaking, this treaty limits our responsibilities to protecting Malaya from foreign aggression and maintaining good law and order. We do not interfere with the lives of the ordinary people, especially where their religion is concerned. It follows therefore that we have to be very careful what we do. We certainly cannot afford to exceed our powers granted under this treaty. The Sultan is sovereign here, let there be no doubt about that. You cannot have failed to notice that the Kelantan stamps you put on your letters bear the State coat of arms or the Sultan's head, and not that of the British monarch as in Singapore. It shows that the Sultan is the constitutional ruler here.'

Stuart indicated he had used the stamps many times but, with some irritation, asked what that had to do with him taking his own son from the orphanage.

'Under the provisions of this formal agreement with Kelantan, and contrary to what many people think, the Sultan does not have to do what we tell him, he merely undertakes to govern in accordance with our advice, and he does not even have to do that when it comes to Malay custom and religion. In those areas we have no right to interfere at all, and without doubt this is a Malay matter involving as it does a Malay child and a Malay father, not to mention the Malay religion.'

'But he is not a Malay child I tell you. He does not have a Malay father. He is as British as you or I. He even has my red hair – and I'll wager you have never seen a Malay with red hair. What right has the orphanage to keep a child from his lawful parents? And as for all this nonsense about 'the Sultan does not have to do what we tell him, he just takes our advice', I cannot for the life of me, see the difference. It sounds like the typical mumbo-jumbo that politicians and civil servants, and lawyers, like to use on these occasions. Let me remind you again – this is my son you are talking about. There is no doubt about it, he is definitely British. One glance is all that is needed to see that.'

And as the image of faceless functionaries in a distant office ordering the affairs of simple folk like himself came flooding back into his mind once again, he ended with a flash of the old she-bear Valerie had admired a few days before. 'And I'm not going to stand by and have his future decided by some petty, self-appointed popinjay shut away in his ivory tower. I don't care what you or anyone else says.'

The B.A. sighed wearily. Arguments tired and upset him. He was used to telling underlings, mostly respectful Malays or Indian clerks, what their duties were, not having to justify his opinions and actions to difficult planters and Mitchell was being as difficult as he feared he might be. His main ambition was to see his time out in Malaya, hopefully, still as the Crown's representative in Kelantan, without doing anything which might risk even the smallest stain on his blameless record of thirty years service in the country. But unless he used all the diplomatic skills he had acquired over the years dealing with Malay rulers and difficult civil servants, the first full of their own self-importance, the remainder over-sensitive to a fault in preserving their precious reputations, this affair looked as if it might do more than just blot his copy book, it could bring his whole career down in ruins. Without careful handling, it had the potential to mushroom into the major political scandal it showed signs of being when it first erupted several months ago – and at the time he had not been able to believe his good luck when, quite unexpectedly, it had died a death.

Now, to his horror, Mitchell's arrogant behaviour at the orphanage had resurrected the whole affair and with far more serious implications. What had possessed this troublesome planter to behave in such a way? Was this baby really his son or was he fooling himself, a case of wishful thinking perhaps?

What he found particularly upsetting at that moment was that, in the course of just one afternoon, Mitchell had managed to jeopardise everything he had striven so hard to achieve since his appointment as British Adviser, Kelantan. To have run full tilt into Malay sensibilities like this, and to have upset no less a person than the Sultan himself was nothing less than a disaster. For years he had done his utmost to ensure the Sultan had maintained a benevolent attitude towards the British Crown, no easy task after the difficulties during the Great War when there had been so much anti-British feeling in the state, and now all his good work had been reduced to nothing by just one act of selfishness on the part of a planter who really, after all his years in the country, should have known better. But by far the worst aspect of the whole business, and the one he could barely bring himself to contemplate, was the threat it posed to his prospects of the customary honour that administrators of his rank could expect to receive at the end of their careers.

He had long cherished the fervent hope that his hitherto unblemished record in the country would receive its due recognition when he retired, which, pleasant as it was to contemplate, was only one further posting away, a posting he hoped might be in the form of a renewal of his tenure as British Adviser, Kelantan for a further term. Now, with this scandal hovering over him, not only was that honour seriously imperilled but the happy prospect of a K.C.B.E. was looking decidedly uncertain. And that could mean the redoubtable Lady B., his loyal companion in marriage of over 30 years, being denied her dearest ambition.

She had long left him in no doubt of her expectation of still being addressed as 'the Lady Beatrice' after their return to Britain – a mark of distinction she considered to be no less than her just desserts for a lifetime of devoted service to the Empire. Her indignation if his knighthood failed to materialise did not bear thinking about. He hardly had to use his imagination to hear her aggrieved voice: 'All these years stuck in this backwater, in this awful climate, and nothing to show for it, and all because a planter and his wife behaved badly, and you were unable to sort it out. It isn't as if we have made our fortunes out here. It's too bad of you.'

Damn Mitchell. He was such a difficult fellow. He tried again.

'Look, we have to keep calm about this. It is not a simple matter of natural justice. We are dealing with a complex situation here. In law this baby may well be Malay, after all he was born in the country and had a Malay father when he was born. All I am asking is that you are not too hasty and stir up local sensitivities. You know how civil disturbances can get out of hand at the drop of a hat in this part of Malaya. The Malays can get really worked up over quite silly little things sometimes and then property is destroyed, rubber production halted, troops have to be sent up from Singapore, and all the rest of it. It happened in 1915, you know, and it is still talked about here.'

If the incident had not been too painful for the B.A. to recall in detail, he would have provided Stuart with the full particulars of the crisis in 1915 when a Malay firebrand, To'Janggut, had staged a revolt in Kelantan at a time when Britain had its hands full coping with the Great War. Sadly, the career of the Adviser who was in Kelantan at the time and had to deal with the emergency, became yet another casualty of that conflict when he precipitately, and as it turned out – unnecessarily, called for a detachment of troops to be sent up from Singapore, and so set had the dovecotes in the Colony's Secretariat a-fluttering.

At that moment this Adviser's much-hoped-for recognition when he retired hung in the balance by a single thread, which, unfortunately, he himself had snapped when he and his police force put down the revolt before the troops arrived. Clearly, the Colonial Secretary was justified in thinking the panic had been of the Adviser's own making and, inevitably, he paid the penalty, which came in the form of only a sideways move when his next posting was due. In the hazardous business of climbing a colonial civil servant's preferment ladder, a sideways move was not to be welcomed as it often signified, when viewed at the end of a long career, to have been the exact moment when the promotion bus had been missed.

But the Kelantan Rebellion, as it became known, and its aftermath was a recurrent bad dream for the B.A. so he went on quickly before Stuart might enquire further. 'However, I am sure that if you give the Malay authorities and the lawyer chappies a chance to verify what you say, they will let the child go eventually.'

'And when is that going to happen? What does 'eventually' mean? And what happens meanwhile?'

The B.A. answered the last question first. 'It will mean you returning the child to the orphanage of course … ' But he got no further.

Stuart nearly exploded. 'Over my dead body! There is no chance of that happening. He is not going back to an orphanage again. He is my son and I intend keeping him. No father would do less.'

'Then you will have to take the consequences. The Sultan has considerable power here you know. You must remember the case of the acting Headmaster's wife in K.L. in 1911, Ethel Proudlock, who shot her British lover and was condemned to death, a sentence that was then commuted to life imprisonment? She was a British citizen, and despite the fact we thought it was imperative she serve her proper term of penal servitude, we were ignored and the Sultan of Selangor pardoned her, sent her off back to Britain a free woman instead of to a British jail, and we could do nothing about it. Made us look foolish in fact. We can be almost powerless at times in a protectorate.'

'And how does that affect me?'

'You also could find yourself on the next available boat home, and not because you had been pardoned like Ethel Proudlock either. In fact, I would say it is almost certain you would find yourself thrown out of Malaya on your ear, to use an expression, and without your child of course. If the Sultan so took it into his head, he could have your baby removed from you by force, you know, and he would be acting entirely within the law irrespective of whether the baby was British or Malay. An order from him to the police to come to your bungalow and take him would be impossible for me to do anything about, even though, as you are well aware, the chief of police is one of our people. I cannot countermand the Sultan on an issue such as this, not constitutionally I can't. Your only remedy would be the courts and I would not fancy your chances there very much.'

'Just let them try it,' said Stuart fiercely but the B.A. shook his head.

'That would only make matters worse. We cannot have expatriates breaking the law. That would never do. Not only would you put yourself outside whatever protection we could give you, you would sacrifice every bit of goodwill on the part of the Administration. Indeed, I think every Briton in the country would consider you had let the side down completely.'

'Damn the side, damn the Administration, damn everyone. It isn't their son's future which is at stake.'

'It doesn't help taking that attitude. I understand how you feel but this is not the time for hasty action which we might all come to regret.'

Despite his anger Stuart suddenly saw, with awful clarity, the reality of the situation he was in. He knew the B.A. was perfectly correct and was not exaggerating the danger he was facing. He had not lived in Kelantan for as long as he had without knowing the Administration had to walk on egg shells around the Malay rulers as well as the religious authorities. He had a vision of armed police on the estate and an hysterical Valerie – not a happy picture or one he wished to see at the end of his career as a planter. On the other hand, he had always been a bad loser so his instinct, even now, was to fight, regardless of the consequences, but he was also enough of a realist to know that battles in which defeat was inevitable were best not fought at all if any kind of alternative offered itself, and something in the Adviser's demeanour suggested he had such an alternative up his sleeve. So he paused. 'Then what is to be done?' he said at last.

Stuart had sensed correctly. The B.A. did have a plan – he had obviously done his homework. The knighthood was not to be given up that easily. 'Look,' he said. 'There is a chance we can get around this problem if we keep our heads and act quickly and decisively. I believe you have some home leave coming up in three months' time. I could ask your company to bring this forward and then we could get you home and out of harm's way before the Malay authorities had a chance to do anything about it. At the end of – is it four months leave you have? – tempers might have cooled and the whole matter might have blown over.'

Privately he thought there was not an earthly chance of that happening but if Stuart took the bait and departed, this whole messy business would at least be out of his hands and end up in someone else's lap. He had no power to prevent Mitchell going back to Britain if his company sent him, and taking his family with him. Planters were not Malayan civil servants after all, so neither he nor His Majesty's Government could possibly keep him here or be held to account afterwards if he had not actually broken the law.

Could taking one's own child out of an orphanage having put him there in the first place be a crime? A legal nicety if ever there was one, but certainly not one worth debating now. The future would have to take care of itself. The Sultan would be incensed of course, and no doubt the fur would fly in the High Commission for a while – a protest in the ruler's name might even have to go off to the Colonial Office – but the Sultan would have to accept the situation in the end, given time, though not perhaps some others in that touchy entourage of his.

He felt most uncertain about the Mentri Besar who would be the one to make the most fuss, but he would have to bow to the Sultan in the end. One thing he would have to make sure of, however, was the part he was playing in the affair – it had to be kept securely under wraps. Under no circumstances must a whisper of it be allowed to escape the Residency and so be laid at his door. There were to be no skeletons left rattling in his cupboard – such things had a remarkable and distressing ability to emerge into the cold light of day at the end of a career, as well he knew from the past. So far, however, he felt his tracks in this matter had been pretty well concealed. He had committed nothing to paper and intended keeping it that way.

As for Mitchell, he could see him wavering as he watched – he had obviously not spotted the inevitable consequences of the plan he had just outlined – and so he felt fairly confident he had nailed his man. The Lady Beatrice's place amongst the minor aristocracy of her native county of Lancashire was looking a lot more secure than it had been even a few minutes before.

'But how can we get over the problem of the baby? '

'If we can act quickly enough you can be out of the country and away before Mentri Besar's staff realise what is happening. Fortunately, they are not known for their swift action. I will phone the High Commissioner as soon as you have gone. Officially, we will know nothing about this at all. You understand that of course. This is entirely between you and your company.'

'I was thinking more of the documentation. Will we be able to get the baby out of the country all right? There could be a problem as he doesn't officially exist – he doesn't even have a name at the present moment, his birth not having been registered as far as we know. He hasn't been christened either of course. Won't he have to be put on my wife's passport or something if he is going to get through immigration? Surely he will need some official identity if that is to happen?'

'Leave all that to me. The Secretariat will see to whatever is needed. A word from the Colonial Secretary will be all that is necessary. Immigration will have things all ready for you when you get down to Singapore. You would be surprised how fast a civil servant can move when he has to. Now, what do you want the baby's name to be?'

Before Stuart had got half way across the well-manicured lawn, the B.A. was reporting to the High Commissioner's secretary in K.L. 'As I suspected, Mitchell would not play ball. There is no way he can be persuaded to hand the child back. We are now in the hands of his company. If they cooperate we should be home and dry, but, of course, I shall have to leave that matter to you. I can stall things here for a day or two, maybe several days, but no longer.'

Two days later a telegram was delivered to Bukit Bintang Estate, the first anyone could remember, and it arrived just as Stuart got back to the bungalow for breakfast. It said: 'Passages booked *Rawalpindi* leaving Singapore 12ᵗʰ inst.'

There was barely time to pack and say goodbye.

* * *

Valerie watched the *kampungs* between Kota Bharu and the state border slip by the train window and it was natural for her to recall, not for the first time, her first drive to Bukit Bintang. On that day she had wondered what daily life in the Malay houses was like. Now she had seen it, shared it, laughed and cried with it, not to mention having been rejected by it. In many ways it was as straightforward and simple as it looked, in others it was as mysterious and remote as only another religion and a different culture could make it.

They passed through an enormous padi field stretching away to the horizon on either side of the track. A farmer, up to his knees in mud and water, was struggling behind a plough pulled by a ponderous, grey buffalo. She had been frightened of the buffaloes in Batu Lima. During the day they had wallowed in the swamp by the river, each one with their complement of yellow-legged mynah birds clinging to their flanks in search of ticks like little brown rock climbers – but at night, they had come out onto the banks to graze. She remembered how their heads had lifted as she passed, their noses discerning she was no Malayan. They had been alert, suspicious, wondering what to make of this figure with a familiar outline but an unidentifiable odour. Like the village elders, they had not been taken in by her Malay dress and her soothing words. They were like that inner Malay society and its religion from which she had been excluded. She sighed as the scene slipped behind her. Perhaps she could never have fully merged with these people in their landscape of perpetual green.

On the other side of the track some Malay girls were planting padi seedlings, the soaked bottoms of their sarongs clinging darkly to their knees, their *selendangs* thrown back around their shoulders or drawn over their heads against the sun. She had never forgotten stepping into a padi field for the first time and finding, to her astonishment, that the brown water was almost as warm as a bath back in Britain. The girls had laughed at her clumsy efforts with the planting fork, and she had laughed with them, happy to be one of them.

Nearby, some boys were dipping their fishing nets in the monsoon ditches at the edge of the field and Valerie remembered similar scenes around the village. The nets were suspended like huge string saucers from the end of a cane pole. Scraps were placed in the middle of the nets and lowered into the water to lure the little catfish, which abounded in the drains. They were then hoisted out, wriggling and twisting, for the curry pot. Truly it was a fertile country when both fish and rice could come from the same piece of land.

The drooping heads of some banana trees broke the blue skyline over the padi field and she was reminded of the plantation across the Kelantan River from the *kampung*. Each evening, almost without fail, the setting sun had etched its jagged fronds in dark outline against a reddening sky to create what she had always felt was one the most quintessential images of the East. She had expected to look at that scene forever and never thought she would be walking the rainy streets of Glasgow again. Now she was shortly to call that city home once more, and she was not looking forward to the contrast.

Even on the brightest days, Glasgow's sun could never match Malaya's. Hanging in the industrial haze over the Clyde, it struggled to illumine the greys and blacks of the Victorian city, a murky and irrelevant backdrop to the lives of the people; whereas here, the sun's almost daily glare from a peerless sky was like God's floodlights, dominating everyone's existence, brightening and sharpening every colour in a perpetually shifting kaleidoscope. She marvelled it had not inspired an impressionist painter by now, just as the clear light of Arles had inspired the genius of van Gogh. Nevertheless, the sun could be a tyrant as it subjected every living thing to its power, and both man and beast ignored it at their peril. It was not to be basked in or enjoyed as at home, and could be merciless to those who did not respect it, but few who had been born under it, when exiled to cooler climes, did not long for its brilliance.

Yet, as someone who had been raised under the grey skies of Britain she was not altogether sorry to be leaving this land of everlasting sun, high humidity and sticky heat. Initially, she had revelled in its lack of winters and the dazzling brightness but then, as it had done for so many of her countrymen, the sameness began to pall and she began to miss the rhythm of the seasons and the varied activities each brought. Malaya, the land of perpetual summer where nature never slept, could not know the renewal of winter or the magic of spring.

The people, too, were never moved by the spirit of the changing seasons. Each day was exactly like all the others, even their length, and this brought dullness and lassitude, and when compounded by the heat and the humid air, sapped the energies, mental and physical, even of the young, and could undermine the strongest European constitutions. No wonder the two commonest English words used to describe it were 'enervating' and 'monotonous'. Remarkably, few Britons willingly ended their days in it – or wished to.

Was there nothing she would miss about the life here? Indeed there was but she struggled to find a word to describe it before she recalled one the Secretary in Kuala Lumpur had used when trying to find a suitable word to describe her affair with Osman. He had said she had 'embraced' a Malayan and indeed she had, but she had 'embraced' Malaya more. She had not been able to help herself as it was an intimate country inviting a close, personal relationship that her native country could never match. Perhaps it was because people in the East could not muffle themselves up in clothes, lock themselves away in houses or even shut themselves up in cars, as many liked to do at home, the suffocating heat would not let them. Air conditioning was as yet almost unknown in the country, even in the smartest hotels, and so the world could not be held at arm's length or kept out in the streets as in Britain. As a result, people always felt involved in what was going on around them in some way or another – the outdoors in Malaya could never be just a simple backdrop to daily life, it was a player in its own right.

It also meant that there was a neighbourliness about the country, which only Britain's slums could emulate. She remembered how the suburbs of her native city on a November evening could be as silent and deserted as the grave, whereas in Malaya at any time of the year, every road in every town bustled with the life and energy of a busy market – a colourful cavalcade of alfresco living – although, admittedly, only when the sun went down. Newcomers from Europe were often swept away by the sheer exuberance of it all.

Unexpectedly, it was the smells of the East which had been responsible for some of her most vivid impressions and so were likely to be among her most lasting memories, and she was still able to recall those which had come to her from the shore when she had been on the deck of the steamer going up to Kelantan for the first time. The sense of wonder and anticipation they had induced that night had never really left her. Not all of the smells, though, had been so evocative of the romantic East. Any European who had driven a car past tapioca drying in the sun, or durians piled high upon a stall, would ever forget the experience, however brief their passing. But they were the smells of the natural world, they were not the fumes of vehicles or the smoke of factories. They were what came from producing, not consuming, earth's resources. Life in Malaya was one of growth and greenery, organic, very different to the urban, manufactured one of home.

She was sharply aware, however, that for much of her time in the country she had been among Malaya's elite, guiltily sharing the best the twentieth century could offer in a land where most of the people were still living in conditions Britain's rural poor of the nineteenth century would have recognised – except that few went hungry in this land of plenty. But how much longer could her countrymen enjoy the privileges of such an existence? Their rule in Malaya could not possibly be more than a passing phase of history no matter what the Administration liked to claim and many expatriates believed. She had to be grateful for her good fortune in having lived here when she had, for the age of empire could not last much longer – indeed, it was already showing signs of having run its course.

Slowly the ship edged away from the quayside and the coloured streamers provided on these occasions were left sticking disconsolately to the white paintwork. Valerie had been parted from Malaya, she sensed for the last time, and she watched with sadness the ever-widening strip of water separating them. She could not imagine there would ever be a cause or an occasion when she might set foot in the country again.

Darkness was descending with its usual swiftness and hardly had the ship slid thirty yards from the shore than the rows of waving figures on the quay began to fade. All she could see now was a row of white-painted bollards, reminding her of the long white socks many planters wore with their traditional shorts when they gathered for their curry tiffins. The garb was quaintly known as 'planters' order' and somehow it seemed fitting the sight should be her final image of Malaya. None of the events during her days on the estate had caused her as much frustration as the popular Sunday gatherings of Malaya's rubber planters. But now, looking back, she thought she may have made too much of Stuart's refusal to let her host one of her own, and so she had elevated tiffins and the social life they represented above their proper worth, just as she had a lot of other things come to that. Batu Lima, however, had applied the necessary corrective.

Her six months in a local village had enabled her to see the daily problems of the great majority of Malaya's inhabitants at first hand and they had put the years she had spent on the estate into perspective. Before going to Batu Lima, her ideas of how the ordinary people in a British colony lived had been very one-dimensional, as anything is when seen from above. However, her life in the village had given her a picture as viewed from a different angle, and thus her image had been given the depth it lacked. Now it was more than just an outline – it had shape, and detail too. The locals were not just lucky to be able to buy a meal for as little as twenty cents – they could not afford anything more!

It prompted her to ask the question she could remember hearing a dozen times in the club in Kuala Lebir: surely the Malays are better off now than they would have been if the British, the wealth-creators, had not set foot in their country? Despite what she had learned from living on both sides of the divide she still did not know the answer, as what did better off really mean?

One day soon, however, it would be time for the wealth-creators to go and she hoped her countrymen would know when that day had arrived and depart without resentment. For the sake of those living in her little *kampung* by the river, and in a thousand of other villages like it, she hoped there would be no bitterness or anger on either side. When the British came to leave Malaya for the last time there would be no reason for them to feel any other emotion than gratitude. For generations they had earned more than just their living in the country and so had every reason to see themselves as the fortunate ones despite having to leave many of their fellow countrymen mouldering in Malayan soil, victims of war and disease. Although they would be leaving much of economic and cultural value behind them – and this was to their credit – the balance would be unquestionably in Britain's favour.

She went below, settled the baby in his cot and returned to the rail to join Stuart and the others prepared to brave the chill breeze whipped up as the ship left the protection of the harbour. Together they gazed at a typical Malayan sunset, spectacular and brief. Already the shore was too dark and too distant to pick out any detail, reminding her of the first time she had viewed a similar scene from the vantage point of a ship's rail – those now seemingly distant days when she had first gone to Kelantan on the little tramp steamer. How much had happened since.

Stuart meanwhile, was silent – obviously intent on keeping his thoughts to himself. Had he also a presentiment that he might not see Malaya again?

Valerie was equally silent as she gazed across the waves, their tips reddened by the last rays of the setting sun. Somewhere over there, far distant, was Osman, perhaps sitting on his verandah talking to friends, perhaps already in his taxi on the way to Karang or Kota Bharu. Would he ever think of her? Not nearly as often as she would think of him, and of the life together they had so very nearly achieved but which would now be a world away, forever.

*   *   *

The letter containing Stuart's dismissal dropped on the mat a fortnight after they arrived back in Scotland. It bore a London postmark so he knew it had come from the fount of all Company wisdom – the Directors. It made no mention of the orphanage affair but alluded several times, in effusive terms in fact, to his long years of outstanding service to the Company. However, the Directors were very definite regarding the reason why, in their view, the time had come for that service to end, and the wording of the main paragraph left no room for uncertainty:

'Having had time to consider recent events, in particular the regrettable incident on Bukit Bintang Estate in Kelantan in March 1934 when company property was damaged as a direct result of the failure on the part of the Manager to enforce Company rules, it is the Directors' unanimous opinion that the time has come for Mr Stuart James Mitchell to be granted retirement to begin on the date at the head of this letter, but without prejudice to his terminal leave entitlements or his pension, and that his present three months vacation in the United Kingdom be regarded as his serving the Company's statutory period of notice.'

The irony of the contents – the incident of the slashed trees had been the only occasion in his entire career when a charge of dereliction of duty could have been laid at his door – and therefore the injustice of his dismissal, aroused all of Stuart's old combative instincts, but he knew an appeal would be a waste of everyone's time, and certainly his. The decision of the U.K. directors was always final and in any case his forced retirement came as no surprise. Valerie's removal of the baby from the orphanage had posed a threat to the delicate balance in relations between the nation protector and its protectorate and so could not have been tolerated or excused. As he now realised, he could never have gone back to Malaya.

At the time, he had rather naively accepted the British Adviser's assurance he would be able to return once the furore had died down, but as he had boarded the boat in Singapore he instinctively knew his time in the East had ended, and before the notice of his dismissal had come through his letter box, he had become convinced of it. It was still too early, however, to say he had become reconciled to the fact. The role of sacrificial lamb was not one that sat well with him.

Nevertheless, he was pleased he had not accepted the alternative solution of returning his son to the orphanage and leaving the decision on his future to the lawyers. He had long distrusted such people and he suspected any arrangement they would have made would have been more to save the face and the dignity of the authorities than settle the long-term interests of the boy.

But to resurrect a two years old minor incident as grounds for the dismissal of one of their longest-serving managers was expediency of the grossest kind as both he and the Directors knew full well but if they had not used that, they would have been forced to find some other excuse. What that excuse might have been rather intrigued him as his record, together with the production figures from all of his estates, had been almost beyond reproach. Apart, of course, from the incident involving the girl from the weeding gang, and even the Board would not have dared to resurrect that indiscretion after all these years.

In truth, however, nothing could have saved his career once the Administration had decided his presence in the country was not conducive to their smooth running of the country and the continued maintenance of their all-important image. And when the lava-flow of indignation, which must have been issuing from the mosque without any sign of it abating, had been added to the equation, irresistible forces would have been brought to bear on the unfortunate custodians of United Estates, rendering them powerless. It made his discharge from their service a formality, despite his long years of devotion to their profits.

But oddly, he had few regrets. His life in Malaya, such as it had become in its last six months, was a small price to pay for the gift of a son and, he hoped, other sons in the future. There was every indication that such additions to his family would materialise as, surprising as it may seem, he had blossomed, not only into a proud and dutiful father but into a more than tolerable husband as well. He did not blame his wife for her aberration with his *syce*, or ever make any allusions to it, fully recognising the part he had played in what he chose to see as her *folie d'amour*. Nor did he, even once, make any reference to the night she had left the baby at the orphanage and so set in motion the chain of events which had brought an end to his career as a rubber planter.

Valerie, for her part, was more than happy to accept marriage on these terms. As she sometimes consoled herself, she was surely not the first wife to enjoy a successful marriage to one man while remaining faithfully, though distantly, in love with another. She had regrets, of course she had, but was there ever a wife who had not been required to compromise somewhere in her marriage? Her union with Stuart had not been made in the most propitious of circumstances it was true, but she had the satisfaction of knowing it had been strong enough to withstand an ordeal which would have broken many others.

Monsoon titles
set in Malaysia and Singapore

Fiction

Olivia & Sophia by Rosie Milne
Bamboo Heart (Vol.1) by Ann Bennett
Bamboo Island (Vol.2) by Ann Bennett
Bamboo Road (Vol.3) by Ann Bennett
Shadow Play (Vol.1) by Barbara Ismail
Princess Play (Vol.2) by Barbara Ismail
Spirit Tiger (Vol.3) by Barbara Ismail
The Red Thread (Vol.1) by Dawn Farnham
The Shallow Seas (Vol.2) by Dawn Farnham
The Hills of Singapore (Vol.3) by Dawn Farnham
The English Concubine (Vol.4) by Dawn Farnham
A Crowd of Twisted Things by Dawn Farnham

Nonfiction

Our Man in Malaya by Margaret Shennan
Out in the Midday Sun by Margaret Shennan
You'll Die in Singapore by Charles McCormac
The Boat by Walter Gibson
Malayan Spymaster by Boris Hembry
The Defence and Fall of Singapore by Brian Farrell
Sayonara Singapura by Parapuram Joseph John
Raffles and the British Invasion of Java by Tim Hannigan
In the Footsteps of Stamford Raffles by Nigel Barley